WHERE DARK HEARTS DEVOUR

VICTORIA HOLLIDAY

*To all the girls who don't like being told what to do…
Unless it's between the sheets. Then it's okay.*

PLAYLIST

Sinister Kid, The Black Keys
White Dress, Lana Del Rey
Last Hurrah, Bebe Rexha
My Love, Kovacs
Chandelier, Sia
Beautiful People, Beautiful Problems, Lana Del Rey
Blue, Billie Eilish
Black, Pearl Jam
I was made for lovin' you, Yungblud, Dominic Lewis

CHAPTER 1

*C*ristiano

I shift on my chair and sink backward into the shadows, where I'm most comfortable. Joe's Bar is the only establishment in this part of the city not under my family's rule, and as I observe my surroundings with detached curiosity, I'm impressed at how the fabric of this place has transformed in just a few hours.

Since I arrived at five p.m., I've seen every type of patron, from workers having a quick beer and young women on a bachelorette party, right through to shady Casanovas out for a slow scotch and a quick lay. And now the sky outside is black and those allergic to daylight have come out of the cracks in the street, it feels like I'm in a different place altogether.

Loud whispers fill dark corners; thick fingers graze bare skin. Deceit and debauchery taste too sweet in the air. As for the dress code, it appears anything goes, as long as you can turn a blind eye to bad behavior.

I came here to prolong the inevitable. As soon as word gets out that I'm back in New York, the days will no longer be my own. The whole city has its eyes on the Di Santos, and just because I left ten years ago doesn't mean I'm exempt from the view. If anything, the changing dynamics of our family and my role in it are sure to make our advisors giddy with the suggestion of returning blood. And that won't please my brother *at all*.

My eyes drift to the clock. It's getting close to midnight.

I pick up the glass of water I haven't touched for several hours and bring the rim to my lips. Glancing across the room one more time, I tip it back and swallow the lot. Only a few heads turn my way as I stand. My height and build make me a little conspicuous, but the tailored suit and black shirt cover up any clue as to who I am.

I'm almost at the exit when a door to my left bursts open and something small and fluttery collides with my ribs. A young woman stares up at me, her large eyes wide with shock, and short, nervous breaths escape her full lips. Her hands are pressed against my torso to steady herself, and I don't miss the way her fingertips curl into my shirt when our eyes meet.

She swallows with some effort. Then she looks down, realizes she's still touching me, and withdraws her hands quickly. Her cheeks are flushed pink when she glances back up.

"I . . . I'm so sorry, I wasn't looking where I was going. Did I, um . . . Did I hurt you?"

Her words are stuttered and slightly slurred, but her *voice*. She sounds like she just tanked a full pack of Marlboro Reds. I almost laugh, but she's being serious, so I bite my cheek before I reply.

"No, you didn't hurt me. Did I hurt *you*?"

She blinks long, dark lashes at me. The movement is lazy and languid, which tells me she's had a few too many drinks. I take in her taut, unblemished skin and delicate build—she can't be more than eighteen, surely. Too young and too fragile to be drinking alcohol in backstreet bars.

"Um . . . no."

"That's good."

The sound of grinding bone vibrates around us, and it takes me a few seconds to notice I'm cracking my knuckles.

"You came at me with some speed."

She wrings her hands together. "I'm really sorry."

Something dark and more Di Santo than I'd like to admit crosses my mind. "Can I see your ID?"

Just like that, the blood drains from her face. "Excuse me?"

"Your ID," I repeat. "Can I see it?"

Any sober person would question my right to ask, but I'm pretty sure this little one isn't sober at all.

"W-why?"

It's a good question. Why *do* I want to see her ID?

At first I just wanted to see her reaction, and I've seen that now, along with everything but the stone-cold evidence she's underage. But I realize even though this is merely a fleeting visit and I'm not here to find a woman I can walk away from in the morning without so much as a backward glance, I want more than just a reaction from this girl. I want her *name*.

"Because I need to know whose secret I'm keeping."

She blinks again, then her wide eyes soften, and she breathes out a resigned sigh. She reaches into a straw basket hanging over her arm and pulls out a driver's license. I instantly spot the telltale signs of a counterfeit.

The photo is genuine and doesn't do her justice. But it's the wording below it I'm interested in.

Trilby Castellano.

A faint thread of recognition winds its way through my mind. There are a thousand Castellanos in this city, but not Trilbys, and I'm sure I've heard that name before.

Her bottom lip trembles slightly when my gaze glides from the license in my hand back to her. Her large eyes are lined with black kohl that flicks up at the outer corners, and her lips bear the remnants of a cherry-red stain that probably wore off hours ago. She looks oddly—interestingly—vintage. Her white dress clings to her waist and flares out at the hips. Her dark hair has been bleached to the tips and curled in the style of Marilyn Monroe. There's even a crystal comb above her ear that looks just like the one my nonna used to wear.

Without another word, I hand the license back to her and shove my hands into the pockets of my slacks. Her lip's still trembling, yet there's a defiance in her expression as she tips her chin upward.

"Did it tell you what you needed to know?"

I wipe the beginning of a smirk from my mouth with a rough thumb. "For now."

She straightens her shoulders, and her bleached hair bobs about her face like cotton candy. "Well then." She goes to step past me. "It was nice meeting you."

She's implying I was on my way out, and I can't tell if she's feeling hopeful about it or regretful, which annoys me, because I can usually read people effortlessly. Managing casinos for the best part of ten years has delivered me an unrivaled education in human behavior.

"I wasn't leaving," I lie. "I was going to the restroom."

Her cheeks flush again. "Well, this is the ladies' restroom." She nods to the other side of the room. "The men's is over there."

I run my tongue across my teeth, taking my long-ass time about it, and enjoy her obvious discomfort. Then I lazily cock a brow. "Thanks."

She tugs the bag higher up her shoulder, turns, and walks clumsily back to the bar.

I silently curse my decision to stay as I head to the restroom. I was hoping to spend an early-ish, quiet night in my Tribeca apartment, lying low for a few hours longer, but for reasons I won't try to understand,

I don't want to give this girl the satisfaction of a reprieve.

I reach the door and look over my shoulder. She's talking to the bartender, and even from the far corner of the room I can see his cheeks flushing and his eyes lighting up. She sits haphazardly on a stool in front of him and then somehow manages to slide right off the other end, landing in a heap on the floor.

I find it hard to believe she's a regular drinker, because she has no tolerance for it at all.

Three grown men rush to her aid and hoist her up.

When she's back on the stool, she turns her head slightly until she can see me out of the corner of her eye. Embarrassment burns up those pretty cheeks. I save her from further mortification by walking straight into the restroom.

The door closes behind me, drowning out the thick bass of "Sinister Kid" by The Black Keys, which thankfully makes the voice in my head clearer.

One week, Cristiano.

That's all I'm here for. To lay Father to rest, congratulate my brother on his new title, and tie up a few loose ends. Then I'll fly back to Vegas, never to return to this coast again. I'll have no reason to. Mama died ten years ago, Papa has gone, and my brother has taken on the top job—one that's bound to keep him far too busy to be bothered with surviving relatives. Sure, we have other family members in the city, but they're more than happy to vacation in one of my casino hotels; I don't need to be in New York to stay in touch.

The bottom line is, I'm not sticking around, so there's no point in making nice with a random woman I just met in a questionable bar, no matter how much she intrigues me.

I emerge from the restroom in time to see the bartender push a cocktail glass into her hand: a bright blue concoction topped with a curl of orange peel and a paper umbrella. Her gaze drifts to the man at her side, then her lids lift, and our eyes lock. My breath sticks in my throat.

She's sitting a good fifteen feet away, but I can see the color of her irises. Turquoise, like the Atlantic.

I walk to the other end of the bar and slide onto a stool.

The bartender looks up, his expression bordering on cocky. "You gonna have a real drink now?"

I wrap a hand around my neck and rub. My life in Vegas is hardly stress-free, but being back in this city makes me feel tighter than a wound spring. "Whiskey. Neat."

"Coming right up."

He pours two fingers and places the glass on a coaster. "So, where are you visiting from?"

"Who says I'm visiting?"

He huffs out a laugh, narrowing my eyes. "Our clientele is pretty steady. I haven't seen you here before, and don't take this the wrong way, but . . ."

My eyes narrow further. Whenever anyone says that, there's never a right way to take it.

"But?"

"If you were from this city, you'd be sitting in a different bar."

I knock back half the whiskey. "Why's that?"

He stares at me like he's trying to figure me out. "You know this part of the city is owned by the Di Santos . . . right?"

"Is it?" I decide to play dumb. People give up more information that way.

His eyes light up. Finally, new blood he can bestow his wisdom on. "Only a few businesses have managed to slip out from their greasy fingers. This is one of them."

"Greasy fingers, huh?"

He leans toward me with a slightly curled lip. "Italian Mafia scum," he says, low and quiet.

I bite back a smile. If only he knew who he was talking to. I may not be involved in the crime side of our family anymore, but the blood still runs through my veins, and the gun in my waistband is loaded. But I'll spare him this one time.

"Why don't they want this place?"

"Nothing in it for them."

He's right about that.

"What do you mean?"

A smirk crosses his cocky lips. "It's a backstreet dive you're sitting in, buddy. The only people who come here are those who don't want to be seen. And in a city like New York, there aren't too many of those, you know? The Di Santos wouldn't get a cent out of this place. Not worth their time."

I knock back the rest of the whiskey and push the glass toward him for a refill.

While the dickwad pours another two fingers my gaze is pulled to the right. The Castellano girl is chatting quietly to two of the men. There's nothing suggestive in any of their body language, but the sight still stiffens my spine. The bartender's words ring in my ears. *"The only people who come here are those who don't want to be seen."*

"What's her story?" I ask as he refills my glass.

"Who—Tril?"

The way he says her name makes my shoulders tense.

He picks up a glass and starts to polish it with a dirty cloth. "You won't see her in here again for another year."

"What?"

"Only comes in once every twelve months," he repeats. "Has done for the past five years." When I don't respond, he looks up. "It's the anniversary of her mom's death."

Something heavy settles in my chest as I look back at her. She's swaying gently on the stool while the two men have a conversation across her.

"Don't expect her to talk to you about it," the bartender warns. "I only know because I asked around. She was real young the first time she came in here, but she looked so broken. She needed to forget something, so I served her." He glances at me, perhaps expecting some kind of reprimand because she must have been a young teenager then. He sighs. "She was fifteen."

I don't say anything.

"Like I said, she needed something, and to be frank, we needed her money."

My brows draw together, and I feel the familiar dark desire to put a bullet between another man's eyes. *His.* There were other ways he could've helped her that didn't involve serving her alcohol or greedily taking the small amount of money she'd have spent to escape her demons. It sounds suspiciously like he took advantage of a grieving underage girl.

He places the dirty glass on a shelf and lifts another one to polish.

My thoughts begin to roam the different ways I could punish him for being a prize dick, but they're quickly interrupted by a warm sensation caressing my right side. I turn to see the girl zigzagging past me. She averts her gaze and walks off to the restroom.

Turning my back to the bartender, I lean my elbows on the bar and slowly sip my whiskey while I watch the restroom door. When it opens again, I don't look up, but as she passes, something possesses me to push out a foot. She stumbles over it, and I catch her from falling. Breath gushes from her lungs, and her eyes fly open in shock.

With my arm wrapped around her torso, she makes no more of an attempt to wriggle free than I do to release her. She's surprisingly small and warm. Her pert breasts press teasingly into my forearm.

She slurs a breathless apology.

"Don't apologize," I say firmly.

When she finds her feet, I reluctantly let my arm slip from her body.

"Are you okay?"

She rubs her eyes, smudging a little of the kohl across her lids. "I guess I drank a little too much."

And I purposely tripped you up. But then again, if she weren't so drunk, she'd have noticed my foot.

I call over my shoulder to the bartender. "Can I get a glass of water?"

It takes a while, but a half-full glass eventually appears. He's probably cursing me for getting her off the hard stuff. I watch as she sips it then cradles the glass in her hands.

"I don't normally drink," she says, her gaze on the floor.

"I can tell. You don't seem to handle it all that well. Why bother drinking at all?"

She looks up with a frown, and there's an unexpected bite in her tone when she replies. "I don't have to explain myself to you." As if she's overstepped a boundary, her skin flushes again. "I'm sorry. That was rude. And very . . . *unlike* me."

I watch her, thoughtful. "You're right though. You don't have to explain yourself."

She laughs darkly. "That's a relief. Most people expect me to." When she looks up again, there's a new boldness in the set of her jaw. "What's your secret?"

I take a long sip of whiskey to steady my pulse. "Who says I have a secret?"

"Everyone who comes here has a secret. Something to hide."

I think about it and how right she is.

"If I told you, it wouldn't be a secret, would it?"

She looks away, but I don't miss the deeper shade of pink inching up her chest. "I guess not."

"Is that why you're here?" I ask. "Because you have a secret."

"Maybe." She glances up timidly. "Or maybe I come to Joe's because it's preferable to every other bar in this part of the city."

I'm intrigued. Not only because every other bar around here is either owned or ruled by my family. [BL4] "How so?"

She looks around. "It's not perfect here, but at least there's no violence."

Something hardens behind my chest. "What do you have against violence?"

She touches the crystals in her hair, and when she answers, there's a bitter burn in her voice. "It's a weapon of the weak."

There's more to this girl than a tragic story and an annual drunken escapade. There's anger and a thirst for revenge. I lived on the dark side of our world for long enough that I can *smell* it.

I neck more whiskey. "Yeah, well, there's violence and there's violence."

Now I feel her gaze.

"What's that supposed to mean?"

I place my glass on the bar and drift my focus to her. "It means there's more to violence than death and destruction."

Her expression darkens. "I doubt it."

"One day, if you're lucky, you'll find someone who can show you." The words are out of my mouth before I can stop them, and I feel her gasp in my gut. I change the topic before I can say anything else without thinking it through. "Do you live in the city?"

She shakes her head. "Long Island."

My ears prick up. "Which part?"

"Near Port Washington."

Interesting. That's not far from the Di Santo residence.

Her eyes narrow. "And before you ask, I'm not telling you which house. I may be a little drunk, but I'm not stupid."

I arch a brow. "A *little* drunk?"

She rolls her eyes to the ground and folds her arms across her chest.

"Why are you here alone?" I ask.

She looks up and coasts one arm in front of her. "Does this look like I'm alone?"

"That's not what I meant. You don't appear to be *with* anyone." I flick a gaze sideways. "And those two assholes don't count."

Her face contorts into a grimace as if I just trod on her cat. "They are not assholes. They're regulars here."

"You're avoiding the question."

She falls quiet and starts to chew on her lip. I feel an unbridled need to pull it out from between her teeth.

"We don't all have idyllic pasts, you know."

I don't know who she's insinuating has had an idyllic past, but I let her continue.

"I have . . . memories. And sometimes I just need a little help blurring them out."

The bartender slides another blue drink in her direction, and she smiles guiltily before wrapping her lips around the straw.

After a long sip, she flashes her eyes up to me. "What's your excuse?"

"Excuse for what? I'm not drunk."

She's about to roll her eyes again, but she stops herself and instead bats her long, dark lashes. "What's a nice gentleman like you doing alone in a miserable dark bar like this?" Those eyelashes are loaded with sarcasm.

I place the glass down carefully. "It doesn't seem all that miserable to me."

When she parts her lips to probe, I cut her off. "And besides, I'm not that nice, and I'm definitely no gentleman."

She laughs bitterly. "Well, if you weren't the most attractive guy in here already, you certainly are now."

I bite back a grin and shake my head.

"Seriously. You show me a girl who doesn't like bad news, and I'll show you a liar."

"You think I'm bad news?"

She rests the straw against her lips, drawing every ounce of my focus to them, and nods.

I swallow and try to remember her original question. "I'm surrounded by people constantly when I'm working. All day every day. This . . ." I look around the bar and try not to smirk. "Is my *me* time."

She folds her arms. "What about when you're not working?"

"I run casinos. I'm always working." I turn to lift my glass and gulp back a larger than planned mouthful of the scotch. My throat isn't too happy about it, but it'll live.

"But you're here on a break?"

I almost choke. "Not quite."

"Well then, why are you here?"

I swirl the whiskey around one more time. I shouldn't have let the conversation go this far. If I tell her I'm here because my father just died, it won't take much for her to figure out who I am. And then she'll run a mile.

I settle on: "Family matters." Then I throw the rest of the whiskey down my throat and place the glass on the bar.

"You want another of those?" Her tone is playful.

Our eyes lock, and in those few seconds I consider indulging myself with another whiskey. But the door to the bar bangs against a wall, knocking the thought from my head.

What the fuck am I thinking? I have duties to carry out, people to console, papers to sign. I'd only be prolonging the inevitable, and I need a clear head for the coming days. I consider inviting her back to my place—

a quick, hard fuck could be just what I need—but there's a timidness about her that makes me think she'd run for the hills at the mere suggestion.

"No. It's time I headed home."

She pushes herself upright and hardens her jaw. "You're leaving?" she asks quietly.

"Yeah. I have a busy day tomorrow."

She smooths a hand over her hip. "Right. Okay, well, it was nice meeting you. I'm Trilby, by the way."

Something pulls at me. Her name really is familiar. I'm sure we've met before, even though she clearly doesn't remember it.

"I'm Cristiano." I watch her face carefully for any flicker of recognition, but it doesn't come. "Can I ask . . . how long have you lived near Port Washington?"

"Why does it matter?"

"It doesn't. I'm just curious."

She shrugs, her eyelids falling heavy. "All my life."

If she was fifteen when she first came in here five years ago, that makes her twenty now—eight years younger than me. Our paths may well have crossed.

She sways side to side.

"Isn't it time you went home too?" I suggest.

Her skin pales. "I don't want to go home yet." As she says the words, she sways too far to the right and stumbles into a table.

I grab her before she can fall, trying not to process how soft her skin feels beneath my fingertips. The bartender appears, looking concerned.

"Yeah," I say. "I think it's home time. Come on—I can give you a ride."

Her eyes flash suddenly, and she yanks her arms from my grip. "I'm not getting in a car with you," she snaps. "I don't even know you."

"Fine." Reaching into my jacket pocket instead, I pull out a thick roll of hundreds. I flick a few out and slap them on the bar. "Make sure she gets home safe." I direct the words to the bartender, but my eyes bore into her.

Her face blanches. "You're paying him to have me leave?"

"I'm paying him to get you home in one piece," I reply.

She narrows her eyes like a seething cat, and there's a flash of fire behind them.

The bartender puts an arm around her shoulders, and every muscle in my body tenses. "Come on, T. Have another glass of water, then we'll get you in a cab."

T.

Blood thumps through my temples.

Her brows knit as she looks at him. "I'm fine, Brett," she slurs.

The bartender flushes pink. "It's actually Rhett, but, you know, phonetically, it's about the same."

She staggers to a stool, and he finally releases her.

I exhale slowly and uncurl my fists. I didn't know I'd clenched them, but I can feel crescent-shaped indentations in my palms.

I unbutton the collar of my shirt and look around at

the clientele. It surprises me how few people I recognize. All day I've been looking for something— anything—that might suggest the opposite of what I know to be true. That my father hasn't just died. That I'm returning to a place untouched by his absence. But all that's become clear while sitting in Joe's is that whether our loved ones are dead or alive, the world keeps on turning. And distractions in white dresses don't help much.

I take one last look at her sitting on the barstool, the dim light casting her pretty features in a tragic shadow, making her all the more beautiful for it.

Then I head out into the darkness.

CHAPTER 2

Trilby

Vomit rushes up my esophagus and splashes into the toilet bowl. I can feel a hand rubbing my shoulder blades, and another one holding the hair out of my face. I press the back of my wrist to my mouth before another retch brings up more fluid.

My head pounds all over again at the sight.

It's blue.

"Ugh, Trilby. What were you drinking last night?"

I reach behind me and grasp my sister's hand. After I've expelled every possible thing from my stomach, I slide from my ankles onto the floor.

Sera passes me a glass of water, then joins me on the tile, crossing her legs. "Are you okay?"

I shake my head. It's fuzzy—which, at this time of year, I've found is preferable to it being crystal clear.

Crystal clear means I remember.

Every. Vivid. Detail.

And I don't want to, because it hurts.

Five years ago today, I sat in the back of my mother's car and watched as she was brutally murdered right in front of me. Whoever said time is the greatest healer has never had to wash their dead mother's blood off their face.

"I can't imagine what it must be like," Sera says softly, "reliving it over and over."

I sip the water and feel the instant coolness soothe my throat.

I'm the eldest of four sisters, Sera being the second eldest. She's only one year younger, so Mama's murder affected her as much as it affected me. But for one thing, she wasn't there when it happened, and for another, she doesn't like to talk about it, preferring to bury her head in horoscopes and tarot cards instead.

Contessa was twelve when Mama died, and Bambalina was ten. Tess has grown into an angry teenager for whom black is the aesthetic of choice, disgust the mood du jour, and anarchy the weapon of justice. Bambi is still a child. A sweet, kindhearted, pony-mad girl who's been raised and swaddled by three strong-willed sisters and a slightly unhinged aunt.

I sigh heavily. "I keep hoping the visions will fade as time goes by, but they don't."

Sera tips her head to one side. "Maybe when you finish school you should move somewhere new. Get a change of scene. It can't be helpful to be around all these places and people constantly reminding you of Mama and what happened. I would miss you enormously, but if that's what it takes to make the visions fade, I'd support you one thousand percent."

"It's a nice idea, but Papa won't allow it," I say with a resigned sigh.

"Talk to him, Trilby," Sera says earnestly. "He knows what you went through—what you're still going through. He might consider it. Even for just a few months."

I shake my head.

Though there's only one year between me and Sera, I know more about Papa's business than anyone else in the family. While he hasn't been sworn in as a made man, Papa's a valued associate of the Di Santo crime family. As the owner of Castellano Shipping Co., he runs one of the city's biggest ports, which has been of some interest to the Di Santos for as long as I can remember.

Until Mama was killed, I was blissfully ignorant of exactly how involved in Mafia activities our family business was. Afterward, I wanted answers, and I found them in Papa's office. Turned out we shipped a lot more than "consumables." Unless you put firearms, ammo, and cocaine into that category.

"It's too risky. Especially now Gianni is dead. Papa has to reestablish himself with whoever succeeds the former don."

Sera strokes a thumb over my palm. "Who do you think it will be?"

I shrug. It's not as if I'm an expert on all things Mafia, but there are a few names I overhear often in Papa's conversations. "Augusto Zanotti? Benito Bernadi?"

Sera wrinkles her nose. "Isn't Benny Bernadi their consigliere?"

An image of his scarred face and iron-rigid jaw crosses my lids, and I suppress a shudder. A consigliere usually advises the family on legal matters, but it's obvious when looking at Bernadi he takes the law into his own hands—literally.

"I think so. And Augusto was Gianni's second-in-command. He's perhaps the more likely option."

"Not his son, Savero?"

I hadn't thought about him. He generally keeps a low profile, so I don't even know what he looks like.

"Maybe," I murmur. I don't actually care.

"He was here yesterday," Sera says, watching warily for my reaction.

"Who was here?"

"Savero Di Santo."

A chill raises the hairs on my skin. "When?"

"While you were, um . . . out."

My pulse thumps, and a bad feeling settles in my gut. "Why was he here?"

"I don't know. I tried to eavesdrop, but Allegra shooed me away. He was in Papa's office for at least an hour."

"It must be something to do with the port," I say. "That will be it. There were contracts . . ." I don't want to say too much. I don't want Sera to worry about our family's livelihood like I now do. "Maybe Savero just wants to be reassured business is continuing as normal."

"That makes sense." She seems appeased—until her brows knit together. That look on Sera is never good.

"What is it?" I ask.

"Last night was a solar eclipse."

I refrain from rolling my eyes. Astrology is her language, and though I don't understand it, I respect the way she uses it to make sense of the world.

"What does that mean?"

"New moons often signal new beginnings," she explains. "But an eclipse is particularly powerful."

"Maybe Papa has signed a new contract," I suggest.

"Hmm. Maybe." Her focus drifts.

"You don't have to stay with me, Sera. I'm going to be fine." I know she'd rather be alone in her room surrounded by textbooks and tarot cards.

"You sure?"

I squeeze her hands. "I'm sure. And thank you."

She cocks her chin like she has no idea just how wonderful a sister she is for staying with me while I puked my guts up.

"I really appreciate you being here."

Sera stands and strokes a hand through my hair. "Anytime, Tril. See you for dinner?"

"Yeah, okay."

"Go back to bed," she says with a smile. "You could probably use a bit more sleep."

I nod and watch the bathroom door close as she leaves.

I'm barely on my feet when the door bursts open again. Sera reappears, her face flushed this time and her eyes wide.

"Trilby . . . Papa wants to see you in his office. Now."

My heartbeat sticks at the base of my throat. Papa *never* wants to see me in his office.

"Did he say why?"

"No, but it sounds urgent. And serious."

Oh crap.

A second hangover lowers itself onto me like a pregnant rain cloud. Did I do something bad last night? I drink to forget, but that means there's always the chance I'll do something regrettable.

"Do you want me to come with you?" she asks. "I could stand outside the door . . . give you some moral support."

I smile weakly. "No, it's fine. But thanks for offering. What would I do without you?"

"Probably everything you do already," she replies in her sweet voice. "There's nothing you can't handle on your own. You've got a thicker skin than any of us."

That might have been true once upon a time, but not anymore. Now, I look twice before getting into a car. I've developed a genuine fear of the dark, and I have such bad nightmares I can't remember the last time I had a full night's sleep. I only hope I can summon some measure of resilience, because I have a feeling my ability to pretend everything's okay, that I can handle whatever life throws at me, is about to bite me in the backside.

Ten minutes and three coffees later, I'm sitting in my father's office, the Advil hasn't touched the sides, and my ass hasn't just been bitten, it's been one hundred percent annihilated, and I can't breathe.

"I'm *what*?"

Papa doesn't move a muscle, but a twitch escapes his right eye. "You're getting married."

I feel his words again like a punch to the sternum.

He averts his eyes to some papers on his desk. The sheet at the top of the pile bears a crest that looks unnervingly familiar. It's a dove in flight amid a tongue of fire. The symbol of saintliness.

Of Saint.

Di Santo.

He sighs with a heaviness that betrays his true feelings. "I know you're aware of some of my . . . business partners, Trilby."

I feel a tremble hardening my spine as I glance back at the crest. It's an image we've been raised to fear.

My lids slowly lift back to my father. "Yes, Papa."

Papa's jaw ticks. "Savero Di Santo came to visit me yesterday. He doesn't just want to continue the agreement I made with his father to ship occasional goods through the port—he wants to make things more official."

I have to force myself to listen, because I don't like the way this conversation is headed.

"In fact, he wants the majority share of the port."

A dark and desperate feeling settles in my stomach. "I didn't think it was for sale, Papa."

He swallows audibly. "It isn't, but that's not how Savero Di Santo operates. He doesn't look for things he can buy—he looks for things he can take."

"Papa . . . I don't understand."

"I can't afford for him to take the port from under me. And I'm under no illusions, Trilby. He has thousands of soldiers working for him now. If I fought him, I wouldn't stand a chance, and I have to support my family and protect the livelihoods of my workers."

Regardless of how many times I swallow, the dryness in my mouth doesn't abate. "So?" I croak.

"So we came to an agreement. You are to marry him to keep the port in our family."

I fight to hear his words over the sudden ringing in my ears. "You want me to marry Gianni Di Santo's son. The son of the don."

"Yes." Papa's tone is firm and nonnegotiable. "But you are not marrying the son of a don, my love. You are marrying the don himself."

"Savero is the new don?" I whisper. My head feels light while my stomach has dropped with the weight of inevitability.

I'm getting married. To Savero Di Santo. To a *Mafia don*.

I can't stop my nostrils from flaring. "Why me?" My voice inclines to a high pitch. "I haven't even met him, Papa! He probably doesn't have a clue who I am."

Papa clears his throat. "He knows exactly who you are."

"But he's never even met me! Why on earth would he want to marry me?"

Papa leans forward, and I've never seen him look so serious. "He wants the port, Trilby." There's a sober weight to his words. "It's as simple as that. If we hadn't come to this arrangement, he would have declared war on me. I would have lost everything—our entire livelihood. He would've found a way to bring our business down."

"That doesn't sound like something Gianni would do," I say quietly.

The notorious mob boss was as morally black as they come, but he never took issue with my family despite Papa owning one of the biggest import-export businesses in New York. I guess this was, in part, because my mother's death gave Gianni and Papa a common enemy. Mama and I were caught up in a misunderstanding between the Di Santos and the smaller-numbered but no less deadly Marchesi mob. I survived. Mama didn't.

There's a sadness in Papa's voice. "Savero is not Gianni. They couldn't be more different."

I focus on breathing steadily, because it wouldn't do

to betray my true feelings to Papa—not when he too has
been through so much and raised all four of us to be
polite and becoming. "Can you explain?"

Papa looks at me for a long moment. "Savero is . . .
passionate."

Normally, that description would prick my ears up,
but Papa's tone suggests it's maybe not a good thing.

"He has a temper . . ."

I can tell he's choosing his words carefully.

"Not with women, I'm reliably assured," he
continues. "But I hear he can be hasty in his actions. It
wasn't expected that Gianni would pass so soon. He was
coaching Savero to conduct himself like the don Gianni
was. I don't know how much success he had before his
untimely death, but what I do know is there are some
nervous people in the Di Santo mob right now. A wife—
someone who can distract him a little—might be exactly
what Savero needs."

I can only tackle one heinous point at a time,
especially when I'm throwing every mental tool I have
at remaining calm for Papa's sake.

"So, I'm to marry a man who just became the boss
of New York's biggest crime family—someone who
isn't liked by his soldiers and is rumored to have a
temper—not because he's long been a secret admirer of
mine, but because he wants to use our port for his own
illegal gains?"

Papa's jaw hardens. "Would you like me to spell out
the alternative?"

I don't need him to. The Di Santo family has owned

New York City's underworld for three decades. The FBI may have clipped the wings of the big five, but all that did was make way for a sharper, cleverer kind of crime. Crimes that come in the form of digital espionage, poll rigging, reputation manipulation, and—most lucrative of all—online gambling. The Di Santo family now wields enough power that its soldiers can kill anyone who denies them on a whim, and the feds can't afford to touch them with a barge pole.

If I dare to deny the don of this family, it won't only be me impaled on the shaft of his pretty yacht; it will be every member of my family, to "set an example."

Gianni Di Santo and Papa had an arrangement, but only because it suited Gianni. One sneaky look through Papa's office when I wanted to fake my ID informed me a quarter of the goods that came through our port were Gianni's, and Papa would've had no choice but to do as Gianni asked.

Papa watches me with a grimace of finality, and I know the time has come for me to accept my fate.

"We're letting the Di Santos take over the port, but by cementing our alliance through marriage, it will remain in our name. Savero has agreed to let us continue running it the way we always have. No one has to lose their job. But we'll be splitting the profits."

"So he does nothing and still gets fifty percent of whatever our family makes . . . *and me*?"

Papa breathes in slowly. I can tell it's taking some effort for him to stay calm too.

"You think I can be happy with a man like that?" I

say quietly. "I won't ever be able to respect him or love him, or even like him. I'm going to be miserable, Papa."

I've only seen Papa lose his shit once, and that was when the cops brought me home and delivered the news of Mama's murder. Once is about to become twice.

He slams a giant hand into his desk and curses so loudly I have to cover my ears. "What choice do I have, Trilby? It's this or we lose it all! Do you want that for our family? It won't just be the lack of income—it will be the shame of having to start again. The *humiliation* of being cleaned out by the Di Santos. There'll be no more college for Tess and Bambi, no more hospitality school for Serafina. We'll have to sell this place, lay off our staff. Is that what you want?"

"N-no," I stammer. "Of course not."

He stands and towers over his desk. Papa has never laid a finger on any of us, but the thought of it alone has always been enough to keep us in line.

"I suppose I am the eldest," I mutter. *And a virgin, of course.*

"It isn't just that." Papa sets both palms on the desk and leans over it toward me. "Your sisters, they're not as . . . *resilient* as you."

I swallow. That simply isn't true anymore, but my family refuses to acknowledge it or even see it.

"With my connections, I half-expected each of you to marry a made man, but of the four, you're the only one who can handle a don. Especially a don like Savero Di Santo." Papa sighs and sits back in his chair. "You might even be a good influence on him."

I swallow the urge to disagree.

"In fact, I'm counting on you to be." Papa levels me with a stare. "Savero needs to be kept under some semblance of control, otherwise I genuinely fear for the people of New York."

My heart stops thundering and limps along quietly instead, as if its very existence has been thwarted.

"I know it's a lot to take in. Go rest up. Tomorrow you'll be introduced."

A little more blood drains from my face. "Tomorrow?"

"After the funeral."

"But . . . we're not going to the funeral."

The church chosen for the ceremony is too small to accommodate all of Gianni's family, capos, soldiers, and associates, so anyone not directly connected to the mob has been relegated to watching the procession from the streets.

"We are now," Papa says with the air of someone who's finally made it but is finding it's not quite as he expected. "We'll be seated inside the church along with Gianni's capos and their families. It's a huge privilege."

The weight of responsibility takes ahold of my chest. "I have one more question."

"Go on."

I look up at Papa through heavy lashes. "What exactly makes you think I can do this?"

He sighs and shifts in his chair, then he *really* looks at me. "Before your mama died, you had such a strong spirit. You were never badly behaved, but you were bold and fearless and resilient. After she died, well . . . you tucked yourself away. You became a smaller version of yourself in front of my very eyes." He leans forward and rests his forearms on the desk between us. "I want to see that brave, bold girl again. I know she's in there, Trilby, but me, Alli, and your sisters . . . we haven't been able to draw her out. I want you to live a big life, my love. Maybe someone like Savero is just what you need."

My throat feels like cardboard when I swallow, so I simply nod and stand on shaky legs. My voice is but a whisper when I reply.

"Of course, Papa. I won't let you down."

$\mathcal{T}$rilby

Black paint splatters in raindrops over the canvas. If I tilt my head and narrow my eyes, it looks like a shower of bullets.

There's no escape.

It's even seeped into my art.

The visions that haunt me every night were bound to work their way into my paintings. It was inevitable. What I wouldn't give for a peaceful night—one where I don't startle awake repeatedly, gasping for breath, or surface feeling like I haven't slept at all because my dreams have exhausted me.

Last night I shunned Sera's offer of a sleeping pill— further proof she knows more about my tortured sleeping pattern than she's letting on—because I didn't want to wake up even groggier than usual. But after

Papa delivered the news I was to marry a Di Santo, my nightmares were filled with more darkness and destruction, so I guess the joke's on me.

I drop the paintbrush into a pot and sit at my dressing table. As I smudge some highlighter onto my cheeks, something sparkles in the corner of my eye. I open the ballerina jewelry box Mama gave me as a kid and pull out the hair comb I usually only wear once a year. Its clusters of crystals shine up at me, a glimmer of light in a sea of gray.

I remember the first time I saw Mama wear this comb in her hair. It was my parents' tenth wedding anniversary, and they were heading out to dinner, leaving me and Sera with Papa's sister, Aunt Allegra. I was six years old. I begged Mama to let me wear it one day. I remember how she laughed. I don't know if her laugh really did sound like silver bells in the wind, but I certainly remember it that way.

I was asleep when they returned home, but when I awoke the following morning, the first thing I saw when I opened my eyes was a cluster of crystals on my pillow. I folded my small hand around the comb and clutched it to my heart. It was then—and still is—the most precious thing I own.

I scoop my hair up on one side and tuck the comb in to hold it in place just as the doorbell rings.

It doesn't take me long to reach the door. My apartment is small, but it's all I need. It was converted from a garage attached to the main house just before Mama died, and I made such a fuss about wanting to move into it so I could grieve in peace that Papa didn't have the heart to deny me. It also meant that when Allegra moved in to take over the care of me and my sisters, she could have my old room.

Unlike most Italian women in our community, Allegra has never married or had children. She's always been a doting aunt, though, even if she sometimes has a funny way of showing it.

As soon as I open the door, Allegra struts past me, curling a lip at my painting outfit and brandishing a hideous pair of shoes, which she promptly places on my bedroom floor. "Trilby, please change out of that sack. We have to leave in five minutes."

I take a steadying breath and step out of the paint-splattered overalls.

"And put these on." She points to the shoes and huffs impatiently. "Now is not the time to be arriving fashionably late."

I arch a brow and peer down at the beige kitten heels. There'll be nothing fashionable about it in those. Only late.

"I'm not in any hurry to marry the Mafia," I say, slipping my feet reluctantly into the ugly shoes.

She yanks a strap a little too hard. "Honey, you're not marrying *the* Mafia. You're marrying one man."

"One man who happens to be head of the biggest crime family in New York." The thought still makes me shudder. I find it ironic that as someone who detests violence in all its forms, I have to marry perhaps the biggest source of it this side of Chicago.

"Come on, Trilby." Her tone's tight, and I can tell I'm testing her patience. "If you cast your net wide enough in this neighborhood, sooner or later you're gonna reel in a made man."

"He's a little more than a made man," I mutter.

Allegra glares at me, sympathy morphing into despair. "We live in modern-day New York, and your father is one of the family's most trusted associates. Marrying a Di Santo man was practically inevitable, and to marry the don himself is the highest privilege of all."

"And a death sentence to boot," I add under my breath.

"Don't be such a pessimist." Allegra folds her arms defensively and nods pointedly at the shoes. "Now look —they're not so bad, are they?"

I'd prefer to take my chances and argue, but it's clear nothing will get me out of wearing these godawful heels. "These aren't really my style."

"They're chic, Trilby. They're befitting of a sophisticated Mafia wife. You're going to have to get used to wearing—"

"Beige?" I cock my head to one side.

Allegra rolls her eyes and stands back to take a good look at the beigeness that is, apparently, my palette for the foreseeable future. "You won't be wearing neutrals entirely," she says with narrowed eyes. "It's a funeral, dear. You're wearing black today."

She reaches behind her and presents me with an outfit only a widow from the 1800s would be seen dead in. In fact, many were probably buried in such a garment. It's calf-length, with an A-line skirt in starched cotton, and a blouse buttoned up to the neck.

I stare back at Allegra, feeling my brows caressing my hairline. "I'm not wearing *that*," I say without thinking. "It is neither chic nor sophisticated."

For a second she looks at me as if I've slapped her. Then I realize my mistake.

"I mean, I'm sure it was sophisticated and chic once upon a time, but, um . . . it's not really the style anymore. I may not want this marriage, but I'd at least like to feel comfortable enough to make a good impression. I'm sorry, Allegra."

She puts the dress back into a suit bag and mutters under her breath something about it being good enough for her grandmother.

I shuffle in the hideous heels to my closet and pull out a 1940s black lace shift dress. This one's also calf-length, but it's pencil cut, with a fitted bodice, long, tapered sleeves, and a sweetheart neckline. It's demure, classic, and subtly sexy.

Allegra rolls her gaze up and down the dress and gives a begrudging nod. "I'll see you outside in five minutes. Please stop drinking coffee . . ." She glares at the half-empty mug on my desk. "It makes your teeth yellow. And don't be a second late. This is the funeral of the century—I will drag you there naked if I have to."

Crowds line both sides of the street as we drive to the church. The atmosphere is disconcerting. Some people lower their eyes and their hats in respect as we pass; others raise a glass of grappa and dance about in celebration.

New York hasn't seen a funeral like this in decades —absolutely not one for a member of the mob. I even spot a policeman or two among the crowd, singing along to the Toreador Song, Gianni Di Santo's favorite opera aria.

When we arrive at the church the mood outside is decidedly more somber. We step out of the car wordlessly and file up the stone steps. Sera slips her hand into mine, and we walk through the double doors together. A man in a Catholic robe directs us to the left-hand side and tells us to sit in row nine.

"I thought this was a funeral, not a trip to the movies," Bambi whispers behind me.

"Oh, sure, didn't you know?" Tess replies in her signature monotone drawl. "It's a special showing of *The Godfather*."

I keep my lips tightly and politely sealed, but I can see what she means. Before us is a blanket of black suits, black hair, and bulges in black jackets where guns are tucked into waistbands. A few women are scattered about sobbing into handkerchiefs, their faces hidden by black satin veils.

I shuffle along the pew and settle at the farthest end from the action. It's intentional. I want to remain anonymous and hidden for as long as possible.

I don't miss Allegra's glare when she ends up with the aisle seat.

Papa continues to the front and greets some of the black suits. I've encountered made men over the years due to the nature of his agreement with Gianni, but none of them have made a memorable impression.

"Oh my lord," Bambi mutters—then she's abruptly scolded by Allegra for using God's name in vain. She lowers her voice to a whisper. "Is that the body in there?"

We all look to the front of the church, where there indeed is the coffin. One advantage of being thirteen is Bambi has been spared from most of the funerals our family has been invited to over the years. Seeing an open coffin is an understandable surprise.

"Of course it is," Allegra snaps. "His family and associates will want to pay their respects."

Tess grimaces. "But do they have to see the dead body to do that?"

Bambi makes a quiet retching sound. "I think I might be sick."

"Can you see Savero?" Sera whispers beside me.

I shake my head. "I don't know who I'm looking for."

"You haven't Googled your future husband?" she asks, aghast.

"No, I haven't had time." I've actually had lots of time—another lovely side effect of nightmare-induced insomnia—but I can't bring myself to face my future yet.

She leans in to my ear. "There he is."

My blood pumps erratically. "Where? How do you know?"

"I *did* Google him," she whispers. "I want to know what kind of person my sister will be spending the rest of her life with."

"And?"

"There. To the right. Papa's approaching him now."

My eyes narrow on the man my father is weaving his way toward. When Papa stops, my gaze pans to a tall figure, slim but solid. From the back, he looks like every other man in the church, albeit a couple of inches taller. But when he turns his head to the left, I see sharp, prominent features, a strong Roman nose and hooded brow, and lips that are full but slightly downturned. He's not unattractive, but he doesn't make my pulse race. Then again, I haven't even spoken to him. He might have a glittering personality.

"He's . . . quite handsome," Sera says, but her attempt at enthusiasm falls flat.

"Yeah, if you like that same old suited and booted Italian greaseball look." I pop a mint into my mouth and suck it to stop any more incriminating words leaving my lips.

"Hmm," she muses. "He doesn't look as greasy as some of them."

I scan the other black suits and tip my head to one side to assess Savero from a different angle.

"Is that him?"

I turn to see Tess staring at my future husband. Her

top lip is curled and her face partially turned away as if she's recoiling in horror. She's never been one to conceal her true feelings.

"Thanks a lot, Tess," I mutter under my breath, while Sera elbows her in the ribs.

"Owww." She spins toward us, then her face falls. "Sorry. I didn't mean to make that face out loud."

"You've really got to learn to be more expressive," Sera says. She leans into me. "He's a Gemini sun. Without his time of birth I can't work out the rest of his chart, but I wouldn't be surprised if he has Virgo somewhere."

"How do you know?"

"Smart, understated. Obviously a perfectionist."

"Aren't Geminis supposed to have split personalities?" I whisper.

She doesn't get a chance to reply before Papa and Savero turn and look over at us. My blood heats from chest to cheek. I hate being the center of attention at the best of times, but like this, I feel like a prize cow being sold at market.

There's no flicker of interest in Savero's eyes when he narrows them in my direction. In fact, they're ice shards perusing me.

"Jeez," I mumble. "Could he at least look like he's pleased at the prospect of marrying me?"

Sera rests a hand on my arm. "Remember, it is his father's funeral, and he's now the boss of New York's biggest Mafia family. He probably has a lot on his mind."

I sigh. It's a fair point, but it doesn't make me feel any less uncomfortable.

The service ends far too soon for my liking. Six of the men who were sitting in the top two pews lift the black lacquered coffin, with its ostentatious gold trim, and carry it down the aisle to the exit. Then what I assume to be *actual* family, as opposed to *Mafia* family, follow next.

I glance sideways at Savero as he passes, but his gaze doesn't flicker my way. It makes me feel invisible and anxious, like I'm about to fall into a deep, deep hole from which no one can rescue me. I look down before the rest of his family passes because I can't face any of them yet. After today, I'll have a lifetime to get to know them. Right now, I want to bathe in ignorance a little while longer.

Papa stands and ushers Allegra and my sisters toward the exit before turning his expectant gaze to me. He finally seems to notice my outfit, and I can't tell from his tight huff whether it's a good choice or bad. No matter—there's no way I could have embarked on this day in the dress Allegra picked out for me.

"Remember what we talked about." Papa's stern warning comes out of the corner of his lips. "Give him your full attention. Only speak when you're spoken to. And always be polite and courteous."

I sigh despondently. "How else would I be, Papa?"

He wraps a hand around my elbow and walks me to the exit, where Savero is talking to the priest. Beyond the church building, the coffin is being carried across

the lawns to the cemetery, where it'll be lowered into
the ground.

We stand to the side of the aisle and wait. Papa may
think this is polite, but I think it's weak. I hate the way
we're already walking on eggshells around the man who
is basically robbing us of our family business.

Finally, the priest nods in our direction, and Savero
turns around. His gaze finds me instantly and rakes over
my outfit before clawing its way back up to my face.
His expression barely moves.

"Mr. Di Santo," Papa says, making me step forward.
"Meet my eldest daughter, Trilby Castellano."

"It's a pleasure to meet you," I say in my most polite
voice. "And I'm so sorry for your loss."

My offer of condolence makes him pause, and for a
second a flash of sorrow crosses his face. But just as
quickly, it's gone, and his eyes lick me up and down as
though I'm an appetizer he hasn't ordered but will, with
some reluctance, eat anyway.

"Likewise, Miss Castellano. And thank you."

Only a few people remain inside the church, but
they all watch our stilted first meeting with ravenous
curiosity. I feel self-conscious and slightly sick. This is
the man I'm going to marry. The man I'll spend the rest
of my life with. The thought hollows my stomach.

"It was a beautiful service." I lapse into my default
state of trying to fill the uncomfortable silence.

"Yes, beautiful," Papa echoes. "Thank you for the
invitation to the church."

Savero looks back at me, his features stoic. "It made

sense. We would have had to bring our families together to celebrate our impending union at some point—why not kill two birds with one stone?"

"Well, it's an honor," Papa says, while I refrain from rolling my eyes into the back of my head. I hate seeing Papa suck up to this man knowing everything he's doing to our family.

Savero shrugs like it's nothing. "We'll be having a simple buffet afterward at The Grand, followed by a toast to my father, then we'll announce our engagement."

"Perfect," Papa replies, patting my arm.

Suits move around us quietly, preparing for the next part of the funeral: the burial. One of them is halfway past us when Savero thumps him on the back. Hearing my father's instructions echoing in my ears, I dare not look away from Savero—but then something otherworldly draws my gaze to the right.

The "back" turns around, and the frigid air heats up.

"*Fratello*, meet my fiancée . . ."

It takes no more than a second for me to recognize the man. Then my breath leaves the building.

I've seen those Barolo-colored eyes before. They swim somewhere between the desire to remember and the need to forget, swaddled in blue lagoons and dark stares. My brain claws around for details until they fly at me thick and fast. Joe's Bar, the dark-eyed stranger whose gaze burned my skin and whose words probed at my story.

". . . Trilby Castellano." Savero's voice sounds faraway, as if I'm traveling through a tunnel toward it.

I'm pretty sure my face has drained of color. Those full-bodied eyes betray no emotion as shame floods my veins. In this moment I can read his thoughts. He's looking at a drunk. Someone undeserving of his family name. Of his *brother*.

He lifts his hand. "Miss Castellano," he drawls. "It's a pleasure."

I blink. We've met before, but he's chosen not to divulge that.

"This is Cristiano, my brother," Savero says.

I slip my hand into Cristiano's, and he wraps his fingers around it until his grip is firm and mainlining fire down my arm.

"Cristiano," I say, weakly. "Pleased to meet you."

Those deep, dark eyes watch me with indifference while blood rushes back to my cheeks. Seconds pass, and he doesn't let go of my hand. His skin warms me like a faint memory, and the sensation of being caught in his arms makes my bones soft.

I try to pull away, but he holds my hand fast, a small smile curling one corner of his lips. Just as I sense Papa's gaze zeroing in on the contact, Cristiano lets go.

My hand feels suddenly cold. I already miss the heat of his grip.

"Excuse me sir. . . " A portly man with a bald head and searching eyes pushes his way towards us. "The service is about to start."

Savero's right eye ticks before he pans his gaze to

the man. His jaw is like steel, his body alarmingly calm. Which is why what happens next makes my heart stop.

"What did I say about interrupting me, Franco?"

Instantly, the bald man flinches as though he's been physically hit.

"Um, I'm sorry sir. I, um. . ."

Savero is unfazed by his blustering, and continues in a patronising tone. "And what don't I like to do?"

Franco swallows, and because the church has fallen silent, I can hear the movement in his throat.

"Um, repeat yourself, sir."

He takes a step backward and hits a pew. Raw fear fills his face.

In the blink of eye, Savero pulls something from his jacket pocket. My gaze catches on a flash of silver before a blade is driven into the side of Franco's neck, then dragged down his chest to his sternum.

Franco's eyes widen in shock. He's alive, yet, he's just been sliced open.

My breath stutters and I snap my lips together. I anchor my focus on Franco's face because that's the only visible part of him that isn't pulsing out of his skin.

Someone hands Savero a crisp white handkerchief which he uses to wipe the blood off the blade before sliding it back into his jacket. I can feel the tension vibrating through Papa as we both hover like reluctant spectators.

Franco's legs buckle and the wooden pew creaks beneath his weight. Before he can slide to the floor,

Savero puts a hand to Franco's throat, plunges his fingers inside and pulls out his jugular.

I finally find the strength to avert my gaze. I don't turn my head—something tells me that if this was a test, turning away would get me an instant fail—but I direct my attention over Savero's shoulder. I don't see anything though. My focus is turned inward, working overtime to stop the tears that want to fall. My mama's face flashes across my lids and I bite down hard on my lip, drawing blood. A frozen chill wraps around me raising all the hairs on my body.

In the distance, I hear Franco's body thud against the flagstones, and the gurgling eventually stops.

It's only when my face warms that I realise my gaze has settled on Cristiano. He's staring back at me, his stance primed, his eyes full yet narrowed. I hold onto that stare like a life raft, half conscious of people moving around us, stepping over Franco's body as though he's roadkill.

I sense Savero hand the bloodied cloth back to one of his men, then he turns to me and Papa.

"Please excuse me. I look forward to seeing you at the hotel."

I drag my focus back to my future husband and ignore the nausea crawling up my throat, burning up my chest. He is eerily calm, as though he extracts body parts from only partially dead people every day of the week—even Sundays.

"Of course," Papa replies. His voice is hoarse.

We both watch Savero leave.

Papa's arm has turned to stone; he doesn't feel the heat of Cristiano's hard gaze like I do, and something in me knows we have to at least *appear* able to take this kind of shit in our stride. I squeeze his arm tightly. Imperceptibly.

Papa inhales beside me and I feel the blood pumping defensively beneath his skin. "We should get going," he says. "It's a pleasure to see you again, Cristiano. You're looking well, and more like your father than ever. You were just a boy when we last met." I close my fingers around his arm to stop him from rambling.

My eyes flick back to Cristiano who smiles stiffly. I try to imagine him as a boy, but I can't get past those sharp cheekbones and strong jaw or his sheer height. He's overwhelmingly *there*, as though his presence has wrapped itself around me, blocking out all the light.

"I'm not sure that's a good thing, but thank you," he replies, smoothly. Too smoothly.

Papa straightens, snapping back to his more professional demeanor. "Well, it's good to see you. I hope we can speak again soon."

Even through the haze of shock, I can tell Papa genuinely likes Cristiano. I know when he genuinely likes someone, and when he doesn't but knows what's good for him.

"That would be nice."

I hear the "but" in Cristiano's tone and dart my eyes toward him. He drapes me in a loaded gaze that weaves a trail of fire from my head to my beige-clad toes.

"But this is only a fleeting visit. I'm not staying."

I feel my heart drop an inch—probably in relief. I don't know how I'd be able to cope living under this man's glare while married to his brother. His sick, callous, *murderous* brother.

What would Savero do if he knew I'd been out in the city alone, drinking and talking to men I don't know? I hope Cristiano doesn't breathe a word about it, because if Savero can tear someone's throat out in the middle of a church no less, at his own father's goddamned funeral, in front of his future wife and father-in-law, without so much as a blink, for simply *interrupting*, I don't stand a chance.

I hear Papa bid Cristiano farewell as though there isn't a dead bald guy at our feet and blood pooling around our shoes. I don't respond. I'm not even engaged yet and I'm done with the tests.

As we walk, numbly, away from the church, oxygen returns to my lungs, along with the strange feeling that I've left something behind.

I check for my purse. It's hanging from my shoulder. I check for my sunglasses. They're on my head. I smooth down my dress. It doesn't help. There's a burning sensation on the back of my neck, and I hope I'm not coming down with the flu.

I turn around on impulse, and all those feelings disappear.

Cristiano is standing on the edge of the circle of mourners, his back turned to them all. He's not paying any attention to the burial taking place behind him, nor to the sobbing women to his left and his right.

Instead, he's staring. Dead ahead.

At *me*.

CHAPTER 4

Trilby

I'm barely holding myself together by the time we pull up to The Grand. Mercifully, my sisters have gossiped among themselves allowing me to hold back tears in the privacy of the car window. Papa has also stayed silent, the two of us bearing a secret that is already eating up my insides.

Witnessing my future husband callously murdering one of his soldiers at his own father's funeral, then stepping over him like he's a dead rat has filled me with the kind of anxiety a stiff drink and a mood-enhancing pill could only attempt to alleviate. And neither of those things are an option. I may not have been born into the Cosa Nostra, but I've lived on the edge of it for long enough to know what's acceptable and what could get us outcast or even killed.

A good Italian Mafia wife doesn't drink to excess, doesn't take drugs, doesn't argue, and doesn't express opinions. She only speaks when it's acceptable to, she dresses conservatively, and she takes good care of her husband and then herself. The only difference between a Mafia bride and a Stepford wife is that the former's white picket fence is bulletproof.

These are rules I have to live by now, if I value my life and that of my family. What's more, there I was thinking the only introduction I'd have to contend with today was my introduction to Savero Di Santo, not the brother *no one* talks about.

I can feel the anger colliding with fear deep in my chest. Papa talked to Cristiano like he was a long-lost son, whereas I didn't even know he existed. That encounter alone has left me dizzy and disoriented, especially knowing what Savero is capable of. If only I could remember a word of my conversation with Cristiano that night. The not-knowing is crippling.

Something pink and blue looms overhead, and we all crane our necks to the sky. Tess is the only one who finds the power of speech.

"What the *hell* is that?"

"*Madonna!* Contessa! It is for your sister." Allegra gasps.

"Seriously," Tess says, undeterred. "What is it?"

I sigh into my lap, while Sera squints and says, "It's a balloon . . ."

"A giant inflatable heart with a crown on it," Bambi adds.

"*Cazzo!* How inappropriate," Tess says, her lip curling into its signature grimace. "It's a funeral, for heaven's sake."

"You don't know Di Santo arranged it," Sera said. "There could be another engagement taking place here."

Tess's eyes widen, and her voice drops several octaves. "That's why it says 'Di Santo and Castellano' on the back?"

I groan inwardly and step out of the car.

"Well, I think it's romantic," Sera says, working overtime to make me feel better. I don't have the heart to tell her nothing she says or does today will work. I've sunk into a pit of despair, yet I can do nothing but plaster a big smile on my face and push pretty words out of my mouth.

As we walk into the hotel, I hear Tess whisper behind me. "Don't you think it's weird he's chosen today to celebrate his engagement? I mean, everyone's dressed in black."

"Some might say it's fitting," I mutter under my breath.

"But his *father* just died," she continues. "He's supposed to be grieving."

"People grieve in different ways," Allegra says curtly. "Mr. Di Santo is doing what his father would have wanted him to do. What respectable Italian man wouldn't want a wife and a family? Settling down with a good woman may be his own way of paying his respects to the late don."

I spin around, unsure I heard her correctly.

"You are a *good* woman, Trilby," she says through a clenched jaw.

"Don't choke, Allegra," I deadpan.

She straightens her shoulders. "Come on, girls. I need you all to be on your best behavior. This is an important moment for our family."

We file into the expansive function room. High, ornate ceilings tower over us, and gold-trimmed walls close us in like caged birds.

"So what did he say to you?" Sera asks.

I swallow down vomit. "Nothing of note."

"Not even 'you look beautiful'?" Tess says, striking another blow to my self-esteem.

"He has a funeral to attend to and far more important things to be thinking about," I reply. *Like dismembering a living being while he's choking to death right in front of us.*

"It was his decision to turn a funeral into an engagement party," Tess says. "I think it's rude."

"Trust me." I smooth the creases from the journey out of my dress. "This is *not* going to be a party."

I glance up to see her looking at something over my shoulder. Turning to follow her gaze, I see several groups of men, all dressed in black, flooding into the room like termites. I watch them enter one by one, their conversations as tight as the lines on their brows. There's only one man I recognize: Benny Bernadi. His quiet and mysterious reputation seems to enter the room before he does, as the volume drops by a couple of decibels when he steps inside.

His gaze does a circuit of the room and lands on our little group—more specifically, on Tess. She's dressed in her usual signature black but has somehow managed to find a way to make respectable look debauched. She's wearing a long black maxi dress that clings to her like a second skin. One bare leg shows through a long slit up the side, and the leather straps of her gladiator stilettos wind up to her knee like a vine. Still, I cough and draw her attention my way. I don't like how he's looking at her—like she'd make a decent meal.

"Not rude . . ." Sera comes to my defense, drawing my attention from Benny's perusal of our younger sister. "*Important.* Tril's about to marry the most powerful man in the city. What do you expect?"

I squeeze Sera's hand.

Tess leans in until her breath whispers across my cheek. "Who's the broody guy by his side?"

I locate Savero and pan to his right. My pulse quickens at the insidious sense of shame. "That's his brother, Cristiano."

"Wow. Even with that dirty scowl, he's the hottest guy in the room."

"From the little I've seen of him, he's a grumpy asshole," I say, hoping that concludes the topic.

I should know my sister better than that.

"Grumpy and *gorgeous*. He could tell me to go to hell and I'd look forward to the trip."

His eyes lift and lock with mine, instantly quieting everything around me. Tess is still speaking, but I don't hear her. I can't tell from this distance if he's angry, irritated, or simply disappointed by the knowledge I'll soon be his sister-in-law. I tear my gaze away. I wish he'd do the same, but the side of my face glows hot, and somehow I know he's still staring at me from across the room.

I turn my attention back to Tess. "I'm sorry, what?"

"Do you know if he's single?"

I inhale sharply. "I literally just met him, Tess. I have no idea."

She jerks slightly. "All right, all right. No need to bite my head off."

"Sorry," I mumble, feeling suddenly guilty and transparent. "I didn't mean to snap."

She sighs and seems to notice my discomfort for the first time today. "It's okay. It's all pretty surreal, being in a room with all these armed men. It's making me feel nervous, and I'm not even marrying one of them. Here —maybe this will help."

She pushes a flute of champagne into my hand then touches it with hers. It makes a ting that sounds decadent and everything this afternoon isn't. I go for a sip but suck in half the glass, hoping to fill the sudden hole in my chest.

"Easy, tiger," Sera whispers. "Don't let the family see . . ."

I take another sip. The champagne is delicious. Light, fresh, just dry enough. It softens the tautness in my temples. "Which one?"

Her brows knit together.

I clarify. "His, ours, or the firm?"

She looks across the room. "Isn't the firm his family? They all seem to be from the same Sicilian stock. Slick black hair, oily skin, same wardrobes, by the looks of it . . ."

I snicker into my flute. "Right?"

Her head tilts to one side, and her eyes narrow. "The women though . . ."

I look up sharply. "What about them?"

Sera covers her lips with her flute and lowers her voice. "They seem to be from a different stock altogether."

I train my focus on her despite the urge to look at what she's seeing. "What do you mean?" I hadn't even stopped to consider there might be other women in Savero's life, but of course there are.

"They're either all of Scandinavian blood or they've paid a truckload of money to look like they are."

I turn enough of a fraction to be in wholehearted agreement. The entire far corner is filled with blonde blow-dries, inflatable busts, and hemlines that showed a little too much skin for a funeral.

"Forget marrying the don," I mutter. "Those women look even more frightening."

Sera clasps my hand and smiles sympathetically. "Come on—let's have a walk."

The evening drags by slowly. We stand through toast after toast dedicated to the great man that was Gianni Di Santo. We eat caviar and foie gras and drink expensive champagne (when no one's looking) and conveniently ignore the fact people would have died so my fiancé could fund this reception.

"What's going through your head right now?" Sera asks as we look through the terrace windows at the darkening sky.

"That I've never seen so many Breitling watches in one room before."

She smirks and nudges me with her elbow.

The sound of the PA system cranking up again makes us turn toward the stage, and my heart starts beating erratically. I can only imagine I've been in denial up until now, because with the announcement of my engagement to Savero Di Santo imminent, I feel an instinctive need to escape.

A host's voice booms over the speakers. "Please join me in welcoming Mr. Savero Di Santo back to the stage."

A rousing cheer fills the room as Savero reappears. The authenticity of it repulses me. He takes the microphone and coasts his gaze across the audience. I feel suddenly faint.

"Oh God, this is it," Sera whispers.

I grip her hand for support.

"Some may say that a funeral—especially the funeral of someone as loved and well-respected as my father—is an unconventional place to announce an engagement. But who knows when I'll have all those closest to me together in one room again?"

"And alive . . ." I mutter under my breath.

"As many of you know, my father enjoyed a

successful business partnership with the Castellanos, and the port has played a fundamental role in some of our import and export operations. With Father's passing, I believe we can only strengthen that partnership. So, not only will we be co-owners of Castellano Shipping from this day forth, but I'm also delighted to introduce my new fiancée, Trilby Castellano."

"Holy hell," Sera mutters under her breath.

"Smile," Allegra says, discreetly jabbing me with her elbow.

A hundred eyes turn toward me, but there's only one pair I can feel. My gaze is drawn to Cristiano, and the weight of his glare almost pulls me under.

I gasp for air as the room spins around me.

"Trilby . . ." Sera grips my arm. "Are you okay?"

"Mm-hmm," I manage through short, panting breaths. "Just give me a moment."

Pull yourself together, Trilby.

I think I'm having a mild panic attack, but I can't let it show on my face. The last thing a Mafia don needs—especially one as unhinged as Savero—is a wife who can barely stand unaided at her own engagement announcement. This marriage means everything to Papa; his entire life's work and our family's livelihood —hell, even our *lives*— is at stake. I can't give Savero any reason to call it off.

Up ahead, my fiancé receives slaps on the back and raised glasses. I may as well not exist for all the congratulations I receive.

On the few occasions I glance across the room with

the hope of a returned smile, at least, from the vast collection of brassy blondes, I get anything but. If a look could cause a thousand cuts, I'd be bleeding out on the function-room floor.

I lock eyes with the matriarch of the female entourage—the wife of one of the capos—and regret it instantly. She sits on a floral club chair, her hair tinged yellow and voluminous, her weathered tan compressed into a too-shiny black bandeau dress. Her head is pulled back, her chin slightly raised, allowing her a view of me through lowered lids. She's flanked on either side by two lookalikes who make a show of swiveling their bodies fully toward her and then back in my direction. They're gossiping about me and not making any attempt to hide it.

For what it's worth, I agree with them. I'm not the right woman for their don. But it's not like I have any say in the matter. My heart cracks a little at the reminder *I'm* not the reason he's marrying me. The man I'm set to spend the rest of my life with only wants me because of what my father can offer him.

Sera does her best to put me at ease, but I can't focus. "Have you eaten anything yet?" she asks.

My eyes round. "You think I can stomach food right now? I can barely stomach life."

"It might help." She nods encouragingly. "Just a little bite. Come on—the food is right over there. I'll go with you."

I huff out a tense breath. "Fine. I'll give it my best shot."

I follow her through crowded bodies, feeling the heaviness of judgment as people watch me pass. Just as we reach the table, Sera stops short.

"What is it?" I ask.

"Sorry, Tril, I just need the restroom real quick."

I swing my head toward the buffet and then back to the chasm now lying between us and the rest of our family. "Now? You can't hold on a couple minutes?"

She stares at me pleadingly.

"Fine. Go. I'll meet you back here."

"I'm sorry," she squeaks. "I'll be as fast as I can."

I grit my teeth and walk up to the table of food. Stretching across the back of the room, it would be piled high with Italian antipasti and other delicacies had the rest of the guests not already devoured half of it. I slide a thin porcelain plate from the top of a pile and eye what's left of the cold meats and marinated vegetables. It's as I'm spooning some limp salad onto my plate that I feel a hot breath across my neck. It's so hot, in fact, it feels angry.

My cheeks warm as I stare at my plate. I can almost taste his presence behind me. My heart races, and I have to force my hands to move mechanically from one dish to another.

The hot breath continues to graze my ear and warm my left side. I step to the right, training my eyes on a dish of pasta salad. As I lift the serving spoon, his voice chafes against my ear.

"You're marrying my brother?"

My heart clatters against my rib cage. I dare not look

up. Instead I focus on scooping another spoon of salad and lowering it onto my plate.

The hot breath continues to burn, searing the side of my face.

"Answer me, Castellano."

Hearing my family name sound so bitter against his lips makes me startle. When I look up, I'm swallowed whole by his eyes. They're larger than Savero's and a richer brown, almost burgundy.

I take a breath. "It seems so, yes."

Shame leaches into my veins as images of the night at Joe's Bar flash blurrily across my lids.

I was *intoxicated*.

So intoxicated I don't remember much about our encounter at all.

I wouldn't have kissed him—I know that much. I've kissed boys before from my school and was so underwhelmed by the experience I simply don't see the point in it. But something about the way he held my hand in the church earlier today . . . it felt familiar.

God, please say I didn't touch him.

Blood rushes into my cheeks as I gaze up at the man who is to become my brother-in-law. "I'm sorry if I was . . . inappropriate. I'd had a difficult day . . ."

"And a bucketload to drink." His voice is sharp, and no smile accompanies his words, only judgment. He also isn't denying I was inappropriate, which means . . .

Oh God.

My face burns. "Did we . . .? Um, did I . . .?" I don't

even know what I'm asking. I wouldn't know how to be forward with a man.

I crane my neck to look up at him. His shoulders are as broad as his height is foreboding. It would take nothing for him to snap me in two—and from the way he's glaring at me, I think he might want to.

"We talked," he says. "That's it."

Relief floods through me, softening my bones to the point I have to steady myself by gripping the table. But something in his expression seems . . . resentful.

"Okay." I force a smile, but it falls quickly when he takes a step toward me.

He bends his neck until his lips skim the comb at the side of my head. A cool shiver coasts down my spine. His whisper is soft, in stark contrast to the sharpness of his words.

"If you hate violence so much, why are you marrying the most violent man in New York?"

I stagger back a step and stare at him. Then I do something completely out of character.

I laugh.

His eyes narrow.

When I speak, my voice is low and thick with bitterness. "You think I have a choice?"

I don't know what has possessed me to be so brutally honest with the one person closer to my fiancé than perhaps anyone else in the world, but instead of feeling terrified—which would be the most logical emotion right now—I feel . . . liberated.

His forehead softens, and a corner of his mouth

twitches into a smile that he erases with a swipe of his thumb. "And there I was, thinking you were going to be just like the rest of them."

My heart pounds against my rib cage. *What is* that *supposed to mean?*

"Did you get home all right?"

The change in topic almost gives me whiplash. "Yes. I did, thanks."

Several seconds pass, and he doesn't move. The heat of his glare is close to unbearable. His jacket bunches where his hands are shoved deep into his pockets, and a glimmer of steel shines through a fold. He's armed, but it doesn't turn my stomach as much as it should.

"When did you and my brother meet?"

I straighten my shoulders. "Today. In the church, after the service."

His eyes widen a fraction. "You only met him today?"

"Just seconds before he introduced me to you, in fact."

His jaw works from side to side. The pause drags out uncomfortably, until I have to look away. But when he leans into my space and whispers hoarsely, I can't mistake his words.

"So you met me first."

I turn my head to see him *staring* at me, his eyes almost black. My lips part as a raw thrill skitters down my spine.

Sera bursts into the space between us. "Ugh, I'm sorry about that, Tril." Oblivious to the tension she just cut like a knife, she coasts her gaze across the buffet table. "Where's all the food?"

Cristiano clears his throat. "Apologies. It appears my family has eaten most of it."

Sera jumps as if she's only just noticed he's there, then she backs up into me. "Oh gosh, I wasn't implying anything. It's food, isn't it? I mean, that's what it's there for."

Ignoring her, his attention rests on me like a heavy weight. "Congratulations, Miss Castellano. I wish you and my brother all the happiness in the world."

My heart pounds as he walks away. I can't believe what I just said. I basically admitted I'm only marrying his brother because it's what others want, not my own choice. Worse, he didn't give me any clue my secret was safe with him. If I was anxious before, I'm positively incapacitated with nerves now.

"Jeez, it's eat or be eaten in this place. Do you think Papa will let us grab a pizza on the way home?" Sera says as Cristiano disappears into the crowd.

I push my plate toward her. "Have mine. I'm not hungry."

She looks up eagerly. "Are you sure? The bride-to-be has to eat."

"I'm sure Allegra would prefer that I don't between now and the wedding." And I don't think that will be a problem given that all I need to do is close my eyes and picture the scene from the church to put me off food forever.

Sera shovels a forkful of pasta salad into her mouth and shrugs in agreement.

While she eats, I scan the room. Not much has changed. The Scandinavian Barbie dolls are still seated in one corner, black suits line the walls and fill half the floor, and my small family hovers near the glass doors that open onto the garden terrace. I feel a surprising urge to join them. I want them to form a protective circle around me and reassure me that, marriage or no marriage, they'll be there for me.

My gaze catches on Papa. The lines on his brow are deep, and though his hands are pushed casually into his pockets, his arms are rigid. He's no more at ease than I am. I feel the weight of our situation settle in my stomach. Our family's future rests on my shoulders. I have to do everything in my power to make this work.

Straightening my spine, I ignore the curious eyes of other mourners as I return—if only temporarily—to the fold.

After several hours of faking happiness and suffering the remnants of yesterday's hangover and today's horror show, I'm exhausted.

"Are we leaving soon?" Bambi whines, and I could hug her for asking the question I'd be scolded for asking.

"Hush, Bambi. It won't be much longer now," Allegra whispers before stiffening and snapping her mouth shut.

I look up to see the cause of her uncharacteristic silence. Savero is heading toward us. My skin breaks out in a cool sweat. On one side of him is what I assume to be a capo. He hasn't left Savero's side since I saw him at the church. On the other is Cristiano.

I train my focus on Savero, afraid of what I might see if my gaze glides too far to the left. I can't be certain I won't start hyperventilating if I look into those eyes again.

Savero stops in front of me, not sparing the rest of my family a glance.

"It's a beautiful evening," I say.

His gaze travels down my black dress and settles on the nude shoes before climbing slowly back up to my face. I search for any clue he might like what he sees, but I can't seem to focus on anything other than the side of his jacket where the blade is hidden.

For some inexplicable reason, my eyes ache to look at Cristiano, but I don't allow it. That could invite a whole other world of fear.

"We're about to leave, but I wanted to thank you for being here," Savero says, and I bite back another urge to laugh hysterically. I'm still in shock—that's the only explanation. "I will see you Tuesday."

I blink. "Tuesday?"

"Yes. Your father invited me to dinner." His face is impassive.

I force another smile. "Wonderful. It will be a pleasure to welcome you to our home."

He doesn't seem to hear me. With one of his hands, he reaches up and grips my chin firmly, making me suck in a breath. These were the same fingers he plunged into a man's throat only a few hours ago. I want to be sick. He pushes my face slowly from side to side as if inspecting a diamond for flaws.

For a few seconds I hold my inhale, not daring to move my eyes away from his. When he releases me, I blink across to where Cristiano is standing.

Was standing.

He's gone.

A hot breath floods out of my lungs. There's immense relief, but I still want to crawl into a hole in the floor.

Savero doesn't notice. Instead he takes my hand and pushes a roll of green notes into it. "Your dress will be couture, the flowers will be white, and the food will be Italian."

I frown, not quite understanding.

Allegra, who is clearly none-the-wiser about the earlier scene Papa and I were treated to, puts a hand on my arm and begins to thank Savero for his generous contribution to the wedding costs, but then an ear-splitting bang knocks us—and everyone around us—to the ground.

That sound . . . It should take me straight back to the car I was sitting in when Mama was shot. It should flood me with grief, send my heart up my throat, and set my pulse throbbing through my temples. Yet I feel strangely calm.

Gradually, I become aware of my cheek grazing the hotel carpet and a few screams from the outer edges of the room. Black suits move around in my peripheral vision, and all the blonde women previously sitting on club chairs are on the floor. They know the drill.

Voices shout above me, and I lift my head to see Savero sauntering toward the terrace doors. They're ajar, and a light illuminates the manicured lawns. The other family members don't seem too alarmed, so I carefully pull myself up and crane my neck to look outside.

A male figure stands out there, silhouetted by moonlight. A curl of smoke snakes upward from a cigarette in his left hand.

I press my palms into the carpet and shift sideways for a closer look. When the edges of the silhouette crystalize, my heart skitters to a halt.

Cristiano is standing alone in the center of the lawn, a gun resting against his thigh. My gaze travels down his legs to the grass, where a now deflated giant heart covers the ground.

Tess crawls toward me on her hands and knees. "Thank God he shot that thing down. Ten more minutes, and it would have been me."

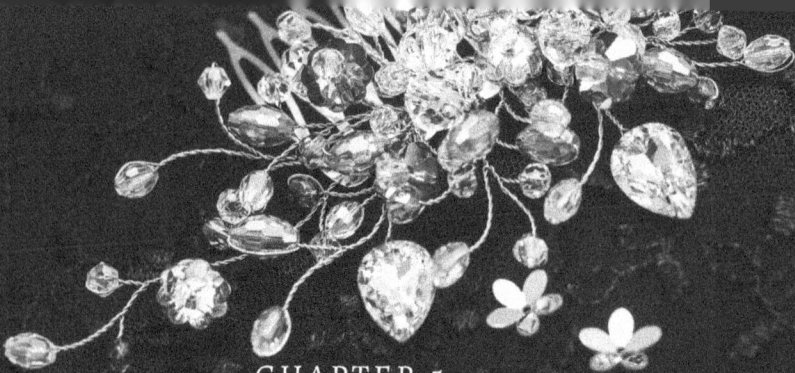

CHAPTER 5

Trilby

I stare at my reflection in the mirror. The sparkle has gone.

Even my painting hasn't pulled me out of the haze of depression like it usually does. Whatever challenges I've lived through, I've learned to cope by pouring all my emotions into my art. Even my outfits. Sera always says she can tell what mood I'm in or what side of my personality will come out that day by the clothes I choose to wear. "Choose" being the operative word.

I stare down at the dress Allegra had delivered. It sits stiffly on my hips and makes a scratchy sound when I move. The label describes the color as "sand," but it's beige. Frustration tenses my shoulders. I've never worn beige clothing, and I refuse to start now.

I step out of the ugly garment and fling it to the bedroom floor, then I pull out one of my favorite outfits: a red silk dress that falls just below my knees but makes up for the conservative cut by hugging my curves a little too hard. Allegra will have a conniption, but I don't care.

I kick off the nude kitten heels she keeps making me wear and slip on my highest heeled stilettoes. Leopard-print patent leather. Clashy, different, perfect.

I stand in front of the mirror. I look more like myself, but since the engagement announcement four days ago, I feel diminished.

Meeting Savero Di Santo wasn't the heart-racing pinnacle of my romantic life I'd hoped for. I don't know what I was expecting, but it certainly wasn't to be given a front row seat to a gruesome kill, then dismissed for most of the evening, and relegated to the ranks of all the other faceless, nameless women in his life crowded into that one corner of the room where the light doesn't shine.

The only memory worth holding onto from that evening is the one of the monstrous balloon lying flat on the ground, my fiancé's brother having fired a bullet into it. But each time I recall Cristiano standing casually over the multicolored foil, guilt, shame, and raw nerves punch me in the chest.

I still don't remember what happened at Joe's, and despite Cristiano saying we only talked, I don't believe him. We touched—I'm sure of it. Why else would the heat of his palm when he shook my hand feel so natural and familiar? And if he's not being honest about that, what else isn't he telling me?

Papa has hardly been home since the engagement announcement. He's been at the port around the clock with Savero's men. It seems my fiancé doesn't want to wait until I've signed the marriage certificate, which makes me question whether I'm needed in this arrangement at all. But then I remember the look on Papa's face when he told me of my fate. He wouldn't have agreed to give me to this man—"the most violent man in New York," according to his brother—if he'd had any other choice.

I just have to hope with all my heart that whatever Cristiano isn't telling me about that night, he isn't going to share it. Because I can't be the cause of my family's ruin. I can't be the next in line to be sliced open with a silver blade.

My phone buzzes on the restroom counter. I glance down and see Allegra's name.

> Allegra: Trilby Castellano, you'd better be on your way. We need to be ready to receive the don. He'll be here any minute now. And don't forget to straighten your hair.

I glance at my hair in the mirror. Messy waves brush my shoulders and trail over my forehead. I sigh and reach for the straighteners, then I put them down again. I'm probably already walking towards my imminent demise for wearing this dress—I may as well fully commit.

It wasn't long after Mama died that I began bleaching my hair blonde. I didn't need a shrink to know it was a symbolic way of detaching myself from the world around me. While we've never been an intrinsic part of the Mafia, we've lived close enough for me to feel its dark red stain and resent the olive-skinned, dark-haired *Italianness* of it. The less I looked like I belonged in its vicinity, the more easily I could stomach Mama's murder.

The sound of the doorbell makes me jump. Allegra must have gotten impatient waiting.

I walk to the door and mutter loud enough that she can hear, "Honestly, anyone would think I was about to hotfoot it to Atlantic City or sell myself to a circus."

I yank open the door expecting to see Allegra's pursed lips, but instead I get a shock that almost knocks me out at the knees.

"Let me guess. Trapeze artist?"

I don't know what takes my breath away first: the Barolo-colored eyes holding mine at three paces, the velvety voice dripping with mild amusement, or the fact *Cristiano* Di Santo is leaning against my doorframe.

My mouth falls open, and he reaches his thumb and forefinger up to scruff the manicured stubble on his chin as he regards me.

"I hope you're not always going to be this surprised to see me," he drawls, "because maybe we should get you on blood pressure medication now."

My heart thuds like a drum. Medication doesn't sound like a bad idea right this second. Nerves are fluttering around my chest like rabid wasps.

"Why—?" I flush at my squeaky voice and clear my throat. "Why are you here?"

His face is so still it could have been carved from granite. Then he sucks in a breath. "Sav is going to be late. I've come in his place."

Of course. Why else would he be here?

But something about his demeanor makes me feel like I'm being played with. All it would take is the mere mention of my drinking to Savero, never mind the fact I talked to Cristiano having no idea who he was, to put this whole arrangement into jeopardy. Cristiano knows my secret, and he could share it with anyone at any time. I'm at his mercy, and despite the fear that lines my stomach, that fact ignites something inside me. Something new and untested and dangerous.

His eyes flicker to the hallway behind me. "May I see your father?"

"Um, sure. I'm on my way around there now." I look for a space beyond the door to step into, but his body takes up the entire doorway. I bite my top lip nervously and glance around—anywhere but at him.

"On your way around where?" I hear the frown in his voice.

I jerk my head to the right. "Next door."

He pushes off the doorframe and anchors both feet to the ground. "Next door?"

A shiver tickles my spine. "Yes. The main house. This is the apartment."

When he doesn't question me further, I cock my head to one side. "Shall we?"

He grinds his jaw and steps aside. "After you."

My thighs tremble as I turn to lock the door, and I feel his warm breath drifting across my bare shoulders. I have to take extra care walking down the steps so I don't trip and make a fool of myself. We reach the main door, and I ring the bell. When I turn a fraction to check he's still there, Cristiano has a knuckle pressed to his mouth.

"What's so funny?"

"You ring the doorbell? You don't just walk in?"

I run my tongue across my top teeth. "I like my entrance to be noticed." I narrow my eyes in a challenge, but the laughter in his expression has disappeared. "What?" I ask.

He swallows. "Nothing."

Before I can press him any further, the door swings open, and Allegra's face instantly contorts as if she'd asked for a crate of Dom Pérignon and got a glass of cheap white wine instead.

"Ah . . ." Her gaze flits between me and Cristiano, and for a few seconds I enjoy her flustered confusion.

Cristiano, it appears, doesn't enjoy it so much.

"*Signora*, my apologies. *Mi fratello* . . . he is going to be a little late. He has some business with—"

"I understand," Allegra replies in a tone that suggests quite the opposite. "No need to explain."

"I found this one on my way here." His fingers lightly tap the small of my back, making me leap forward into my aunt. Out of utter embarrassment I try to make it look as if I'm going in for a hug, even though I rarely do that despite how much I adore her.

"Hey, Allegra!" I unravel my stiff arms and smile like a lunatic before stepping past her into the house. I need to get away from the owner of those fingers before the mortification burns me from the inside out.

I feel his hot glare at my back as I skip down the hall. Thankfully, Allegra, in a bid to impress the family I'm marrying into, holds him captive at the door.

I tuck my head around the entrance to the living area and see Papa deep in conversation with one of the port managers. I continue on by and almost run for the stairs. I need to get to a restroom to splash cold water on my face and then seek solace in one of my sisters' bedrooms.

"Not so fast, Trilby." Allegra's voice is stern, and I turn to see the kind of expression I've learned to just deal with, because an objection simply isn't worth it.

Cristiano's voice filters through from the living area. He must have been swiftly steered toward Papa.

"I was just going to the restroom," I say weakly.

Allegra's brows rise. "I thought you'd just come from one." She looks down over my outfit and mutters, "Supposedly…" She coughs and gives a little shake of her head. "Now, our guest would probably like something to drink, wouldn't he?"

I shrug like a moody teenager. "I don't know."

Her spine straightens defiantly. "Then I suggest you go find out."

When I don't move, her face drops as though I'm fast becoming the most disappointing sister of the four of us.

"Fine." I sigh and push myself off the bottom stair.

I drag my feet past Allegra and hesitate in the doorway. The three men have moved to Papa's desk, where they're looking through plans of the port and the surrounding area. Part of my heart wilts at hearing Papa transfer some of the control of his pride and joy. His father built that place from the ground up, and Papa has run it since he turned eighteen. The port is part of our family, and it feels like we're losing it.

I take a deep breath and walk quietly into the room. Papa and his manager keep their heads down, focused intently on the maps. Cristiano is the only one who senses me entering. For a moment our eyes meet, and my pulse picks up speed. His gaze betrays no emotion, but it tunnels into me like a laser beam.

". . . and that's where the private consignments are checked in," Papa says as if he still has the attention of the second most prominent member of the Di Santo family, when, in fact, it's settled wholly on me.

Cristiano's lips move mechanically. "I look forward to seeing it in the flesh."

I stop in the middle of the room and shiver. His gaze somehow makes me feel naked. "Mr. Di Santo, would you like something to drink?"

"Yes, I would." His voice sounds as gravelly as my mind feels foggy.

I hold in a lungful of air, hoping for strength. "What can I get you?"

"Whiskey, please. No ice."

I nod and turn slowly, trying not to run out of the room the way I want to.

Then his words halt me. "Actually, I will take ice."

I twist to see him yanking at his collar, his jaw rigid with tension.

"Thanks."

Biting my bottom lip, I walk out of the room. It's only when I reach an empty kitchen that I release a hot, wretched breath.

My brain claws around for some explanation as to why I'm feeling so unhinged all of a sudden. I'm about to marry a *don*. And not just any don—the downright ruthless head of the Di Santo family, the most notorious crime family for miles. A don whose brother knows my secrets—that I get drunk in backstreet bars and that I don't want this marriage at all. Those are reasons enough for why I can barely think straight.

I reach for one of our "best" crystal tumblers and place it on the counter, staring at it for several seconds. We never use the "best" glassware for anything—what are we saving it for? For this? For a man my family feels is above us in some way? I'm suddenly infused with a sense of injustice. What makes Cristiano Di Santo more deserving of our "best" glassware than we are?

No one looks up as I enter the room.

I place his whiskey gently on a coaster and take three steps backward. The men continue their deep discussion as if I'm not there.

Cristiano's gaze glides from Papa directly to me, and he reaches for his drink. Without glancing at the vessel, he lifts it to his lips and takes a sip.

It's Papa's gasp that turns everyone else's head. "What th—?"

Papa's manager snorts and then quickly tries to cover it up.

"Oh, um . . ." Papa gently wraps his fingers around the mug I've served Cristiano's whiskey in. "I'm so sorry. Let me . . . um . . ."

Cristiano refuses to let go of the mug.

Our eyes are fixed on each other.

A rumbling beside him begins to infiltrate my consciousness until Papa's voice breaks out in a growl. "TRILBY!"

I pan an innocent glance his way. "Yes, Papa?"

"Get rid of it and serve Mr. Di Santo's drink in a proper glass. Now."

"No." Cristiano sets his hand firmly on the top of the mug that has a giant pair of naked boobs and the words "What would Dolly do?" printed shamelessly across it.

Tess bought the mug for my eighteenth birthday, and no matter how often Allegra tuts and purses her lips, I refuse to throw it out.

His eyes never leave mine, but something behind them dances. "It's fine. It doesn't matter what the poison comes in." A corner of his lips lifts before his expression settles into something else. Something deadly and accompanied by a low, sinful voice and eyes that burrow beneath my skin. "As long as it *comes*."

Blood rushes like an avalanche up my chest, flooding my collarbone, my neck, my entire face.

Cristiano pans his gaze back to Papa's, effectively dismissing me.

I turn on wobbly legs and walk back to the kitchen, wondering—not for the first time since I met him— what the hell just possessed me and why such simple, innocent words from the mouth of my future brother-in-law make me feel like I've just been doused in lava.

CHAPTER 6

*C*ristiano

I turn back to the conversation and try to curb my flaring nostrils.

Cazzo.

If the sight of that woman in a red silk fucking *slip* wasn't enough to make me itchy and irritable, then the sheer balls on her could make me feverish.

I saw the mug out the corner of my eye the second she walked into the room. It's as if our bodies are connected through heat. Whenever she comes within a few feet of me, my skin burns. I felt it in the bar, then again in the church, and I felt it just now as she entered the room.

Part of me wanted to crack up laughing at her little joke, because the *nerve* it takes to serve something like that to a Di Santo . . . But I'm here representing my brother, the *don*, and it won't do to find practical jokes amusing.

"As Savero has said, this alliance will be beneficial in many ways . . ."

I turn my attention back to her father, though my gaze wants to remain on the door she just disappeared through. "How so?"

"Not only will it strengthen our defenses at the port and open up opportunities for a broader variety of shipments . . ."

Well put.

I've been under the impression Tony Castellano doesn't have much say in this "alliance," but it seems he's just as on board with it as my brother is. Either that or he's putting on a damn good show. I suppose there's nothing like opportunistic butchery to incentivize loyalty.

". . . it will also mean we can join forces against some of our common enemies, such as the Marchesis."

My eyes narrow. "What do you have against the Marchesis?"

Tony pauses, and grief floods through me. I know that pause.

"They killed my wife, the mother of my four girls. Right in front of Trilby."

I suck in a ragged breath as pieces of a puzzle fall into place. I knew I'd heard his daughter's name somewhere before. "Fuck," I say softly. "I'm sorry to hear that."

The temptation to kick myself is real. I haven't

forgotten the bartender's explanation of why Tony's eldest daughter only ventures out drinking once a year, but it never occurred to me her mother might have been murdered, and I never would have *dreamed* she was at the scene when it happened.

My stomach twists into a guilty knot. We're not so different, the Castellano girl and me, after all. I lost my mother at seventeen, ten years ago; she lost hers at fifteen, five years ago. Both our moms were killed by the Marchesis. The biggest difference between us is that I was allowed to leave the Cosa Nostra, while she's about to be swallowed up by it whole.

"Appreciate it." Tony sighs tightly. "They were sending a message."

I rarely use the gun in my waistband—I carry it out of habit more than anything—but right now it's warming my back, making its presence known.

"What kind of message?" I ask.

"They didn't like that I was working with your father. They offered me bigger contracts, greater profits, but I refused to work with them."

"Why?"

Tony turns to me, and the emotion in his features is genuine. "I respected your father. I know a lot of what he did was below the law, but at least he did it with integrity. He had principles, and that's hard to find in anyone these days."

Sadness curls a fist around my heart. Since finding out about my father's passing, I haven't given myself a moment to grieve—but it will come, along with a barrage of guilt for having fled so young and stayed away for so long.

Tony exhales heavily. "With the opportunities my port can offer and the partnerships your brother is looking to develop, we may be able to drive the Marchesis out of New York altogether."

Although I don't always agree with my brother's approach, the blood in my veins runs hot. "I agree."

Tony stops and looks at me. "Are you back in the family? I know your father hoped you'd return."

"No, I'm not. And I'm only staying a short while, then I'm heading back to Vegas."

"It's a shame," Tony says. "I like you."

I smile. "You should probably keep that to yourself."

"Ah, who fucking cares? We're in business now."

"Correction—you and my brother are in business. I simply run casinos. I have good connections with the authorities. Valuable ones. They'd be seriously compromised if I were to come back into the family."

We both stand and button our jackets.

"But you're loyal to Savero, no?" he asks.

"Of course I am."

"You would never side with the authorities?"

"Not when it comes to family."

Tony side-eyes me. I know what he's thinking.

"I prefer to think of it not as hypocrisy but compartmentalizing," I explain.

He grins. "He's lucky to have such a loyal brother."

I'm pleased Tony can't see my face as I follow him to the dining room. Savero doesn't see it that way. He puts on a good show to the rest of our "family," but I know he's counting the hours until I leave. He's never particularly wanted me around, and I've never known why. Still, I can't afford to hold a grudge.

"I'm lucky to have him," I say. "He saved my life when I was eight years old. I'd never dream of being anything but loyal."

Tony rests a hand on the back of a chair and turns to face me. "What happened?"

I push my hands into my pockets to keep them from fidgeting restlessly. Telling this story stirs up strange emotions I can't always explain.

"We were playing down by our boathouse. Nonni, my grandfather, used to keep a boat down there, and we'd sometimes sneak on board with some sodas and hide from our father. This one evening, we were play-fighting, and I fell overboard. I wasn't an experienced swimmer back then, so when I kicked my legs, they got caught up in one of the boat ropes, and I was pulled under. Savero dove in and cut me free."

Tony simply stares at me. It's a common reaction. I've given up trying to explain any further, because it is what it is. Savero saved me from drowning, and I will be forever indebted to him for that.

"Good heavens. That sounds horrific."

"Yeah, well, thankfully, I don't remember too much about it."

"That was some quick thinking on his part." There's awe in Tony's voice, which isn't something I hear very often when it comes to my brother. "He must have had a knife or something. Boat ropes are tough old things."

"Hmm." I pause. "I haven't given much thought to the details, to be honest. I was just glad to be alive."

"*Cavolo*," Tony says quietly. "He saved your life."

"He did, and I will never be able to repay him. We don't often see eye to eye anymore, and we go about our businesses *very* differently, but we're blood, and I will always support him in one way or another."

"That makes him a very lucky man." Tony says, a belated smile not reaching his eyes. "Please, take a seat. I'll go see where dinner is."

My throat is suddenly dry, and I could use a moment. "Actually, do you mind if I use your restroom?"

I follow Tony's directions down the hall and close the restroom door behind me. Then I stare at my reflection in the mirror. For the first time in a long time, I don't feel sure of my next move, and for someone who runs casinos for a living, that's not a good place to be.

I like Tony. He doesn't deserve to be handing over his life's work and his eldest daughter to someone who only has eyes for blood, gore and a quick, dirty buck. Although Father's business ventures were hardly legal, they weren't short-termist, and there was at least some political motivation, some rational thought, behind them. Savero is like a hyperactive kid in a china shop; he doesn't care what he breaks, as long as he gets a kick out of it and enough money to blow on a lineup of hookers. I don't agree with the way he does business, and neither did our father.

I splash some cold water onto my face. It isn't just the conversation with Tony that's turned up my inner temperature—it's been flaring since the second his daughter opened the door. She can't be given to my brother. He won't have the first clue what to do with a thinking, feeling human who doesn't expect payment for her services.

When I first met her, I thought she was meek and misguided, but the more I learn about the Castellano girl, the more I see a kind of fire behind her eyes that she can't help but release. But then as soon as she does, she shuts down as if it's the worst thing she could have done.

I'm under no illusions about what life is like for Cosa Nostra women. My mother was one after all. I know what the expectations are.

The Castellano girl is doing everything in her power to appear the perfect potential Mafia wife, but there's more to her than a pretty dress and polished words. I've seen glimpses of her true character, and it's only served to whet my appetite. I want to know exactly who my future sister-in-law is, and importantly, how the hell she's going to handle my brother.

I press the towel to my face and close my eyes. An image of her walking across the bar, her white dress fluttering around her thighs, glides across my lids. I brace my hands on the vanity and stare down at the faucet. I can never conjure that image again. Not if I'm to get through the rest of my life with her as a *sister*.

As I wrench open the restroom door, I immediately collide with something soft, smooth, and *rippling*. Castellano falls backward and only misses hitting the wall because I've got a hand wrapped around her arm.

A gasp parts her lips, and I realize I've just broken the only promise I've ever made to myself.

I was never meant to touch her again.

And now . . . it's too late.

CHAPTER 7

Trilby

I knew I wasn't imagining it when I suspected Cristiano's touch was familiar. There's a ring of fire around my arm where he's holding me upright, and like a thought treading a neural pathway, my body fizzes with recognition at the contact.

His words are harsh and at total odds with the way he's been looking at me since he came to the wrong door.

"Have you been drinking again, Castellano?"

My mouth drops open.

"I should be asking you the same question. Don't you look where you're going before you walk out of a room?" I snap, but I regret it instantly. Why, when I'm around this man, do words fly out of my mouth before I can even consider them? I've never spoken so curtly to a man before—not least one who wields just as much power over my family's future as my fiancé does.

He coasts his gaze over me slowly. The way it falls across my stomach and glides over my hips makes me shiver. We're standing in each other's space in the middle of the corridor, staring each other down. If anyone were to find us like this, there'd be questions. For me, not him, let's be clear.

His eyes morph from opaque to sparkling. "What's with the Dolly Parton mug?"

I glare up at him through my lashes. "I was flustered."

His hands slide down my arms slowly and drop away. Then the corridor echoes with the sound of cracking knuckles as he stares at me.

"So flustered you forgot where the glass cabinet was?"

My nostrils flare. "It's easily done. I don't use the glass cabinet too often."

"You don't serve drinks to other male visitors?" Another crack.

"Not usually." I turn my head for some oxygen. The air in the gap between us is too heated. "Was the whiskey to your liking?"

Out of the corner of my eye, his Adam's apple bobs up and down.

"It was perfect. Maybe I should drink from a mug more often."

I can't help but let a slow smile creep across my lips. "Don't be thinking you're going to borrow that mug," I warn. "It's my favorite."

His eyes widen, and I could kick myself. I just told my new brother-in-law I gave him my favorite mug. Is that flirting? I think it's flirting. Is it obvious? I truly don't know. I've never had to worry about anything like this before.

My breath sticks in my throat when he dips his mouth to my ear, and his words are slow, low, and deep. "Then, Castellano, I'm *honored* you served it to me."

It's a few seconds before he straightens, and by then I'm pink-cheeked and flustered. I must be the ideal opponent at this game. All the man has to do is breathe a whisper in my direction, and I don't know right from left.

He pushes his hands into his pockets and goes to walk past me, stopping at my shoulder. "Can you do me a favor?" he asks, looking straight ahead.

"Um . . . of course," I reply, remembering my manners.

"Don't wear that dress when you're with my brother."

My heart thumps with dread. "Why?"

"Because he'll destroy any man who can't take his eyes off you. And I don't want to be cleaning up his mess for the next month."

He walks away before I can respond. Not that I have a response—only a question.

Did Cristiano Di Santo just give me a compliment?

Why is it that sometimes you're faced with a meal that simply doesn't disappear no matter how long you look at it?

I curl another string of spaghetti around my fork and stare at the wall ahead as I feed it into my mouth. Then I chew it for longer than normal, because my throat simply won't entertain the idea of swallowing it.

The invisible blinkers I've attached to each side of my face don't stop his voice from wrapping itself around my ears and sliding its way inside, making me hot from the mere sound. I didn't know sound could do that.

Since Cristiano delivered that loaded instruction, I haven't been able to stop thinking about him. It doesn't help that he's sitting at the far end of the table, next to Papa, coasting his gaze over to me every thirty seconds. He's attempting to make Allegra feel comfortable about the fact he's here and his brother conspicuously isn't.

"I'll be sure to let him know exactly what he's missing, *signora*. I haven't tasted spaghetti like this since my mother was alive."

He's trying to put her at ease, but I can tell by the way her fork drops into her bowl the topic of a deceased parent has caught her off-guard. I look up sharply—not at the sound of clattering cutlery but the realization he too lost a mother.

"Perhaps you can give me the recipe to share with our cook."

"Of course," Allegra replies, composing herself. "It's a family recipe, but . . . well, I suppose you are about to become family too."

His eyes burn the side of my face. My invisible blinkers are useless; I don't need to see him to feel the weight of his gaze.

"How is the waste-disposal business going?" Papa asks. "I hear you're doing well in the north."

Cristiano looks down at me as he takes a long sip of red wine. "Yes, Nicolò just won a few major contracts with the help of some friends in Washington."

I suspect this is code for dirty politicians sending government contracts their way in return for backhanded payments.

"We've also financed a new division. Private residential. I believe Sav plans to launch it in the next few months."

"Do you have branding for it yet? A logo? Trilby could design something for you—right, honey? She's about to finish up art school, just in time for the wedding."

My gaze snaps to Papa. "What about the other courses I talked to you about, Papa? And the galleries that offer management programs?"

Papa continues as though he didn't hear a word I

just said. "She's a qualified designer. Top of her class."
He jabs a fork in my direction, then he spins his last few
strands of spaghetti around it.

My jaw would hit Allegra's fancy tablecloth if I
weren't so incensed.

"*Was* top of the class." I pick up my napkin and dab
the corners of my mouth before laying it gently to one
side. "Unfortunately not qualified though, and it sounds
like I never will be." My chair scrapes the wooden floor
as I stand. "Excuse me," I say, sweeping my gaze across
everyone except Cristiano. "I have a headache. I'm
going to get some fresh air."

Allegra inhales tightly. "Take some Advil, Trilby.
You'll be fine to join us again in thirty minutes."

Guilt tingles across my skin as I walk the short
distance to the library. I'm behaving like a child, and it
isn't like me at all, but I feel like I'm walking barefoot
into a fire with no protective clothing to keep me from
getting burned.

What on earth was Papa thinking when he said I was
the only one of the four who could handle marriage to a
don? I haven't even married Savero yet and I'm
struggling to keep the resentment at bay. How will I
handle a whole lifetime of dinners with my husband and
his capos and associates if I can't even handle one
dinner with his brother?

Cristiano's voice echoes in my ears, and I can still
feel the burn where his fingertips dug into my skin. He
doesn't even need to be in the same room as me to haunt
my every thought.

I shake the sound of his velvety voice from my head. It's fine to not be attracted to my husband-to-be. People have arranged marriages all the time to people they're not attracted to. But to be more attracted to his brother would be *unthinkable*.

I leave the door of the library ajar and walk to the window. Mama's rosebush in the center of the lawn is beginning to bud. I miss her so much it's like I have a permanent hole in my chest. Mama would tell me what to do and how to behave. She'd make sure I don't jeopardize my family's future. I wish she were here. I need her to stop these traitorous thoughts, because I'm not sure I have the strength to do so myself.

Resting my hands on the windowsill, I look out over the gardens. Papa has worked so hard for everything we have—I won't let him down. But despite my loyalty I feel angry at him, and it's taking everything in me to contain it.

I had plans before Papa decided to marry me off. I wanted to graduate art school and work for a gallery. I wanted to champion new artists and give them spaces to show their work to potential investors. I wanted to counteract all the death and destruction in the world with beauty.

I'm incapable of producing such great beauty myself, as evidenced by my black splatter marks, but I could beam others' sunshine into the skies. However, it's clear Papa has other plans for me. Namely, not taking my education any further and having me deliver work for just the one client: Di Santo Incorporated.

A figure moves past the open door, casting the room in shadow. I look over my shoulder to see Cristiano leaning against the doorframe watching me.

I turn around, rest back against the window, and stare back at him. The hem of my dress rises up my thighs, and I make no move to tug it down like I normally would in front of any other man. He's in *my* space after all.

The longer his gaze holds mine, the hotter I become, until I'm sure my burning skin is the same color as the red silk dress.

Without waiting for an invitation, he steps into the library and walks toward me. My gaze follows him, and my heartbeat quickens.

He stops a couple of feet away, his chest level with my face, and uncurls his palm. "For your headache."

I drop my gaze to the two white pills in his hand then glance up at him. "I think we both know I don't have a headache."

I cross one ankle over the other, knowing it will elongate my legs, but not knowing why I can't *stop* myself.

"You don't have to design any logos or branding for us. We have agencies on our books."

"I'm sure you do."

He pushes his hands into his pockets and regards me.

"How about we start over? Let's forget about the night at the bar and pretend we just met at the church."

"The church? Seriously?" I smile thinly. "What's to forget? I barely remember anything anyway."

For a split second he looks at me as if I slapped him, but he resumes his blank expression instantly. "You told me I was attractive."

Blood freezes in my veins. "No, I didn't."

"Yes, you did." He folds his arms across his chest, and his biceps fill out the white shirt, dark ink filtering through the soft cotton. "In fact, your exact words were, 'If you weren't the most attractive guy in here already, you certainly are now.'"

My vision swims.

His gaze feels searing against my shoulder blades as I turn back to the window. Even looking in the opposite direction I can't escape the heat.

"That was inappropriate of me. I'm sorry," I whisper.

He takes another step toward me. "Don't be. I would have been flattered if it weren't for the fact you only thought that because I might be bad news."

My peaked nipples chafe against the fabric of my dress. "And are you?"

There's a long pause before he replies.

"It depends who's asking."

My mouth is suddenly dry. "What if it's me asking? As your future sister-in-law." I stare out at the garden, too afraid to read his expression.

His soft sigh touches my skin from a few paces away. "No . . ."

I hold my breath.

". . . because I'm not staying."

The thump of my heartbeat threatens to drown out all other sound. "But you'd be bad news if you were?" I turn my head far enough to catch his presence out of the corner of my eye, and my blood pulses in my ears.

Seconds pass.

His jaw works softly from side to side.

Then he nods slowly.

I shiver as I exhale. I feel like I'm levitating, unable to keep a handle on solid ground.

I turn back to the window, afraid to look at him. "I'll see you in the dining room," I say quietly.

When I return to the table, rain is lashing against the windows, the late spring weather reflecting my volatile mood. One minute I'm upbeat and the sun's shining; the next I'm as low as I can possibly be and thunderclouds are emptying themselves over every corner of my world.

I'm attracted to my future brother-in-law.

And if his cryptic response to my last question was what I think it was, he's attracted to me too.

I feel sick and lightheaded.

Cristiano and Papa are discussing something at one end of the table, with Allegra and my sisters at the other. Sera and Bambi are doing something on Bambi's phone, while Tess and my aunt bicker over something inconsequential. I sigh inwardly and sit next to Tess and Allegra, feigning interest in their low-key quarrel.

"Can we talk about something else?" Tess whines, jerking her chin toward me. "The wedding. What's the latest?"

My stomach drops, and my eyes involuntarily find Cristiano's. His face is turned toward Papa's, his chin resting on his curled fist, but his eyes keep flicking sideways, watching me.

I turn away before my cheeks heat. "I don't know anything about it."

Tess lifts a glass to her lips and extends a finger toward Allegra. "Do you?"

"I've had some ideas. I was hoping to talk to Savero about it this evening," Allegra replies, looking personally offended he didn't show.

Tess flashes me a glance.

I look down at the linen napkin I'm bunching between my fingers. "He's not coming."

"How do you know?" Tess places her empty glass on the table, the loud clang turning Papa's head.

"It's ten p.m. already." I shrug. "And he sent his brother in his place. At least I know what his priorities are before I marry him. My expectations won't have to come crashing down after the wedding—they'll already be on the floor." I pick up a glass of whiskey that hasn't been touched and throw half the double measure down my throat.

"Trilby Castellano," Allegra hisses. "What's gotten into you?"

The whiskey burns, but I manage to swallow. "What?"

"You don't know the reasons why he didn't show . . ."

"And I never will," I say tightly.

"What do you mean by that?"

"I'm never going to know where he is, what he's doing, who he's with. It's not my place, is it? Not in his world. I have to sit back, do as I'm told, and live with it." I circle the whiskey glass, watching the amber catch the light. "So there's no point in speculating. I'll only ever know as much as you." I glance at her wide-eyed expression. "Which is nothing at all." Then I down the rest of the glass.

Allegra seethes silently, while Tess gleefully scours the table for more whiskey. What could be more entertaining: me having another disagreement with Allegra, or me having another disagreement with Allegra, drunk?

My aunt and I stare at each other until a shadow falls over us both.

"Excuse me, ladies."

His voice brings me out in goose bumps. I glance up —a long way up—until I find his face.

"Oh! Mr. Di Santo . . ." Allegra springs up from her seat, but Cristiano puts his hand on her shoulders.

It's then I think the one thing I never thought possible: Right now, I'd give anything to be my aunt.

"Please sit." He coaxes her back down. "And please, call me Cristiano."

Allegra gulps loudly.

"I'm about to leave, but may I have a word with your niece?"

Allegra frowns. "Serafina? Well, yes, of course."

"Serafina?" Cristiano's brow dips.

"Yes. You're interested in marriage, no?"

Both Cristiano and I gasp at the same time but for probably very different reasons. I suspect any marital involvement with my family is low to nonexistent on his bucket list, and nausea overcomes me at the thought of him marrying one of my sisters. One Mafia man in the family is more than enough.

"No. Trilby, *signora*. I owe her an apology."

Allegra flushes deeper than a ripe raspberry.

"No, you don't." My words come out too high and too fast. "It's fine. I understand. Savero has business to attend to."

His eyes darken. "Still . . ." He pauses, his gaze burrowing beneath my skin. "Would you mind walking me out?"

Nerves sizzle across my shoulders. Allegra pans to face me slowly. Tess returns from her search empty-handed and with an obvious awareness of the uncomfortable vibe. Her gaze flits between me and our aunt.

"Um, of course," I mutter. I can hardly refuse him. "In fact, it's time I went home anyway."

If I leave now, I might save myself the Spanish Inquisition for at least twelve hours.

I kiss Allegra's stone face and wave good night to

Papa. Then I numbly follow Cristiano out the dining room to the front door. Before he opens it, however, he shrugs off his jacket and slides it around my shoulders.

"It's been raining out, and I noticed you didn't bring a jacket."

He opens the door before I can think of a response.

Our pace is slow as we walk along the path. When we reach the steps to the apartment, an image from the night at Joe's flashes across my lids, and I burst out laughing.

"What's so funny?"

I pinch the bridge of my nose. "I just remembered something. When I got home from Joe's Bar that night, I was so relieved to see these steps. I had the cab driver doing circuits of this whole neighborhood, because I couldn't for the life of me remember my address."

When I look up at him, he's not laughing. It sobers me right up, even though the only thing I drank tonight was the one glass of whiskey.

"Didn't the bartender tell the driver? He knows where you live, right?"

I gawp at him. "Yeah, he does, but . . . why would Rhett tell my cab driver?"

In a beat Cristiano has my arm in a tight grip. "Who called the cab?"

"Cristiano, that hurts . . ."

He growls through clenched teeth, "*Who called the cab?*"

"I did. What's the matter?"

"Who paid for it?"

"Me!" My voice is high-pitched, and I look around the gated development, hoping no one is witnessing this. "Who else?"

When he doesn't respond I glance back at him, and for some unknown reason, I'm afraid of what I might see.

It turns out I'm right to be, because a shadow has descended over him like *thunder*.

CHAPTER 8

Cristiano

My heart has been hardened against everything my family stands for. My brain has been rewired to focus only on what can be achieved *without* resorting to firearms and a ton of ammo. But my blood will always be Di Santo through and through, and right now, it's boiling.

I can barely conceal the tremor in my voice. "Say that again?"

"How many times?" she snaps impatiently. "I called myself a cab, and I paid the driver."

Chaos breaks out behind the solid wall of my chest. Utter contempt for the bartender who, with zero regard for her safety, let her stagger out onto the fucking street alone and pocketed nearly a thousand bucks of *my* money. I don't care about the money—although I vow to break as many bones as it takes to get that back—it's the damn principle. She was *inebriated.*

"Do you know where Rhett lives?" I narrow my eyes.

She blinks. "Is this a test?"

"No. Why would it be?"

She looks affronted. "I haven't . . . *been* with him, if that's what you're concerned about."

Well, it wasn't, but it is now.

"He's not just the bartender—he's the landlord. He lives above the bar."

I grind my jaw and pull her away from the steps. "Come with me."

A slither of panic crosses her brow, but she does as I say. "Where to?"

"You'll see," I snap. "We won't be gone long."

Her skittering heels set the nerve endings dancing across my skin, moreish and unbearable all at once.

I pull her to where my car is parked on the street. "Get in."

When she hesitates, her baby blues as wide as saucers, I wrap my other hand around the back of her neck and push her into the passenger seat.

"Buckle up," I say before slamming the door.

Tires screech across the asphalt as I burn through the gates, and I try to block out the sound of her almost hyperventilating. She's marrying into the biggest crime family the States has ever known; what she's about to witness is nothing. Child's play. She should consider this Mafia 101 "lite."

"Have I done something wrong?" she asks as we round the corner.

"Nope. Someone owes me money, that's all."

"What does that have to do with me?"

I bite back a growl. "You'll see."

We draw alongside Joe's Bar, and I ram my foot on the brake. Her hands fly out to the sides and grip the window and the stick. I walk around to her side and open the door.

"Come on."

Her dress rides up her thighs as she steps out of the car, and I force my gaze toward the bar. I can't be distracted by the smoothness of her damn calves right now. It's hard enough averting my eyes when we're just sitting at her father's dining table.

"Is that the apartment?" I nod to a door next to the bar entrance.

"Yes." She goes to smooth her dress down, but I tug her around the front of the car, those skittering heels messing with my mind. "Why are we here? The bar doesn't open on Tuesdays."

I don't answer. Instead I ram my fist repeatedly against the apartment door.

I'm rewarded when, seconds later, the little shit who took my money opens it. At first he looks confused. Bless him. Then he gets over his temporary amnesia, remembers why I might be hammering his door down, and starts to back away.

There's a corridor behind him—he could run. So I

reach behind my back, pull out my gun, and aim it at his head.

Castellano screams until I wrap a hand around her face, covering her mouth. Her hot breath dampens my palm, almost distracting me.

I cock my head to one side. "Remember me?"

"I-I . . . Yes, sir."

"I'm guessing you don't remember the instructions I gave you, though, right?"

His eyes widen and flick to Castellano. He knows exactly what I'm talking about. "Look . . . I—"

"You what? Had a change of heart?" My voice is thick and saccharine. "You took the money I gave you to get this girl into a cab safely, and you kept it for yourself. Was there something more important you had to spend it on?"

His mouth opens and closes like a fish.

"And if I were you, I'd think very carefully before answering that," I warn.

He entwines his fingers as though he's praying for mercy. "I'll g-give you the money," he says. "I have it right here."

"Hands," I demand, making him jump.

Castellano sobs against my palm. She's stopped screaming but is holding my hand against her trembling face as if to shield herself from what's about to happen.

"Wh-what?" He pulls his fingers apart.

"Show me your fucking hands," I say in a low, evil voice I honestly thought I'd buried a long time ago.

He slowly opens his palms toward me.

"This is what happens when you choose greed over a woman's safety."

I pull the trigger and send a bullet through his left hand. Castellano jumps and tries to turn her face away, but I hold it firm. She needs to see this.

Tears stream down the guy's face, and his mouth opens slowly, though no sound comes out.

"And this is what happens when you steal from a Di Santo."

I pull back the trigger a second time and put a hole through his right palm.

He finally releases a wail that sounds like a dying animal. Castellano spins into me, pressing her body to mine as if she can disappear into it. I wrap my arm around her shoulders and keep her there. I can feel her heartbeat thundering against mine, and it makes me want to *kill* someone.

"Now get me my money, or I'll take off your kneecaps."

Bent almost double, he turns to a jumble of coats hanging inside the door. With difficulty, he pulls out the same wad of notes I gave him. I don't bother counting it. In fact, I barely even look at it before I pass it to Castellano, who clutches it to her chest.

I tuck the gun back into my waistband. "Now get the fuck out of my sight."

He tentatively closes the door with a toe, and then I hear his footsteps as he runs the hell away.

Keeping an arm around Castellano, I walk her slowly back to the passenger side and help her in. She's shaking like a leaf, but as much as I want to hold her through this, I also know she has to thicken her skin against this shit. She's going to start seeing a hell of a lot worse.

Once I'm seated behind the wheel, I lean across her to grab her seat belt. Tears stream silently down her cheeks. Her salty scent drifts across my cheek, and I freeze. Our breaths collide in the small space, and neither of us move.

I become aware of a tightness in my pants and realize I'm hard.

When and how the fuck did that happen?

My gaze drops to the roll of notes she's white-knuckling. They're soaked in blood, and it's rubbing off onto her bare chest.

It's the sexiest thing I've ever seen.

I propel myself back into my seat, fastening her in at the same time, then I force myself to drive back the way we came.

I thought I'd changed.

I thought I'd buried the Di Santo side of me long ago. But no.

All it's taken is a cheat, a lie, and a coward's blood leaking onto a girl's collarbone, and it turns out I'm as dark and dangerous as I've ever been.

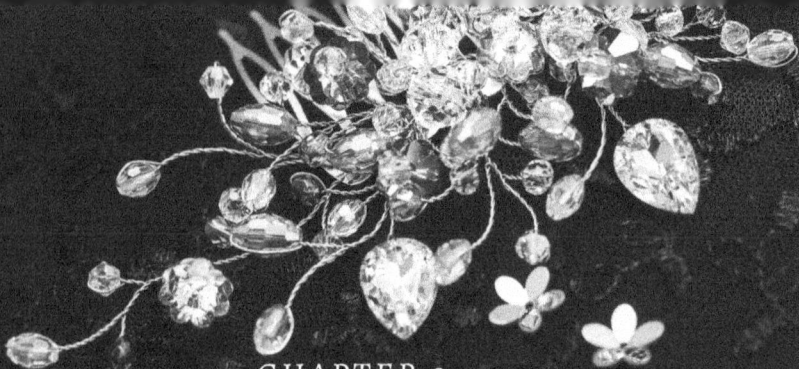

$\mathcal{T}$rilby

"Serafina, button up. I can see your bra." Allegra tuts as she flicks her eyes away from the offending outfit.

Sera rolls her eyes. "It's supposed to peek over the top. It's the style."

Allegra huffs. "Underwear is much like intelligence, my dear. It's important to have but not necessary to show off in public."

"That's such a sexist thing to say," Tess says.

Allegra lifts a chin in the air. "It applies to everyone."

"Even the heads of the Cosa Nostra?"

"Well, not those, *obviously.*"

Sera holds back a smirk, but Tess isn't quite as successful, and hers slips out via a snort.

"And you, young lady." Allegra wags a finger in

Tess's direction. "We've already had words this morning, so . . ."

"I am *not* wearing a pink dress to Tril's wedding. And forcing me to will only result in me repressing my anger and shame at not being allowed to express myself authentically."

Allegra goes to speak, but Tess ploughs on impressively.

"I will go through the rest of my life pretending to be someone I'm not, masking my true identity, because I fear I'll never be accepted for who I really am. And I'll let others treat me poorly, because I don't feel worthy of being liked. Then, when it all becomes too much, and I begin to suffer from anxiety—that's if the depression hasn't already taken hold to the extent I can no longer leave the house—I'll be relocated to a therapist's couch and made to dig up stories about how my childhood experiences effectively ruined my life."

Allegra halts, her mouth open wide enough to catch flies. Tess, to her credit, manages to maintain eye contact with her, while my gaze flits about as if trying to locate an escape route.

The only sound is the *clip* of each button as Sera fastens her jacket.

Allegra's mouth snaps shut. "Fine." She concedes slowly and through clenched teeth. "I won't make you wear pink. But you are not, Contessa—I repeat, *not*— wearing black to the wedding. Do I make myself clear?"

Tess flicks her long hair over one shoulder with a huff. "I'll think about it." Then she strides ahead in black leggings, a bodysuit, and pointed-toe boots that make her look like a raunchy Catwoman.

I turn to Allegra and shrug. "I really don't mind what she wears to the—"

"I do." Allegra wrings her hands together. "She is *not* wearing black. This is a Mafia wedding—it's dark enough as it is. The very least we can do is bring some color."

Sera's eyes flick to me. It's the first time Allegra has expressed a view of my upcoming nuptials as anything other than bright, breezy, and law-abiding.

"Come on." Sera threads her fingers through mine. "It's burning out here. Let's go inside."

I give Allegra a smile, and she follows. It dawns on me then her hand-wringing isn't born of exasperation. She's terrified. As am I.

It's been two weeks since Savero killed a man in front of my eyes. It's been only one since Cristiano dragged me to Joe's Bar and effectively disabled Rhett by shooting through both of his hands, and I'm still a bundle of nerves. I've only seen one other person get shot, and that was my mother. The sound at Joe's took me right back to that day. But in the days since, I've realized with stark clarity the gun isn't the enemy; it's the person firing it. In some ways Cristiano *is* an enemy. He's jeopardizing my ability to protect my family just by *breathing*. The more I try not to think about him, the harder it becomes to keep his deep eyes and seductive voice out of my head.

But his actions were not the actions of an enemy.

I stand by my hatred for violence when it's used for death and destruction. The only thing Cristiano destroyed that night was one man's inclination to steal from another, and possibly the use of his hands. But one thing I was able to deduce from the madness was the fact Cristiano gave Rhett close to a thousand bucks to make sure I got home safely. And Rhett didn't do as he was told.

I personally wouldn't have shot through his nerve endings, but I can understand why Cristiano was a little perturbed about Rhett stealing his money.

What I don't understand is why on earth I was worth that much.

I smile at something Sera is saying, but in the past few days I've lost the ability to be present with my own family. I spend long moments daydreaming about the wedding being called off so I can stare back at Savero's brother without worrying someone might see. Those long moments should be spent throwing myself into becoming the best fiancée I can be to keep my family's jugulars in place.

Logically, I know if the wedding were to be called off, I'd never see Cristiano again. He has a life in Vegas and businesses to run; he's only here to bury his father and be a best man. The thought sits like a lead weight in the pit of my stomach.

The house is enormous. So enormous, in fact, the word "house" doesn't do it justice. It's a complex. A network of opulent buildings connected by intricate covered walkways, terraces, and gardens. A doorman walks us through an entrance hall and outside, to a path painted yellow and white with the last of the snowdrops and the first of the daffodils. Birds twitter in manicured evergreens peppering a central garden.

Tess sucks in a breath and releases it with a low whistle. "Is *this* where you'll live?"

I can't answer her for two reasons. One: I don't know. And two: I can't form a sentence—even a one-word sentence.

"I had no idea a place like this existed here," Bambi whispers.

It's clear this home, this *compound*, is worth more than most homes around here put together. Even the knobs turned by the doorman's satin-gloved fingers look like they cost more than the average family's life savings.

"It's certainly unique," I eventually say, forcing an element of wonder into my voice.

We're taken straight out to a pretty terrace, where a long table has been laid with bowls and plates of delicious-looking seafood and salads. Three men stand at different corners of the terrace, each one talking on a phone. Only one I recognize—the one who never left Savero's side at the funeral. I believe his name is Nicolò.

Savero looks up as we approach and slides his phone into an inside pocket of his jacket. It must be about ninety degrees out, but still, these men insist on wearing their suits.

"Welcome." He strides toward us and makes straight for Allegra.

"Tony is on his way," she explains. "He's coming from the port."

"Of course," Savero replies before kissing her on the cheek. "I apologize for my no-show last week. I'd been looking forward to dinner, and Cristiano told me the spaghetti was *perfetta*."

Allegra has either the good grace or the poor sense to blush.

"Unfortunately, I had a pressing matter to deal with." His expression sobers quickly, and I understand straight away. It's an expression I'd hear a lot when eavesdropping on Papa's conversations with Gianni. I gathered pretty quickly the "matter" was usually a person who'd betrayed the mob, and "deal with" was generally code for "shot in the head."

I swallow and glance at Bambi, whose face has paled. I take hold of her hand and give it a reassuring squeeze. I don't know if Papa or Allegra have had "the conversation" with her yet—not so much about the birds and the bees but about clans, codes, and consequences. She's about to be joined to the New York Mafia through her sister's marriage, and she's fourteen now, so it's well overdue.

Savero pans his gaze to me, and my spine stiffens. "Trilby," he says, casting his eyes over my outfit.

I felt bad for my aunt after she put in so much effort to welcome Savero, only for him to send his brother in his place, so I gave in to her nagging and compromised with a strappy summer dress in sunshine yellow and navy heels that lift me by a meager two inches. I've even straightened my hair.

"You look . . . radiant." He reaches for my hand and lifts it to his lips.

Every nerve ending I have fires up, willing me to run. "Thank you for having us," I say mechanically. "Your home is beautiful."

"Oh, yes. Stunning," Allegra adds, having recovered from the unexpected compliment.

Savero walks us to the edge of the terrace, and we genuinely gasp at the view.

"This is spectacular," Sera says, arriving at my side.

I look behind us to see Tess and Bambi tentatively giving their drinks preferences to a servant.

"Come," Savero says. "Let's eat."

We help ourselves to small plates of antipasto and sit at round bistro tables. Everyone else settles into lighthearted conversation while I fight to keep the image of Franco as far from the backs of my lids as possible.

Thankfully, Papa arrives and shoots me a reassuring look. When he sits down next to Nicolò and another man I quickly figure is a capo, called Beppe, Savero edges closer to my side. I bristle when he lowers his face to my shoulder.

"Do you like the house?"

I swallow a mouthful of food and dab the corner of my mouth daintily, like Mama taught me. "I do. I like it very much."

"You'll be the lady of this residence very soon."

I'm sure his words are designed to please, but his voice carries a foreboding note.

"It would be my pleasure." I sneak a timid smile at him, but a flash of his harsh eyes sobers me.

"*Will*, Miss Castellano. It *will* be your pleasure."

"Of course," I rush out. "That's what I meant."

I cast my eyes downward and curse my brain for emptying completely. I have a million questions prepared, but I cannot for the life of me think of one. "How are you finding your new position?" I ask, internally kicking myself when his brow creases and his top lip hooks upward.

"I won't ever talk to you about my work, Miss Castellano. So don't ask me again."

"Oh, um, of course," I splutter. "I'm sorry."

"Do you have hobbies?" he asks, though his gaze wanders as if he couldn't care less.

For some reason I decide not to disclose the truth about my love of art. I feel so unbearably uncomfortable that I don't want to bring a part of the real me into this conversation.

"Tennis," I say, confident he won't ever ask me to demonstrate my skill—which is fortunate, because I have zero hand-eye coordination.

His lips thin out into what could be a smile, but I'm not sure, and I follow his gaze toward a figure darkening the door to the house.

My heart, God damn it, pounds at the sight of Cristiano. He's wearing a suit, and he must be boiling in this heat, but I can tell even from this distance he's barely broken a sweat. He prowls onto the terrace, greeting two men I've yet to be introduced to, then Beppe, Nicolò and Papa, and Savero.

After exchanging a few coded words with his brother, his gaze lifts to mine. My heart trips over itself, and I curse the stupid thing.

One glance at him and I'm right back in the passenger seat of his car, the road spinning around me even though Cristiano drove as smoothly as if he'd just popped out for gelato, not to shoot straight through both of a man's hands.

I can still taste the nausea that crept up my throat, mixed with guilt and regret. It's my fault Rhett may never have the use of his hands again. If only I hadn't gotten so drunk that night at Joe's.

I can still feel the roll of notes curled inside my fingers, the wet blood trickling down my chest. It stained the neckline of my dress. I should have been repelled by it, but I couldn't tear my eyes away.

I knew unequivocally there was no such intention behind it, but as my eyes burrowed into the blood-soaked bills Cristiano had just shot a man for, I couldn't help but think it was the most romantic thing anyone had ever done.

Sera coughs beside me, and I realize my gaze is still locked on Cristiano. He's looking back at me, and though his expression is indifferent, a smile pulls at his eyes.

I spin away as if I've just been caught stealing red-handed.

After the food has been eaten and the plates cleared away, servants bring more trays of drinks for us all. The mood is light and strangely enjoyable.

Cristiano stands and lifts his glass of whiskey in our direction. His voice is thick and dry when he commands everyone's attention. "I'd like to make a toast."

"*Grazie fratello*," Savero says. No smile reaches his eyes, and his expression isn't friendly as he looks sideways at Cristiano.

It occurs to me I haven't seen them exchange many words together.

"To my brother and future sister. May you enjoy much happiness . . . together. *Congratulazioni.*"

His gaze doesn't leave mine as he tips back his glass and drinks the entire thing.

CHAPTER 10

*T*rilby

The evening at the Di Santo residence was short-lived. I was both aggrieved and relieved about that. No matter how many times I tried to make conversation with Savero, he would give me a one-word (or one-line, if I was lucky) response then walk away. I didn't particularly revel in being dismissed repeatedly, but feeling the weight of Cristiano's gaze the entire night? Now, that . . . That I could live with.

Before we went home, Savero announced the date of the wedding, and my stomach dropped to the floor. It's four weeks away. *Four weeks.* Just the thought of being married to that man in such a short time makes me lightheaded. I feel as though I only have four weeks left *to live*. And that's a dangerous feeling.

So when Sandrine, my classmate at art college,

invited me to her birthday party at a club across town, I agreed.

Only Sera knows I've come here tonight. Everyone else in my family is none the wiser. Living in the apartment next door to them can be lonely at times, but it has its advantages.

Since I'm out on the down-low, I've dressed accordingly. My navy dress is reasonably conservative in that it covers the essential bits, but it's as snug as a dress can be. I've shunned the beige kitten heels Allegra keeps trying to force me into, and I'm standing four inches taller in a pair of my mama's favorite stilettoes.

Sweat drips down the walls, and my skin pulses to the music. Sandrine's two friends are making out with each other on the sofas, while we hover at the edge of the dance floor, sipping our drinks while swaying our hips to the music.

"Honey, we need to do this more often," Sandrine says, pulling on a Long Island iced tea. "I didn't realize how well you let your hair down, mocktail aside."

"It's because they never let me out," I shout over the music before slurping my virgin mojito through a straw.

She laughs because she thinks I'm joking, but it's going to become my reality before I know it. I'm pretty sure if Savero knew where I was right now, he'd have security lining the walls. I've already noticed a few curious heads turning. It hasn't taken long for word to get around that I'll be a part of the notorious family in a few short weeks. The only person entirely oblivious to my predicament—partly because she refuses to acknowledge the Cosa Nostra exists, and partly because she wants me to be perpetually single with her—is Sandrine.

Her gaze catches on something, but I'm too happy and adrift to give it much thought. Then she leans into my ear.

"Don't look now, but there's a fucking gorgeous guy sitting by the bar, and he's *staring* at you."

My skin tingles—until I remember that's not a good thing. In fact, it's terrible. As demonstrated by my future brother-in-law's propensity for disabling bartenders who don't call cabs for drunk women, a man coul meet his maker if he so much as *looks* at me the wrong way.

"Ignore him," I shout over the music. "Besides, I'm engaged. I told you."

Sandrine flicks her hair back over one shoulder and bats her lashes in the direction of the bar. "I'll believe you have a fiancé when I see him for myself."

I roll my eyes, because the day Savero lets me parade him around in front of my friends will most likely be the day hell freezes over.

"If you're not going to make a play for him, I will. How have I not seen him around here before? He'd be a permanent fixture in my *dreams*, let alone my fantasies. God, he'd make the cutest babies."

I'm not the type of girl to make a play for anyone, but curiosity gets the better of me. I feign a slow twirl to the music, panning my gaze past the object of her obsession.

The idea was to keep on going, but his stare roots me to the spot.

The look in his eyes is *lethal*.

"It's Cristiano," I say on a gasp.

He's leaning against a stool, his legs spread as if he's much too tall to be accommodated. His elbows rest on the bar, his jacket falling open. The top few buttons of his shirt are undone, revealing just enough bare chest to make a woman's throat go dry.

Sandrine stops at my side. "You know him?"

His eyes have locked mine into a battle of wills.

"Unfortunately, yes."

"Honey, there is no 'un' about it. Who *is* he?"

"My fiancé's brother." As I say the words, they feel foreign. He's more than that, but it's way too much to articulate.

Her mouth hangs open, yet she still manages to speak. "Shit. I hope for your sake those 'I want to bend you over and fuck you from here to Peru' eyes run in the family."

"I have to go talk to him." His expression says it's nonnegotiable. "I'll be right back."

The music pounds in my ears as I weave my way across the dance floor through writhing, sweaty bodies.

He doesn't move an inch as I step right up to him. Doesn't even sit up.

Cristiano has seen me on a night out once before, but this time feels different. This time he knows I'm engaged and that I probably shouldn't be here.

I drop my eyes to the tumbler of whiskey he's

dangling between a finger and a thumb. I slide my hand around the glass, brushing against his, before lifting it to my lips. I'm shocked at my own behavior, but the way his gaze follows the movement and fixes on my mouth makes me feel bold.

I swallow and feel the smooth scotch heating my throat. Then I lick my lips and place the glass back in his hand. "Meeting someone?"

His gaze trails over my outfit, and frustratingly, his expression doesn't register a thing. "No."

"Then why are you here?"

He doesn't owe me an explanation, but this boldness that's come out of nowhere demands one anyway.

A corner of his mouth ticks up, but he wipes it away with a knuckle. "To keep an eye on you."

A chill coasts over my shoulders. I raise a brow, impressed he doesn't feel the need to sugarcoat it, and rest a hand casually on my hip. "Why?"

"Because my brother has had to go away on business, and I don't trust you're not going to get blind drunk again and embarrass our family."

I don't tell him I'm as sober as a judge. I shouldn't have to explain myself.

"Excellent. My own personal bodyguard. I always wanted one of those." In a move so uncharacteristic I hardly recognize myself, I lean past him to rest my forearms on the bar. "Do you offer driving services too?" I glance over my shoulder. "And fast-food delivery? Because I do love a thick, juicy burger after dancing all night."

I can sense the irritation rolling off him, and it lights me up like nothing I've ever known.

"Don't push it, Castellano." Even with the thudding bass making the room vibrate, I don't miss the threatening tone in his voice.

I turn my head another fraction. "Don't push what? You're the one following *me*. I'm just here with my friend, having a nice time. Besides, you shouldn't care what I'm up to. I'm not married yet."

"You're engaged to be." His voice is so low I can hardly hear it over the music.

I give up waiting for a bartender and spin around so I'm facing him. "So? That doesn't mean I can't enjoy myself."

My breath escapes when I see the look in his eyes. His gaze is aggressive as he roams it over me. "This dress . . ." he hisses. "It's *inappropriate*."

I'm surprised and slightly offended. Mostly, I'm sated. My dress is not inappropriate, but he's noticed it, and that makes my pulse dance.

I cross my arms, his observation emboldening me even more. "Says who?"

His glare feels like a shock. I've called his bluff, and he doesn't like it. He knows it's not his place to say whether I'm dressed inappropriately or not.

"You need to stop telling me what to do. I'm not your *principessa*."

His eyes remain indifferent, but his jaw works from side to side.

I continue, emboldened. "I'm the daughter of a

hardworking businessman, and I've earned the right to stand here in this club with whomever I want, wearing whatever I want."

Cristiano swallows, drawing my gaze to his throat, and without thinking, I stroke my tongue over my dry lips.

A tight grip around my wrist snaps my gaze back to his. He pulls me toward him—so close his lips warm the tip of my nose. He speaks slowly and quietly, yet the force of his words makes them unmistakable.

"I don't give a *fuck* who your father is. I don't give a *fuck* what you have and haven't earned the right to do. I don't give a *fuck* who you're about to marry. I don't want you getting drunk out of your mind, because I could really do without blowing another man's hands off." He pulls back and stares into my eyes. "If that's all right with you."

I yank my wrist from his grip but don't move. I can't when I'm panting so hard I'm lightheaded. Thank God he can't hear how *bothered* his words have made me over the volume of the music.

I'm hot and restless.

I'm also *fuming*.

I spin around and strut toward Sandrine, grabbing her hand as I pass.

"Trouble in paradise?" she says, giggling.

I pull her impatiently to the restroom and walk straight up to the mirrors. With the sound dulled, I turn to face her.

"Do you have any scissors in your purse?"

"Yeah." She cocks her head to one side. "And I have a chainsaw, a length of rope, and some gag tape, if you need those too."

"Sarcasm is the lowest form of wit," I remind her.

"What can I say? I left my sewing kit at home."

My gaze skates across the counter. "How good are you at ripping fabric?"

She stares at me as if I've lost my mind. "What?"

"He's here to babysit me, Sandrine, and I'm a grown woman, for God's sake. I do not need a chaperone. He just had the nerve to tell me my outfit is inappropriate. I haven't even married into the family yet! Can you believe it? Well, if he wants to see inappropriate, I'll *show* him inappropriate."

Sandrine has no concept of just how risky this is, my fiancé being the don of the city's biggest Mafia family and all, and it's evident in her squeal of, "Hell yeah!"

Before I can stop her, she's on her hands and knees, a nick of fabric from halfway up my thighs jammed between her teeth. I grip the vanity for balance as she tears a thick ribbon clean off the bottom of my dress.

I gape open-mouthed at the small amount of length leftover.

Sandrine spits out the fabric and holds it up, studying her handiwork. "Thou shalt not bend over in this, my lady," she says.

"I bloody shall." I grin despite the crazed butterflies zinging around my abdomen and turn to look in the mirror. "What about the neckline?" I tug it down to where my cleavage is visible.

"The neckline is fine," Sandrine says, standing. "But you could do with showing off these babies." She tugs the thick straps down over my arms, showcasing my shoulders and illuminating my collarbone.

Next she pops open her purse and squirts something iridescent onto my skin, until my cleavage shimmers under the lights.

"Holy crap. If he doesn't jump you, I will." She smacks her lips together and studies me with intent. "You need to put your hair up. You have such a gorgeous slim neck. Make him want to sink his teeth into it."

I feel a surge of intention and fish a band out of my purse. I twirl the strands into a messy bun and turn my head from side to side.

Wow.

I like to dress up, and I have a tendency to wear slightly outlandish vintage garments, but I've *never* taken it this far. If Papa could see me now, he would actually kill me.

Out of the corner of my eye, a girl shakes a can of what appears to be hair lacquer. When it sprays out, her platinum strands turn a gorgeous baby pink. I catch Sandrine's eye and know she's thinking the same thing.

She confronts the girl. "Would you exchange that can of spray for a kidney?"

The girl darts her eyes between the two of us and laughs. "No body parts necessary."

She holds out the can, and Sandrine swipes it from her hands, getting to work immediately. When she's finished, I glance in the mirror, and my jaw drops. I still look like myself, but . . . I look like myself *on acid.*

Part of me can't wait to show Cristiano what he's driven me to. Another part of me is about to crap right here on the floor.

"You ready?" Sandrine says after she's handed back the spray and exchanged numbers with the girl. It never fails to impress me how easily she collects friends.

I force a nod.

Her eyes narrow mischievously, and she takes my hand. "Let's go."

We walk out into the club and have to resort to shouting again over the music.

"Shots?" Sandrine calls over her shoulder.

I coast my gaze over the bar, and my heart sinks— way more than it should. He's gone.

"Sure," I shout back, my tone flat. If ever there were a time to succumb to the lure of a fluorescent alcoholic beverage, this is it.

We reach the bar, and I feel every single male pair of eyes on me. "Self-conscious" doesn't even begin to explain how I feel. Maybe mix it with a bit of mortification and a dash of disappointment, and we'll be on the right track.

Sandrine turns around brandishing four shot glasses filled with something pink. "To match your hair, baby doll," she says with a wink.

We clink glasses and down them both.

My throat burns as the alcohol sears its way to my

stomach, but as soon as the flame sizzles out, I feel calm. I feel invincible.

I feel . . . *hot*.

Before my brain has a chance to catch up with the message my skin is sending, Sandrine confirms my worst fear and my most dangerous bet.

"Babysitter. Ten o'clock."

I slowly pan my gaze across the dance floor. He emerges from the men's room and walks purposefully toward us. The crowd seems to part for him without him even sparing a glance. In fact, his focus is entirely on me.

A whole-body tremor racks me from head to toe.

Sandrine turns her head so the movement of her lips is indecipherable. "You show him inappropriate, girl."

I reach out to grab her hand—I suddenly don't want to be left alone with him—but she's gone.

My heart thumps at the bottom of my neck, my pulse rivalling the heavy bass bouncing off the walls of the club.

Each step Cristiano takes toward me extracts a little bit more of my breath. By the time he's standing mere inches away, forcing me to tilt my face up to his at an uncomfortable angle, I'm dizzy.

"What are you doing?" His lids are lowered, his irises almost black under the neon lights, and his voice is a low growl that rumbles beneath my skin.

I gulp warm air. "I'm enjoying a night out with my friend."

His words are bitten out. "Where's the rest of your dress?"

"The restroom."

His pupils are like sharp stones, but I can still see a world of annoyance dancing behind them.

"You have ten minutes."

My throat heats. "Until you leave?" I'm stunned at myself. I've never spoken to another man this way. I've never taunted someone like this or flirted so *brazenly*. And don't get me started on the fact I already belong to the most powerful man in New York, yet I'm toying with *his brother*. If my nights weren't already busy with recounting the hell I've lived through, this would be the stuff of nightmares.

His chest rises and falls with measured breaths. "Until I drag you the fuck out of here."

I've gone too far already, and I'm in so deep I'm struggling to see the benefit in pulling back at this late stage. "Why ten minutes? Why don't you just drag me out now?"

He leans forward until I can feel the bristles on his cheek against the side of my face. "Because I figured you'd want to say goodbye to your friend, and I just saw her disappear out the back with one of my brother's soldiers."

What?

She'll have no idea who he is, and I can't let her get involved with this family. If I can't save myself, I can save Sandrine.

I step backward and hit the bar. His body seems to

wrap itself around me, trapping me into the small space. He presses a hand to my chest, and heat radiates out from where his skin meets mine. He doesn't push hard, but it's a warning. *Don't fucking move.*

His warm timbre rumbles in my ear. "He's young. She's hot. I give him five minutes max."

Something inside me twists painfully. He thinks Sandrine is hot.

I mean, she *is* hot. She's drop-dead gorgeous. He wouldn't be a red-blooded male if he didn't notice her in that way. But why does it bother me to the point I might need a painkiller to ease the tightness in my chest?

I draw my focus back to what he just said. "They went outside? Like, together?"

I feel his smile against my jawline.

"Yeah."

Wetness collects in my underwear, and I blush from my breasts to my hairline. *What on earth?* She's my best friend—why do I feel like I'm turned on? I don't care a dime when and where she gets off, as long as she's safe.

When he doesn't withdraw his hot breath from my skin, I turn my head. I need air. I need to cool down. I twirl a few strands of pink hair around a finger and say the boldest thing I can think of.

"Why do you want to drag me out of here anyway? It's not like I'm marrying *you*."

His form solidifies, and heat radiates from him. "You may as well be."

That knocks the wind out of me. My cheeks burn up.

His hand takes hold of my neck and grips it tightly.

"You're marrying a Di Santo. And not just any Di Santo."

Irritation scratches at my patience. "If I have to hear one more time it's because I'm marrying *the don* . . ." I start, but then the feel of his lips dragging across the shell of my ear makes my stomach collapse.

"You're marrying my *brother*. My flesh and blood . . ."

A shiver travels down my stomach and lands squarely between my legs.

"You will treat our name—*my* name—with respect."

My vision narrows to the veins on the side of his neck. They're corded and throbbing. And for a man whom I've yet to see break a real sweat, his skin sure is glistening with a damp sheen.

I feel a depraved urge to reach forward and lick a line from his collarbone to the soft skin beneath his ear. It's not the first time I've thought about doing something so wholly inappropriate with this man, and these strange urges are making me feel untethered. I can only hope they disappear once I've grown used to him being around.

When I'm a part of his family.

I lean back so I can look him in the eye. His jaw is as firm as his grip.

"How many minutes do I have now?" I ask with half-lidded eyes.

His teeth grind slowly. "Five."

"Are you going to let me go?"

He breathes deeply. "Go where?"

I dart my gaze to the dance floor. "I came here to dance, so if you don't mind . . ."

His grip loosens, but instead of withdrawing it completely, he lays it flat against my throat and strokes it down to my collarbone. It lingers there—only for a second, but it's long enough to make me feel a chill when he removes it and pushes it deep into his pocket.

He steps aside and watches me as I strut past him to the edge of the dance floor. I don't know anyone here except for Sandrine and her two friends, but I feel an unbridled need to let off some steam; rid myself of the tension that man coils inside of me.

As if by divine intervention, "Chandelier" by Sia kicks off, and I lose myself far more easily than I anticipated, with Cristiano's gaze glued to my every move. I close my eyes and let my hips swing decadently. My legs part, and my skirt rises above the crease of my ass. The skin around my thighs *burns*, and I know he's watching.

I'm instantly addicted. I have his undivided attention, and it feels dangerous. For someone who loathes violence in all its forms, I suddenly want to feel his anger—or whatever it is that makes him treat me this way—in whatever form I can get it.

A warmth envelops me from behind, but I'm too lost in the music to question it, surrounded by sweaty bodies grinding to the bass. Two hands rest on my hips, moving with me as I gyrate. My lids open a little, and I see Cristiano out of the corner of my eye still standing at the bar. His cheekbones look like razorblades from this angle, and his eyes seem darker. I let whoever owns the hands on my hips move closer until I feel something pressing into my lower back. It feels obscene and too intimate, but I've come this far . . .

In what is quite possibly the most uncharacteristic thing I've ever done, I arch into it, relishing the sensation of one man's arousal against my backside while I bask in another man's thunderous glare.

The music is my excuse. I'm completely lost, living vicariously through it. My fingers interlace with those on my hips, and I rest my head back against a shoulder.

Short, sharp breaths stutter past my ear. "Fuck, you are so sexy."

I quirk a lazy smile and look at Cristiano as I skim against the other man's erection. I'm so lost in the moment my brain doesn't catch up with what my eyes are seeing until it's too late.

Screams break out in every direction as the hands on my hips disappear, unbalancing me.

I land hard on the floor and find myself staring up at the man who just had his hard-on practically between my ass cheeks. He's holding his hands up in a kind of surrender. Then I pan to his face and see why.

He has the barrel of a gun pointed at his head.

I follow the outstretched arm to a thick chest I'm fast becoming far too familiar with. Cristiano has this poor, innocent guy held up at gunpoint. If that fact doesn't shake my core, the next one I recall sobers me up and rocks my foundation.

I was *flirting*.

I'm engaged to be married, and I was brazenly flirting with another man. In front of my fiancé's brother. And not just any fiancé—the head of the Di Santo crime family.

I clamber to my feet and reach for Cristiano. "Put it down," I plead. "Put the gun down, Cristiano. He did nothing wrong. It was me—all me."

"What was you?" His focus doesn't waver from the guy now sobbing and shaking like a damn leaf. "What *exactly* did you do?"

I take a deep breath. I have to come clean, be honest, and hope it's enough to get him to lower the gun. "I was flirting. I was dancing up against him. It was me. I did that, not him."

"He fucking *liked* it," Cristiano says with gritted teeth.

"It doesn't matter." Panic lurches into my bloodstream. "He doesn't know me or you. He doesn't know who I'm engaged to. He didn't mean any harm. Please . . . put the gun down. Please, Cristiano."

A small hand rests on my arm, and I almost collapse with relief at the sound of Sandrine's voice. "What the f—?" She leans into me and whispers, "He's got a gun, Trilby. Step the hell away."

I turn and mouth, "I know."

She jerks her head back toward the exit. "Come on." Her face is filled with panic. She truly does have no idea what family I'm marrying into.

I furrow my brow in apology. "You go. I'll call you in the morning."

The music has stopped, and the club is now almost empty. Security guards are dotted around the edges, and it strikes me they haven't stepped in to stop Cristiano and help this innocent guy being held at gunpoint.

I glance at their faces. They wear the same expressions as the bartenders and the waiters. They're not surprised by Cristiano's actions, because . . . they've seen this show before.

It dawns on me even this place, situated at the opposite end of the city, is owned by the Di Santos.

Sandrine's gaze darts between me and Cristiano. She shakes her head in confusion.

"Seriously," I urge. "Go on home, Sandy. I'll be fine, and I'll make sure this guy is too."

She backs away slowly, her eyes wide and terrified. Yep, she likely has no idea what her lover boy is involved in either.

I turn back to the scene to find nothing has changed. Cristiano still looks as calm and lethal as a sniper with a thousand lives in his holster. The guy I was dancing with looks like he's actually pissed himself.

It's already become clear Cristiano doesn't listen to me, so I have to try something else.

I walk around the back of him and slip my hand into his free one. It's bone-dry, no sweat to speak of, and as still as a sleeping baby. If his pulse has ratcheted up a notch for holding someone at gunpoint, there's absolutely nothing on his person to make that obvious.

I look up at his face. It's completely still. But then

his jaw squeezes tight, just for a second, and his fingers curl around mine.

My heart flutters up my chest.

"Come on," I say. "Let's go."

He doesn't respond, but the feel of his fingers sends tendrils of fire up my arms.

"Cristiano," I whisper up at him. "Take me home."

His chest expands, then he shoves his gun into the guy's head, forcing him to stagger to the ground. His voice is pure venom as he directs it at the trembling mess now scooting backward along the floor.

"If you so much as *look* at this woman again," he hisses, "you won't be alive to see dawn. Do you understand?"

The man turns his face and nods manically. "I-I promise . . ."

Cristiano faces me, and I feel the full strength of his loaded stare. It's hard and flinty—the polar opposite of his soft fingers, which are threaded through mine. His voice dips even further. "And don't even get me started on what will happen to you if you so much as *breathe* in another man's direction."

My instinct is to argue, because I don't let anyone tell me who I can or can't look at, speak to, breathe in the vicinity of . . . But Cristiano isn't bluffing. There's something dark and unequivocal in his expression, so I just blink at him rapidly.

A sinister growl erupts from deep in his chest. Before I can question it, Cristiano's striding toward the exit, and since my hand is still enclosed in his, I can do nothing but try to keep up.

CHAPTER 11

Cristiano

Never before has a walk to the car tested so much of my patience.

Good *God*, this woman.

I'm so angry I can feel my blood searing hot beneath my skin. My temples are throbbing, and the urge to gun down the next jackass to cross my path is overwhelming.

I unlock the car and don't bother opening the passenger door for her. I'm far too angry to be chivalrous.

"Get the fuck in and sit the fuck down."

She does as I say without a murmur, which makes my toes fucking tingle. I start the engine and grip the steering wheel until my knuckles turn white.

"I want you to do three things when you get home," I start.

I can't bring myself to look at her; I'm already boiling over with *something*, and I can't guarantee the sight of her in that strip of fabric will help matters.

"One. Go straight to your room, and don't come out till morning."

Her eyes dart to me. I know she's not a child, but not thirty minutes ago, she was behaving like one, so . . .

"Two. Call your friend and tell her to erase Damiano's number from her phone. She can do a thousand times better."

I hear her swallow beside me.

"And three. Take off your dress . . ."

She gasps. It's a breathy, sexy sound that makes me want to see the look in her eyes—but I stay focused on the road.

"And throw that fucking thing in the trash."

Her head pans slowly back to the windshield, and it's a few seconds before she speaks.

"And what are you going to do?" she says quietly.

"I'm going to have words with your father."

"You're what?" She turns her whole body to face me, and I hold my breath before glancing at her.

"I don't want you going on any more nights out with friends. You can't be trusted to not get yourself into trouble, and I will not have you risk our family name because you had one too many fluorescent drinks."

"You can't stop me from seeing my friends." There's

a warning in her tone that weakens when I harden
my jaw.

"Yes, I can, Castellano. And I will."

She sits back in her seat and folds her arms. "I'm
going to talk to Savero."

I chuckle lightly. "He'll honor my recommendation.
You want to know why?"

"Why?"

"Because he's charged me with keeping an eye on
you," I lie.

She spins around again. "No, he hasn't. He would
have told me."

Despite the fact my brother wouldn't even think to
have anyone keep an eye on this hot mess, we both
know he wouldn't inform her if he had. I can't help the
sadistic smile turning up a corner of my mouth.

"Yeah, well, he asked me to let you know."

She sits still and chews on her bottom lip. I want to
pull it from between her teeth, because it's a nice bottom
lip, and it doesn't deserve to be eaten.

"Scaring off my best friend and holding a gun to
some poor, innocent guy's head isn't 'keeping an eye on
me,' Cristiano."

"What is it then?"

She considers her response before—quite frankly—
impressing me with her bravery. "It's blind irrationality.
Idiotic bravado. It's throwing your weight around in a
place where you know no one's going to stop you . . ."

I spin the wheel and pull the car up short. She
presses back into the seat when I lean into her.

"You don't have the faintest clue who I am, do you?" I say quietly.

"Yes," she whispers. "You're the brother of a don."

I shake my head. "I'm more than that, Castellano. I'm the *son* of a don. I was born into this life. I know every governor's gambling secret, every fucking fed's indiscretion, *and* I have Mafia blood running through my veins. There's nothing in this world more lethal than someone who can manipulate a prosecutor and a .45 with zero emotion and equal finesse. If I'm blinded by anything this second, it's you. And if I'm an idiot, I dare you to say that right now, to my face, because God help me, I've seen you cry, and *fuck*, it's pretty."

She presses those lips together and swallows. Damn right she's tongue-tied. She needs to know who she's dealing with, because I've seen her up close and personal with another man, and I almost killed him. It's for her own fucking protection that she knows.

I can't save her from me, but I can save her from herself.

Her breaths are short and—damn it—delicious, and there's nothing I want more in this moment than to taste them. But I'm also furious. At her and, right now, the fucking world.

So I settle back into my seat, thanking God I'm still wearing my jacket, because it's the only thing shielding my rock-hard erection from her flittering eyes as I pull back out onto the road.

Most of the house is dark when we arrive. Only one light glows, and I assume it's from her father's office.

She walks behind me as I approach the door to the apartment, but before she opens it, I turn to her.

"What was number one?"

She blinks again. I wish she wouldn't do that, because it makes me lose track of thought.

"Go to bed."

I arch my brows and glance at the door. "So go."

She anchors her feet to the ground and wraps her arms around herself. "I want to know what you're going to say to my father."

I regard her as plainly as I can. "What I'm going to say to your father is none of your business."

She lowers her gaze to the ground. "Please, Cristiano."

I raise my face to the sky, shove my hands deep into my pockets, and release a long breath. "I want him to keep a closer eye on you." I roll my head toward her. "It's for your own sake."

She has the good sense not to argue as she looks up at me.

"You need to slow down on the drinking, okay? It's not a good look on anyone, in my opinion, but you . . . You seem less able than most to handle it."

She rubs a hand over her face, and to my surprise, she doesn't object. "You're right. I can't handle it. Which is exactly why I do it."

"It has to stop, Castellano, before you really hurt yourself."

"Why do you care if I hurt myself?" she whispers.

My throat tightens. "I'm not going to dignify that with a response."

She renews her gaze, and it's resigned. "What else?"

"No more nights out. Your friends can't be trusted."

"But Sandrine—"

"Can't tell the difference between a regular punter and a made man. That lack of awareness could cost your friend her life. You owe it to Sandrine to keep her as far from this world as you can."

She knows I'm right, and her lack of response confirms it.

"Anything else?"

My jaw grinds as I contemplate the other rules I want to impose on her, but not only are they not mine to impose, but they'd also be transparent.

Instead I shake my head. "That's all."

She glares at me as if "that's all" is everything, when she doesn't know the half of what I want to do.

I watch as she opens the door and slips off her shoes, and I continue to watch as the door slowly closes, eclipsing her from view. I stand and stare at a closed door for several seconds too long, then I make my way to the main house to speak to her father.

$\mathcal{T}$rilby

"Oh, Trilby, if your mama could see you now . . ."

I'm standing on a pedestal, facing a large oval mirror. A white bodice peppered with crystals hugs my ribs, and a long satin gown flows to my feet and trails behind me in a small, tasteful train. The halter neckline shows off my shoulders, and a subtle fishtail skirt makes a decadent meal of my curves.

An attendant hands Allegra a box of tissues, and she promptly blows her way through four sheets.

"You look stunning," Sera whispers beside her. "That dress was made for you."

I smooth my hands over my hips and marvel at the way the light bounces off the ripples it creates. "It is a beautiful dress," I agree.

Penelope, one of New York's most coveted

seamstresses, takes a pin from her mouth and tucks it into the skirt. "I've been in this business a long time, madam, and the dress is only ever as beautiful as the woman who wears it." She smiles up at me. "I have to agree with your sister."

I turn to my family. "Do you think Savero will like it?" I ask weakly.

Do I want him to like it?

Is it him I want to impress as I walk down that aisle?

I can't allow myself to follow that train of thought, so I turn to my aunt. "He said couture, didn't he?"

Allegra sniffs. "Yes, he did, and that's what this is. But it's irrelevant really. No one is going to wonder who the designer is when you look like this. They'll all be too blown away to care."

Penelope stands back and assesses her handiwork. "I'll take the dress back to my studio. Can you come along in a couple of weeks for another fitting?"

I take a last long look at the dress and permit myself a small smile to counteract the sinking of my stomach. If the final dress fitting is in only two weeks, that means the wedding day isn't too far behind it.

"Yes, of course."

The seamstress helps me undress and conceals the gown in a bridal bag. It's a good thing she does, because the moment we open the door, the unmistakable sound of Di Santo drifts up the stairs.

My heartbeat turns erratic. It's only been a few days since Cristiano pulled me out of the club with a gun in his hand, his finger poised on the trigger. After Rhett,

I've been determined not to let him shoot another man as a result of *my* actions. I didn't anticipate his propensity to put bullets into flesh to raise its head again so soon.

"I'll walk you out," Sera says, leading Penelope down the hallway.

Allegra turns to me with raised eyebrows.

I sigh. "Don't worry about me. I'm going out to the garden to finish my painting."

"Make sure you stay out of trouble," she warns. "I don't want you to give either of those men cause to speak to your father again."

My chin jerks with the effort of holding back a bold retort, and I settle for sticking my tongue out at her departing back. Not too long ago, I would have felt shame—so much shame—at the thought of giving a man reason to "speak to" my father, but these days . . . I feel like I have bigger problems. Like, how am I meant to marry a man whose brother makes me so mad, so angry, so *hot*, I can barely think straight?

The voices congregate in Papa's office, and I hear the word "port" as I get closer. The door is slightly open, and I can't stop myself from glancing through it as I pass.

All three men are standing over Papa's desk. Papa and Savero have their heads down, studying a spread of documents, but Cristiano's eyes rise the second I pause at the gap.

I mentally kick myself. Now I've been spotted, it

would be rude to continue on by without greeting my husband-to-be.

I push the door wide and wait for him to raise his head. When he doesn't, I make a play of clearing my throat. Papa opens his mouth to presumably dismiss me from the "men's work," but Savero beats him to it.

"Miss Castellano." His lips twitch into what I assume is a sort of smile.

"Mr. Di Santo."

He draws in a tight breath. "Making the most of the sun, I see."

I glance down at my outfit and mentally kick myself again. I didn't know we were expecting company for a start, and I needed something I didn't mind getting covered in paint. Hence why I chose to wear my faded old denim cutoffs and a red bikini top.

"I'm painting," I reply, my cheeks heating under his scrutiny. "And it's a beautiful day out."

"It is." He looks at me with no emotion. "Well, I'll let you get back to it."

It takes me a few seconds to realize I've been dismissed.

I can't stop my gaze from darting to Cristiano. He has a pen resting against his bottom lip, and his focus on me is thoughtful. I suddenly need the breeze of the outdoors to cool my skin.

Feeling acutely self-aware, I turn my back on the three men and walk out to the garden.

My easel is where I left it, along with the landscape watercolor I began just before Penelope arrived.

While our garden isn't enormous, it backs onto an orchard, and with it being late spring, the blossom is abundant. I've already captured the pale blue of the sky warmed by the blistering white sun, so I mix some greens and browns and set to work.

I'm so absorbed in trying to capture the scene I don't hear footsteps approaching from the house until Cristiano squats down beside me. I'm suddenly infused with nerves, and when I look back at my painting, it seems stupid, like something a child might paint.

"Don't stop on my account." His tone of voice is softer than I expect, but I still hate that he's eyeing my painting and probably seeing all of its imperfections.

I try not to look at him. "Shouldn't you be in Papa's office discussing the port?"

There's a long pause before he replies. "The port is Sav's thing, not mine. If I were still invested in the family businesses, I'd probably have sided with our father on this, but I'm not. Sav's in charge, and this is important to him."

I swallow. I need to ask him something even though I don't particularly want to know the answer. "If you're not invested in the family's businesses, why are you still here?"

He watches me casually as I soak the brush in water and catch a little paint on the tip.

"Moral support. Even though Sav has been Father's head capo for years now, becoming the don so soon was . . . unexpected. Not all our soldiers and associates have accepted him yet. I'm staying a while longer to reassure the rest of the family he's the right man for the job."

Something in his words strikes an uncomfortable chord. "If he's been head capo for years, why hasn't he been accepted as the natural successor?"

Another long pause follows, and I try to study him out of the corner of my eye. He grinds his jaw quietly.

"He has a different character to our father, that's all. He has different ideas and priorities. People can be funny about change."

I always thought I was one of those people, fearing change, fearing growth, fearing the idea that things move on. Sadness pricks at the corners of my eyes. Every second I move on is another step further from having my mama in my life.

I remember being in pieces, inconsolable for days, when I started art college. The change, the moving on, was terrifying. Even moving into the apartment felt wrong. It was so different from anything I'd known when Mama was around, but I had to do it. It was one thing for me to suffer through the night but a whole other thing for me to put everyone else through it too.

I've felt the guilt of moving on for five long years.

But for the first time since I lost Mama, I'm feeling it less. In the past few weeks I've found myself seeking change. I've consciously and unconsciously rebelled against the norm; the "what has to be." It doesn't take a genius to know who and what I'm running from. I never wanted to marry Savero, and I still can't reconcile myself with that vision of the future. But, what's harder to confront is what I *do* want.

Neither of us speak for the next few minutes, amplifying the sound of brushstrokes against canvas. One question sits on the tip of my tongue and makes my throat itch. I take a deep breath before asking.

"How long do you think you'll stay?"

He pushes a hand through his hair and then rubs it down his face. It's a slow, simple movement, but it's a reaction I can read into—a step away from the cool, still exterior he usually displays. My heartbeat quickens.

"I don't know," he replies, his tone weary.

I hold my breath. "Will you stay for the wedding?"

This man is the king of long-drawn-out pauses. He watches each brushstroke until even my hand feels self-conscious. I try my hardest to focus on the painting and not on the weight of his response.

"Of course. I'm going to be Sav's best man." He wraps a hand around the back of his neck and kneads it lightly. Then, almost as an afterthought, he adds, "But then I have to get back to work."

I roll back my shoulders. Although his response makes my stomach hollow, we're on safer ground now. It doesn't feel any less dangerous though.

"At the casinos?"

His shoulders relax. "Yeah."

I swallow and pretend to focus on the view I'm trying my hardest to replicate.

It's for the best that he isn't going to stick around. If I'm finding his presence challenge enough *before* I marry his brother, what will it be like when I'm his sister-in-law? I realize, with dreaded clarity, I don't want Cristiano to leave, and that alone is a clear sign he should. Hopefully, his visits will be few and far between. I have to limit my contact with this man. The survival of my family depends on it.

"Where are they?" I peek sideways at him. "Vegas, the gambling capital of the world?"

A sigh escapes his lips. "Mostly, yes. I do have interests in Atlantic City and also Chicago, but the main money is in Vegas."

"Wow," I breathe. "I've never been there, but I'd love to go one day."

"You like gambling?"

I try to conceal the horror in my features, because gambling is right up there with my views on violence. "No, but I love Elvis."

"You're an Elvis Presley fan?"

I glance sideways, and he's smirking. "More importantly," I say with a frown, "who *isn't* an Elvis Presley fan?"

He attempts to grimace, but nothing is going to make that face of his appear unpleasant. "I can think of at least one person."

I flick my hair back with a huff. "Well, that one person is a heathen."

When he doesn't throw a quick retort back my way, I look across at him, with my brush midair.

His expression is devious. "If that one person ever heard you call him a heathen, he might throw you over his shoulder and spank your ass to Memphis and back."

My cheeks *flood*, and I have to look away before I pass out. Cristiano chuckles darkly. I have no idea if he's joking around or being serious.

I paint in silence for the next few minutes, feeling his gaze flicking between the landscape and my painting.

"You're talented, aren't you?" he says eventually.

I laugh nervously. "Not really, but I enjoy it."

I can see him frown out of the corner of my eye. "For fuck's sake, Castellano, I just gave you a compliment. Own it."

His scolding smacks of impatience, which irks me. I train my eyes on the canvas, afraid to look into his eyes.

"Fine. Yes, I'm talented." I purse my lips to stop anything leaving my mouth that I might regret.

"There's a but . . ."

Damn, he's annoyingly astute.

I drop the brush and glare at him. "But . . . it doesn't matter, does it? It isn't like I'm going to be able to put it to good use. I'm being married off. I have to say goodbye to further education and work and anything that means—heaven forbid—I might fulfil my potential . . ."

"Hold up," he says, frowning. "Who said you have to give up your education?"

"Papa," I snap. "And don't act all surprised—you know it's the Cosa Nostra way. I can't work when I'm a Mafia wife. I've done enough research to know it doesn't reflect well on the husband if his wife works too."

Cristiano's stare pierces my skin until it hurts to look at him. The desire to paint is gone, so I busy myself putting away the colors. The sun is dipping behind the clouds anyway, and I'm beginning to feel a chill.

Without warning, he gets to his feet and brushes his hands down his slacks. It's only then I realize he's been squatting for the past twenty minutes. My leg muscles would have burned to a crisp by now.

I tear my eyes away from his thick thighs, but not quickly enough. His lashes flick upward and catch me staring.

As the flames of humiliation flicker up my neck, heating my cheeks, I turn away from him so he can't witness my embarrassment. I needn't have worried, though, because when I do finally turn around, thankfully, he's gone.

I breathe out a sigh of relief. I can't afford for him to get even the smallest glimpse of my true feelings—how weak I feel the second he enters a room. It shouldn't matter that Savero isn't out here with me and Cristiano is. And I absolutely, unequivocally, shouldn't prefer it that way.

CHAPTER 13

*T*rilby

I've never been one to speak ill of the dead, but I wish Giovanni Luigi Marioni the third had picked a different day to die.

I haven't even met the man, but his reputation as one of Gianni Di Santo's favorite capos preceded him, and as with most things shaped by violence, I find it hard to feel sorry for him.

As is tradition in the Marioni family, a funeral must be held exactly ten days from the second the deceased became, well . . . *deceased*, regardless of whether the last breath was taken at midday or midnight.

Exactly nine days, twenty-three hours, and ten minutes ago, Gio Marioni was shot between the eyes in the heart of Queens for beheading a close Mexican acquaintance of the Marchesis. Which is why I'm now sitting in a long black vehicle, playing the role of spare wheel to my fiancé and his phone, instead of presenting my final art show at the college.

I gaze out the window, watching the gray buildings pass by. We left the homely boulevards of Long Island an hour back and have now entered the more industrial streets of Williamsburg.

I turn to face the other view—that of my future husband. His focus is entirely on his call, which I gather to be "work"-related since it's peppered with words like "tracks" and "boxes." It doesn't take a genius to know he's talking about cocaine smuggling.

I tune out the voice and concentrate on his face. I've only had a handful of moments to study Savero, so I seize the chance to do so as discreetly as I can.

I study him objectively, like a piece of work I have to critique for a college project. His jaw is molded with hard lines to match the immovable frown covering his brow. His lips are full, though often pursed into a thin line when things aren't going the way he likes. His brows are thick like his brother's, but his irises are lighter—more bronze than burgundy—and his cheeks set lower.

My gaze runs downward, taking in his neck— thinner and leaner than Cristiano's—and his shoulders —slim and sharp compared to his brother's thick, rigid form. I've seen them stand side by side only a few times, but I remember there being about three inches between them, Cristiano being markedly taller.

I find myself wondering if I'll ever feel the same

pull toward Savero that I seem to feel for his brother. I wonder if that's why I feel so strongly for Cristiano . . .

Because he's the wrong man. The man I can't have.

I haven't seen him since he sat with me while I painted. That was over a week ago.

Savero doesn't even know I paint.

I look out the window again, just as we pull into the gravel parking lot of the St. Augustus Church. I sit up sharply. I didn't know we were coming to this church. Of all the Catholic churches in Brooklyn, why this one?

My chest tightens.

Feelings I thought I'd buried start clamoring for oxygen.

Savero's phone snaps shut, and he rests a hand casually over mine. I drop my gaze to it, wondering when the warmth might penetrate my skin, or when butterflies will take flight in my lower abdomen, but there's nothing. Then again, my heart is stuttering with the aftereffects of trauma. I haven't been to this church in five years. And I vowed never to set foot in it again.

"Wait here for five minutes."

I nod and look into his eyes, seeking some kind of softness, but I'm met with only flint.

"There's some business I need to take care of."

The door closes with a little too much force. The leather squeaks as I drop my head back against it and close my eyes, for the first time *willing* them to fill with Savero or Cristiano—anything but the memory of when I was last here, saying goodbye to Mama.

I can't do this. Blind panic fills my throat, and I try

to slow my breaths, my fingertips gripping the leather seat like I might levitate off it.

Pull yourself together, I scold.

The past isn't important right now. The future is everything. My *family* is everything. I focus on my breathing, deliberately slowing my inhale, my exhale, until I feel almost normal. Gradually, the tightness in my chest eases enough that I can step out of the car.

Other mourners are walking my way, dressed from head to toe in black. I don't recognize any of them. I'm an outsider at this funeral, unsympathetic to the plight of the deceased, no tears brimming in my eyes, only shock pulling at the corners.

I draw the net down over my face and walk in the same direction as the other mourners, toward the entrance to the church.

Out of nowhere, his presence warms my side, matching my racing heart step for step, his large hands shoved deep into his pockets, his expensive shoes making a soft click against the paving stones.

"The Cosa Nostra world suits you."

With each step I take, my breath shakes a little more. "Well that's a relief," I say, remembering his lack of response to my assessment of what is now expected of me. "I'd say it suits anyone who can dress in black and keep a few secrets."

"We're back to keeping secrets, are we?" Cristiano says, a smile tugging at his lips.

I'm only half paying attention even though his arm grazes mine, challenging my determination to keep my distance. "Aren't secrets the same as currency in this world?" I try to keep my tone light, but in all honesty, I'm struggling to place one foot in front of the other.

"True. But you're not a part of this world *yet*, so yours are of little value."

I stop and stare at him, though the vision of him is faint and graduated. "You're saying my secrets are worthless?"

"It depends who you're asking,"

The same words he said to me in the library scratch at my patience.

I narrow my lids. "I'm asking *you*."

His eyes flash as if he's just stumbled across a moment he's been waiting his whole life for. He steps into my orbit despite the fact I'm spinning, untethered and so disoriented I feel slightly sick.

"Your secrets will only be worthless if you share them with the wrong person."

A short gasp leaves my throat.

He can't know.

I have only one secret, and it's *him*. But he can't know that. No one can.

The realization I'm in deep collides with the memory that I'm still rooted in so much loss.

I start walking again and somehow reach the steps, where I pause at the bottom. Cristiano takes two before realizing I'm no longer by his side. He turns and coasts his gaze over my frozen form.

"Come on—we should get inside. The ceremony's about to start."

"I-I can't," I stutter. I'm rigid with shock. My legs won't move.

He's at my side in a heartbeat. "What's wrong?"

My brow feels clammy, and I raise a trembling hand to wipe it.

"You're shaking. Are you feeling okay?"

"Um, I'm fine." Even as I say the words the steps are swimming before me. "But I don't think I can go inside."

I feel his large palm cradling my elbow and guiding me to a bench.

"Put your head between your knees."

When I don't respond, his hand moves to my nape and pushes me down gently. I close my eyes and focus on my breathing, and slowly, my head begins to feel normal again.

After a few minutes have passed, I look up at the doors to the church. They've been closed. "Shit," I mutter. "I need to be inside. Savero . . ." I go to stand but wobble precariously.

Cristiano's hands find my hips and press down firmly, until I'm once again sitting beside him. "Savero will be fine. He's survived without a woman by his side for thirty-two years. He can get through another day."

I cast my gaze to Cristiano. "Thirty-two? I had no idea he was twelve years older than me."

His expression darkens. "What happened just now? I thought you were going to faint on me."

I stare at my hands. "The last time I visited this church, it was . . ." I swallow, but the dryness grows tighter, the lump in my throat larger. "It was for my mama's funeral."

Cristiano lifts a hand to his face and presses his thumb and middle finger to the bridge of his nose. "Fuck," he whispers coarsely. "How long ago was that?"

"Five years." I take deep breaths and look up at the building. "It feels like it was only yesterday. I can't believe five years have passed since I last saw her."

"What happened?" His voice is surprisingly soft.

"She was driving me to an art class." My voice sounds faraway, and the image in my mind crackles like a vintage movie that's been played too many times. "I didn't want to go, but she'd already paid for it. We got into a huge fight, so we were late getting into the car."

That will always be my biggest regret: fighting with Mama that day.

"Even though she was driving fast, we noticed a car following us. We were used to being trailed, and we often had a couple of Papa's security guys with us for protection. But that day we were too late for my class already, so we didn't call the guys, and we didn't try to lose the car like we normally would. When we stopped at a set of lights, a guy jumped out of the car, ran over to us, and smashed in the driver's window. My face got all cut from the glass."

Cristiano stills beside me, but I can hear his breathing, slow and steady, matching mine to his and grounding me while I recount the moment my life changed forever.

"He was screaming at Mama, and she screamed back at him. I can't remember what they were saying, because I was terrified. Then he reached into the car and started strangling her . . ."

I stop to catch my breath. I never again want to feel as helpless as I did that day.

"Then another guy came out of nowhere, pulled out a gun, and before I could even figure out what was going on, he'd shot Mama. She died instantly."

I slowly become aware of a hand stroking the tears from my cheeks. "I can't forget the look on her face. So angry and afraid. Then, as the blood drained away, her expression changed. She looked peaceful."

Cristiano continues to breathe steadily. "What did you do?"

"Nothing." I lift my lids to check for a reaction, but there is none. "I couldn't move. I couldn't breathe. No sound would come out of my mouth at all. It was the gunshots that raised the alarm. The police took me home and broke the news to Papa."

Out of the corner of my eye, Cristiano scrubs a hand across his face. "Does Sav know any of this? That this is the church where you held her funeral?"

I drop my lids and shake my head slowly. "It wouldn't make any difference," I say with a trace of bitterness. "I know people die in this life all the time. I can hardly boycott the biggest church in the city, can I?"

He stares straight ahead with an almost angry glint in his eye.

Nerves skitter across my skin as I prepare to ask him his story. "You lost your mama too, right?"

He inhales a deep breath and exhales it through pursed lips. Then he rubs his hands over his knees.

"You don't have to answer that. I just—"

"No," he cuts in. "We did lose her. She was also shot dead. A drive-by, to get to my father."

Oh.

"I'm so sorry. When did it happen?"

He shifts slightly, and his arm brushes against mine, raising the hairs across my skin. "Ten years ago. I was seventeen."

I shake my head at the horror of it all. Between Cristiano and Savero, and me and my three sisters, that's six kids deprived of a mother, all because of the criminal underworld lurking around every corner.

I look sideways at him and momentarily admire how composed he is when talking about something so personal; so emotional. "What did you do?"

"I moved to Vegas soon after. I got special dispensation from my father to leave this world behind. I wanted nothing to do with it. I still don't." He shakes his head as if he's the one who needs convincing. "At least, it's what I keep telling myself. The life I have now, the businesses I run—sure, it's not always straight and legal, but I *chose* it. I run these businesses entirely by myself. Every bit of success I've had, I made it on my own. And I haven't had to put a bullet in anyone's head to make it happen."

I nod as though I understand, but I don't.

Unlike Cristiano, I don't have a choice. Unlike Cristiano, I can't marry whomever I want, because apparently, I have to be pawned off to "save" our family. Cristiano can come and go as he pleases; his family accepts that from him. But me? I'm stuck in this way of life, and I'll never be able to leave.

I feel his eyes settle on me as if they can reach into my soul and hear every thought.

"I'm fortunate," he says softly. "I got to choose a different path. I chose not to follow in the footsteps of my father and Sav. I didn't want that kind of life. I felt like I owed it to our mother to create a different life, to improve the chances of at least one of us living till we're sixty."

I hesitate, unsure my next question is appropriate given how short a time ago it was, but I figure we've probably gone past the point of appropriate by exchanging the details of our mothers' bloody murders. "How old was your father when he died?"

He laughs, low and bitter. "He was six months shy of his sixtieth birthday."

"Oh man," I whisper.

"Yeah." He sighs heavily and with a note of suspicion. "He went too soon. None of us expected it. He was fit and healthy."

"I'm sorry. It must have been a shock."

He cracks his knuckles and stares at the ground.

"Savero seems to be handling it okay," I suggest.

"My brother will never show his true emotions." His

gaze seems to darken as though he doesn't necessarily approve.

I wring my hands and then realize I've picked up the damn habit from Allegra. "Not even with me?" I ask quietly.

His jaw hardens, and he turns to face me. The heat of his unwavering focus on the surface of my skin will never get easier to bear. Every cell of my body wants to turn from him, but like an addict who just laid eyes on their next fix, I can't draw my attention away.

"I don't know the answer to that." He speaks softly, but there's an edge to his tone. "As far as I know, he's never shown his true emotions to anyone his entire life."

Does he even have emotions? I want to ask, but I realize how dark and judgmental that might sound.

"That must be very tiring," I say instead.

Cristiano smooths his hands down his suit pants and then stands and holds out a hand. "I'm sure it would be," he says with a taut smile.

I can't hear anything properly as I place my hand in his, because my pulse is thundering at the feel of his fingers wrapped around mine, but I swear he mutters something that sounds like, "If he actually cared for anyone else."

We walk up the steps to the church, and I make no attempt to withdraw my hand from Cristiano's. I know he's only holding it because I very nearly passed out on him, and he probably doesn't want to be burdened with a comatose woman at the funeral of his father's favorite capo. Still, a small part of me imagines he's holding my hand because he wants to. Because, if he's anything like me, he's *craving* this touch, and he can't seem to think of anything else, as inconvenient as it is.

At the top of the steps, the doors open, and he drops my hand, leaving the sensation of his heated skin on mine to evaporate into the thick Brooklyn air.

The church looks smaller somehow, as if my recollection of that day is slightly less poignant than this moment I'm sharing with someone else who also lost their mother. Someone who understands.

Thankfully, no heads turn our way as we walk quietly down the aisle and slide into the first empty pew. I can see Savero sitting several rows ahead, but he doesn't turn around. Not that it matters, because Cristiano's thigh is pressed against mine with a possessiveness I want to devour, and despite the memories nudging at my consciousness, I can't think of anything else.

$\mathcal{C}$ristiano

Growing up, I was always the calm one, the steady one.

Mama's words still ring in my ears a decade after she was run down on the street by the Marchesis. *You can't figure out Cristiano. You'll never know what game he's playing until he's wiped the floor with you.*

I was the cool customer to Sav's hothead; the ice to his flame.

While Sav often drove headlong into battle lines, fuck to all consequences, I knew what power lay in caution; in holding back and staying out of sight.

It's for this very reason I can't still my bones as we follow Sav's car away from the church, through the heart of Newark, in broad daylight. This place is home to the Marchesis—the biggest rival family in New York. I don't understand why we've taken the scenic route. Is he gloating about the fact we found and quartered the guy who shot Gio?

His car alone has a price on its head in this neighborhood. Driving it beneath the beams of the sun and the heat of the enemy's gaze isn't just ballsy—it's irresponsible as fuck. It isn't just his own life he's risking. It's Castellano's too.

My eyes scan the streets as we drive along slowly and then come to a stop at a red light. A few people turn to take in our two blacked-out cars before walking away quickly, pulling kids and elderly companions with them. A woman to my right trips, drawing my eye for a second. A young couple help her up, and she nods vigorously, letting them pull her to her feet and guide her along the road in the opposite direction to our cars.

A heaviness grows at the base of my chest, then the sound of gunfire brings everything to a halt.

"Mother FUCK!"

Donato, who pulled the slightly longer straw of driving me around today, throws open the car door and leaps out, a pistol raised in his outstretched arms.

I jump out onto the sidewalk, trying to make sense of the scene before us. Savero's driver has been pulled out of the car and is lying limp on the ground, blood seeping from a bullet hole in the center of his forehead.

From a short distance away my gaze scans the rest of the car, measured and fast. I see movement in the back seat, and my chest blooms with relief. Sav stands over his driver's body for all of half a second, then he's gone, sprinting down the road after whoever it was that pulled the trigger. Donato runs after him, his yelled directions probably falling on deaf ears since Sav will be singularly focused on killing someone.

I scan the road. Pedestrians have scattered like mice at the sound of gunshots. My eyes spin back to Sav's car.

Castellano.

I run to the car so hard my thighs burn, yanking open the back door and bending down to see where she is. A scream pierces the air as she scrambles to the opposite side of the car.

Marchesi assholes could be anywhere—I don't have the luxury of being able to coax her out in her own sweet time—so I grab her ankles in one hand, pull her roughly toward me, and lift her with my other arm. Her fists beat against my shoulders, panic lacing her shrieks.

I run back to my car, drop Castellano in the front seat, buckle her seat belt, and slam the door before sliding in behind the wheel. The engine is still running, but it's barely audible over the sound of more gunshots. I slam the accelerator and spin the car across the road, straight through the lights. I don't take notice of what color they are, but I figure if the sound of screeching wheels and honking horns is anything to go by, red is a likely bet.

With one palm ramming the steering wheel left and right, I reach out to take Castellano's trembling hand in mine. I can feel her seat vibrating from her terrified sobs and gasping breaths, but as soon as my fingers graze hers, she snatches her hand away.

My teeth clench, and I put my foot down harder.

I'm not angry at her. I'm angry at Sav for putting her through this. She's just lived through a repeat of what happened to her mother, only to be abandoned because her husband-to-be values anger and revenge over protecting his future wife.

He's the don now—he has capos and soldiers who can do the chasing for him. In fact, each one of them would relish the opportunity to exact revenge on whoever shot Sav's driver on the hostile streets of Newark. Savero has other priorities now; he needs to man up and deal with them. I shake the thought from my head, because it only adds to the already sour note I'm beginning to taste when it comes to my brother.

Tension stays with me as we cross the bridge to Manhattan. Only the midday traffic stands between us and my Tribeca apartment. The urge to damage someone settles in my veins, doing nothing to convince me I changed when I fled to Vegas. I've been back on Long Island for all of three weeks, and it's as if I never went away.

It's a relief in a way.

In Vegas my days are spent navigating wins and losses, profits, deficits, and middle grounds, and punishing bad behavior with bans and loaded threats. Lots of gray. Too much gray. But here, it's easy. It's black or white. Right or wrong. Life or death.

There's no in-between. No gray area. You're in or you're out.

It's hard to believe just how easily I've settled back

into the Cosa Nostra ways. Distinguishing black from white is as easy as breathing.

Which might explain why being around Castellano makes it hard to fucking breathe.

With her, I can't be black or white, in or out. "Out" means I leave now and never come back. "In" means I satisfy this insatiable hunger to know how she tastes on my tongue, how she feels beneath my fingertips, destroying my relationship with Savero forever. I can't do that, because he's all I have left in this world. Not only would Father have been devastated, I owe Savero my life. And as questionable as his actions and his morals are, he's still my brother.

We drive through the security barriers and arrive in the underground parking lot, where I open the passenger door and hold out my hand, but she doesn't move.

"You're safe here." I shift impatiently. In principle it's true, but I don't want to push our luck. "You can either come with me or sit out here alone. I'm armed, and I have a secure penthouse apartment, so I strongly recommend the former."

Her eyes flick upward, a frown battling against a light flush of her cheeks.

"Come on." I swallow. "I'll take care of you."

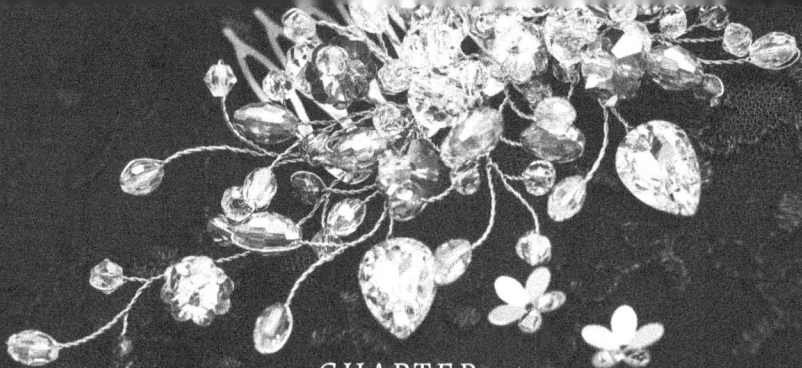

$\mathcal{T}$rilby

It isn't fear that makes me look away as I hold out my hand. It isn't trust either. It's pure, unadulterated confusion.

I'm pulsing beneath the black silk that covers my body.

I just witnessed a man being murdered, shot at point-blank range and dropped to the ground three feet from where I sat. I watched, frozen and unfeeling, as my fiancé flew out of the car in pursuit of the attacker, without so much as a backward glance. Then I allowed the shock and disorientation to drag me under even as Cristiano yanked me out of the car by my ankles and clutched me to his beating heart.

This whole day has brought back memories I've tried so hard to bury. First, the church where I buried

Mama when I was just fifteen. Second, the shooting that took me right back to the day I sat in the back seat of my mother's car with her blood raining over me.

But now, in the quiet of the underground parking lot, under the dark shadow of the man who's driven me to safety—the man whose eyes I can't get out of my head —I'm a weak, boneless mess. I'm itching and aching, in need of *something*. And a terrifying voice in the back of my head is convinced Cristiano is the only person who can give it to me.

Thick black elevator doors slide apart. Cristiano pulls me inside and presses a series of buttons. I watch the doors close with a sense of detachment. In seconds they're opening again with a silence that reeks of money.

His hand warms my back, coaxing me into a bright, airy space. My ability to describe my new surroundings is impeded by the fact I've never seen anything like it. This place has no windows, just clear glass walls that seem to stretch around the entire outer edge. The view —not just of lower Manhattan but beyond it, to Staten Island and even as far as the Atlantic—tells me we're almost as high as the clouds. And the furnishings, which initially appear to be minimally chic, are anything but.

Cristiano walks across the floor delivering voice commands to an unknown entity, creating mood lighting, darkened glass, and soft music. When he circles back and comes to a sudden standstill, his brows draw together as if he's only just realized I'm standing in his apartment.

"Why the mood lighting?" I ask. "It's mid-afternoon."

He slowly pushes his hands into his pockets and watches me carefully. "You should try to relax."

I look around some more. There may as well be bars on the windows for all the freedom I now have. It's for this reason I can't keep the irritation out of my voice. "For whose benefit?"

He doesn't skip a beat. "Yours, of course." He nods toward a seating area. It's probably a living room, but it looks too slick and *unlived-in* for me to comfortably call it that. "Go sit down."

When I don't budge, his jaw tics, and he turns to walk into a sleek, modern open-plan kitchen.

I walk up behind him, quietly seething. After witnessing a man being murdered just inches away from me, less than an hour after I sat outside the church of memories I don't wish to revisit, I feel vengeful. And I'm not about to let anyone tell me what to do.

Fury is suddenly so near to my pores it burns.

I stand close enough to him that I can smell the sweat rising from his back. I fight the urge to place my palms over his thick muscles and feel the damp exertion beneath his shirt. Lust collides with hatred, and for some inexplicable reason, I want to hurt him.

His voice is soft as he turns his head a fraction. "Do as you're told, Castellano. Go sit down."

Mine is silky and spiteful as I reply. "Or else?"

His pause drags, and his breaths become heavy. "Don't test me."

His tone is thick with warning, but I can't stop myself. I want to push him. I want to see how hard I can press his buttons before he lashes out at me.

And God, I need him to.

I need a reason to *hate* him.

It's suddenly crystal clear. The only way I can get through this marriage to Savero and have Cristiano in my life is if he gives me a reason to despise him with all my heart—every inch of it.

I speak slowly and with as much venom as I can muster. "Don't tell me what to do. I am not *yours* to order around."

My heartbeat thumps in my ears as I feel his temperature rise. The heat between his spine and my chest feels oppressive.

I don't even get a chance to take a breath. In the blink of an eye, I'm spun around and pressed up against a counter, my spine bent backward, with an enormous hand around my throat.

My windpipe is unrestricted, but the threat of its closure is darkly present. My eyes stretch wide, absorbing the stark white ceiling, until his face moves into my view.

He growls through clenched teeth. "What part of 'don't test me' do you not understand?"

The whites of his eyes gleam at me, and a knot twists deep in my gut. It feels like satisfaction.

"And what part of 'don't tell me what to do' do *you* not understand?" I can only squeeze out a whisper.

A whisper and a smile.

Confusion clouds his face, along with something else. Something darker than he's let me see before.

Then I'm disoriented beyond measure.

A giant fist slams down on the kitchen surface, and my jaw is freed. I stagger backward and spin around to see Cristiano facing the counter.

His arms are braced, his knuckles white from where he's gripping the edges. I only notice the way his back rises and falls as he gasps for air because the movement mirrors my own. I can't seem to catch my breath.

"What just happened?" I whisper.

He squeezes his eyes closed and then curls both his hands into fists on the countertop. "I nearly kissed you," he says slowly. "That's what just happened."

My gut implodes.

The few kisses I experienced as a young adult left me wondering what the fuss was all about, but right now, my lips are *tingling* with the need to press against his. It's an urge so raw, so brazen, and so foreign to me, but I need it like oxygen.

My entire pelvic area has turned to jelly, while he seems more solid and defiant than ever. Myriad responses flash through my mind, but none of them feel appropriate. There really is no appropriate way to say "I wish you had." At least not when it's being said to the brother of one's fiancé.

So instead I do whatever any self-disrespecting Cosa Nostra fiancée would do: I take full responsibility and apologize.

"I-I'm sorry."

He turns his head a fraction but keeps his eyes closed. "Don't you *dare* apologize for a man's behavior."

I go to open my mouth, but his lids ping open, spearing me to the spot.

"I nearly kissed *you*," he repeats. "You did nothing wrong."

Despite his assertion, I can hear Papa and Allegra's words ringing in my ears, chastising me for drawing his eyes, riling his temper, and using my feminine wiles to lead him astray.

Everything stills—even my beating heart.

"What if I wanted you to?"

I lower my gaze to the floor, afraid to look at him. The burn of his stare mellows into a warm caress on the side of my face.

"You can't say things like that to me, Castellano." His voice is soft, but it carries a dark warning.

I inhale a shallow breath. "But it's true. I wanted you to kiss me."

A glance through the corner of my lowered lids makes my breath hitch. He's released his fists from the counter and is now stretching and flexing his fingers while his eyes scan me intensely.

He takes a slow step toward me, then another one, until his chest is almost brushing my nipples. My spine cries out to arch a little so I can press my breasts into him, but the look on his face is agonized, as though he's debating the merits of ending me and putting himself out of his misery.

He brings a rough palm up to my face and lets it rest there gently. "Listen to me," he says, his voice lucid and low. "There's no room in this life for wanting something you can't have."

My breath stutters inside my chest as his deep burgundy eyes make my skin burn.

I part my lips to speak, but his forefinger moves across them and presses down gently.

His voice dips with the stroke of defeat. "Sometimes the best memories are the ones we can't make."

He drops his hand from my face and walks out of the kitchen toward the expansive windows. The sky outside is darkening with thunderclouds. With the oppressive humidity we've been having, we're due a storm.

I follow at what I think is a safe distance, my head spinning with thinly veiled warnings and the burn that comes from realizing the chemistry I thought was all in my head is actually real, and he feels it too.

In the heat of this moment I don't know what's worse: wanting this man in some raw, carnal way, believing he's blissfully ignorant of it; or knowing the feeling is mutual but that an entire underworld stands in the way of it ever being more than an inconsequential feeling.

"You will stay here tonight," he says without looking around. "I don't know when Savero will be finished."

I know what that means. Savero will be pursuing every single person who might be somehow connected to the man who shot his driver at point-blank range, and that's a task impossible to put a timeframe on. But Cristiano's warning still echoes in my ears.

"Maybe it would be better if I went home."

He turns and looks at me, almost weary. "Even your father, someone who's lived a life on the edges of this world, hasn't seen the kind of threat we Di Santos have been under for as long as we've been alive. A lot of people want us dead and will keep trying to kill us—and those closest to us—until they get what they want. You're at risk now, Castellano, and your father can't protect you anymore."

He lets the weight of his words settle on my shoulders, then he jerks his head toward the back of the room. "You are exhausted, and I have a spare room you can sleep in."

I am exhausted. I've seen enough in one day to last me a lifetime.

"Is it okay if I use the bathroom?"

His jaw tics from side to side. "There's one in the spare bedroom, but if you want to take a shower, the best one is in the master. I'll show you."

He strokes his gaze down my neck and lingers on my collarbone one last time, then he walks past me.

I take in his gait as I follow. It's smooth, assured, and purposeful—everything I wish I were. He opens a set of doors and takes out two unfathomably fluffy towels. When he catches my widened eyes, he shrugs.

"I have a housekeeper when I'm in town."

Two seconds later, we're standing in a tastefully

decorated bathroom. There's an enormous waterfall shower enclosed in polished glass panels, and enough shampoos and lotions to last a year. I can't stop my jealous thoughts from veering to the question of whether other women have been here.

"Have you had company?" I ask before I can stop myself.

I feel him smile beside me.

"No." He turns to leave but stops in the doorway. "My housekeeper is a wishful thinker." His gaze caresses my face, sending me into a hazy spin.

I want to know what he's thinking. We came close to *kissing* back there, and now I'm staying in his apartment. And it's not weird. I feel like I'm meant to be here.

His voice softens like a damn pillow. "Just come back out when you're done. Take your time."

I stare at the door he just left wide-open and wonder how he can be so mindful of my honor yet so selective about it.

My stomach is roiling after the past few hours. Being in the church brought back memories I never want to relive again in any lifetime. Witnessing cold-blooded murder just inches from my person made me yearn for my family, when in reality, they're slipping from my fingers. And having Cristiano's lips so close to my own has made me feel, for the first time since my mother died, like a living, breathing, *aching* human being. Someone who wants to feel *everything* again, without the protective layers of grief and loss.

I leave the door exactly where it is and slowly peel off my clothes. I let them scatter like breadcrumbs along the floor until I reach the shower, then I step inside and let the water pummel me.

Steam floods the room, and I drench myself in it. I need to cleanse myself of all the dirt and grime tunnelling under my nails and into my dreams.

I stand there for about ten minutes relishing the sizzle of hot water on cool skin, until I can barely see further than my nose. I wipe a hand across the glass separating me from the rest of the bathroom. As my eyes readjust to the light, I see movement beyond the door.

My breath stutters. Standing in the center of the living room, feet braced on the wooden floor, and *staring* at me like he wants to devour me limb from limb, is Cristiano.

My pulse thuds through my temple like my own personal bass drum. Every throb punctuates another second in which neither of us move.

He's looking at me.

Really *looking* at me, and it makes me feel even more naked than I am.

My legs tremble as I force myself to hold his gaze.

Cristiano slowly rolls his head, loosening the tension in his neck. He doesn't break eye contact. As more seconds pass, the shock and embarrassment I feel give way to defiance; to challenge. He wanted this to happen. This is why he left the door open. He *wanted* to see me. He wanted to see more of what he can't have.

This man is a masochist.

As my fingertips rest on the glass, I realize that although I've been standing under the shower for the past ten minutes, I haven't actually washed myself. And since Cristiano's obviously now seen all of me stripped bare, I have nothing to lose.

I break eye contact to locate a bottle of very expensive soap. I squeeze some onto my palm and rub it slowly to a lather. When I lift my gaze, I feel the hot spear of his focus instantly. His hands are in his pockets, but his shoulders are rigid. Something pulses between my legs, threatening to distract me, but I don't stop.

I rub the soap onto my arms, working it up to my shoulders, across my chest, and down to my breasts. My palms catch the sharps peaks of my nipples, and a soft gasp darts out of my throat, taking me by surprise.

Cristiano tears a hand from his pocket and pushes it roughly through his hair. He's standing too far away for me to read his expression through the steam, but his stance hasn't changed. He's still *looking*.

I rub the soap across my rib cage and slowly down over my stomach. My cheeks tighten with warm shame as my hands reach a part of me no man has ever seen. I tremble at the contact and allow the soap to glide my hand between my legs, back and forth. I only intended to clean myself, but holy crap, it feels good. I've been down there before—not always with much success—but right now I could collapse with the need for release.

Even at this blurred distance I don't miss Cristiano tugging his bottom lip between his teeth. I want nothing more than to tip my head back and rub myself until this torturous *urge* implodes, but I force my hands down my thighs.

The same hand that Cristiano pushed through his hair now wraps itself around the back of his neck, squeezing at the taut muscles lining the tops of his shoulders.

My mouth has achieved the impossible—in a steam-filled room, it's as dry as a desert. I don't want to stop this exhibitionist display, but I have to. Because if I don't, and nothing comes of it, I might die.

And if I don't, and something does come of it, I might be killed.

I step back beneath the powerful spray of the shower and close my eyes as the suds run off my skin.

When I eventually turn off the water and open my eyes, Cristiano has gone.

$\mathcal{C}$ ristiano

"We've found the guy. He's not a Marchesi, but he was paid by one, and we know where he's hiding."

I feign interest in Sav's update, keeping one eye on the bathroom door. I've had to take the call in the kitchen so the sound of falling water won't trigger any questions. Not that it would. When Sav is on a mission, he's single-minded. He can only entertain violence. Dramatic, bloody, all-consuming violence. The sound of a shower in the background that potentially holds his future wife is an unnecessary distraction as far as he's concerned.

Sometimes I wonder if we're from the same parents, if not the same planet.

I stare at the door, half-listening to my brother. From here I can only see the doorframe, but that's for the best.

I stared at her for too long.

I shouldn't have stared at all.

She's about to become family.

A lead weight settles in my stomach. She'll share his bed; bear his children.

My grip tightens around the phone until I'm sure it would only take one more squeeze for me to crush it into small pieces.

"What happened to the Castellano girl?" he asks, rather late in the day.

I settle back against the island. "She's safe. I've got her."

"Are you at the house?"

"No. My apartment in the city. She can't stay at her father's."

"No. You're right. They'll want her, and his place is wide-open. Okay, good. Keep her there. I'll collect her when I return."

"And take her where?" It shouldn't matter to me where he takes her, but it does.

"She can stay at the house," he says with an undertone of boredom. "She's going to be living there after the wedding—she may as well start getting used to it."

I rub the ache from my jaw. At some point during our conversation, it's tightened.

"When do you think you'll be back?"

"Couple of days. I'm sorry to burden you with this, *fratello*. Especially when this is only a short visit."

"I'm fine," I say tightly. "It's not a burden."

"Okay, listen. Call her aunt—what's her name . . .?"

My brows knit. "Allegra."

"Yeah, her. Invite her over, or one of her trillion sisters, so you don't have to engage in too much small talk."

I almost laugh down the phone. Small talk is the least of my problems.

"Don't worry about me. Or her. You just focus on finding that son of a bitch."

I can hear the relief in his voice now he's off the hook from domestic responsibilities, and I wonder how he's going to manage once he actually has a wife.

"I will. I'll call when it's done."

There's a click on the other end of the line, and I slowly lower the phone, my gaze floating like a feather to the woman standing in front of me. She's wrapped in a large towel, but her shoulders peek over the top, still carrying droplets of water, and her hair hangs in wet ringlets around her face. Her cheeks are pink from the steam, but her eyes are wide.

"Was that Savero?"

I nod and slide the phone into my back pocket.

"Is he okay?" she asks in a whisper.

Something inside me burns. "Yes, he's good. You're staying here until he returns."

She swallows. "How long will that be?"

"Couple of days."

Something fearful flashes across her face. "Why can't I go home?"

"We've discussed this. You're not safe there."

"We didn't 'discuss' it—you told me and assumed I agreed."

"You're staying here. End of story."

She blinks rapidly, as if it's finally dawned on her what this engagement actually means: her life will never be the same again.

"I have a gown fitting tomorrow," she says, staring at the wall behind me.

"I'll take you."

She looks back at me sharply. "*You* are going to take me to a bridal gown fitting?"

I shrug. "Sure."

"I don't think that's appropriate."

"Why wouldn't it be?" My eyes narrow in a challenge. "I'm going to be your brother soon enough. This is a brotherly thing to do."

Her lips part, and her neck flushes pink. I know what she's thinking. A brother wouldn't confess to wanting to kiss her. A brother wouldn't blatantly stare at her while she showered.

Her shoulders deflate. "I was going to go with Allegra."

"Well, now you're going with me." I ignore Sav's recommendation to invite her entire family over to save me the inconvenience of actually speaking to her. I've already made the decision that while she's under my protection, I'm keeping her to myself.

"Are you hungry?"

She hugs the towel around herself and chews her lip while she thinks. Then she shakes her head.

"You haven't eaten a thing all day."

"I'm not hungry."

It's becoming increasingly difficult to see her standing in front me with nothing but a towel separating the heat of her skin from mine. I turn my back to her and walk to the refrigerator.

"I'm making you dinner. Go get dressed."

"I don't have any fresh clothes."

I take out tomatoes and place them on the island, along with olives and some garlic. She watches me warily.

"Fetch a shirt and some shorts from the master. I'll have more clothes for you by the morning."

"You don't know my size."

I coast my gaze over her. "I can hazard a guess."

She swallows and clutches the towel even tighter.

I jerk my head toward the master bedroom. "Go."

One of her brows arches, and I can see the old Castellano emerging. "You're going to let me rummage around in your room?"

I lift a sharp chef's knife from the drawer and turn it in my fingers. "I have nothing to hide."

Her eyes sparkle. "Great. I may be a while." She spins on the balls of her feet, sending droplets of water flying in every direction.

When she's out of my sight, I rest my hands on the island, stretch out my arms, and let my head fall. I've never envied my brother. I've never wanted what he's inherited as the firstborn son. But she's the one thing he has that I want—that I *crave*.

Savero has never been the most amenable brother, but now I know he has something he doesn't deserve, I'm finding it even harder to like him.

I shake the thought from my head, take a few long breaths, and then straighten and get to work.

CHAPTER 17

*T*rilby

I step inside Cristiano's bedroom and close the door behind me, letting my towel drop to the floor. Standing beneath his scrutiny wearing only a square of fluffy cotton felt obscene, but I couldn't bring myself to slip the black dress on—not now it carries the memories of being back at that church, sitting in a car, with a gunman right outside, and having my jaw held tightly by a ravenous man who apparently wants me as much as I want him.

Standing naked in his bedroom feels wrong and rebellious. He could walk in here at any moment. He could touch me in any place he wanted. My cheeks grow hot at the realization I'd let him.

Or . . . he could simply stare.

I know what it feels like to be turned on. I've read

plenty of kissy books and let my fingers wander south enough times to know what triggers it, what draws it out, and what kind of pressure brings relief. But I've never felt the space between my legs weigh so heavily until Cristiano's disinterested gaze lingered on that part of me. I've never felt scorching blood course through my pelvic bone, making me throb in places I didn't think possible. I've never yearned for another person's touch like I did when I stood beneath his waterfall shower.

I can feel myself getting hot and heavy again, until I remember. He isn't the one I'm marrying. I shake my head, but no matter how brisk, he won't leave. So I shove the image of his burning eyes to the back of my mind and get back to the task at hand.

I head to the closet. Light illuminates the rails as soon as the large doors open. This is the closet of someone with a serious case of OCD. The hangers are spaced at equal distances apart, and the clothes are pressed to within an inch of their life. Suits are ordered by shade: black to charcoal, steel to midnight-blue. Shirts, too, in only two color groups: black and white. His ties hang on the inside of the door, again ordered from dark to light and largely monochrome.

No sign of a T-shirt or shorts.

I close the doors and open the next set. Another downlight illuminates five rows of shoes, all luxury Italian leather and polished until I can see nearly a hundred of my faces reflected back at me.

I swallow.

Apparently, it's entirely possible to be intimidated by a closet.

The next closet contains drawers. A brief look into each reveals Cristiano is a fan of Marie Kondo, or his housekeeper is. I've never seen underwear rolled and stacked in real life before, and he doesn't make a habit of storing secrets in his clothing. No guns, no business cards, no mementoes.

I pull a pair of running shorts from a drawer dedicated solely to this particular breed of shorts and pull a T-shirt from one of the hangers above me. Both drown me, but I have very few other options. Stay naked or walk around in a towel all day.

I cast my gaze across the rest of the room. It looks like it's never been slept in. The bed is enormous and made of solid wood. The sheets are dark and pristine. There are two nightstands, each boasting simple but very expensive-looking lamps. On one sits a John Grisham thriller and a pair of reading glasses. I try to imagine Cristiano wearing reading glasses and then immediately squash the idea, because even *that* makes my legs tremble.

I leave the room and walk back to the kitchen. Cristiano glances up and does a double-take. Then he wipes the back of his hand across his forehead.

"It smells good." I perch on one of the stools around the island. "Arrabbiata?"

He scoffs as if creating something so simple is beneath him. "Puttanesca."

My stomach rumbles despite the fact I don't feel any form of appetite.

A corner of his mouth curls slightly before he wipes that away too. "It's a specialty," he adds. "Whore's pasta." He picks up a bottle of vodka and splashes some into the sauce.

"Shouldn't a good little Italian boy leave the cooking to the mamas or the wives?"

He arches a brow and reaches for two bowls. "Who says my wife will know how to cook?"

Something flares inside of me, and I laugh nervously. "All Italian girls are expected to be able to cook."

"And who says my wife will be Italian?"

I frown. "But isn't that the Cosa Nostra way? All made men must marry an Italian woman."

"I'm no longer a part of the Cosa Nostra," he says, spooning pasta into the bowls. He picks them up and turns to face me, his eyes hard and dark. "So I can marry whomever I want."

I feel his words like a punch, and it knocks my gaze to the floor. "Are you trying to make me jealous?" I ask quietly.

I hear him place the bowls on the counter. "No." His footsteps grow nearer until he squats down and brings his face to mine. "I'm simply telling you the facts."

Emotions collide in my chest. Part of me wants to push him away, because being this close to him is taunting me. *Tainting* me. But another part of me wants to push my fingers through his hair, dig my tips into his scalp, and pull his lips onto mine. I breathe heavily, sure he can smell the lust on my breath.

"No one ever leaves the Cosa Nostra," I whisper.

His eyes take on a heavy tincture. "As I said, I'm the exception. On account of my mother's murder."

"Didn't you want to stay and get your revenge?"

He grinds his jaw. "Yes. More than anything. But I moved on. For her. She loved my father, but she hated this life. She lived in fear every day that one of us would be taken too soon. I made a vow to stick around for as long as I could, and that means getting out of this life. Of course, it helped having the city's most lethal don for a father."

My gaze roams his face. He really is staggeringly beautiful. It makes my knees weak and my heart hurt. Without thinking, I draw my bottom lip between my teeth, and his eyes dip. His chest seems to swell, and his breathing deepens. Then he stands quickly. He pushes a bowl and a fork toward me.

"Now eat."

Cristiano sits on the other side of the island as though he doesn't trust me or himself. But he watches me intently as I push the food around.

"It's delicious," I say, feeding another piece of penne into my mouth. It really is delicious, but there are so many butterflies racing around my stomach I'm worried I might throw up if I force any food down.

"Is that why you've only taken three bites?"

"I told you, I'm not very hungry."

"When you're in my house and under my watch, you'll do as I say. Eat three more bites."

My eyes widen. I'm about to protest, but his steady, threatening gaze halts me.

I count in my head as I swallow three more mouthfuls, then I place my fork in the bowl. His scrutiny has me tied up in knots. I burn under his eyes, but at the same time, I can't bear the building tension. It feels like something has to burst or erupt for it to simmer down.

I pull back my now dry, *unruly* hair, pull a band off my wrist, and tie it in a knot on top of my head. He watches me, his gaze thoughtful.

"I don't have my straighteners," I say by way of apology. "This is the best I can do."

He runs his tongue across his top lip and lets his gaze weigh heavy. "I prefer your hair like this." His voice drops to a cavernous whisper. "It looks like you just got out of bed."

My stomach rolls inward, and I realize I don't have the energy to make sense of it. "I'm tired," I say with a sigh. "Is it okay if I go lie down now?"

He sits back abruptly, as though he's just been broken out of a trance. "Of course. I'll show you to your room."

I follow him to a door a little farther down from the master. A blush threatens the edges of my cheeks at the memory of standing in that shower. He holds the door open and lets me walk inside. This room is the polar opposite of the primary. Light, airy, peaceful, and inviting, not dark and oppressive like his own.

"This is perfect. Thank you." I turn to face him and swallow a gasp. He looks *agonized*.

His gaze licks up from the hem of my shorts to the collar of my tee, and his jaw tenses. "When I close this door, lock it. Do you understand?"

Nerves that are already bristling near the surface of my skin cause the hairs along my arms to prickle. "Why?"

He inhales deeply, his chest filling out. "To keep yourself safe."

My brows knit in confusion. His apartment is like Fort Knox already—I haven't missed the myriad security systems. Not only that, but the building is managed, adding another layer of security.

"From who?"

He releases his breath, his gaze darkening even further. Then he straightens and draws the door closed.

I guess I'm not getting an answer.

CHAPTER 18

*T*rilby

I wake up disoriented. Despite the fact my restless dreams were filled with gunshots, memories of my mother, and the overpowering presence of my fiancé's brother, it still takes me a few minutes to recall the previous twenty-four hours and the reason I'm in Cristiano Di Santo's spare bedroom.

I get out of bed and unlock the bedroom door. When I remember Cristiano's warning, I open it with trepidation. When nothing on the other side of it seems amiss, I pad on bare feet to the kitchen. Or at least I try to. Blocking my path is an enormous box in the shape of a closet, bearing the name of the city's most exclusive designer boutique.

"Open it."

His voice on the other side makes me half-jump out of my skin.

"What is it?"

"Your new closet."

I huff. "I don't need a new closet. I have a perfectly good one at home."

"You're not going home. I told you."

"Then ask Allegra to bring me some of my clothes when *she* takes me for my gown fitting."

"*I'm* taking you to your gown fitting. Don't you remember anything, woman?"

I seethe quietly at the thought of being caged in, and then again at being branded "woman."

"Remembering isn't the same as agreeing." I step forward and pull the handle to the box. An unwitting gasp leaves my throat. Every single dress I've ever coveted is inside this box, and a quick skim through tells me they're all in my exact size.

"Pick one. Get dressed. We're leaving in ten minutes."

I pull a face at the command, safe in the knowledge he can't see me. "What about breakfast? I thought you said I had to eat."

"We're eating out." A smile nips at his tone. "And stop making that face. It doesn't suit you."

I glance to my right, and of course, there's a damn mirror.

"Fine." I huff again, then I pull out the shortest, skimpiest, raciest dress I can see and walk back into the bedroom, locking the door behind me.

Ten minutes later, we're standing in the elevator, and I can feel the anger rolling off him in waves. I allow myself a small, satisfied smile. After all, he did buy me these clothes. Did he expect me not to wear them?

The dress I selected is fuchsia-pink and reaches only a third of the way down my thighs. It's meant to be worn with shorts, but since he only ordered bikini briefs —and small, lacy ones at that—my bottom may very well be on display should I happen to drop something and, well, need to pick it up again.

The halter neckline shows off my shoulders, and the midriff is cut away, displaying my stomach, which is even flatter for having hardly eaten anything in the past forty-eight hours.

Come to think of it, I haven't eaten a great deal since the engagement. I'm not trying to starve myself; I simply haven't had an appetite since that fateful day.

The heels aren't as high as I'd have liked, but at three inches, they're still formidable. I was careful to choose a pair that gives good toe cleavage. And if the way Cristiano's eyes keep dropping to them is proof they do the trick, I chose well.

He doesn't utter a word when we reach the car. He just opens the door and averts his gaze while I slide into the low seat.

When he starts the engine, I glance sideways at his

expression. He's feigning indifference, but his jaw is tense, and if he grips the wheel any tighter, he'll pull the whole thing off.

"Where are we going for breakfast?"

He keeps his eyes on the road and his words crisp. "Lucio's."

I swallow. Lucio's is only the most popular restaurant in this neighborhood. Anyone who's anyone dines there—not only for the amazing food but to be *seen*.

Does Cristiano want us to be seen?

"Is that the best idea considering you're supposed to be keeping me out of sight?"

"I never said I was keeping you out of sight. I think 'safe' is the word you're looking for. God, woman. You're either immensely forgetful or you're purposely trying to infuriate me."

"Wow. Someone got out of the wrong side of the bed this morning."

"I didn't sleep."

My eyes dart back to the road. I want to interrogate that, but I'm worried about what I might uncover.

"I'm not sure 'woman' is an improvement on 'Castellano,'" I say. "You know, you can use my given name. I even answer to it."

He doesn't reply. Not with words anyway. His knuckles on the other hand grow a paler shade of white as they threaten the steering wheel's very existence.

"It's an expensive restaurant to go to just for breakfast," I point out.

"So?" He snorts, and I roll my eyes at how even *that* sounds sexy. "What does it matter anyway? It's not like you eat anything."

I turn my head away and resolve to order everything on the menu.

Cristiano parks right outside the restaurant— illegally, but I doubt anyone will challenge a member of the Di Santo family, whether they're active in the mob or not. I don't wait for him to open the door before I stretch out my bare legs, which I can tell bothers him. He huffs out a tight breath as I brush past and make my way to the entrance, my heels tapping soft clicks across the warm asphalt.

A male host greets us. He's already flustered before we step inside. "Mr. Di Santo, your, um, table is ready. Please come this way."

We're taken through the middle of the restaurant, and I can feel the heat of heads swiveling to assess us. When they realize we're not famous, some return to the more exciting prospect of a freshly made mimosa. Others linger on the impeccably dressed man walking behind me, his eyes on my dress, muttering about how he's going to "send it back and get a fucking refund."

We reach the table, listen to the list of specials as we sit, and then settle into an uncomfortable silence. Cristiano finally rests his eyes on me with an air of thinly veiled annoyance.

"Is everything okay?" I twirl a wavy hair around a finger and beam at him.

"Couldn't you have chosen something more . . . conservative to wear to breakfast?"

I tip my head lightly to one side and bat my lashes. "What can I say? I assumed since you picked it out, it was okay to wear it."

He regards me with a lethal glare. "It's an evening dress, not a breakfast dress."

I smile sweetly. "I've had breakfast in less conservative dresses than this."

I've never been this bold with anyone, but for some reason, I feel safe with Cristiano. Perhaps knowing he almost kissed me last night bought me some insurance against him betraying my words and my behavior to his brother.

He swallows and unashamedly coasts his gaze over my bare shoulders, down my collarbone, to my breasts. I feel my nipples harden until they're standing to attention under his stare.

A smile pulls at the corner of his mouth before he slowly drags his gaze back to mine.

"Any word from Savero?" I ask, masking a shiver as it coasts down my spine.

Just like that, his eyes darken, and he shakes his head once. "Not since last night. He's safe though."

I swallow and look across the other tables— anywhere but at him. "Where will I go when he returns?"

After a long pause, I glance at him to see his teeth grinding together.

"You'll go to the main house—the Di Santo residence. That's where you'll be living."

"Yes, *after* the wedding. I want to go home until then. I want to be with my family."

"It's not possible." His reply is laced with boredom. "I've already explained. You're not safe at your father's. To be frank, neither is the rest of your family. I've already drawn up plans to install new surveillance tech at the house and to reinforce the perimeter. Now your father has formed an official alliance with Savero, you all have a price on your head." He sits back in his chair, still regarding me with measured indifference. "*You* have the highest price of them all."

I shiver again, feeling the cold, conditioned air touching my shoulders.

He summarizes for good measure. "You'll be safest at the house, so that's where you'll be."

A waiter appears at the table and looks at Cristiano expectantly. I know we're living in contemporary times, but doesn't the waiter usually ask for the woman's order first?

Then I understand. He expects Cristiano to order for me.

Over my dead body.

I clear my throat, drawing the gazes of both men to me, and sit tall.

"I will have the porcini omelet." I give the waiter my most sugary smile.

"Um . . ." He glances nervously at Cristiano, whose head hasn't moved but casts a suspicious glance at me out of the corner of his eye. "Would you like that with or without Périgord truffle?"

"With," I say brightly.

The waiter scribbles something with a trembling hand and then turns his body back toward Cristiano.

I clear my throat. "I would also like the fruit cup— no pineapple—and a turmeric shot to start, a small bowl of coconut yogurt, with granola on the side . . . and can you bring a small jug of maple syrup? Actually, no. I hear you do a sensational blueberry compote. I'll take that instead. And . . ."

Cristiano's gaze is narrowed. He knows exactly what I'm playing at. I smile like I just hit the jackpot.

". . . an espresso."

The waiter's gaze flits between me and my breakfast partner as if he's experiencing a panic attack, while Cristiano and I embark on an all-out staring contest.

"And for you, sir?"

Cristiano keeps his glare fixed on me while he hands his menu back to the waiter. "I'll just take the eggs Benedict."

"Thank you. I'll be right back with some water." The waiter scurries away as if he's just been electrocuted.

Cristiano shrugs off his jacket and maintains eye contact as he hooks it over the back of his chair. Then he rolls up his shirtsleeves, rests his forearms on the table, and leans toward me.

"No fruit cup for you?" I force a thread of innocence into my voice in the hope of disguising the avalanche of lust crashing over me at the sight of his thick, inked, and corded forearms.

The waiter returns quickly and pours us each a glass of water. I barely wait for him to finish before I gulp mine down in one. A trickle slips down my chin, and I finally avert my eyes to dab at it with a napkin.

"I'm not as hungry as you, it seems," Cristiano says.

I arch a brow. "Didn't your mama ever tell you growing men need to eat?"

"I kind of hope I've stopped growing." He tips back his own water, and unlike me, he doesn't spill it down his chin. "It would be a pain to have to go up yet another shoe size. Sixteens are already hard to come by."

I gulp and lean backward, only to silently curse the tablecloth for concealing everything south of his waist.

I lift the drinks menu and fan myself. I was shivering a minute ago—why has it suddenly become so damn hot in here? The last thing I want is to coat my body in a sheen of sweat before I change into my bridal gown.

"How did you sleep?"

His abrupt change of topic startles me.

"Um, I slept well, thank you . . . Relative to how I normally sleep."

"And how do you normally sleep?"

"Fine." I force a smile onto my face.

"Fine?" There's a note of impatience in his voice, and somehow I know I'm not going to get away with confessing anything but the truth.

My breath shortens. I've lived with erratic sleep patterns, insomnia, and night terrors ever since Mama's murder, but I've never talked to anyone about it. Living in the apartment helps. If no one can hear my screams, no one will ask any questions.

Oh.

My cheeks heat under his determined scrutiny.

"You won't lock your door tonight."

It isn't a request; it's an instruction. And it sets my pulse racing.

Shame creeps across my skin, making me shudder. What did he hear? I don't know what I sound like when I have nightmares—all I know is I wake up drenched with sweat, my throat hoarse, and my limbs shaking. I don't want to bring that part of my life into this one—although, admittedly, that ship might have sailed.

I don't want to bother anyone with my problems—least of all Cristiano. They're my problems, not his. And I'm not his responsibility. Nor am I his charity case.

"Whatever you heard . . ." I'm not sure what I'm trying to say. "It's nothing. I'm fine."

He watches me steadily, but he looks pissed. "Yes. So you've said." His nostrils flare as he breathes in a ragged breath. "You still won't lock the door."

I stare back at him. "I thought I had to for my *safety*."

He swallows and wipes the pad of a thumb across his mouth. "Let me be the one to worry about that."

Not wanting to draw attention to my now quivering hands, I wring them together beneath the tablecloth.

The food arrives mercifully quickly, simmering the tension that's settled over the table, and I feel full just looking at it.

Cristiano rests his chin on his hands and watches me, his brows raised in a challenge.

I push back my shoulders and swallow the turmeric shot. A flame erupts in my throat.

Fuck, it's spicy.

I smile sweetly and spear a piece of fruit, then I glare at Cristiano as I chew and swallow. "Are you going to eat your eggs, or do you prefer to just stare at me while I eat?"

He runs his tongue over his teeth as if he's only just getting started, then he wordlessly cuts into his breakfast. By the time he's devoured it in four mouthfuls—and yes, I counted—I've managed to put a two-strawberry dent into my three dishes.

I gently push the fruit to one side and pick up my spoon. I lift a scoop of granola-laden yogurt up to my face, and my stomach tightens. Why did I choose yogurt? It's thick and oozy and impossible to swallow at the best of times.

Cristiano's gaze warms my face, so I do what any worthy opponent would do and go in for the attack. The yogurt sits unmoving on my tongue, and I attempt to smile as I squish it around my mouth. The texture is all wrong for how I'm feeling. The second it slides down my throat, I'm going to puke.

With my mouth still full, I pour out another glass of water and suck a load back before swallowing everything in one go. Then I keep swallowing, because the nausea is already creeping up my esophagus.

Cristiano frowns. "Are you okay?"

"Mm-hmm." I tap the base of my throat. "It's a little sour, that's all."

He cocks his head to one side. "That's funny. I thought coconut yogurt was sweet."

I purse my lips and push the offending dish to one side. Maybe I'll have better luck with the omelet.

The scent of truffle invades my nostrils, putting my eyeballs on the brink of watering. *What the hell was I thinking?* I take a deep breath and feed a morsel into my mouth. I'm pleasantly surprised. The taste of porcini is subtle, and the eggs are soft. I can do this. With a look of triumph, I feed more forkfuls into my mouth.

Cristiano sips his espresso and watches me with uncomfortable intensity. If I didn't know better, I'd think he was glued to a pornographic movie.

I'm about to cut another piece of omelet when my stomach groans. I'm full already. I look down to see I've barely eaten anything. Defeat makes my cutlery clatter against my plate.

Cristiano clears his throat. "You've finished?" There's a note of glee on the edge of his tongue.

I lift my chin. "No. I'm having a rest."

A smile tugs at the corners of his mouth. "You can't do it, can you? You can't eat any more."

"Yes, I can," I protest, but the conviction in my voice is weak.

He allows his lips to curve into a satisfied smile. It's the smile of a winner.

"You put up a good fight, Castellano." He reaches over and takes my plate. "Now let's leave the real battle to the big guns."

He winks playfully, and it's *devastating*.

I could watch him eat for days, so imagine my disappointment when only another six mouthfuls later, he's devoured not only the omelet, but the yogurt and the fruit cup too.

To his credit, he doesn't gloat any further, but he can't hide his smile behind his curled fist.

And neither can I.

I thank God when Penelope helps me into my dress, because my fingers are too clammy and shaky to do it myself. We're behind a thick velvet curtain, but I can feel Cristiano's presence as though he's standing inches away breathing hot air onto my neck.

"Have you been starving yourself, Miss Castellano?" she hisses, my lack of appetite clearly an inconvenience to her. "I've never had to take a dress in so many sizes. This is going to be double the work."

"Then Savero will pay double for your time." Cristiano's voice sails over the top of the curtain, and the blood drains from the seamstress's cheeks.

"I apologize, Mr. Di Santo." Her fingertips fumble with the pins. "My surprise got the better of me."

"Let me see the dress."

His instruction makes us both jerk our heads up.

"Um, Mr. Di Santo, I believe that may be bad luck," Penelope responds, with wide eyes fixed on me.

"It's only bad luck if it's the groom who sees the dress. I am not the groom."

If I didn't know better, I'd detect a trace of bitterness on the edge of his tongue. As it stands, I've amused Cristiano enough throughout breakfast to know he's more than likely relieved to not be marrying me.

Penelope continues to stare at me until I realize she's asking if I'm okay to do this. I nod once, and she lets the gown fall to its full length. She walks around me, nipping and tucking the edges into all the right places, until it looks like I was born wearing the beautiful garment. Then she stands to one side and pulls back the curtain.

I have my back to Cristiano, but I can see his reflection in the floor-length mirror. He's sitting on the black velvet couch, his knees spread and his elbows resting on them. When the curtain pulls back, his expression is stunned.

Then, as he takes in the backless dress, the waist dipping low toward my buttocks, the skirt clinging to my hips and my thighs before floating outward in a graceful fishtail, his gaze darkens, a treasonous glint drawing in the light.

I've seen those eyes before.

He held them over me right before he slammed his fist into his kitchen island.

I move my focus back to the bodice of my dress and concentrate on counting the glass beads and pearls— anything to avoid the rolling thunder in his eyes.

"Is it to your liking, Mr. Di Santo?" Penelope asks nervously.

I listen to the beat of my heart.

B-bum, b-bum, b-bum.

Then he answers.

"It's exquisite."

My stomach liquifies, and I lift my gaze to meet his. His stare is no longer indifferent. It's frighteningly possessive, and I have to look away. I stroke my hands down my hips, distracting myself with the beautiful finish and the craftsmanship.

"Is everything okay, Mr. Di Santo?" Penelope asks.

I look over my shoulder to see Cristiano's back disappearing in the direction of the exit.

"I have to make a call," he replies without looking around. Then he yanks open the door and leaves.

My stomach drops. That look in his eye . . .

How will I ever be able to face Savero on our wedding night, let alone our wedding day, when all I'll be able to see is the way Cristiano stares at me with eyes as black as a starless sky?

$\mathscr{C}$ ristiano

I haven't bummed a smoke off a total stranger since I was fifteen years old, but I need something to calm my racing pulse.

I stand on the corner of the street watching the sun bounce off the hood of my car and fill my lungs. The cigarette's harsh enough to distract me until I can reassemble my thoughts into something less obscene; less inconvenient.

I type one-handed into my phone.

> Me: Any news?

I blow a curl of smoke into the air and watch as Sav types a response.

Sav: It's done.

I breathe out a long sigh of relief.

Me: So you're on your way back?

Sav: Tomorrow.

Fuck. I chew my bottom lip. I can't have Castellano at my apartment another night regardless of what I said about her not locking her door. The temptation was too great *before* I saw her in that dress. And now that I have. . .

I shake every thought from my head. There's really only one thing for it.

I press the phone to my ear and take another long drag of the cigarette.

Someone picks up on the other end. "Allegra Castellano."

"Allegra," I say, feeling a small sense of relief. "It's Cristiano. Would you like to see the bride-to-be?"

An hour later, the voices of five semi-drunk women are grating against my temples. This *was* a good idea, I remind myself. The alternative would be a lot worse.

Annoyingly, I've opted for Savero's recommendation to avoid small talk by inviting over the entire female contingent of Castellano's family. I'm not avoiding small talk exactly, but the solution is the same. I need to *not* be alone with her. Not in the wake of that gown fitting.

Bridal gowns are meant to be virginal, for crying out loud, not the clothing equivalent of a slow, decadent fuck laced with ravenous bite marks and quiet gasps of desperation.

Cazzo. Cazzo. Cazzo.

Hidden by a velvet curtain, I turn to face the wall and bang my forehead against it repeatedly.

"I have your water here."

I turn to see the seamstress holding out a glass, her eyes averted.

"I may have given them a little too much champagne," she says apologetically.

"It's fine," I say, taking a sip. "I suppose she'll only get married once."

The thought sticks in my throat, and I suddenly want to hurl the glass at the wall. Instead I smile and place it on a side table, away from any inclination to vandalize this innocent woman's property.

I walk with a great deal of reluctance into their gathering. "How are we doing, ladies?"

They all look up, their cheeks pink and their faces shiny from all the laughing. I absently wonder what it must be like to get along with a sibling to the extent one could have a good laugh with them. My relationship with Sav has never been like that. Even when we were kids, he was intense. Too intense to joke about with.

I've never understood why he was always so

competitive. Papa gave me a lot of attention, but I figured that was because Sav was the eldest—the one who'd inherit it all. He was the heir; I was the spare.

But so many of Sav's actions smacked of jealousy. There was the time he set fire to my toy cars, torching them until they were steel nubs, and the time he threw Father's favorite Rolex into the ocean because he'd let me wear it to church one Sunday. It was always explained away as "passion." I was calm and measured. Sav was "passionate." I never understood how that was supposed to be a positive thing. It never felt positive to me.

Allegra scrambles to her feet despite my urges to the contrary.

"Thank you so much for inviting us, Mr. Di Santo. It's just nice for us girls to spend some time together before the wedding."

"Do you like her dress?" The next eldest sister, Serafina, looks up at me expectantly.

"Yes." My voice feels tight. "It's beautiful."

"Do you think Savero will like it?" The youngest sister blurts this out, and the other one elbows her in the ribs.

I can't honestly answer that, because I have no idea what Sav likes and doesn't like. He certainly doesn't advertise it. So I give a noncommittal—and truthful —answer.

"He wouldn't be human if he didn't."

The younger sister blushes and bats her eyes away, and for some inexplicable reason I feel protective of her, as if she's my own sibling. At the feel of something warming the side of my face, I turn to see Castellano watching me curiously. Truth be told, despite working day and night in casinos, I haven't been around this much life in ages.

I rub my hands together and address them all. "How about an early dinner? I know a great little place down the street."

"God, yes." One of the sisters—the one dressed in an all-black ensemble despite it being early summer—clambers to her feet.

Allegra follows and sighs in agreement. "We could probably use some food to soak up the bubbles."

Castellano doesn't say a word, but neither does she remove her gaze from me as we bid farewell to the seamstress and head out onto the street. I become aware of her closest sister whispering something in her ear, but she bats it away.

I take them to an Italian restaurant owned by an old friend of my father and order everything on the menu. The table fills with chatter as they help themselves to prosciutto crostini, fried olives, and herbed ricotta. Even Castellano manages to eat a few bites.

"Will you be Savero's best man?" the sister in black asks.

"Tess!" Castellano hisses.

"What? It's a perfectly reasonable question."

I smile, but it feels stiff. "Yes, I will be. But I'll be heading straight back to Vegas soon after, unfortunately."

Tess's mouth falls open. "Really? But . . . it's going to be the wedding of the year. Surely, the festivities will go on long after the bells have stopped ringing?"

"Contessa," Allegra warns. "It's not any of our business."

"It's a fair point." I shrug. "We Italians do love a wedding . . ." My attention catches on Castellano. Her face has paled, and she's lowered the fork to her plate. "But I have unavoidable business to attend to."

She holds my gaze as talk of the wedding rumbles around us. Before she looks away, her left eye flickers as though she's caught onto something. Maybe she has. It doesn't change anything though. Whatever I feel for my brother's fiancée is irrelevant. It's better I remove myself from the object of my temptation sooner rather than later.

The sky outside darkens, the bottles of red wine littering the table now empty. The youngest sister lies across Allegra's lap sleeping, while Tess talks her aunt's ear off with what sounds to me like utter drunken nonsense. Castellano and Serafina are talking between themselves, so I pretend to check my phone while intermittently flashing my gaze toward my future sister-in-law. Sometimes she meets it; sometimes she doesn't. The times she does, I feel a spasm of longing clench around my heart.

This was actually a bad fucking idea. The more time I spend around her, the less I want to leave. Now I'm certain we met before, when we were both younger. Vague memories come back to me in fragments, but I'm knitting them together piece by piece, bit by bit. With each passing day, it's becoming harder to think about releasing her to Savero, especially when I know he couldn't give two flying fucks about this woman, which boils my blood. I don't remember much from back then —trauma often gets in the way of clarity—but I do know this: the girl has spirit, and Savero only knows one way to deal with that.

Break it.

Allegra straightens her back. "I think we should get going," she says, stifling a yawn. "We've overstayed our welcome long enough."

"Nonsense," I say, slipping the phone into my jacket. "It's been my pleasure. Let me call you a driver."

"Oh, no, you mustn't. We've burdened you enough. A cab will do just fine."

"No." My sharp tone makes all five women turn toward me. "I won't hear of it. My family has drivers in the city—I can have one here in no time."

"Oh, well, um, thank you." Allegra wipes a flustered hand across her brow.

I step outside to make the call and relish the cool night air. It's a relief after the stifling heat of her presence. But it's short-lived.

"Make sure the car can fit five."

I ignore her and speak into the phone. "Hey, it's Cristiano here. Yeah. As soon as you can. La Trattoria. Back to Port Washington. Four, please."

I hang up and reluctantly let my gaze drop to hers, feeling almost thankful looks can't kill.

"I said five."

"I know you did. I'm not deaf, Castellano."

She breathes in and out tightly. "Why can't I go home with my family?"

"I already told you. You're not safe there, and Savero wants me to look after you until he returns, which won't be until tomorrow."

She crosses her arms and lets out a small noise of frustration. "I don't understand you."

"That's probably a good thing," I answer smoothly.

She continues as if I haven't spoken. "One minute you're buying me the best designer clothes in the city and chaperoning me around as though I'm made of porcelain. The next you're glaring at me across the dinner table as if I just insulted you, and you can't bring yourself to stay after our wedding. I'm beginning to think you weren't telling me the truth yesterday, in your apartment."

"Oh? What do you think then?"

"That you secretly hate me."

I choke out a laugh, but the sincerity in her stare shuts my mouth.

"There's no other explanation," she insists. "You hate that I'm marrying your brother—that he's spending his money on me. That I'm going to be the lady of *your* family home. That has to be it." She shrugs her arms out to the side while I look on at her, stunned.

I suppose I should be grateful. If she hasn't read any further into yesterday's admission, I'm safe from Savero's wrath, and so is she.

Her voice drops to a whisper. It's a seething one, but a whisper at that. "If you hate me so much, why don't you just leave the city now?"

My eyes pop.

"Take me to the Di Santo residence and leave me there. I'll be safe until Savero comes home. And you'll be free from ever having to watch over me again." She turns to face me square and levels me with a pointed glare. "You can go back to Vegas, to your *precious* casinos, your cabaret singers, and your dancing girls, and live happily ever after."

I stare at her for a long moment. Then my patience snaps.

I grab her arm and drag her down the side of the building, out of view of the restaurant. "Are you jealous or something?" I hiss.

She physically recoils, which twists a nerve in my chest.

"When have I *ever* talked about cabaret singers and dancing girls? What do you take me for?"

She shrugs but continues to glare at me.

I breathe out, my nostrils flaring. "Now you've insulted me, the least you can do is listen to my defense."

She works her jaw, not letting up.

"I have saved you from yourself and others too many times to mention. I have made you eat—I've *cooked* for you—and kept you alive despite your obstinate determination to starve to death. I've closeted you in my apartment when it was unsafe for you to stay anywhere else. I've practically shot a man's hands off because he didn't follow my order to get you home safe. If all of these things are symptomatic of my hatred for you, then fuck me twice, Castellano, I hate you with my *entire* being."

Her lips have parted, and her chest rises and falls with a quickened tempo.

I step into her body and soak up the warmth of her breasts again my hard chest. "You think I hate that my brother is spending money on you?" I can't conceal the growl at the base of my throat. "I hate that he's not spending *enough*. There isn't enough money in the world that would make him worthy of you."

Her breaths reach my ears, sending me even deeper into insanity.

"You think I can't bear the idea of you being the lady of my family home?" I laugh low and dark. "That doesn't bother me in the slightest. What bothers me is that *he* will be your lord."

I shift my feet out to each side and dip my mouth toward the crook of her neck. I can taste the sweat rising off her collarbone.

"Only one of your accusations is spot-on, Castellano." My words drift over her skin, my lips brushing the hairs at her nape. "I do hate that you're marrying my brother. I hate that it's him." I start to pant in her ear from the exertion of holding this back, then my voice falters. "It should be *me*."

I linger until that statement has worked its way into her bones, then I push myself hard away from the wall and coast my eyes to the street. "Your aunt's car is here."

I ignore the sexy sound of her breathless gasps and pull her back out into the evening light.

I let her lead the way back inside, but "lead" is too generous a word. She can barely put one foot in front of the other. I didn't see her drink a whole lot of wine, but maybe she really is as incapable of handling alcohol as she's admitted to being.

I said too much, but she has to know.

She *needs* to know I'm on the fucking edge, and that this is killing me.

I can't stop myself from falling, but she can stop herself from pushing. And if she weren't aware of that before, well . . . now she is.

$\mathcal{T}$rilby

Lower Manhattan is only as large as it is busy. When the traffic quiets, it takes no time to get anywhere. Which is a pity when the last place I want to be is in Cristiano's apartment, alone with him, after everything he just said.

He wants me.

His statement was unequivocal and I don't know what to do with it.

I haven't been able to look at him the whole drive here. But I have been able to watch the streets go by in a blur, not one of them registering in my consciousness.

Instead of holding the door like he normally would, he stands to one side as if he's afraid to come near me. Even his gaze is directed somewhere over my head.

I follow him in silence to the elevator and stand against the opposite wall when the doors close. Like

strangers we stand apart, watching the floor numbers zip
past, until my ears pop, the bell dings, and the doors
slide open again. I wish I could say I feel relieved to be
walking back into this apartment again, a place where I
feel safe and looked after, but I don't. I'm on edge; a
bag of nerves. I don't know what to say or do or how to
behave.

I turn around, and we both speak at the same time.

"Thanks—"

"I—"

"You go first," he says with a nod.

"Oh, um, nothing. I just . . . I just wanted to say
thanks."

He buries his hands deep in the pockets of his slacks
and leans his shoulder against a wall. "For what?"

I shrug and look around his apartment, taking note
of little things I missed before, like the framed black-
and-white photographs of Long Island, a cabinet filled
with rotating wristwatches, and a tasteful bar lined with
crystal decanters and heavy-bottomed lowballs.

He watches me taking note of all the little details
that make up *him*.

"Would you like a drink?" He walks to the bar and
pops the top off a decanter.

The fact he's offering me an alcoholic beverage
when he's made it clear I'm the last person who should
be touching the stuff suggests he's past caring. I nod,
and he pours a finger of scotch into two lowballs before
passing one to me.

The tips of our fingers touch and our eyes meet

before he pulls his hand away. I sip the liquor and feel its heat spreading out from my chest.

"Thanks for doing all those things," I say.

"What things?"

I drop my gaze to the floor. "Looking out for me. Cooking for me. Keeping me safe."

Silences stretches, and I become painfully aware our breaths are mirroring each other's.

"I can't thank you for shooting Rhett though." I turn my head slowly from side to side.

"Fine." His mouth ticks up in one corner. "But I'd do it again."

I can't help but smile as I cast my gaze back to the floor.

We stand in the center of the room sipping the scotch and watching each other as though this is our last chance. I feel like we're exiled from the world, locked up in this penthouse apartment miles above everyone we know. No one could get up here without Cristiano pressing a few security buttons first. No one would know if we crossed a line.

Awareness prickles between us, along with the weight of his words.

It should be me.

He voiced what I thought was impossible. What *is* impossible.

I shake the illicit thoughts from my head. If we did cross that line, we could never turn back. It would risk everything I need to build on with Savero for my father's sake.

It's for the best that Cristiano is leaving.

I swallow the rest of the whiskey and place the glass on the bar. I run my fingers along its surface, admiring the polished mahogany and the solid gold trim. It's tasteful and understated—not something I'd expect from a man with Mafia blood running through his veins.

"I need to sleep." I go to walk past him, but his fingers encircle my wrist. It feels like an electric shock, jolting my gaze to his. My heart pummels the wall of my chest as we stare at each other.

Cristiano grinds his jaw and swallows hard. His voice breaks when he speaks. "Remember what I said. Don't lock your door."

He grips me until I nod once, then the tips of his fingers trail down the palm of my hand, making the nerve endings dance across my skin.

The second I close the door I exhale a long breath. I'm proud of myself for walking away. The temptation to step up to him and run my fingers through his hair, pull his lips onto mine, is so great it makes me ache *everywhere*.

I open the closet and pull out the brand-new shorts-and-top pajama set Cristiano bought, and change into it. I'm so tired, but every inch of my skin is on fire. I can't even pull the shorts up my bare thighs without having to pause and take a breath.

Eventually, I pull back the covers. I'm about to collapse onto the soft mattress when I remember his words. Not the ones where he instructed me to leave the door unlocked, but the ones where he told me to do the exact opposite.

I now know what he wanted to keep me safe from. What he doesn't know is that task is now mine. I'm the one *he* needs to be kept safe from.

His confession this evening told me everything I need to know. He doesn't have the strength to stay away, so I'll have to find it for us both.

With this resolve I walk to the door, ignore his instruction, and click the lock. Then, in minutes, I'm lying under a soft, newly laundered comforter, fast asleep.

CHAPTER 21

*C*ristiano

I lie awake, my hand wrapped around my semi-hard cock, but I can't get myself off. I seem to have a permanent semi these days, but nothing I do will sate it. With my gaze trained on the ceiling, I listen for the smallest noise coming from the spare bedroom down the hall, but unlike last night, there's nothing but silence.

I should be relieved for her. No nightmares tonight.

I wanted to ask her about them, but she seemed to close off the second I asked how she slept. I respected her wish to change the topic, but if it happens again, I'm coaxing that shit out of her.

I glance at the clock, but time has only moved on by five minutes. I sigh and avert my gaze back to the ceiling. It's going to be one hell of a long night.

I've half-drifted off when I hear it.

A wounded moan seeps beneath my door, and I sit bolt upright. My pulse pounds through my ears, but she's so agitated I can hear her above it.

The moaning intensifies. It's dragged out in long breaths and builds up to quiet, terrified screams.

At the first "No!" I leap out of bed and run down the hall. Something tells me this isn't a rare occurrence, and I'm not letting her go through another night of this alone.

I reach the door and turn the handle, but it's jammed.

I blink and try again, my heart beating faster at the pitch of her cries.

It's locked. *Damn it.*

I ram the side of my body up against it, but—security-obsessed maniac that I am—I had all the doors and locks reinforced when I bought this place. There's only one thing for it. I run back to my room and retrieve my gun from the nightstand.

When I return to her door, I hear the bed creaking under her sobs. It sounds like she's clawing at the mattress.

I stand back and aim the gun at the lock, then I fire three silenced bullets through the steel. The door swings open, and my gun clatters across the wooden floor. In a beat I'm on the bed, on my knees, my hands cupping her shoulders.

"Castellano, wake up . . ."

I gently shake her, but she's so lost to her nightmares she doesn't even flinch. Her body is curved into the fetal position, and sweat pours down her temples. I have to wake her.

"No!" she cries out again. "Please don't . . ."

I freeze as the realization hits me. I know exactly where she is. She's sitting in the back of a car, pleading with a gunman to not shoot her mother.

I sit back on my heels.

She's held this in on her own for far too long.

I know why she's done it, and I can hardly blame her. She doesn't want to burden her family with the horror of what she saw that day. But enough is enough. She has to share her pain with someone, and selfishly, I want to be the one who takes it all away.

I release her shoulders and lift her up. Her small fists press against me, trying to push me away, and her screams rock her entire body. "Please, no . . . Please don't . . ."

"Shh." I shift slowly to the head of the bed and pull her into my chest. Her cries have mellowed into distraught, uncontrollable sobs that shake the length of her spine. "Shh . . . I've got you."

I stroke the damp hair out of her face and hold her while she trembles in my arms. I match my breathing to hers and then slow it down until her thundering heartbeat returns to a more normal speed. The shorts and top I bought for her are wet with sweat, soaking through to the skin beneath my T-shirt.

"Oh God," she whimpers. "Oh God, no . . ."

I hold her tightly and whisper that everything's going to be okay, on repeat, until her body softens and she slips into a calmer sleep. When I'm sure she's through the worst of it, I loosen my hold, rest the back of my head against the headboard, and close my eyes. Her chest expands and contracts lightly against mine with her gentle breaths.

I continue to stroke her hair absently, just because I want to hold onto the moment for as long as I can. As soon as she walks out of this apartment tomorrow, she's all his.

My heart cracks a fraction, and I hold her a little tighter.

I yawn, but I don't succumb to slumber.

I don't want to miss a second of this.

I'll sleep when I'm dead.

CHAPTER 22

*T*rilby

The first waking thought that enters my head is, *How on earth is this bed so comfortable?* The second thought is, *I feel strangely rested, as though I* actually *slept.*

I snuggle deeper into the bed. Then the bed moves.

My eyelids snap open, and my breath escapes. My palm is pressed flat against a wall of skin. Skin that isn't mine.

"Good morning."

The vibration of his voice makes me freeze. It came from beneath my palm.

I slowly piece together the rest of the picture. My bottom is cradled in his lap, and his arms are entwined around my shoulders, pressing me firmly into his hold.

Wait a minute . . . I thought I locked the door.

I glance upward, momentarily lost for words. The

whole top half of his body is bare, his hair is adorably messed up, and his inked skin is covered in a silky sheen. I swallow as his eyes roam my face, searching for any evidence I might have fallen apart in the night. It's not likely if he's been holding me as tightly as he is now.

My limbs turn solid in his grip. This is so far beyond appropriate I might as well be humping his leg.

"Cristiano . . ." I whisper.

"You had a bad dream."

My chest hollows out. I only ever know what it feels like when I wake up screaming; I have no idea how it sounds.

"How do you know?"

He loosens his grip, but only a little. "I heard it. You were crying . . . and then you were screaming. I couldn't just lie in my room and listen."

My heart sinks. "Your neighbors . . ."

His chest heats. "Fuck my neighbors. I couldn't let you carry on suffering like that alone."

I breathe out steadily, my head spinning from trying not to register every single spot where our bare skin touches.

"I've managed for a long time. What's another night?"

A low growl rumbles in his chest. "Does this happen every night?"

I shrug. "I don't know. Most nights, maybe."

One of his hands leaves my shoulder, and he scrubs

it down his face. Exasperation looks good on him. To be honest, any damn emotion would look good on him.

"How . . . um . . . how long did it go on for?" I watch my forefinger trace a circle on his left pectoral muscle before realizing too late what I'm doing. Then I curl it into my palm.

"It was going on for about five minutes before I came in here. You calmed down not long after I picked you up."

"So it was just once?"

"Yeah. Just once."

I don't let him see my widened eyes. I usually wake up screaming several times in the night. It's no wonder I feel rested.

The breeze from an open window somewhere in his apartment makes the door to the bedroom sway, and my focus narrows on it.

"What happened to the door?" There's a shoulder-shaped dent in the side, and its handle is falling off.

He doesn't turn his head to look, and his voice is firm. "You locked it when I told you not to."

I repeat. "So what happened to the door?"

"I put a bullet through the lock. Well, three, to be precise."

I lift my gaze to his and force myself to keep it there. It's frightening, because the longer I look at him, the harder I fall into those Barolo-drenched depths.

My eyes narrow. "You shoot a lot of things when I'm around."

He cups my chin between his thumb and his forefinger, and the urge to lean into him is excruciating.

"I would shoot a fuck of a lot more if I didn't think it would make you run a mile."

I wet my lips, and he watches as if he's starving. Then I reluctantly pull away from his chest. I haven't moved off his lap, and it's been several minutes. I should probably show willing.

"At least there's one thing to be thankful for." I try to make light of the situation.

His tone is bland. "What's that?"

"We didn't have sex." I shoot him a shy smile and hope it comes off as relief. It only makes his eyes darken.

"Oh, Castellano. If we'd had sex, you'd know about it."

The breath whooshes out of my chest, and my body seems unfeasibly heavy as I try to move myself off his thighs. He said that with such *promise*.

"How so?" I sound breathless.

He waits until my stilted journey onto the comforter is complete, then he swiftly stands and brings his half-naked body close to mine. His fingertips trail down the side of my face, which mainlines fire straight to my clit.

There's a smile teasing the edge of his words. "Because you'd still be feeling me in your stomach, little one."

His fingers drop, and I follow them to where there's an obvious—enormous—erection inside his shorts.

Then he turns and is gone, leaving me short of breath and so utterly frustrated I want to cry.

When I emerge from my room showered, dressed, and slightly less *bothered* than I was in the bedroom, Cristiano is suited and booted and spooning cereal into his mouth while scrolling through messages on his phone.

I hover by the kitchen island, unsure of where to put myself.

He doesn't look up, which makes me question everything I've heard and felt since I woke up. "Sav will be here in one hour," he says.

My stomach drops.

He gestures to some bread and cereal boxes laid out on the counter. "You want some breakfast?"

I stare at him.

Breakfast?

Breakfast?

He's just dropped the bombshell that in one hour I'll walk out of here to live permanently with a man I'll be serving for the rest of my life as a Cosa Nostra wife, when I'm falling fast for his brother, and he thinks I might want *breakfast*?

I grit my teeth and walk across the apartment to take a last look at the view.

Minutes pass silently, and I can't believe he can feel comfortable about it.

"What will you do when I've gone?" I ask.

He swallows a mouthful of cereal. "Pack."

I feel the skin across my brow go taut. I want to cry.

"So you're leaving."

"You always knew I was going to."

"Doesn't mean I'm happy about it."

He stands and faces me as I turn my back to the window.

"I'm not happy about you marrying my brother, but I have no choice but to deal with it."

I sigh heavily. "I—"

He holds up a hand. "And don't try to find a way we can make this work. I've been through a thousand different scenarios in the past four weeks, and it always boils down to two nonnegotiables."

"Two?" I whisper.

"You can't let your father down, Castellano. If you were to back out of this marriage, my brother would pull the plug on the whole arrangement. He'd use the strength of his army to screw over your family, and unlike me, he wouldn't hold back on the bullets. He's had his eye on your family's port for years. Our father wasn't interested in pulling it from under you, but now he's gone . . ."

My blood runs cold, my awareness latching onto the sinister fact the very man Cristiano is speaking of is about to come in here and drag me back to his home.

"You sound like you don't approve," I say

accusingly. "Why would you let him get away with doing this?"

He tears a hand through his hair, gripping at the follicles, then drops his arm to his side. "Which brings me on to the second nonnegotiable," he says, his tone weighed down with defeat. "I don't agree with how Sav does business. I don't want the same things he does. And I certainly don't approve of his methods. But . . ."

I take two steps toward him. I need to hear the reason why Cristiano is letting his beast of a brother get away with treating me and my family like pawns.

". . . I owe him my life."

I swallow and take a step back. "What?"

He cracks his knuckles, drawing my gaze to the tension in his hands. "When we were kids, I fell over the side of our grandfather's boat and got stuck in the ropes. Savero cut me free and pulled me out. I was unconscious, but I eventually came around. If he'd been only a couple of seconds later, I would have died."

The thought of Cristiano not making it that day suddenly overwhelms me, and I walk to a sofa, almost collapsing onto it. He follows and bends at the knees, bringing his face level with mine.

"I don't like my brother." He enunciates each word with care. "I don't understand him. I certainly don't deem him worthy of you . . . But I wouldn't be alive right now if it weren't for him."

My mind empties of all the happy-ever-afters I've dared to dream of with the man crouching in front of me, taking every drop of hope with it.

He reaches up and takes a curl of my hair between his fingers. Then he closes his eyes as he lets it slide from his grip.

"If he hadn't saved me that day, I would never have met you."

I nod slowly, and a tear rolls down my cheek to splash on the polished floor.

"So . . ." He lifts my chin gently. "We're going to be brother and sister, Castellano. And even though it's not exactly what I want, it's preferable to what we could have been. Which is nothing at all."

I force a smile through my quivering lips. "Brother and sister."

CHAPTER 23

*T*rilby

The thick, heavy bass is welcome music to my ears as we walk back into the house. I'm lightheaded from the cigarette I just took a few sips from. I don't smoke—I don't like the taste or the smell—but I'm in the mood for rebellion, and no one knows I'm here. Well, no one except Lorna, one of Savero's maids, who saw me escape under the veil of darkness.

Since the night I met Cristiano I've hardly recognized myself. Not since I was a young girl have I felt the need to rebel. It's as though that young girl is still inside of me, itching to get out, but years of concealing my grief and trying to protect my family from the strength of my feelings have muzzled her.

Savero barely spoke two sentences to Cristiano when he arrived to collect me two days ago. I'm beginning to wonder how close they really are. I sat in the back of his car watching the streets pass by, getting no prettier as we entered the sunnier streets of Long Island. My fiancé spent the entire journey scrolling through his phone and occasionally ranting in Italian to his browbeaten capos. Then, if I weren't already feeling surplus to requirements, he deposited me in a deserted wing of the house, which had been sparsely furnished with little to no heart, and promptly left again to go who knows where for who knows how long.

I felt relieved, when I should have felt disappointed. I still have no idea where he's gone, and forgive me, Father, but I can't bring myself to care.

While I hated being alone in that enormous, silent house, I needed the space to process the fact I'll have to forge a relationship with my new "brother." The thought makes me want to crawl into a hole and never come out, and I don't especially want to deal with it now.

I just want to dance my sorrows away.

That's why I took the risk and slipped out from beneath the noses of Savero's security guards, under the guise of visiting my supposedly "sick" sister. And now, as the lights of the house party follow the swirling nicotine in my brain and ill-advised punch as it trickles down my throat, I'm beyond smug that I did.

"Not going for the ripped hem and pink hair tonight then?" Sandrine jokes as we walk toward the makeshift dance floor. We're at a fellow classmate's house party – a venue I'm pretty sure isn't owned by a Di Santo.

I arch a cocky brow. "No need. No one knows I'm here."

She high-fives me as I twirl around, then she slurps on her drink. "What happened with the gun-toting pimp?" she asks, laughing.

"He is not a pimp," I gasp with an eye roll.

"He certainly behaved like he owned you, honey. And jeez, how did he get into that place with a gun? There were metal detectors, like, everywhere . . ."

I groan into my glass. "His family owns the bar."

"Well, that's one way to get around the rules," she replies. Another slurp. "So he's going to be your *brother-in-law*?" She has a glint in her eye that makes me feel uncomfortable.

"Yes, that's right."

"And . . . is he single?"

My chest hollows. "I think so."

"In that case, honey, I need an invite to that wedding."

I gulp down half the liquid then force a smile.

"Did you know, something like thirty percent of women meet their future husbands at their friends' weddings? This could be it, Tril. He could be the one. And we could be *sisters*. Wouldn't that be amazing?"

Something bitter twists inside my chest. "I think you're forgetting you snuck out the back with a stranger that night."

She stops dancing and stares at me. "Trilby, what on earth do you take me for? I'm *joking*. The man couldn't take his eyes off you, and when I came back inside, he'd cleared out the entire club because—what, you danced a little too close to some guy?"

Every part of my body tenses. I know I just got caught in that forbidden land of acting all jealous over someone who isn't mine, then getting called out for it by someone who's seen the truth.

I don't have time to dwell on it, because Sandrine's focus narrows on something over my shoulder, and her face pales.

"Um, Tril, are you sure no one knows you're here?"

"Yeah. Why?"

A loud crash stops the music dead, and a few screams of surprise ring out from the edges of the room.

I spin around to follow Sandrine's gaze and immediately wish I hadn't.

"Castellano . . ."

My heart trips over itself as Cristiano Di Santo roars his way toward me. My instinctive reflex is to put my hands up—if not to surrender, then certainly to slow him down so he won't humiliate me in front of my friends.

But he's not getting the hint, and he's not slowing down.

I start to back away, but it's too late. He reaches me too quickly, bends forward, wraps an arm around the back of my thighs, and hoists me over his shoulder.

Everything is a blur when he turns sharply and strides back the way he came. Gasps follow us out of the house like little gusts of wind.

As soon as the cool night air kisses my skin I come to my senses.

"Put. Me. *Down!*" I scream, but it's breathless.

When he doesn't even acknowledge me or break his stride, I beat his back with my fists. The hits are small and insignificant, but I keep at it. I once read somewhere that if you think you're too small to make a difference, you've never shared a room with a mosquito. Well, I'm determined to be one hell of a mosquito.

If only my fists would leave just a fraction of a mark on him . . .

I lift my head to see people flooding out of the house to gawp at me being hauled out to the street upside down. I'm so mortified it burns.

Behind me a car door opens, and then I'm floating through the air, only to land with a humiliating thud in the passenger seat of Cristiano's car.

The second he lets go of me, I grab the door and push it hard in a vain attempt to escape. In response he drags the seat belt across my body, the back of his hand brushing against my breasts, and fastens me in tightly. When I try to release it, he whips off his tie and yanks my hands above my head, and with more speed than my half-drunk brain can handle, he ties my wrists together behind the headrest of my seat.

I wriggle uselessly even as the passenger door slams shut.

Cristiano walks calmly around the front of the car and slides in beside me without so much as a glance.

"You can't keep me tied up," I say, practically spitting. "It's unsafe."

"Not as unsafe as you trying to shove open the door

while I'm driving down the freeway," he answers smoothly.

My chest expands and contracts as I pant with frustration, and I'm mortified further by the fact with each breath I take, my breasts are pushed out brazenly.

"I'm not comfortable," I huff.

"You should have thought about that before you put up a fight."

He starts the engine and pulls serenely out onto the street.

My chest rumbles with frustration. "Where are we going?"

"Back to my apartment. You clearly can't be trusted to stay in the house alone."

My awareness darkens. "How did you know where to find me?"

"It's amazing what the promise of a new car and a few personal days can get you, especially from those who have nothing to bargain with."

Lorna.

Guilt quietens me. "Please don't punish her."

He chuckles darkly. I pan my glare out the window.

"Why were you at the house?" I snap.

"I was checking on you."

I shake my head, exasperated. "It's not your job anymore. You don't need to keep checking on me."

"No? I should just let you run out to parties at the wrong end of town with no protection?"

"No one is going to hurt me," I say, rolling my eyes.

"Don't be so sure about that. Besides, pain isn't the only thing you need protecting from, Castellano."

I grind my teeth together. "Then what?"

"Capture." He strokes a hand across his chin. "You'd make excellent ransom collateral."

Oh.

His words twist like a knife in my abdomen. He doesn't care that someone might want to hurt me to avenge my new family; he only cares about preventing his family from having to spend money on protecting me.

My lip curls. "So don't pay the demands. Just keep your money and let them have me."

His voice is like flint. "That might be the most ridiculous thing I've ever heard come out of your mouth."

Savage.

I don't understand why, but I like that I got a rise out of him. I want to do it again.

"Better yet . . ."—I narrow my eyes—"do it after the wedding. That way, Savero gets his share of the port but doesn't have to contend with a wife he doesn't actually want."

A low growl erupts from his chest, setting my skin alight.

"I swear to God, Castellano, if you say one more word tonight, I might have to shove you out that door myself."

I'd hide my smile behind my fingers, but my hands are tied, so instead I turn to look out the window, content that he can probably see my triumphant expression in the reflection.

We drive in silence for a long ten minutes. All the blood drains from my hands.

I turn to him accusingly. "I can't feel my fingers."

"Good thing you don't need them for anything right now."

I pout. "I'll need to pee when we get there. How do you propose I'll remove my underwear?"

His jaw grinds, the sound audible over the smooth engine. "What did I say about talking?"

I tip my head. "You said I couldn't say one word. You didn't specify several."

"I said 'one *more* word.' Are you baiting me, Castellano? Because if you are, let me say this. When it comes to dishing out punishments, I don't discriminate."

"You mean you don't play favorites?"

"I don't *have* favorites."

I chew my lip, weighing up the sense or senselessness of my next retort. "Not even your new sister?"

He stops working his jaw and swallows hard. His voice thins when he replies. "You're not my sister yet."

"No, but I bet you're counting the days," I taunt.

"Not exactly."

"Whyever not? I've got lots of experience being a sister. In fact, if you were to ask Serafina, she'd say I'm the *best*."

His jaw continues to grind as he focuses on the road.

"I give the best cuddles," I joke, determined to get more of a rise out of him.

"I'm not a cuddler," he bites out.

"You could have fooled me," I say, in reference to the way he held me all night after my bad dreams.

"That doesn't count," he says through gritted teeth.

"I bet I can convert you." I arch my brow in a challenge. "At the very least, I'll tickle you until you submit."

"If you dare tickle me, I'll break your fingers."

"Bit harsh," I mutter, secretly pleased to be getting a response—*any* response. "I make the best midnight feasts at pajama parties."

He pulls his bottom lip between his teeth but doesn't manage to completely stifle a smile. "I don't wear pajamas."

A bolt of fire barrels toward my pelvis and takes my breath away. I swallow, bat away the image of Cristiano wearing zero clothes, and press on.

"I'm not very good at pillow fights, so you'd win at those," I muse, almost to myself. "My upper-body strength is terrible. Even worse now the blood has drained entirely from my arms."

Cristiano drives the car down the ramp into the parking garage with more speed and force than necessary.

"But I promise you this," I say with a cunning smile, "you'll *never* beat me at hide-and-seek."

He spins the car into a space and switches off the

engine, then he turns slowly to face me. I almost gasp at the heat in his glare.

"Wanna bet?"

My brows knit together as my tipsy brain struggles to understand. He reaches behind my head and releases my bound wrists. They flop into my lap and immediately start throbbing as blood courses back through the veins.

Then he leans forward and pushes his fingers through my hair to my nape, tugging me into him. His lips brush across my jaw, and he breathes heavily.

Hotly.

"I'll give you a head start, *sis*."

When he releases me, his eyes are the darkest I've ever seen. They look like blood moons against a ravaged sky. He breaks eye contact to lean across me for the door handle. He pulls it toward him and opens the door up. His shoulder presses into my breasts, and God help me, I push them into him, devouring the way he halts with awareness.

The sound of our heavy breathing fills the car, and as he draws back slowly, his hand brushes across my thigh, skimming over my pelvic bone and making me jump in shock. When his face is level with mine, he stops and drops his gaze to my lips.

There's only an inch or two between us.

I'd barely need to move to feel the brush of his lips against mine, and suddenly, it's all I want. A throbbing sensation ticks up between my legs, and my breaths shorten.

As his lips part, he runs his tongue slowly along his bottom lip, chasing it with his teeth.

I'm watching every movement as if I'm studying him beneath a microscope, so when his eyes flick to mine and he silently mouths, "Run," I'm already one step ahead.

The seat belt snaps into place, my shoes clatter to the footwell, and my bare feet touch the ground. I turn back once to see his eyes fall shut and his head drop back against the seat, then I run.

I search for the most obvious places I could hide— under cars, in doorways, behind a dumpster. Then I look some more. My heart pounds as the sound of his voice counting backward travels up my spine with the adrenaline.

When I finally settle on a hiding place—one I'm convinced will fool him—I hear the sound of a car door closing softly.

His voice is thick, molten steel.

"You asked for this, Castellano. Ready or not, here I come."

$\mathcal{T}$rilby

I press my back against the pillar and hold my breath. The only sound I can hear is the beating of my pulse as blood pumps through my temples, and it's getting faster.

This is what foreplay must feel like.

For almost a month I've been moving around Cristiano, testing the boundaries, seeing how far I can push it before one of us snaps. I've felt the burn of electricity whenever he's entered the room and wondered what would happen if his fingers coasted just a little bit higher than my wrist or my arm. What if they stilled across my breast? What if they lingered on my hips? What if they went to places forbidden to anyone but the man I've been ordered to marry?

The thought makes my bones weak and my core smolder.

I strain to hear the soft click of an Italian leather shoe or the rustle of designer cotton, but nothing comes. I slowly breathe out and press my palms to the cool concrete.

In the distance something scurries along the edge of the garage, and every hair on my body bristles. What was I thinking when I leveled this challenge?

It's simple. I wasn't thinking. I was taunting.

I was doing everything I could think of to provoke him, to push his buttons, because I can't keep up this act anymore. Something has to give.

Someone has to give *in*, and I'll be damned if it's me.

The tension between us is so taut it's about to snap, and neither of us can afford for it to snap in full view of Savero, or my family, or even the friends I keep at the wrong end of town.

I don't know what the snap will look like. All I know is I can't take this tension anymore. It needs to break; to leach out into the air. The pressure needs to release, otherwise I'm going to explode.

My virginity feels like a chain around my neck. A broken hymen and a high-five. That can't be all this comes down to. This moment, this anticipation, is so much more. I feel as if this is what I've waited my whole life for, not a tick in the box that supposedly determines my worth and my value as a woman.

Every cell in my body sings for Cristiano. I'm crying out for him to touch me, to feel me, to hear the song my body's performing for his ears only, before it's obliterated by a false sense of duty.

I breathe in again slowly and turn my head to the right. Nothing. Not even the dart of a shadow.

I lean over a little, careful not to overbalance. My fingers grip onto the concrete as I brush my cheek along the smooth pillar, then I turn my body until my front is flat against it.

The cool wall is soothing against the heat of my chest and my stomach. I bring my hands up to steady myself and lean toward the edge of the pillar a little more.

He's nowhere to be seen. Everywhere is silent.

Then the hairs on the back of my neck shiver under a hot breath.

"Caught you."

His whisper drips with promise, and my eyelids flutter shut.

A shudder rolls down my spine as he closes in on me.

"Now, what am I going to do with you?"

I don't miss the dark teasing behind his tone. It warms my pelvis and turns my stomach to liquid. I want to turn my head, but I can feel his heat right there, tantalizingly close.

His breath strokes my nape, and his lips press softly against my hair.

The suspense, the not knowing what he'll do, has me teetering right on the edge of sanity. If he doesn't do something to ease this unbearable tension, I'm going to lose it.

My heart is in my throat, every sense on high alert. Then I feel his fingers pushing between mine, his hot flesh pressing my hands into the cool concrete.

Slowly, he works his fingers beneath mine, curling them into my palms, and *finally*, his body pushes up against my back.

A satisfied sigh leaves my body, along with a soft moan. He's pressing his erection into the small of my back and holding it there, like a warning.

A low, desperate growl rolls through his chest. "This is what you've done to me. I've been walking around with a fucking hard-on since you strutted into that damn bar. My cock has never been so fucking needy. It won't settle for anything less than you. I can't even sleep when you're in the next room. I can't *breathe*."

His words light me up like a flame. He's halfway to explaining just how deeply I feel. Like a brazen cat, my back arches, lifting the cheeks of my ass so his hard-on slips between them. My head drops backward onto his shoulder, and an untethered sound I've never made before in my life curls its way out of my chest.

His breath scorches my collar bone as he dips his mouth toward my shoulder. His teeth graze along the sensitive skin, from the tip of my shoulder to the curve of my neck. I tilt my head to the left to give him access, because the need for him to sink his teeth into me *burns*.

His voice trembles with restraint. "I'm afraid if I taste you, I'll never stop."

One word leaks from my lips. I never thought I'd

resort to this, especially not with someone like
Cristiano.

"Please . . ."

He pauses, his lips drifting lightly over my skin,
making me raw with need.

I hold my breath.

And then I weaken under his strong hold as he pins
me to the concrete.

"You drive me *fucking* crazy." His low murmur sets
my skin alight, but he cools it with soft brushes of his
lips. It's maddening, and it's doing nothing to burst this
tension.

"Cristiano . . . *please* . . ."

"Please what?"

My breath leaves my lungs in short bursts. "I don't
know," I admit honestly. "I don't know what I need, but
I can't bear this anymore."

Very slowly, he pulls my right hand in toward my
body. He takes a long breath and then extends my arm
down until my hand is about level with my underwear.
The throbbing between my legs grows needier, as if my
body knows something I don't.

With his fingers threaded through mine, he pushes
them beneath my dress. I don't know what he's doing,
but it's balancing on a fine line between torturous and
darkly promising. His fingers guide mine toward the
soft cotton of my panties, and then, with my mind
dancing to an uneven rhythm, he presses softly into
them.

A loud, uncontrollable sigh rushes out of my lungs.

God.

"Is this what you need, little one?"

I swallow repeatedly, unable to speak.

As he presses my fingers more firmly, a strange wetness coats the tips through the fabric, and a shocked gasp makes my spine rigid.

"Yeah, you're soaking." His smile is unmistakable against my skin, and in that split second I decide that's enough to live for. We're doing this, and I've never felt so desperate yet sated in all my life.

Gently and slowly, he works my fingers in circles against my panties. I turn my face and cool my forehead against the pillar. I want this unbearable need to give, but also to never end. Small notes of desperation drip off the edge of my tongue in time with the rough breaths caressing my neck.

"You're shaking so hard," he says gruffly. "Is that for me, little one?"

I can't respond. I can only gyrate between the growing burn at the top of my legs and the dark promise pressing into the base of my spine.

I open my mouth to speak, but he nips me with his teeth, halting me.

"Don't tell me we can't do this." His voice is edged with desperation, making my legs weak.

An image of Savero crawls across my lids, a replay of his fingers shoving into the depths of a man's throat. Ice cold fear winds its way from my heart to my fingertips, but still it doesn't cool the burning embers coating my skin. As terrified as I am of Savero, it's his brother I want, with every dying fraction of my soul. I breathe out with absolute conviction. "I wasn't going to," I whisper, my own voice in tatters of need. "I want you to put an end to this feeling."

His tone softens. "What feeling?"

"Like I'm going to explode. I don't know how to live with it, and it's burning me up."

Suddenly, the heat against my back disappears, and I hear him settle on one knee behind me. He wraps a hand around my left ankle and lifts it up to rest it on his raised thigh.

"What did I say about wearing these short dresses?" He teases the hem with his tongue, tickling the curve of my bottom. Lust pools between my legs, and I'm mortified, because his face is so close to it, yet I'm desperate for him to put an end to this longing.

He feeds his hand through the lace, curls it into a fist, and then yanks, ripping it clean off.

The tips of my fingers are sore from where I'm gripping the pillar, and my breaths are short and needy.

Then something hot, wet, and firm presses against my clit.

Oh *God*.

He hums his approval, sending tendrils of fire across every inch of my body.

Taking hold of my hips, he licks me hard and slow, from the uppermost tip of my clit to the puckered opening of my bottom. An animalistic moan escapes my throat, but I'm too far intoxicated to care.

His tongue circles my entrance, and when I'm

thoroughly soaked and slippery, the cool underground air dances over me. He leans into me again and laps at my pussy with a focus bordering on obsessive, the pressure increasing gently with the speed of his tongue.

I press my forehead harder into the cold concrete and close my eyes.

"Jesus. Fucking. Christ," he murmurs between licks. "I didn't know sin could taste so damn sweet."

He makes a long humming sound and then pulls back before turning me around in his thick hands. My eyes remain closed, because I don't want to lose this feeling. I know how treasonous this is; I know I should put a stop to it. But, for the life of me, I *can't*. I want to be the sweet sin on the flat of his tongue for as long as I live.

His palms spread my thighs until I'm standing wide-open, my back against a pillar, with a dangerous man's hot breath on my pussy. His fingers pull my folds apart, and he leans in and flicks his tongue lightly over my clit. A groan of desperation leaches from my lungs into the damp air.

He presses a finger to my opening and rims it, the sound of wet flesh filling the stone-cold silence. My arousal drips to the floor, and I couldn't care less.

"Fuck yes. Shiver for me, my beautiful girl."

He rests his hands lightly on my trembling thighs as though he's relishing the fact I'm incapable of controlling my body's response to him. When he leans into me, coating his whole face with my arousal, I sob with relief.

He works his mouth over my entire pussy, fucking my opening with his wicked tongue and suckling at my clit like it's a nipple.

My head falls back while I grip his thick hair between vibrating fingers.

With his lips firmly attached to my swollen nub, he shifts his angle and slips a finger halfway inside of me. My moan is high and breathless.

He finds a delectable rhythm between circling my pussy and lapping at my clit, which has me panting breathlessly, riding the edge of bliss.

Then, as if he isn't getting enough, he lifts me off my feet and brings me down onto his face.

My hands reach overhead and grip onto the edges of the pillar as he rocks me back and forth over his mouth. Untethered, desperate breaths are pumped out of my chest as I barrel toward absolute ecstasy.

"Cristiano," I whisper hoarsely. "Make me come."

He moans onto my clit and curls his tongue inside my heat. Then my vision explodes into a million stars. He doesn't let up. He keeps rocking me on his face, and I keep coming. It's so dirty and so wrong, and I never want him to stop.

My legs are shaking so hard he doesn't lower me to the floor. Instead he drags his mouth to my upper thigh and French kisses it all the way down to my knee, while I shudder weakly on his shoulders.

He stands before I can protest, and I almost choke on the hunger in his eyes.

His earlier words dance in my ears. *"If we'd had sex, you'd still be feeling me in your stomach."*

Suddenly, I want to feel him in my stomach. I want to feel him everywhere. A shadow drapes itself over my consciousness.

"What is it?"

I lift my gaze to his. "It hasn't worked."

"What hasn't worked?"

"I thought scratching that itch would help me . . ."

"But . . .?"

I look away, the shame burning me from my bones to my skin. "It hasn't."

His fingers clasp my chin, tilting my face up to his. Without saying a word, he demands I finish that sentence.

My thoughts come out in a trembling whisper. "I need more."

He leans in and grazes his lips across the shell of my ear. "Say that again."

My breath stutters, and I whisper, "I need *more*, Cristiano. I need *you*."

He wipes a hand down his face before lifting both hands and pushing my hair back, resting his fingers on my nape. "Fuck," he drawls.

Then he closes his lips over mine.

For a moment he doesn't move. He just presses his lips against me, breathing deeply. Then his tongue darts out and softly licks the underside of my top lip.

A groan escapes him, and he pulls away, resting his

forehead against mine. It takes a second or two for me to realize his breathing is labored. He's holding back.

"Kiss me," I whisper.

His hands reach up and grip the sides of my face. Then, with his lashes lowered, he brushes his lips across my eyelids, over the bridge of my nose, and down my cheeks. When he reaches my mouth, he traces my lips with his tongue, the sensation setting every inch of my skin alight. I moan helplessly, and he folds his mouth over it, sucking it into his lungs.

Then, *fuck*, does he kiss me.

He presses me back against the pillar while his tongue swipes against mine from every angle in a hungry waltz. It's messy and delicious and *heated*.

Those kisses that failed to light me up before? They were *nothing* compared to this. This man can kiss like it's his dying breath, and I want him all over me.

"Don't stop," I groan as he pulls his mouth away.

He chuckles darkly, smooths his hands below my bare buttocks, and lifts me up. My legs wrap themselves around his waist, my ass brushing the top of his erection.

Just being in his arms with his lips on mine is enough to make my world shimmer. I've wanted this for more than mere weeks. The way I melt into his embrace as if we were designed for each other, and the way my heart has expanded to fill my entire being, tells me the cool, hard truth: I've wanted this all my life. I don't understand why or how I know this—I just do. Cristiano and I must have met in another life. We were meant to be. And nothing can take that away from us.

His tongue laps at mine, tasting every crevice of my mouth with deep, focused curiosity. It's like he's cataloguing every fraction of me. I open up and let him.

"God, I need this," he moans.

I'm transcending to another reality, one in which I'm treasonous and trapped, but at the same time fed and free.

He continues to kiss me, hard and deep, as he carries me to the elevator. He doesn't even wait for the door to close before he's ramming my back against the wall.

His fingers thread up through my hair, his fists pulling at the follicles. With some of my weight taken away, he grinds into me, slowly rolling his cock up and over my clit, drawing more moans from my throat. I lean back against the mirrored wall and watch the way his eyes feast on my swollen breasts. They ache to feel his fingers.

All too soon, the elevator doors ping open, and he walks with me wrapped around his waist into his apartment. I feel my back pressed up against the refrigerator, and he grinds into me again, letting me know just how turned-on he is. The feel of his solid cock against my soft pussy is maddening, and I let out helpless moans, one after the other.

He runs a hand from my throat to my chest and holds it there as if he's keeping me literally at arm's length. Then, slowly, he lowers me to the counter. When the bare skin of my ass touches down, I jump.

"It's cold, huh?" A slow, devastating wink. "I'll warm you up in no time."

He leans forward and catches my bottom lip between his teeth. His warm breath caresses my skin as his tongue chases the sharp graze his teeth left behind.

A wilt of a moan passes from my mouth to his, then I glance down at his pants. They're wet.

He follows my gaze, and a darkness drapes over him. "I came when I was licking you out."

"You . . . But—"

"Yeah." He pushes his hands through my hair and presses kisses to the side of my throat. "Never happened before."

My head is spinning. Can he come again? I want to be able to give him this.

He senses my questions, stops still, and stares heavily at me. "Don't worry, Castellano. I'm just getting started."

Breath gushes from my mouth, and he laughs again. It's the most beautiful sound I've ever heard.

I'm lifted again and carried to the master bedroom. He lays me gently on the bed and crawls up over me. His gaze is intense and just *hot*.

"Let me see your body," he says softly.

"The zipper is at the back," I say in a whisper.

"Roll onto your front."

He sits back on his knees to let me do just that, and I smile as a murmur of approval reaches my ears.

My hair tickles my nape as it's brushed to the side. He pulls the zipper down slowly, the cool air nipping at my bare skin. The zipper reaches to my sit bone, and he swallows as his finger strokes a circle on the small of my back. His palms touch my back and slide up, until his fingertips are beneath the short sleeves of my dress. As he pushes them outward, he lowers his body and kisses the top of my spine. A shiver coasts down it despite his warmth covering me like a blanket.

One by one, he pulls my arms through the straps, then he reaches a hand beneath me and touches my chest. Back on his knees, he pulls me up with one hand while smoothing the dress down to my stomach. He shifts backward and lifts my hips as I sink my face into the comforter, partly out of embarrassment that I literally have my ass in his face, and partly because I'm still so turned-on I could cry a river.

The dress is pulled down my thighs, baring my bottom to him. He pauses, every second heightening my arousal.

Then he leans forward and sinks his teeth into the left cheek. I yelp and melt under him when he licks away the sting.

"I'm going to make a meal out of your ass, Castellano." His voice is so gravelly I almost turn to check it's still him. "And you're going to kneel there like a good girl and let me."

I don't get a chance to object when he does the same to my other ass cheek. I moan like an absolute hussy. I'm heated and restless *everywhere*, but I don't want to move. This must be what delirium feels like.

He bites and nibbles until the skin is sore and

buzzing, and then he licks and kisses until I'm chasing his teeth again.

"Keep still," he commands, pushing my bottom forward. "Greedy girl." Then a hot, wet tongue dips between my legs and licks all the way to my puckered opening.

"Oh yeah," he murmurs, almost to himself. "You're still so fucking wet."

I shiver again.

"Come up onto your hands."

I do as he says, but it's slow. I'm so decentered I can barely coordinate my limbs.

He unties my bra and then reaches his hands below me to cup my naked breasts. They rest like pendulums in his palms, and I moan restlessly as he kneads them.

"I want to see you," I say, slurring my words.

His hands leave my breasts, and he gently rolls me onto my back. I may be as naked as the day I was born, but he is still one hundred percent fully clothed.

He gets off the bed and stands, soaking up my hungry gaze while he drops his jacket to the floor. First he unbuttons his shirt. He untucks it and lets it hang open while he thoughtfully removes his cufflinks. His eyes don't leave me once. When his cufflinks are removed, he shrugs the shirt from his shoulders, and I heat up like a kindled fire. His upper body is perfect. I gobble up his broad shoulders and cut biceps before my gaze falls to his ink.

A dove in flight amid a tongue of fire takes up the whole left side of his torso.

I sit up. "Is that the . . .?" My voice trails off.

"The Di Santo crest," he answers. "Every made man in our family has it."

I swallow. "Were you . . . made?"

"Not officially, but Sav and I got the ink at fourteen. Being born into the family made it kind of unavoidable."

I'm so glued to the intricate details—the feathers of the dove and the licks of the flame—that I don't realize he's removed everything from his bottom half until my gaze focuses on the enormous cock in his hand.

Cristiano is leaning back against his bedroom wall, slowly moving his hand up and down his shaft while he watches me watching him.

He jerks his head toward me. "Touch yourself."

"No!" Anxious sweat leaches through my pores.

"I've eaten you out, little one—you have nothing to be embarrassed about."

I stare at him, unable to put into words why I'm not on board with this despite his logic.

"Come on, Castellano." His eyes drop to my thighs. "I want to *see* you. Spread your legs for me and let me see the beautiful pussy I just fucking worshipped."

An intoxicating throbbing picks up between my legs.

He drops his head back against the wall and groans. "Castellano, I'm hanging on by a thread here . . ."

He is?

"Have you any idea how much I've wanted this since the first fucking second I saw you?"

My pulse races.

"Please, just put a fi—"

He stops short as he pulls his head up, because I'm doing as he asked. I've pushed a finger inside of myself, coating my fingers in my arousal.

"Oh, Jesus fucking Christ." The words emerge as a strained, hoarse whisper.

I can't believe how this is affecting him. His eyes glaze over and don't waver from the movement of my fingers. His hand grips his cock tighter, and his chest is *heaving*.

I slip a second finger inside of myself and then rub the juices around my clit. But I'm so wet there's no friction.

"Cristiano," I gasp. I need him to do this for me.

His eyes darken, and he takes two strides to the bed, still rubbing his cock. "Lie down. Spread your legs."

Alarm zaps through me. "Cristiano, we can't . . . I . . ."

I can't bring myself to say the words. Not here—not when there's a beautiful spell to break. *I have to remain a virgin.* I want this night to be perfect. I want to feel every long, hard inch of this man, but . . . losing my virginity to him could ruin us both. Seeing how distant Savero and Cristiano are with each other makes me think no love will be lost between the two of them, but a lot of face would be. In fact, Savero might even kill to restore his reputation. Would he kill his own brother? The fact I don't know the answer to that makes me even more wary of giving my virginity to someone other than the Di Santo don.

He gently pushes my legs outward, the fire in his eyes no less dim for me. "We're not doing that," he says, and my anxious thoughts slow. "But we're doing the next best thing."

And just like that, my thoughts bounce back to the beat of, *What the actual fuck? Has he forgotten I have zero experience?*

I keep my mouth shut and lie back on the comforter with my legs extended outward. He nestles himself carefully between them and lets his cock fall heavily onto my clit. It makes me startle, but the sensation of having his hard lines and ridges resting against my sensitive nub makes me dizzy with desire.

He continues to lower his hips until his cock is applying a firm pressure against the cluster of nerve endings. He looks into my eyes as if he's waiting for permission. I give him a light nod, and he starts to rub his cock up and down my pussy.

At first it feels strange, but very quickly, it makes me hot and breathless. In fact, I'm panting, and the need to find that release again is overwhelming. How can having a cock rub up and down on my clit make me want to come so fast?

I bite down on the top of his arm, and he lets out an annoyed growl. His cock doubles down on its task, pressing me just hard enough into the mattress. I wrap my legs around his back, pulling him closer, firmer.

"Fuck." He breathes hot, reckless air into my ear, and I shift my hips, needing more.

Lost in mindlessness, I don't realize how full I feel until he freezes above me . . .

"Trilby . . ."

. . . and says my name.

I drag my awareness back to his face and almost recoil at his expression. He looks anguished and . . . *haunted.*

"What—?"

His voice cracks. "I'm inside you."

Suddenly, the sensation makes sense. It isn't just his wide body keeping my legs apart; it's the crown of his cock inside of me.

"Do something." His eyes are narrow and pleading. "Before I lose my fucking mind."

What?

I battle with his demand. I don't want to move. I want him to inch deeper and fill me completely. I want him to fuck me into the mattress, virginity or no virginity—I don't care.

"Trilby!" The bed shakes beneath his braced arms and barely contained growl. He sucks in a tight breath and pushes his cock in by a fraction.

We *both* groan.

How can we deny ourselves and each other when we both want this *so badly*?

My head is spinning, and my ability to think straight has evaporated, along with my conviction.

He drops his head. His shoulders are glistening with sweat.

Another fraction.

I mewl like a cat, and the already tight walls of my pussy close around him like lips sucking on a popsicle. My body knows what it needs better than I do.

He pumps lightly and groans like a lion taunting its next kill.

This is too good to stop. The sensation is strange, unfamiliar, but so right I can't argue with it.

"Stop me," he whispers again. "Don't let me ruin your life."

He pumps again, and I cry out, the need making my pussy throb painfully.

"I want you," I purr. "Don't pull out, Cristiano, please," I beg him mindlessly.

He pumps a few more times, refusing to push his cock more than a quarter way in. It's agonizing.

He fists a hand in my hair, forcing my eyes up to his. "You have no idea how much I want to push through your barrier, break in your walls, and come deep in your gut while I swallow your moans."

There's a "but," but it doesn't come. Instead he lowers his face into the crook of my neck and groans.

I use all my strength to squeeze myself around his cock. He jerks against me, and I hear his teeth gnash together.

I'm losing my damn mind. I can't do this slowly— it's going to hurt. But if he moves just another inch, he'll break me in. Do I want that?

I don't know. I just want *him*.

Eventually, his breaths soften, and he lifts his head, casting a warm gaze across my frazzled features. "I'm pulling out," he says quietly. "Just give me a minute."

He bends his arms, and the veins pop out with the pressure of holding himself up for so long. I feel his lips caress my ear, and he nuzzles my lobe. I'm dying of need.

My heart sinks. I know he has to pull out, but I don't want to stop.

A thought crosses my mind. "I want to taste you," I whisper shyly.

"Are you sure?" His lips brush the side of my throat.

"Yes, I am."

I feel hollow when he keeps his word and withdraws his cock. When he crawls up over me, bringing his cock to lay on my chest, I feel terrified. First, I've never done this before, and second, I might die of suffocation.

"What . . . um, what do I do?" I blink up at him.

He swallows loudly and strokes his hand down the shaft, cupping the crown in his palm. "We can take it slow." His voice cracks. "Start by maybe licking it a little."

I nod and pull him towards my lips, then I press a kiss to the crown—long, hot and slow.

His jaw unhinges, his mouth curling around a throaty gasp. "Or that," he grunts, swallowing again.

I'm instantly addicted to the look on his face. I push my tongue out tentatively and flick it over the beautiful glistening tip. He releases a string of curses, and it makes my eyelids pop, because, again, I hardly did anything.

A pearl of moisture collects on the edge, and I lick it away. It tastes salty and foreign, but it's *him*.

That thought alone propels me forward, and I wrap my lips around him.

His hands plummet into the comforter on either side of my head.

"Fuck. *Fuck.*"

I close my eyes and suck him into my mouth, swirling my tongue around the circumference. I bring my hands up to his ass, and a deep lust sweeps over me at the feel of his rock-hard glutes. He's shaking, and it only feeds my frenzy. I pull him deeper, opening my throat instinctively.

Italian profanities gush from his lips, and I entangle myself in his desperation. My tongue sweeps and swirls, swallowing more of his pre-cum, and my cheeks hollow as I pull him in and suck.

In the midst of it all, his fingers find my pussy. I don't know what the hell he's doing to it, but I never want him to stop. He strokes it, tweaks it, and spanks it, and I groan my approval around his cock.

"I'm going to come down your throat," he chokes out. "Are you ready for that, little one?"

I nod, and I'm rewarded with two fingers inside my pussy. I buck my hips up toward him, coaxing them deeper. He growls with frustration, and I realize he doesn't want to break my hymen with his fingers either.

"Suck me, Trilby. Oh God, that's perfect. Your lips are so soft, so warm."

I pull his ass toward me in reckless thrusts. He massages my clit with maddening focus, and I feel it sharpen beneath his fingers. I'm going to explode.

"Yes, baby. Harder, deeper. *Fuck*. You suck me so damn good."

His filthy praise drives me over the edge, and I jerk up into his hand. As I spasm beneath him, my mouth fills up with his semen.

"Don't stop," he bites out, fingering me with relentless rhythm.

I keep swallowing until there's nothing left, then I slowly ease him out of my mouth. When he collapses onto the bed, I set to work.

I lick him clean.

Every rock-hard inch of him.

I crawl up to my hands and knees and lick around the base, the tops of his thighs, up the length to the crown, and across every ridge. His fingers work through my hair, soft moans coasting over my ears.

"You're so fucking beautiful," he whispers.

I look up and drown immediately in those deep brown eyes. He gently pushes me back onto the bed and brings his mouth to my tits, then he proceeds to spend the next ten minutes making out with them both.

I'm a soaking-wet mess by the time he comes up for air, and all it takes is a swipe of his tongue over my clit and I'm coming again.

We can't fuck, but we can do everything else.

And we do.

I wake up with an awareness of warmth around me. I'm curled into Cristiano's large, firm body, my face nuzzled into his chest. I breathe him in, not wanting to break the spell by moving.

"You didn't have nightmares," he says softly, the vibration of his voice touching my cheek.

I let my eyes drift closed. "Did you hold me like this all night?"

He presses his lips into my hair, and I feel him smile with his whole body. "Yeah."

I lift my head and immediately drown in the look he's giving me. Like I'm the most precious thing he's ever held.

"Thank you," I say softly.

"What for?"

I stroke my fingertips down his chest. "For everything. But especially for last night. And . . ."

"And?"

"And for not taking my virginity."

His chest turns suddenly rigid.

"It would have made everything so much more complicated. And if Savero ever discovered this . . ."

A chill winds its way down my spine at the thought of Savero finding out about me and Cristiano.

I hear his teeth grinding above me.

"You know why I'm leaving after the wedding, don't you?"

My lack of response leaves the air to fill with heavy breaths.

"I can't stand by and see you become married to another man, least of all my own flesh and blood. It will kill me."

"I don't want to marry him," I whisper. "I have no choice."

His tone is laden with defeat. "And if I try to stop it, it won't be me who pays—it will be your family. I'll never be able to live with myself."

I squeeze my eyes closed in the hope tears won't fall. My heart drops, knowing there's nothing he can—or will—do to keep me.

"Will you do me one favor?"

I look up.

"You said yourself you don't handle alcohol well. Will you please refrain from drinking it? I can't bear the thought of you getting into a . . . predicament . . . and I'm not there to look out for you."

"I managed just fine before you showed up," I mutter.

His tone is gentle. "Will you please just do it for me?"

I sigh. He doesn't have to know. In fact, he'll be on the opposite coast. "Okay."

We fall silent again, and I listen to the steady beats of his heart. Then his fingers draw circles on my back.

"That comb you wear in your hair . . ."

"Yes?"

"It's special to you."

I nod and look up. "It was my mama's."

He bends his head and kisses the tip of my nose. "It suits you."

A warm glow settles over me, and I snuggle into him.

"Will you promise me one more thing?"

I nod against his chest.

"Will you wear it when you think of me?"

I suck in a breath and lift my gaze to his. "Why?"

"Because as soon as you walk out that door, we'll have to pretend this never happened. But if I see you wearing that, I'll know it really did."

I pull myself from his embrace and crawl up to his lips. He moans when I kiss him hard.

After a few minutes, we come up for air, and he holds my face in his palms.

"You know what pisses me off the most?"

"What?" I whisper.

"I fucking found you first."

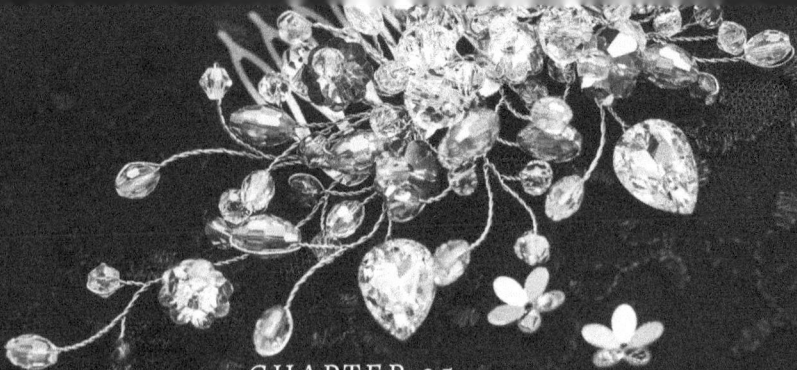

CHAPTER 25

Cristiano

Sav doesn't look up when I enter Father's office. "What are you doing here?" he says with a clipped tongue.

"This is my home too, in case you'd forgotten." I use the sharp retort to cover up my surprise at his blunt tone. "And I thought you might be happy to see your little brother."

He rests our father's favorite Montblanc pen on the leather surface of the antique desk and releases a tight breath. I'm impressed at how quickly he's made himself at home in Father's office.

He stands without looking at me. "I thought you were staying at your apartment. According to my staff, you seem to find it preferable to take my fiancée there than to keep an eye on her here."

My blood runs cold. He can't suspect there's

something between me and Trilby, can he? He hasn't been around enough to see anything that would give him pause. Besides, I find it hard to believe he even cares.

"It's just easier," I say, following him out to the kitchen. "You shouldn't leave her alone so much, Sav. She's too . . . spirited. Twice I've found her in nightclubs . . ."

"Is she a drunk?" His lip curls.

"No." I flinch at his brevity. "But the same can't be said for the company she keeps." I wouldn't categorize Sandrine as a drunk, but I wouldn't say she was a positive influence either.

He turns and presses a hand onto the kitchen counter before glancing at the clock on the wall. "What are you saying, *fratello*?"

"I'm saying she's not wise to this life. She doesn't realize every Marchesi asshole on the street would give his left fucking testicle to kidnap her, torture her, and send you the sound of her begging for mercy."

He pins me with a glare. "Didn't she lose her mother to this life?"

My fingers flex automatically. "Yeah, but she doesn't live in the Cosa Nostra. Not in the thick of it like you do. She certainly doesn't have much comprehension of the kind of threats you and I get on a daily basis."

I watch for some hint of understanding to cross his face, but it doesn't. He just shrugs.

I fight the urge to curl my fists. "Don't you care?"

His eyes narrow. "Not as much as you, it seems."

Fuck. I run a hand through my hair. "If anything happened to her . . ." How can I appeal to him without looking like I'm in over my damned head? "It wouldn't be good for business," I say with a sigh. "Your business or mine."

He folds his arms and tilts his head slightly. "Why wouldn't it be?"

My jaw stiffens as resolve hardens my heart. "Would you be comfortable doing business with someone who can't even keep his own fiancée alive?"

His teeth grind as he considers my response. "Fine. I'll get some guys on her."

I knead the back of my neck. "Good."

"You know . . . you don't have to stay for the wedding."

I snap my head up. "Why?"

"Well, I'm sure you have business to get back to, and Nicolò can be my best man."

My chest tightens. "Are you being serious?"

His expression remains sober.

"I know we aren't the closest we've ever been, but I'm still your brother, Sav."

He emits an ugly laugh. "We were never close, you and me. You assumed I liked you, and I never cared enough to correct that assumption."

A vein at the base of my throat throbs. *Why is he being such a dick?* Has he always been this big of an ass, or is he only revealing his true colors now Father has died?

"So why did you bother to pull me out of the river when I almost drowned all those years ago?"

His eyes grow dark and cold. "Would you be comfortable doing business with someone who didn't save his own brother from drowning when he had the chance?"

His sharp retort is astonishingly revealing. He only saved me because of how it would look if he didn't? He was *twelve*.

"Why do I think there's more to it than that?" I ask.

He levels me with a glare. "Were you really so oblivious to it?"

I shake my head, confused. "To what?"

He smiles, but it's cold. "I guess you were too wrapped up in the glow of Father's admiration to see it."

"See what?"

He pans his gaze to his glass and swirls the amber liquid around it. "That you were always his favorite."

I'm stunned. I knew Father and I had a different relationship to Father and Savero, but that was because tougher things were expected of Sav. He was the eldest; the one who would inherit the title. I had no idea he harbored such resentment toward me. When Father was around, Savero at least pretended he liked having me visit. But now . . . he can't seem to get rid of me fast enough.

"If I hadn't saved you that day . . . he would have ended me."

That is simply not true. I never remember Father

treating Savero as anything other than a much-loved son.

"*Fratello* . . ." I start.

"Save it," he snaps. "I've made my peace with it, brother. I just want to move on and rule this place like I was born to. You may as well leave now."

I glance at the framed photographs above Father's desk. Generations of brothers standing by each other, working together, supporting one another, being *best men* at their weddings. If I left now, as Sav's asking me to do, we'd be breaking a long-held tradition in our family—one my father was so vocal about having us uphold.

That's not the only reason I can't leave yet. I need to make sure Castellano is safe and settled. But even as I think those thoughts, I know they're excuses. Staying an extra few days won't make her any safer or more settled. If anything, my presence will *un*settle her. It'll make it that little bit harder for us both to say goodbye.

Besides, I don't think I can act as though I'm not in over my head with her, and I know my desire for her will be as transparent as the water in Savero's pool.

"I will stay to the end of the wedding." I force out a breath, along with words that taste sour on my tongue. "Then I'll be gone, and you'll never have to see me again."

His brow drops over calculating eyes. "Fine."

"But promise me you'll get some surveillance for your fiancée. She doesn't want to be caged in, and she's demonstrated that multiple times in your absence. If you go ahead with this marriage, Sav, I suggest you get protection on her twenty-four-seven."

Sav's eyes darken further. *"If?"*

"If what?"

"No . . ." His tone is measured. "You said 'if' I go ahead with the marriage. Why wouldn't I go ahead with it? I want that port. This is a business transaction, and I don't back out of those."

I raise my hands. "Fine. *When.* And until then, you will treat me like a brother," I say with grit in my voice and sadness in my throat. Then I walk out before he can object.

I can still feel his accusatory glare burning into my back as I step out into the harsh midday sun. I should feel hurt by his coldhearted dismissal, but the main sensation I have is one of sheer relief. I've never wanted to admit it before now, but being friendly to Savero has always been a struggle. His cool eyes have never reciprocated warmth, and his harsh words are often so hard to swallow. Even Father avoided him on occasion. But the relief is tempered by guilt. I'm leaving Castellano in this man's hands. If anything were to happen to her while under his watch, I don't think I'd be able to stop myself. I'd cause him equal harm without a thought.

I stand on the stone path leading to the gardens, close my eyes, and breathe in deeply, trying to fill my lungs with the same conviction I felt when I last left this place ten years ago. Back then I couldn't wait to get away. Mama's murder was still fresh at the front of my mind, and Father had disappeared on a rampage that resulted in more than a hundred bloody deaths.

This time feels very different. Much as I want to be out from under my brother's hostile gaze, I don't want to leave. And the reason why is shaped like an hourglass and tastes like sweet hope and dangerous distraction.

I could so easily stay. I have easy access to Savero's movements; I could find out exactly when and where I'd catch Castellano alone. All I'd need to do is press those pretty lips to mine and wrap her legs around my waist, and I just know she'd be as far gone as I would be. Despite our resolve to pretend nothing happened, I know for a fact the conviction went only skin-deep. The second my soul speaks to hers again, we'll be fucked.

Her panties are still tucked into my pocket, and her sweetness still sits on my tongue. I'm so far under her spell I can hardly think straight. When I'm not making plans to head back to my businesses, I'm scheming, dreaming up ways I can see her again, get her alone, have a taste of her just *one more fucking time*.

I've seen enough addicts in my lifetime to be able to spot them a mile away. They loiter around every dark corner of my casinos, their fingers sizzling with the need to stack some chips.

That's me in the corner.

She's my winning hand, my lucky dice, the millions that no matter how hard you gamble you can never quite grasp. And that's why I'm leaving. No matter how much I crave her, she isn't mine to have.

I open my eyes and focus them on a cluster of

planters across the yard. Mama adored her flowers and insisted on doing all the gardening work herself. When she died, Father didn't have the heart to get rid of her beloved plants, so he hired a full-time gardener. Mama had a particular fondness for yellow—I remember growing up in a sea of sunshine. She hated dark pink, and especially red. Said she saw enough of that whenever she stepped out of the house. I never really understood what she meant until after she died. Then everything looked red to me, and I quickly grew to detest it too.

This is what makes me look twice at a plant nestled in the center of the cluster. Its berries are white, which isn't unusual for this garden, but the stalks are the color of fresh blood. It looks eerie, the fruits resembling the eyes of small children. A shudder uncoils down my spine.

That's my sign.

It's time for me to go.

CHAPTER 26

*T*rilby

Sera clasps my hand beneath the table and gives it a squeeze. It drags my thoughts from where they seem to reside permanently in the master bedroom of Cristiano's apartment to the present. We're sitting on the terrace of what is about to become my home, and it doesn't feel real.

Living with my fiancé before we've wed is unconventional, but no one is going to argue with New York's deadliest don. Still, Allegra doesn't like the thought of me being thrown headfirst into this world without some sort of support, so she's sent Sera to keep me company. And on evenings like this, where I'm expected to dine with Savero and his top capos, I'm so grateful for her.

I squeeze Sera's fingers beneath the table and dip

my head. "Thanks for coming. I'm sorry you're missing out on the college trip. I know you've been looking forward to it."

"Don't worry." Her small smile doesn't convince me. "There'll be other opportunities to meet top hoteliers. And with Savero's connections, I might even secure some good positions where I can train while I work. Maybe I'll get to do an internship in the Hamptons. I've always wanted to go there."

Guilt gets the better of me. "Hey, you know, I could try to talk to Savero now . . ." My voice tapers off, because even now, that feels like a stretch of the imagination. Despite living in his house, I haven't seen him around much, let alone had a chance to talk to him.

"You don't have to do that," Sera says quietly. "Give it time. You have enough to be worrying about with the wedding in only a few days."

At the word "wedding," I glance across the table at Savero. Apart from a brief exchange of greetings when we sat down to eat, he hasn't looked at me once. Then again, I'm not sure I'd know if he had; his gaze doesn't leave the same burn on my skin as his brother's.

My eyes travel to his side, to the empty chair where I expect Cristiano would normally sit, and my chest aches. He would have pushed it back to accommodate his long legs, and he'd be resting his head back, looking down at everyone, rubbing his jaw in thought. I imagine his upper body lounging casually like he has nothing to prove.

I force myself to blink and immediately feel

anxious. Savero is watching me, and the look on his face isn't pleasant. In fact, it's almost hostile. I smile nervously and focus my attention on my plate of largely uneaten food.

"Penelope's going to kill you," Sera says as I push a piece of fish around with my fork. "She's had to take the dress down three sizes already. I know this is a big deal, marrying the don, but you can't starve yourself. You'll be a bag of skin and bones before you know it."

"I'm not starving myself." I pop a small piece of fish into my mouth and chew to prove it. Swallowing it, however, isn't easy.

Sera's brows dart up her forehead. "Whatever you say."

We spend the next thirty minutes chatting about small matters that are mostly insignificant, designed to make us feel like normal, law-abiding US citizens and not a soon-to-be ordained part of New York's criminal underworld. We talk about Sera's tourism and hospitality gig, Bambi's summer work at the local kindergarten, and Tess's dance recital.

"Allegra is still dining out on the fact Savero's brother asked her for the recipe for her spaghetti." Sera giggles lightly, but the sudden thought of Cristiano makes my skin heat.

I lay my fork delicately on the plate and dab the corners of mouth with a napkin that may as well be a shield.

"Where is he anyway? He's usually only a couple steps away from you."

I swallow and try to calm the chaos that erupts in my stomach. There's something wrong with me. How can the mere mention of a person make me physically incapable of functioning like a calm and normal human being?

I shrug and hope it comes off as genuinely nonchalant. "I don't know. He's leaving anyway." I reach for my untouched wineglass, Cristiano's warning still reverberating around my head, and take a long sip.

I force myself to believe his warning means nothing. I'm not important enough for him to stick around for, so how can I be important enough for him to truly care whether I have an alcoholic drink or not? My head instantly softens, and I take another sip.

"I still can't understand why he'd leave so soon after the wedding and abandon his brother to run the business alone. Shouldn't he be an underboss or something? I'm sure that's what his father would have wanted . . ."

I lower my voice, and it inadvertently comes out as a hiss. "Sera, I said I don't know, okay?" I lift the glass to my lips and finish it off.

A thin line appears across Sera's forehead as her eyes follow the disappearing wine.

"Okay," she says, but she's unconvinced. "I just find it strange. I mean, being head of the Di Santo family . . . there's no more powerful a position. Running a few casinos certainly doesn't compare, if you ask me. And he's spent so much time with you . . . It's not fair that he's invested time in getting to know you—his new sister-in-law—to then drop you all to go back to the other side of the country. Does he have a girlfriend over there?"

A knife twists in my gut. The thought of Cristiano seeing someone else is physically devastating.

She ploughs on, oblivious to my discomfort. "There must be a good reason he wants to be somewhere else. I can't imagine Savero will be happy about his brother moving away so soon after his father's passing and his own wedding . . ."

I bite back a glare. "Sera, the man barely speaks to me. I don't even know his favorite movie, let alone what he thinks about his brother moving back to Vegas. Can we please drop the subject?" I lift my glass again and briefly notice it's been refilled by a discreet waiter.

Sera watches me drink back half of it with narrowed eyes. "I'm just trying to understand. Your fiancé's brother follows you around town for three weeks, dragging you out of bars and parties, holing you up in his apartment and rescuing you from murder scenes, but your fiancé hasn't deigned to speak to you yet?"

I gulp back the rest of the wine. "Yes," I snap. "You got it pretty damn straight."

Sera looks away, flicking her gaze briefly across to Savero, who's deep in conversation with Nicolò. Her hand finds mine again beneath the table. "I'm so sorry, Tril," she whispers.

I breathe out a long sigh. "It's okay."

She continues to look across the table, but at nothing in particular.

"Hey." I draw her face toward me. "It's okay. Really. I'm going to be fine."

One small tear collects in a corner of her eye. At least I think it's one—the wine has very quickly made my vision fuzzy.

I turn my body toward her and take both of her hands. "I'm doing this for Papa—for all of us. It's my duty, and I've made peace with it. Please don't make it any harder."

"But . . ." She leans in toward me. "You'll be in this house all the time, on your own, probably. Won't you be lonely?"

The tear trickles down her cheek, and I wipe it away with a thumb and smile. "No. Soon I'll have children. I'm sure they'll keep me busy. And until then, I have you and Tess and Bambi, and Papa and Allegra. I'll be able to have visitors whenever I like."

I don't know if it's true, but I need to tell this to myself as well as Sera, otherwise I won't have the strength to drag myself down that aisle in a few days.

I settle back in my chair and reach again for my wine. When I bring it to my lips, I almost spit it out. Forcing down the bland liquid, I lift the glass to the light and study it. There's no golden hue as the candlelight flickers through it.

Someone has filled it with water.

As I lower the glass, my eyes catch on a glare that makes my bones weaken. Sitting across the table from me, in his rightful place next to Savero, with a look on his face that could *kill*, is Cristiano.

$\mathcal{T}$rilby

I hold his stare for longer than I should, feeling an irrational anger bubbling up in my chest. Sera is right. Why has he been the one who's followed me around, protected me from danger, laid down rules, and taken me to breakfast? Why him and not Savero?

I shake my head as his eyes catch on the crystal comb I'm wearing in my hair.

It's all his fault. Because of Cristiano Di Santo, I feel completely at sea. I'm not in control anymore.

Since he stalked into my life, I haven't been able to think straight. Because of his insistence on "keeping an eye on me," I've formed an attachment to him. Part of me depends on him, and he knows it. And now he's going to tear that away, because sticking around is uncomfortable for *him*.

The low chatter around the table slowly grinds to a halt, and I realize too late that everyone is staring at us staring at each other. I glance left to Savero, and a shiver of fright freezes my spine. His head is turned, and his eyes flick between me and his brother. His brother who's still *glaring* at me as if I just murdered his firstborn.

My head feels too light, and it isn't from the alcohol. If Savero suspects there's anything between Cristiano and me—anything that goes beyond a brotherly sense of duty—God knows what he'll do. I didn't miss the blood on his hands when he arrived which he calmly washed off in the ornamental fountain near the head of the table. And I will never forget the way he sliced open a human torso as emotionless as if it were prosciutto.

I've never had to worry about it much before now, because he hasn't been around to see the way his brother looks at me, or the way I dissolve into a hot mess whenever Cristiano's near.

My heart is racing. Even if he doesn't add me to his kill list, I can't afford for this marriage to not go ahead. I need Savero, because my father needs Savero. If we don't have him on our side, if we don't keep this amicable, we'll lose the port and everything my father has worked for.

I suddenly need air, and I'm not going to get it sitting at this table under the oppressive eyeballing of the Di Santo mob.

"I'll be right back," I whisper to Sera. She's staring at me, but her mind is elsewhere. She's unaware my world has tilted on its axis and is hovering precariously on the edge of collapse.

I place my napkin on the table and stand. Then, without a backward glance, I walk back inside the house.

I don't know where I'm going—I just need to get away. I need to get my thoughts together. What if Savero questions me about my relationship with his brother? How can I explain without revealing too much or blushing?

I walk through the house from the back to the entrance hall. The grand driveway is illuminated white by the sun, but I hardly register it. I step outside the bulletproof doors and walk across the lawn to the pavilion. The stone seat is cool under the shade of the canopy, and I welcome the fresh temperature against my burning skin.

I lower my body and sink my head into my hands. Just a few minutes, then I'll head back. Hopefully, the atmosphere will have thawed some, and Cristiano will have found something else to glare at.

"You defied me."

I look up, almost jumping out of my skin. A small sense of relief seeps through me at the sight of Cristiano, not Savero. But the sharpness in his tone feels bitter and distant.

"What are you doing out here?" I whisper. Low-level panic makes me turn left and right to check no one is watching.

"Answer me, Castellano."

I grip the seat on either side of my legs. "Oh, we're back to using my last name, are we?"

I shouldn't complain. We should be doing everything we can to reverse what happened, and that includes him not calling me by my given name as if it's his to keep.

He steps forward, his gaze brimming with warning.

"You didn't ask me a question," I point out.

"Don't mess with me. I told you expressly not to drink alcohol again. You can't handle it—it makes you behave irresponsibly."

"What does it matter anyway?" My heart thunders at the sight of him; at the debilitating grief I feel at the thought of him leaving. I stand with my fists balled at my sides. "You won't be around to watch me make a fool of myself, *Di Santo*."

His teeth mash together, and a growl leaves his throat. He grips the nape of my neck hard and pulls me up off the seat and toward him until our breaths brush each other. "Call me by my name," he whispers hoarsely.

I can't help it. "Cristiano," I gasp. "Call me by *mine*."

His gaze drops to my lips, and a full-body shiver coasts from my head to my toes. Then his eyes flick upward, giving me a glimpse of the darkness behind them. "Trilby." His voice breaks. "God help me," he groans, then he puts his hand to the back of my head and pulls me onto his lips.

Relief floods through my bones and softens my muscles. I melt into him.

His mouth forces mine open, and he licks at my tongue with a wild hunger. When I attach myself to him, his hands release my neck and cover my face. Fingers push through my hair and trace an impatient line from my nape to my sit bone. I wriggle restlessly under his touch, and he breathes desperate-sounding Italian curses into my mouth.

He falls back onto the seat, pulling me with him, and my knees come to rest on either side of his thighs. He reaches up to my hair again, mussing it up the way he seems to like, and tugs it while plundering my mouth.

My heart races, the fear of getting caught hovering on the periphery of my consciousness.

He lifts my dress so my underwear is pressed against his pants. Then he pulls me onto his erection and swallows my moan.

My head swims as he stops kissing me to hold my face between his hands. "I need to feel you against me. Skin to skin. Just one last time." His eyes are filled with a deep desperation, and I nod, because in this moment, I'll give him anything.

He releases one hand and drops it to his zipper. The sound of it lowering echoes around the pavilion, and I scan the garden again, terrified someone might have followed one of us out here. When I turn back to Cristiano, my eyes almost pop out of my head. He's released his cock from his pants and is running his fist up and down it.

"Come here."

He slides his hands beneath my ass and lifts me until I'm sitting on his cock, which is laid flat against his stomach. The second my pussy wraps around him, I collapse into his shoulder. He releases a moan that sets my soul on fire. God, it feels like every last thing I need in the world.

My entire body throbs with anticipation, and when he places his hands firmly on my hips, I inhale a breath. He moves me softly, until my whole body sings with desire. His head drops back against the stone wall, and his eyelids flutter shut.

He's hard and soft, feverish and freezing, off-limits yet impossible to resist.

He grips my hips and moves me slowly up and down, the friction making me see stars.

I no longer care that we're in my fiancé's garden and that anyone could walk out of the front door and see us. We haven't even had the sense to hide around the back of the pavilion; we're inside of it, on the balcony, on show to anyone who might walk past.

He places his palm over my mouth, making me realize I've been moaning recklessly.

Neither of us speak, because it feels just so . . . damn . . . good.

I'm racing toward an orgasm and picking up speed. I press down harder, feeling the ridges of his cock as they roll beneath me. Even though I can feel the climax getting closer, I have the sudden realization it won't be enough. It will never be enough.

I want him inside me deeply.

The thought should terrify me. I'm a virgin. No one has broken my walls down, and they've been promised to the most dangerous man on the east coast of America.

But then . . . Cristiano.

I trust him. I *need* him.

I want it to be him.

My hips still, and I pull back to stare into his eyes.

His lids lift and his gaze locks onto mine.

I press my palm to his cheek and suck my bottom lip between my teeth. His cock swells beneath me as I try to communicate what I need without saying a word.

His eyes narrow for the beat of a second. It's a question.

I nod slowly.

Then his large hands are beneath my arms, and I'm being carried across the pavilion to the back. He spins around and rams me up against the wall, where he holds the back of my neck tight and silences me with his tongue. His other hand draws my knee upward and hooks it over his forearm before he lifts me up the wall. It all happens so fast. And I want it.

I want it *all*.

With neither of his hands free to guide it, the crown of his cock searches for my pussy, driving me mad with anticipation. When it finds my opening, our mouths pull apart, and we both look down at where our bodies are about to join.

Our breaths are deep and desperate, our chests rising

and falling in tandem. He curls his tailbone and pushes his cock up by an inch. A breathy cry leaves my lips. It doesn't hurt, but the pure shock of having a forbidden part of him inside of me is incredible.

My forehead rests on his, and I inhale the steam rising off his shoulders. "Do it," I command. "I want it to be *you*."

He shakes his head slowly, and I'm suddenly terrified he's going to back out.

My words trip over themselves. "I don't care if it hurts. I just want to feel you. All of you." I dip my head and lick my tongue across his lips.

An unbearable few seconds of silence pass before he grinds out his final resolve. "You're mine, little one."

Then he drops me.

His cock slices through my hymen in one fell swoop that steals every ounce of breath from my lungs. I feel like I'm being ripped apart and stretched outward, fit to burst.

"Oh fuck," I pant. "Fuck, fuck, *fuck*."

"Trilby . . . are you okay? Tell me you're okay." The words come out fast and urgent as his kisses decorate my face.

I nod, because even though I'm in unadulterated agony, I'm okay. "I want you . . . to do . . . one more thing . . . for me," I say through short gasps.

"Anything," he replies between tender licks and kisses.

"Come inside me."

He stops. "Trilby, I—"

"I just had my period," I say hurriedly. "I know how it works. Please . . ."

He grips my face again, but with a gentleness that softens me around him. Then he presses his lips to mine and starts to move. At first it feels as if someone's running a razor blade up and down my soft virgin walls, but as I loosen and relax I begin to sense something else. He was right about me feeling him in my stomach, but what he didn't say was that I'd feel him *everywhere*.

I loosen around him, and he moves slowly in and out. Every now and then a low growl passes from his lips to mine, along with whispers of praise.

"You're such a good fucking girl, Trilby. You feel like *heaven*. I can't get enough of you. You take all of me so well."

That last one has me moaning too, and he laps up the sound with his tongue. I'm too far gone to kiss with any sense of order or decorum, so I let him take control. He nibbles my lips and tastes every inch of my mouth and tongue as he thrusts long, deep, and slow into my core.

He fucks with his whole body, as though it's as easy and natural as breathing.

I've never done this before, but somehow I know sex isn't always like this, which makes this one-time slip so delectably bittersweet.

"You're getting so tight," he murmurs, then he thrusts a little harder. "*Un.* Fuck, you feel so damn good."

I lost the power of speech a little while ago, but my shortened, gasping breaths communicate everything I feel.

He frees my mouth and drags hot, wet lips down the side of my throat to the sensitive skin where my neck meets my shoulder, and there he straight up makes out with my collarbone. His rhythm doesn't break.

When his teeth sink into the neckline of my dress and drag it down over my chest, my gasps become louder no matter how hard I try to contain them.

His tone is urgent. "Bite down on your fist," he demands.

I do as he says, almost feeling a little stupid. My fist is the last thing I want in my mouth right now.

But then I understand.

He dips his scorching tongue into my bra and flicks my right nipple out into the warm summer air. He sucks it into his mouth, along with half of my swollen, aching breast, and devours it.

I thank God my fist is in my mouth as I bite down hard. With the relentless thrusting into the center of my core and the cannibalistic plundering of my breast, I can't contain a sound—I just have to plug it.

He moans as he sucks, sending zaps of fire down my spine, and growls as he lets the nipple pop out before moving to the left. I'm delirious. I need to let go, but I don't know how.

"Cristiano," I whimper.

He swirls his tongue around the circumference of my breast one last time and then looks up at me with dark eyes. "You are the sexiest thing I've ever seen," he whispers huskily. "Even more so when you're coming undone." He works a hand between us and presses his thumb on my clit while he thrusts faster.

"Oh *God*, Cristiano . . ."

"Trilby . . . Fuck, you feel so good."

"I love it when you say my name." I gasp through the words.

"Then I'll say it every day until I die."

My head falls into the crook of his neck, and he thrusts firmly, repeatedly. I can feel something building, but it isn't coming from where that kind of release came from before. It's coming from *inside* of me. Whatever he's doing, it's dissecting me limb from limb.

"Oh!"

"Fuck, Trilby, that's your spot, isn't it?"

I can't speak.

He does something with his ass that I can't even describe, and suddenly, everything implodes.

I bite down on my hand and grip his firm body everywhere that I can.

"Un, un, fuck, un."

The sound of him losing control is like a symphony to my ears. My free hand has curled around his nape, which is now slippery with sweat, and my back is bouncing against the pillar.

And I'm rolling.

Dear *God*.

"Trilby . . ." His voice is breathless. "Oh God, fuck,

I'm coming." He jerks forcefully and bites into my shoulder.

I feel his roar in my bones.

Then he comes.

And for the first time in my life, I smile around the curl of my fist.

CHAPTER 28

Cristiano

I jerk into her soft body, pumping so much of myself into her I feel dizzy. My lips are pressed to her cheek. Slowly, she frees her knuckles from between her teeth and then sobs. It's only a hiccup, but it draws my heart up my throat.

I put my palms to her face and lick a tear from her cheek. "Are you okay?" I whisper.

She pins her lips together and nods, then I let her bury her face in my neck.

I gently lower her feet to the ground and hold her steady as she lets it all out. "Shh, Trilby. I've got you." I hold her close and match my breaths to hers.

A few seconds after her sobs subside, she lifts her head, and I almost drown in her damp lashes. She licks her lips and peers up at me.

"That was incredible," she says in a gentle voice.

"*You* are incredible," I say, dropping a kiss on her nose. There's more I want to say. So much more. But it would be meaningless, because I have to leave. Not just because I have business to get back to, or because I feel indebted to a brother who only begrudgingly saved my life, but because I now worry what he might do to his new wife if he gets even a hint that I want her for myself.

I drop my gaze to her thighs and see the streaks of red mixed with my cum sliding down the length of her legs. Without a second thought, I rip off my shirt and get to my knees.

She gasps in shock and sobs behind a clamped hand.

I clean her up with single-minded focus, using my fresh white shirt to mop up every drop of blood until she's perfectly clean, then I press kisses to the flesh between her legs, silently thanking her for trusting me to be the first one to go there.

A shard of grief rips through me when I remember I won't be her last or her only, and I stagger to my feet, shoving the soiled shirt into my back pocket. When I lift my gaze, hers is on the gun tucked into my waistband.

"I'm not going to stay for the wedding," I say. My chest tightens until I can barely breathe.

She looks back at me thoughtfully, then she nods. "I'm glad it was you," she whispers.

I drop a kiss on her lips. "So am I. But I don't deserve it."

She smiles sadly and shrugs. "It was always yours."

I inhale deeply and pull a pen out of my pocket. "May I?"

She gazes back at me confused, but she nods anyway.

I push the neckline of her dress to one side and write out my cell number on her right breast, where it will be hidden from everyone but her. "If you need anything— anything *at all*—you call me." My voice cracks. "Do you understand?"

She swallows loudly. "Yes."

I place my hands on her shoulders and dip my head so she can't avoid the seriousness of my stare. "Your safety is the most important thing in the world to me."

Her bottom lip quivers.

"If you ever feel like you're in jeopardy, don't waste a second, all right? You call me."

She nods again, and I pull her close one last time.

"What about your shirt?" she asks eventually.

"I have a clean one in the car. Don't you worry about me. Just get back to the dinner. Say you got lost in the maze out back—it isn't unheard of."

She's about to pull away when I press my cheek to her ear. "I . . ."

For some reason the words won't trip off my tongue. I fucking love her. But I can't tell her. It wouldn't be fair to either of us. So I drop my voice to a low moan.

"I will never forget this."

Her eyes catch mine before she turns away. "Neither will I."

I feel Savero's eyes on me as I walk back to the table. Trilby is already back in her seat and talking animatedly with her sister. I made sure to leave it a good ten minutes before I returned, but Savero still eyes me with suspicion.

He turns his face from the table as I approach. "Anything I need to know about?" His voice is quiet, but his tone is severe.

"Just a work call. Things are getting heated though. I should probably head back sooner than planned."

His gaze is pointed when he looks up at me. "So what's keeping you?"

I blink. "Nothing."

His glare doesn't falter. It's as though I'm looking back at a plastic figurine. Something in his manner has darkened since Father died, and it reminds me of the child he used to be. He can sense there's something I'm not telling him.

"My bags are all packed. If I leave tomorrow afternoon, I can be back at my desk first thing Monday."

He arches a brow.

I rest a hand on his shoulder, and his gaze tracks it like it's a foreign object. "You know where I am if you need me," I say, now suspecting I'm the last person he'd contact if he needed anything.

His gaze pans back to mine, and there's a calculating

look in his eyes. "Drop in before you go. I'd like to say goodbye without all *this* around." He flicks his hand in the general direction of the table.

"Sure." I nod. "I'll come by on my way out of town."

He watches me carefully as I say goodbye to the two capos seated either side of him. As much as I want to, I don't let my gaze flicker to the girls across the table. I leave the terrace without looking back once.

I walk around the outer edge of the house, not wanting to be reminded of where I was just thirty minutes ago, with Trilby Castellano riding my lap. It's taking all my energy just to leave her behind. It feels wrong. All of it. I know all the reasons why, but there's something else too. A feeling I just can't put my finger on.

I slam into a small figure, knocking them back into the side of the house.

"What the f—" I recognize the man. It's J. W. Ranch, Father's head gardener. I'm amazed he's still alive—he must be about ninety years old.

"Mr. Di Santo, I'm so sorry. I didn't mean to get in your way. I—"

"Nonsense, Ranch. That was my fault. I wasn't looking where I was going." I reach out to guide him back onto the path. "Are you okay? Are you hurt?"

"No, no, sir. I'm fine."

His skin is weathered and his limbs all bone and hardly any flesh, but his manner is still spritely, and I bet his mind is as sharp as a spear.

"Ranch, I've been meaning to ask . . ."

He looks up at me eagerly. "Yes, sir?"

"There's a plant at the front of the house. I've never seen anything like it before. Mama always wanted yellow flowers, but these have dark red stalks. I've been wondering what it is."

A shadow falls across his face. "I know exactly which plant you mean." He starts walking toward the front, and I follow.

He stops by the terracotta pot where the eerie-looking berries sprout out of the blood-red stalks.

"They look like eyes," I say.

"Yes, they call this 'doll's eyes.'" I notice he doesn't bend down to lovingly stroke the fruits like I've seen him do with most other plants and flowers.

"I can see why. Who put it here?"

"Truthfully, sir . . ." He shrugs apologetically. "I don't know. It appeared here one morning about six months ago. The late Mr. Di Santo knew nothing of it, but I'm afraid he was too preoccupied with business to give it much thought."

"Let's get rid of it," I say, knowing Mama would be turning in her grave at its sheer creepiness.

"I did try, sir." Ranch looks at the floor, and it draws my brows together. "Mr. Savero Di Santo told me not to bother with such small matters. He wanted me to dig out a new pond, you see. Over there."

I follow where his finger is pointing, and sure enough, there's a new pond in the middle of one of the lawns.

"I'm sure Mr. Di Santo will want it removed when he has children though." Ranch says this casually, as if my chest didn't just harden like drying concrete.

"Why?"

"This is one of the most dangerous plants in North America, sir. It's said that the berries taste real sweet, but they're deadly."

I force back a shudder and repeat my instruction.

"Get rid of it, Ranch. And make it a priority."

He nods and backs away. "Yes, sir."

Instead of heading straight back to my apartment, I drive around the coast and head north. There's someone I want to see before I leave this place behind.

I pull up to an entrance and peer into the camera. Within seconds the gates swing open, and I drive past the security guards, eventually parking up outside a redbrick house.

The front door opens, and a thick-built man with graying hair and errant eyebrows opens his arms.

"Cristiano, my boy. I thought you were never coming."

I grin as I approach and let him clasp my face, planting three kisses on my cheeks.

"*Zio*," I say, smiling. "It's good to see you."

Augie Zanotti isn't really my uncle, but he's as good as family.

"You too, my boy. How long are you home for?"

I follow him into the house. "I'm leaving today. I just wanted to pay my respects before I go."

He turns to me with a frown. "You're not staying?"

"No. That was never the plan, *Zio*. Savero has everything under control, and I have businesses to get back to."

He stops mid-stride and pins me with a serious look. "You think Savero has everything under control?"

I shrug. "Yes. Why?"

Augie's eyes narrow. "Who's his underboss?"

"Nicolò. He's a good capo."

"Not good enough."

I'm surprised at the roughness of his tone.

"What about you?" I ask. "We haven't seen you around since Father died."

"No . . ." He turns and continues walking, and I follow him into the living room. He waves a finger at a servant before we both sit. "Your father and I agreed I would continue as underboss, but only if . . ."

His pause makes me look up.

"Only if what?"

"If you were to succeed him as don."

I blink, confused. "That would never happen. I'm the second son—that was never my destiny."

Augie closes his eyes and pinches the bridge of his nose. "It would have been, if Gianni had moved faster."

"I'm not following."

Augie sighs and lifts his gaze. He looks suddenly

tired. "Your father wanted *you* to succeed him, Cristiano, not your brother."

My head thumps as if it's in a vise. "What? Why?"

"He didn't think Savero was ready to lead."

I shake my head slowly. "He's far more ready to lead than I am. I'm not involved in the family anymore. And Father permitted that."

"And he regretted that decision till the day he died."

I swallow. "He didn't say any of this to me. How do I know you're telling the truth?"

Augie stands, and his arms flop by his sides. "He wanted to show Savero the respect of having this conversation with the two of you, but it wasn't easy getting you both together. Why would I lie about this, Cristiano? Why would I lie to you? You're like a son to me."

I frown. "And Savero isn't?"

Augie rolls his eyes and then settles them back on me. "You know as well as I do that Savero was never an easy boy. He gave your father a lot of trouble. He didn't like how close I was to Gianni either. He could be a calculating son of a bitch sometimes, you know."

"No, I don't."

"You don't remember him slashing my tires so I couldn't visit my mama in the hospital? You don't remember him putting bullets into two of my soldiers? Blowing up the laundromat? Those were things he did to spite *me*, Cristiano, all because I took his father's attention away from him a few too many times." He sighs as the servant returns with a pot of coffee and some fresh water.

A distant memory prods at my mind: Savero at twelve years old, his back pressed against the boating shed, with the barrel of a gun aimed at his forehead. It's an image I've recalled many times, usually in the haunting depths of sleep, but I can never see the person holding the gun. This time, as Augie keeps talking, I trace the arm holding the gun. It looks familiar. It's an arm that held me often as a child; a hand that shook mine as I became a man.

I shake the vision away. It's almost twenty years old. Unreliable.

It couldn't have been Father.

Especially after Savero saved me from drowning.

My brother may not be the most likeable or honorable made man in this city, and he may not like me, but I owe my life to him.

"You were never like that," Augie continues. "You accepted things as they were. You understood this world at a young age. You were unemotional, logical, sensible. Savero is hotheaded, irrational . . . He has a temper he simply can't control. He's a loose cannon, and in this world, that is a dangerous thing indeed."

A thought makes my stomach reel. "Did Savero know this was Father's plan?"

"No. God no." Augie, rightly, looks horrified by the prospect. I can't think of a single thing more painful than to hear you're not considered fit for the role you were born for.

"What was Father going to do?"

"He was planning to talk to you both on his sixtieth birthday." Augie shakes his head again. "You know how your mama always said she wanted at least one of you to . . ."

". . . live past the age of sixty," I finish. "Yes. That's why I chose to leave."

"Your papa never made it that far."

"I know. It was a shock to us all," I say. "I still can't believe he died of a heart attack. He was fit and healthy." A thought occurs to me. "The autopsy . . ."

Augie presses his lips together and nods. "I insisted Savero show me the report, but it was all there in black and white. Cardiac failure," he says with a sigh. "It really was down to his heart."

I pick up a glass of water and drink it down in one go. The summer heat is getting to me more than usual.

"I wouldn't have accepted the job anyway," I say, standing to button up my jacket. It's time for me to go before the thought burrows itself any deeper. "I don't want to be don any more than my brother wants to be anything else. I couldn't take that away from him."

Augie stands. "You're leaving already?"

I sigh heavily. "There's nothing for me to stay for." The lie settles uneasily in the pit of my stomach.

"Please think about it. It's what your father wanted." There's a grave note in his tone.

"There's no need," I say with finality. "I could never do that to Savero."

Then I turn to leave, and though Augie's gaze tugs at me like a rope, he doesn't stop me.

CHAPTER 29

Trilby

Sera looks up, and a shadow falls over her face. I follow her gaze, craning my neck upward.

"Savero," I say with a forced smile.

I hate how timid my voice is with him. I wonder if I'd still sound this way if I weren't so petrified he might see through to my true feelings.

"You can leave."

My heart leaps into my throat. *He knows.*

Then his gaze flicks briefly to my sister. "I will take Trilby back to her rooms."

He wasn't speaking to me. My pulse thrums in relief but is now fueled by the fear of being left alone with him.

"Um . . ." Sera glances at me. "Okay."

Savero stares at her with a hard look. Then, in a split

second, he smiles. It's sharp and disarming. "I'm going to look after her, don't worry. I'll be the perfect gentleman. After all, I'm not just marrying this beautiful girl here . . ."

Sera swoons a little, making me want to vomit.

"I'm marrying into your family. I want to make the best impression I can."

"Of course, yes," she replies sweetly. She pushes back her seat and stands, ignoring my panicked glare.

I don't want to be left alone with him.

"Trilby, shall we?" He holds out an arm. It's thinner than Cristiano's, and his veins are more prominent beneath the purpling ink.

I take it even though every nerve in my body screams at me not to. I can't shake the fact I'm positively repelled by my future husband. I hate what he's doing to my family. I cannot stomach the way he treats death so theatrically. And now I know how it feels to fall hard for someone else, to be touched at the core by a man who truly wants me, I couldn't be more against the idea of marrying him.

Sera shoots me a wary smile. "I'll call you later."

I feel a small measure of relief in those words. They mean she's going to check in.

My nerves are prickling with anxiety. He *could* do anything to me, and my father wouldn't be able to back out of the arrangement—not unless he was prepared to lose our legacy and an unhealthy number of lives.

Cristiano's number burns a hole into my skin. I can only hope Savero is as traditional as I've been led to believe and that he won't try to get a sneaky pre-wedding glimpse at the goods he's purchasing. If he saw his brother's number written across my breast, he would kill us both.

We pass the library and the lounge, and as we reach the entrance hall, my heart ratchets up a notch. The staircase looks shorter than usual, and Savero's grip around my arm is tight as he walks me up each step. My head starts to tingle when we turn left and head toward my rooms in the east wing.

I glance sideways at his face. It's set like stone, his lips a thin, downturned line and his eyes hooded by a long, furrowed brow.

The lights along the corridor are spaced farther apart than elsewhere in the house, making it appear darker. I find myself hoping for witnesses in the shadows—not that anyone would stand up in a court against Savero Di Santo.

We reach the door to my rooms, and I hold my breath. My heart is racing, because I don't know why he's walked me this far or what he's planning to do next.

He tugs me backward and then *shoves* me into the wall. It's so unexpected my head slams back against the coving, disorienting me.

His face cuts through my blurred vision. "Do you have something to tell me?"

"What?" My heart is thundering so hard I'm sure he can hear it. "Savero, what are you talking about?"

"My brother," he hisses. "The two of you seem . . .

close. Closer than a woman should be to her brother-in-law."

Oh . . . *fuck*.

My legs tremble, making my teeth chatter. "Savero, you're scaring me."

He continues talking as if I haven't just confessed to being terrified of my own fiancé.

"It wouldn't do to have a wife who only has eyes for my brother," he seethes. His gaze is pinned to the wall above my head, but his lips move close to my own, each word tasting bitter as it falls across my face. "*I* am the don of this family, of this city, *not him*. Do you understand?"

"I-I . . ." *What?* "Of course I understand. I'm marrying *you*, Savero. I *want* to marry you." I inhale deeply and then breathe out every doubt I have about my ability to lie, because I cannot fail now.

Savero could end me right here if he chose to, and as the thinly veiled rage pulses beneath his skin, I wouldn't put it past him.

"I can't *wait* to marry you, Savero. I want to be your wife. It's all I want—for our families to be joined. I want the shipping business and your businesses to be the success you and my father want them to be. I wouldn't dream of standing in the way of that. You must believe me."

The words scratch my throat, but I chase them with a look of desperation, like I want this marriage more than anything in the world.

"Please don't doubt me, Savero. It would break my heart."

He lowers his gaze, but it disappears into the shadows, making me shudder.

"You're not attracted to my brother?" His voice is low, challenging me.

I force my head to shake firmly. "No, I am not."

"We'll see soon enough."

My heart races. "What?"

"He's stopping by tomorrow on his way back to Vegas, and I will be watching you. Both of you." He leans in close so his lips brush against my cheek.

I fight every urge to move away, because it doesn't feel warm or friendly; it feels hostile.

"And if I can be convinced of your loyalty to me— the *don*—I will break you in softly."

My breath catches in my throat. I've already been broken in, merely a few hours ago, and I can feel the aftereffects still. We'll be married by the time he *thinks* he's taking my virginity, so the deal with my father will have been sealed, and hopefully he won't care.

One look at his devious eyes tells me that's wishful thinking. Of course he'll care. His ego and pride will demand it. I need to come up with a way to convince him I'm still a virgin on our wedding night, and fast.

And that's only if I manage to convince him I'm not in deep with his brother first.

I want to ask what will happen if I can't convince him, but I already know the answer.

CHAPTER 30

*C*ristiano

My footsteps are quiet as I walk through the hallways, and I take advantage of the silence to search for any sound of Trilby's voice. She lives here now. In my childhood home. With a brother I hardly know anymore.

I notice the doll's eyes plant has been disposed of, as per my instructions. At least no future nieces or nephews will be at risk of plant poisoning. That's something to feel thankful for.

There's no sign of life anywhere. Even the staff seem to have disappeared. I round the corner to the terrace and see Savero sitting alone, looking out over the ocean. Not only are there no servants present, but there are no soldiers and no capos either.

I walk around my brother and join him in admiring the view. "Where is everyone?"

"The staff have got their work cut out preparing for the wedding reception, so I gave them a half-day."

"And Nicolò? Beppe?"

"There are some issues with the union. I sent them down there to clear up."

"Both of them?"

Savero looks sideways at me. "They're pretty big issues."

I nod instead of probing further. He doesn't want me involved in this business—he's made that quite clear.

"Come." He stands abruptly. "I told Trilby we'd meet her in the kitchen. I know she'd like to see you before you go."

Something slams against the inner wall of my chest, almost taking my breath away. I close my eyes against the sensation of her unraveling in my arms, the sound of her screaming around her fist as I not only broke her in on these very grounds but gave my little one her first penetrative orgasm. It will be etched onto my brain for eternity.

"Sure." I fake nonchalance and follow him back inside.

There's something about his manner that doesn't sit right. I feel as though I'm being set up, much as that doesn't make any sense.

We walk into the kitchen, and my gaze searches for her. I don't have to look hard—she's standing at the end of the kitchen island as if she's waiting for us. She shifts from one foot to the other, her eyes lifting to mine and then darting away quickly.

I walk around the island and avoid her gaze as I graze a kiss across her cheek. "Trilby. Looking lovely as always. How are you?"

Her chest rises with a deep inhale, and her lips set into a thin smile. "I'm great, thank you. And you?"

"I'm doing good." I walk back to the other side of the island to put some distance between us. "Just stopped in to say goodbye. I'm sorry I'll miss your wedding."

She swallows, and I notice the outer edges of her eyes are red. She's either been crying or she hasn't slept.

"That's okay. We understand." She glances nervously at Savero, who has his arms folded, watching us both. She pans back to me. "I'm sorry, I'm forgetting my manners. Would you like a drink?"

"Just water's fine," I say. I'm not thirsty, but I could use something to occupy my fingers, otherwise I'm just going to stand here cracking my knuckles.

Savero hands me a glass and pours out two more for him and Trilby.

"No Dolly Parton mug?" I ask, wiping the smirk off my face with a thumb.

Instead of sharing in the joke, Trilby looks alarmed. Her gaze flits between me and my brother.

"So, what are your plans after the wedding?" I don't ask because I want to know—I'd rather poke out my eyeballs than torture myself with images that could haunt me for the rest of my life—but because it's what a brother would do.

Trilby looks to Savero for help, and I wonder if they've even discussed life beyond the wedding.

"I have to go to Mexico," Savero says with a shrug. "We have a meeting with some associates from the cartel."

Trilby looks down at her hands.

"Depending on when I get back, we might go to Rome for a couple days."

"Rome." I nod slowly.

Trilby looks up at us both through sweeping lashes. "Nice."

"Yeah. It's about time I dropped in on some of the family."

We don't have any immediate family in Rome, so I assume he means the "family" we work with when it's mutually convenient to. And it's usually Cosa Nostra-flavored.

"That'll be fun."

Savero's gaze drops to my glass, then he tips his back and places it on the counter, empty. "I hear you paid Augusto a visit." He wipes a hand across his mouth.

"Yeah. Thought it strange he hadn't been around since Father died."

"He's not my biggest fan." Savero's lip curls. "That's why he hasn't been around."

I'm now certain I'm being tested. I get a fleeting sense of discomfort at the thought he might know what Father's plan was. But no, it isn't possible. Father took his plan to his grave, and Augie was so loyal to Father he would die too to keep that quiet.

"It's not like you need him. You have Nicolò, Beppe, Benny . . . And Donato is a good capo too. Some good guys have stuck around."

The corner of his mouth ticks up slightly. "Oh, I'm not worried."

I raise the glass to my lips, then a thought occurs to me. "You know, I've been thinking a lot about that time you saved me from drowning."

A flicker of something passes over his expression.

"Something Tony Castellano said to me, actually."

Trilby's gaze flitters over me.

"You'd have needed one hell of a sharp knife to cut the boat rope my leg was tangled up in. What did you use?"

He blinks in slow motion before answering smoothly. "I used the penknife Nonni kept in the hold. We'd been carving pictures into the wooden boards on the deck."

I don't remember carving pictures, but it sounds like something we'd do. Besides, it was a huge trauma to experience as a kid; I was never going to remember every detail.

"That was some quick thinking, *fratello*."

Trilby looks from me to Savero with one hand clasped inside her other.

He eyes me with suspicion. "So tell me, what did Augusto have to say?"

"Nothing." I shrug. "He just talked about Father. You know how close they were."

"Hmm. Too close sometimes." Savero tips his head back so he's looking down his nose at me.

"Why do you say that?"

"They were secretive. They kept things even from me."

He walks toward the window, and I move around the island to follow. With his back turned, I place my glass on the counter next to Trilby's and brush my fingers over hers as I pull away.

Just one last touch.

Her breath stutters, and a flame ignites in my belly at the contact.

"The connection between a don and his underboss has to be unbreakable—you know that. Hundreds of lives and billions of dollars are riding on it. They kept things from me too."

Sav stares out the window, his expression cold as he replies. "Even when I turned twenty-one, older than Father was when he became underboss, they still kept me in the dark. And don't think I wasn't aware of all the times Father begged you to reconsider your departure after Mama was killed."

I don't deny it. There's no point.

Savero speaks through gritted teeth. "He begged you more times than he *ever* confided in me."

"Why are you bringing this up now?" I rest my hands in my pockets, but I'm acutely aware of the gun I'm still carrying in my waistband and the trembling woman still standing at the kitchen island, listening. "Because I went to visit Augie? I've visited with him many times before now, and you've never had a problem with it."

"That was when Father was still alive and you were wedded to your life in Vegas."

I keep my heart rate steady as I answer. "What's different now?"

His head turns slowly in my direction. "You don't seem quite so keen to leave this time."

"I'm leaving now, aren't I?" I can almost feel Trilby's bones shaking. "I thought I was stopping by to bid farewell, not to get the Spanish Inquisition."

Savero spins suddenly and walks toward Trilby before stopping abruptly. She takes two steps back, away from the island. She looks fearful of him, which makes the hairs on my arms rise. *Has he done something to her?* That thought alone roots me to the ground. If I got even the faintest suggestion he'd raised a hand to her or threatened to, I don't think I could be held responsible for my actions.

Savero and I stand on either side of the island glaring at each other, and I wonder what happened to our brotherly bond. I don't remember the last time I felt it. I only remember feeling indebted. He once saved my life, which is why I still find the vision of Father holding him up at gunpoint at the side of the boat shed so disturbing.

"It's not the Spanish Inquisition." His smile is

sudden and not authentic. "I'm just curious to know what you discussed with Augusto."

I let my shoulders drop. "Nothing of importance." I narrow my eyes. "Is everything okay here?"

Savero rests a hand on the island, and I notice Father's ring glinting in the late-afternoon light. "Everything's fine," he says serenely. "Isn't it, Trilby?"

She jumps a little but covers it up quickly. "Yes, Savero."

My heart squeezes painfully, and I suddenly feel tired and parched. I reach for my water and knock it back.

"I have to go."

Trilby sucks in a breath, but I can't look at her. I can't think while I'm here. I need to get away; get some distance. I've already asked Augie to keep an eye on her. I'll give a couple of Father's soldiers a call too.

"Of course." Savero's lips curl up at the corners. It's the most I've seen him smile since I came back. "Thanks for coming by."

He walks me to the door, making it easier to not look back at what I'm leaving behind.

"Safe travels *fratello*." He holds me a little too tight around the face and kisses me on the cheek. "Don't leave it so long next time."

I shake my head slowly. "I won't."

$\mathcal{T}$rilby

My chest is about to burst with the breath I've been holding since Savero and Cristiano walked out of the room. I knew Savero wanted to see if I was telling the truth about not being attracted to his brother, but there was more at play here. Way more. And none of it makes any sense.

Who is Augusto, and why is Savero so pissed Cristiano went to visit him? When did Cristiano visit him, and why? Didn't he know Savero would be pissed?

Something is going on between the brothers. Something that involves the rest of the Di Santo family —not just the blood family, but the made one too. I have an uncomfortable suspicion Cristiano will forever be entangled in this world, whether Savero wants it or not.

My head spinning with questions, I lower myself

onto one of the stools. Cristiano has gone. I just watched him walk out of this house without looking back once. I'm relieved he didn't, because Savero was waiting for a sign. It's almost like he wants a reason to screw over this deal so he can just walk into the port, rip the doors down, and take everything from my father without going through with the hassle of a wedding. Cristiano would be in danger too. Not that he wouldn't be able to defend himself—I've seen the darkness that glows behind his eyes. I know he'd kill before someone could kill him. But he was right to leave.

Still, that doesn't mean my heart hasn't cracked down the middle.

My throat aches from all the effort it's taking me to not cry, and I lower myself onto a stool. I take a few sips of water before realizing it isn't my glass. There's a small chip on the rim. That means Cristiano drank mine. Still, he pressed his lips to this one before placing it next to my hand and tracing the tips of his fingers across my skin. I bring it to my mouth again and hold it there, my lips touching the same spot as his, and inhale every last breath of him.

I don't look up until Savero walks back into the house. There's a look of morbid satisfaction on his face.

"You're either innocent of my suspicion or you deserve an Oscar for putting on quite the act." His presence seems lighter as he walks past me. "Not that it matters anymore. I don't think we'll be seeing my brother again."

My gaze follows him out, then I stare at the island. I

can't show my true feelings—I'm balancing on a knife's edge already. If he believes for a second I'm lying to him, the deal with Papa will be off, and he'll simply take the port from under us. He'll ruin us all.

As his footsteps fade to black, my focus seems to move in and out, left to right. I hold onto the kitchen island even though I'm seated. "Lightheaded" doesn't even begin to describe how I'm feeling. It would be more accurate to say if I were to let go of the counter, I'd pass right out.

"Savero, I . . ." My voice sounds impossibly weak and too quiet for him to hear. I vaguely hear him leave the house and close the main door behind him, without another word or a backward glance.

Is this what it feels like to have a broken heart? To have all the blood drain from my head and my limbs? To ache in places I didn't know I could ache?

I lean forward and rest my forehead on the island. The surface is cool against my skin, but I feel even more dizzy for moving.

My shoulders hurt; my chest hurts. Everything hurts. Then a blissful darkness descends over every inch of me. I slip away from the dizziness and feel the earth beneath my body. Cool and firm.

Then my eyes drift closed.

$\mathcal{C}$ ristiano

In my rearview mirror I see the gates closing behind me. My heart *aches*, the grip of regret closing tighter with every mile I drive. I've never had a girl get under my skin like this before. It goes deeper than flesh; deeper than bone. My brother's wife is inside my beating heart and swimming in my soul.

Every cell in my body screams at me to turn back, and I'm right on that edge, my fingers tingling around the wheel.

Savero and I have grown apart more in the past few weeks than in the past fifteen years of my life. I can't shake the image of him as a twelve-year-old with a gun pressed to his head. I can see the arm of the person clearly. It looks exactly like Father's, but there's no way

Father would have done that. Like Augie said, Savero wasn't an easy son, but Father loved him.

Still, a relentless feeling of unease makes me pull over and take out my phone. I find Augie's number and press call.

"Cristiano. I thought you were leaving today," he says.

"I am. But something's bothering me."

"I wondered when it might." His cryptic response draws my brows together.

I take a deep breath and hope this comes out right. "I've been having these dreams—or flashbacks. I'm not entirely sure . . ."

"Go on," Augie says patiently.

"I keep seeing an image of Savero being held up at gunpoint. He's a young boy, about the age he was when he saved me from drowning. I can't see who's holding the gun to him, only the outstretched arm. It reminds me of Father . . . Tell me I'm going crazy."

"You're not going crazy, Cristiano. You're right to have questions. But that wasn't your father's arm."

I pull over but leave the engine running. "Then whose was it?"

"Think about it," Augie says. "Who else in your family has the same build, the same inked right forearm? Who might have been hanging out near the boat shed?"

My mind scrambles, but only for a second or two. "Nonni."

When Augie doesn't confirm or deny, my stomach drops.

"Why would Nonni hold my brother at gunpoint?"

A long sigh of resignation mixed with decades-old relief winds its way down the phone. "Because he'd just caught Savero trying to drown you."

What?

In less than five seconds, I know what it feels like to have my face drain of all color.

"No," I say sternly. "I fell overboard . . . I couldn't swim . . ."

"He pushed you, Cristiano."

"No . . ." I don't remember. I've never been able to remember, and now I wish with all my heart I could. "But . . . the rope?"

"What rope?"

"The rope that got caught around my ankles."

"There was no rope," Augie says in a low voice. "He was holding you down with his bare hands."

I can't speak. I have a million questions on the edge of my tongue, but none of them will take shape or form.

"Your nonni was inside the boat shed. It was late at night, and Savero thought no one was around. Nonni pulled you out and pumped your stomach until you vomited. You were seconds away from drowning to death. I don't know how long your grandfather had your brother at gunpoint, but that was the way your papa found them both."

"Wh-why didn't Father tell me this?"

"Your father and nonni had a tense relationship. You

were probably too young to remember. Your nonni never liked Savero, and in this case, it was your brother's word against his. Your father never knew who to believe."

"But you believed Nonni?"

Augie sighs again, and I hear him scrub a hand over his thick eyebrows. "One time, not long before your nonni passed, I had a drink with him. He told me he regretted very little in life, but the one thing he regretted the most was not shooting your brother in the head for what he did that day. He was afraid of what Savero would grow into. When I looked into your nonni's eyes, I saw nothing but raw, genuine regret. I don't think I'd have seen that had it not been true."

I sink into my seat.

Savero tried to drown me.

Cars burn past me on the freeway as though my world hasn't just collapsed. Everything I thought I knew about my life needs to unravel, and fast.

"Why didn't you tell me this sooner?"

"I couldn't do it to your father. He didn't trust Savero to succeed him as don, but that doesn't mean he believed him capable of killing his own flesh and blood. I had to honor your father's belief."

"What am I supposed to do?" I whisper the words, but I know exactly what I need to do. My fingers are burning to spin the car in the opposite direction, because if Savero could do that to me—to his own brother—then what the hell is he capable of doing to his fiancée— someone he's marrying for pure convenience? I need to get Trilby out of that house, and I don't think I'll be able to breathe until I do.

"I have to go, *Zio*."

"What are you going to do?" His tone is anxious.

"I don't know yet. I just need to get back to the house."

I hear doors opening and closing in the background. "I'll see you there."

"You don't have to. I'll be okay," I assure him.

"I know you will." His reply is firm and filled with conviction. "I'll still see you there. And Cristiano . . ."

"Yeah?"

"Tell me you still carry a gun."

"I'm a Di Santo," I say. "I never leave the house without one."

I hang up and throw the phone onto the passenger seat. Then, with zero regard for oncoming traffic, I spin the car into the opposite lane and put my foot to the floor.

As I drive, a series of recent images flashes across my eyes like a seventies home movie: Trilby's fearful face, the house cleared of people for the first time in my living memory, suspicion tunneled through a sideways glance at last night's dinner.

My chest tightens.

Savero wanted to kill me when we were just kids. Does a desire like that ever go away?

The decision I made to move to Vegas probably saved my life. I'd never been a threat to him . . . until I stuck around after Father died.

Until now.

Another image spins into view and makes my pulse thunder. The doll's eyes. What was it that Ranch said?

"One of the most dangerous plants in North America."

"Deadly."

I hit a red light, so instead of burning through it, I reach for my phone and search for the plant. Photos depicting its white irises with black pupils on blood-red stalks pepper the screen. It's also known as white baneberry, or so Wikipedia informs me.

Then, as my eyes scan the words, blood pumps loudly in my ears.

"Poisonous."

"Cardiogenic."

"Ingestion of the berries can lead to cardiac arrest and death."

It can't be. I swallow around a sharp lump in my throat. *He wouldn't.*

He wouldn't poison his own father. Poison is a fool's folly. He couldn't be so *weak.*

Father's death wasn't suspicious, the rational part of my brain asserts. *But he died of heart failure despite never having had heart issues before*, another part argues.

My mind darts back to the living room, where Savero found Father lying on the sofa, dead. That morning, the staff were dismissed, and Sav spent the day and night at the private mortuary, holding vigil by Father's bedside. When I stopped by the house to drop off my things, I saw nothing suspicious. Nothing to suggest Savero had a hand in our father's death. I don't even remember seeing the eerie plant. Everything appeared to be normal—from the drapes fluttering by the window to the half-empty glass of water on the table.

Water.

Sav has never in my life offered me a glass of water. The only times he's offered me a drink, it's been beer or whiskey.

This afternoon he passed me a glass that had already been poured, then he poured his own and Trilby's from a pitcher. I drank it all. And I feel fine.

Unless . . .

I placed my glass next to Trilby's so I could touch her one last time. It was on her right. The glass I drank from was on her left.

I drank hers, not mine.

Not the one meant for me.

My mind spins as I wait for the lights to switch.

Trilby.

The light turns green, my heart drops, and my chest caves. I ram my foot down and weave through the cars in front. Horns sound behind me, but if anyone dares pull me over, they'll get a bullet between the eyes.

Please don't touch that water.

The end of the street is in sight, but cars collect, slowing to a standstill at another set of lights. I mount the sidewalk and burn along it, the car half-on, half-off. Tables and chairs scatter; people scream. Tires squeal

along hot asphalt and metal scrapes against metal as I
slide the car past those waiting patiently for the lights to
change. I spin past oncoming vehicles and race down
the remaining part of the street.

Less than a minute later, I'm burning back into the
parking lot outside my childhood home. Security guards
stand back to watch as I pull out a gun and shoot open
the main gates. I don't have time to recall any codes
right now, and the intercom would be useless—I'm the
last person Savero will want to see, especially if he
hopes I'm already dead.

When the gates swing open, I sprint to the house.
More security guards step into view, but they know
better than to challenge a Di Santo who must look like
he's prepared to burn the fucking world down. The
doors are still open, so I run through them, pulling up
short in the kitchen.

Savero has gone.

Three glasses sit on the kitchen island. Two empty,
one half-full.

With my heart in my throat, I step around the island,
and my gaze falls to the floor.

Trilby.

In a beat I'm on my knees, my fingers pressed
against the side of her throat. I can't feel a pulse. I lift
her wrist and run my thumb over the soft skin. Nothing.
I press my ear to her chest. A weak thumping sound
gives me hope, but I have to move fast. I scoop her up
and get to my feet. Her head flops toward the ground, so
I lift an arm, bringing her to my chest. The way her

forehead smacks against my ribs sends shivers through my bones.

Minutes.

I might only have minutes.

I run with her back to my car and thank God I left the door open and the engine running. Just as I'm placing her along the back seat, Augusto's car screeches to a halt.

"Call the hospital!" I yell at him. "She's been poisoned. Her heart's failing."

A dark shadow of realization falls over his face, and he presses a phone to his ear. When I look in the rearview mirror, I see him speaking.

Then I focus on nothing but the road up ahead and my heart in the back.

CHAPTER 33

Cristiano

A medical team is already gathered at the doors of the hospital as I crash through the barrier and swerve to a halt. The Di Santo family has been keeping this place in business for the past decade with all the patients we send its way. They'll do whatever the hell they can to save the one in the back of my car—I'll make sure of it.

They've opened the doors before I've even rounded the hood, and I press a knuckle to my mouth as they gently lift Trilby out and arrange her boneless limbs on a trolley. My heart is pounding through my rib cage. I can't think of anything but keeping her alive.

The fact hits me like a bullet between the eyes.

I love her.

And if she dies, it won't just be Savero I annihilate; it will be anyone who crosses my path in the process.

Words are shouted between them, and a medic rushes over with what looks to be a portable defibrillator. Another places herself in front of me, gently pushing me backward.

"Stand back please, sir."

I look over her head—I need to see what's happening.

"You might want to look away too."

Screw that.

I glare at the woman, and she steps to one side, just as a jolt of electricity surges through the two pads pressed against Trilby's breastbone. Her body jumps into the air. One of the nurses counts, and the words blur into one in my distorted mind. The pads are taken to her lifeless body, a loud bang sounds, and she jumps again.

I take a step back involuntarily. It's not working. Whatever they're doing, it's not working. The only thing competing with my sense of utter helplessness is the steel barrel burning a canyon into my back.

Two more medics run out of the building, one carrying a large syringe. I watch distantly as they plunge the needle into Trilby and pump her full of some chemical. Then the pads are applied again.

I close my eyes before I hear the next bang, and this time I feel it deep inside my chest. Everything goes quiet—even the blood in my own veins.

"We have a pulse!"

My eyelids burst open.

Four medics take each corner of the trolley and run

inside the hospital, while another medic packs the equipment away.

"Follow me." The nurse who kept me back is now cupping my elbow and urging me toward the door.

We jog after the trolley, down a corridor, and through some double doors marked "ER." I've been here before, many times, but never for someone I care about this much. Never for someone I'd *die* for.

The nurse leaves me outside the room they've taken Trilby into. As she walks away, I grab her arm.

"Is she going to be okay?"

The nurse looks back at me, her expression morphing from one of fearful reverence to one of sympathy. "I'll have the doctor come speak with you." She nods toward the team of people quietly but quickly attaching tubes and monitors to their newest patient. "It may be a little while."

I swallow. "No. I need an update. Now."

The nurse almost runs away, leaving me staring at the woman on the bed.

She looks so small and innocent, but I know better. She's stronger than most men I know. She let me—no, *commanded* me—to rip through her barrier and leave my seed deep inside of her. It was defiant, as if she were laying claim to her own body before she was forced to let someone else take it. She's carried the burden of saving her family without complaint. She turned her cheek while I walked away, leaving her to her fate. I'll never forgive myself for walking away so easily.

My thoughts are disrupted by the arrival of a doctor.

I've hardly breathed in the whole time I've stood here. I haven't thought about anything other than this woman's survival—not even the fact I should be telling her father she's in the hospital or considering in grave detail exactly how I'll punish my brother for this. All I know is the answer starts with "kill" and ends with "him."

"Mr. Di Santo." A male doctor appears by my side. "Can I ask what your relationship is to Trilby Castellano?"

Augusto must have given them details of who she is, but ice threads its way down my spine. "She's my sister-in-law. She's family."

She's mine.

"She's married to Mr. Savero Di Santo?" A ghost of a frown crosses the doctor's face. He's right to question it. The whole city would know if Savero had married her already.

"Not yet." *Not fucking ever.*

"I'm sorry, sir." The doctor swallows nervously. "I need to see a blood relative if possible."

"I'll call her father." I hold his arm as he tries to walk away. "As soon as he's confirmed he's on his way, you'll tell me the status of her condition."

The demand in my tone reliably roots the doctor to the spot as I press the phone to my ear.

Castellano answers his office phone on the second ring. "Cristiano. I wasn't expecting to hear from you. Savero is here at the port—do you need to speak with him?"

"No," I rush out. "And do me a favor. Don't tell him

I've called. I need you to trust me. Can you come to the hospital?"

A door closes, dimming the sound of trucks moving shipping containers around in the background. "Is everything okay?"

I inhale and glare at the doctor. "I hope so. You need to get over here though—fast."

"Who is it? Is it Trilby?"

I can't afford for Tony to let anything slip to Savero, so I don't answer. "Just get here as quickly as you can," I say, and then I hang up.

I raise my eyebrows expectantly. The doctor motions to a couple of chairs.

I take a long look at Trilby lying motionless on the bed and then perch on one of the seats, my Di Santo muscles primed to jump up and gun down anyone who might dare to cross my path at any second.

"She's in a critical condition, sir. We're working hard to stabilize her heart, and we've taken tests to understand what caused the attack."

"It was poison," I say. "White baneberry."

The doctor narrows his eyes. "How do you know?"

"Because . . ."—my breath feels scratchy against my lungs—"it's what killed my father."

The doctor smiles kindly. "With all respect, sir, the great Gianni Di Santo died from heart failure."

"And what is it you suppose Trilby Castellano just experienced?"

A shadow falls over his features. "Why do you think it's white baneberry?"

"Because my brother kept it at our family home. I believe he may have killed my father."

Saying the words out loud feels like a dagger to the chest. My breath escapes, and I have to pause. How did I not see it? If it was so clear to Savero that Father wanted me to succeed him instead of my brother, why wasn't it clear to me too? Was I so blinded by the grief of losing our mother that I couldn't see anything else?

If I'd stayed, would it have been clearer then, or would Savero have felt even more threatened?

And then the hardest question of all settles over me like a gravestone. Could I have prevented all this? Could I have saved our father? Perhaps if I'd been less interested in pursuing my own success, I would have more easily spotted someone else's downfall.

The doctor watches me intently.

"And I think he tried to kill me."

He frowns. "You?"

"Yes. It was in a glass of water." I nod toward the room where Trilby's lying. "But she drank it instead of me."

"You're sure it's white baneberry?" He doesn't look convinced.

"Yes. Why?"

"We'll need to run some different tests. If that is in her system, we'll administer specific medication."

He stands up and begins to walk away, but then he turns back to me, alarm fresh on his face.

"Do we have to worry about the don, sir?"

Now that's something I *can* answer with confidence.

"No. You will never have to worry about him again."

I wait for Tony to arrive and stand by while the doctors explain the condition of Trilby's heart.

"Is this why you need to see Savero?" Tony asks. His voice is woven with panic, and I see a kind of terror that's filled those eyes before.

I rest a hand on his shoulder. "He was the last person I saw her with. I want to find out what he knows."

His voice drops. "Do you think he was responsible for this?"

I'm absolutely certain of it, but I don't want to distract Tony from being at his daughter's bedside.

"I don't know, but believe me, whoever was behind this . . . I'll make sure they don't wake up from their next sleep."

Tony grits his teeth and nods, and a silent agreement passes between us.

My legs feel solid, my spine lengthened, my conviction through the fucking roof.

"I'm going to get to the bottom of this."

Tony levels me with a determined stare and then grits his teeth. "You'd fucking better."

I leave him staring disbelievingly at his daughter and go off in search of my car. Fortunately, someone had the foresight to move it out of the path of emergency vehicles. A young medic is standing beside it, looking in awe at me as I approach.

"Mr. Di Santo," he says, practically bowing his head before stepping to one side.

"Thanks, buddy." I toss him a roll of bills before sliding in and starting the engine.

CHAPTER 34

Cristiano

I close the car door softly and look around. I've never had cause to set foot in Tony Castellano's port, but I should have come here sooner. It's clear this is a business that's cared about. The roads are clean and tidy, and the port workers seem mostly relaxed and happy. Only those whose gazes flicker my way appear uncomfortable.

Three large containers are lined up side by side. There's a sign on one of the doors signaling which one is the visitor's office. I'm guessing the other two are Tony's management office and a workers' breakroom.

I open the door of the visitor's office, and two women look up. They're older, around Allegra's age, and looked like they were immersed in work until I showed my face. Now they look mostly alarmed.

One of them rises to her feet. "Mr. Di Santo . . . How can I help you?"

"Is my brother still here?"

"I believe so, sir. He was in the portside warehouse at the south end of the yard. Or at least that's where he said he was going."

"I haven't seen him leave," the other woman says, her expression hopeful.

"Thanks." I go to let myself out but stop mid-stride. My brow furrows in thought before I glance across at the women. "Do me a favor. Whatever you hear in the next fifteen minutes . . . don't call security, okay?"

Both of them widen their eyes at me.

"Or the cops, or Tony, or anyone for that matter. Understand?"

They nod timidly.

I follow the port road to the bottom of the yard. The walk takes ten minutes. I really should have given myself a longer window. When I reach the warehouse, I walk around the outer edge slowly and quietly, until I hear voices coming from inside. I close my eyes and let the sounds help me decipher a view of where everything is. I tune in to the three voices and acclimate to the accents, then I focus on the words.

This is what I do.

I listen and watch for cheats.

Savero seems to be doing most of the talking. "You don't need to concern yourself with what's going to happen to them when they arrive on these shores. I'll handle that, Miguel."

Miguel?

The only Miguel I know of works for one of the Mexican cartels. Our father had an ongoing dispute with him over the importation of illegal firearms. Is that what Savero is doing—setting up another firearms transportation deal?

"All you need to worry about is getting them onto the boat. How secure are the containers? Do they have air holes? I mean, I'm guessing they'll need to breathe." He emits a dark chuckle, and I press my ear to the side of the warehouse.

"No need for air holes. They'll be sedated, and there's enough oxygen in those things to last the journey across the Atlantic."

What the fuck are they talking about? Animals?

"Trust us, Savero. We've done this a thousand times before. Only a couple die each journey, but that's the risk. They know the risks."

"Promise me, no children."

Savero's words slice through my chest.

"Dead children are bad for business."

I've heard enough. It's clear my brother—my own flesh and blood—is plotting with the Mexicans to traffic humans into the country via Tony Castellano's port. It makes complete sense now why he was so keen to get his hands on it.

A lot of other things make sense now too.

This is why Savero poisoned Father—because Father got wind of his ambitions and didn't want him to succeed as don.

This is why Savero wanted me out of the way—so I wouldn't jeopardize his marriage to Trilby. It needed to be *him*, because *he* needed the port.

This is why he tried to drown me as a kid, and why I've *never* felt close to him—because he's a fucking psychopath. I mean, made men are hardly model citizens, but this takes "morally gray" to a whole different level.

"I'll do my best, Savero, but, you know, some slip through."

The nonchalance of the heavily accented tone makes me sick.

I draw a glock from my waistband and turn back the way I came, toward the entrance. The door, understandably, is closed and probably bolted. I can either wait out here until they emerge or shoot my way inside. Either way, I guess I have the element of surprise on my side.

I weigh up my options.

Out here is pretty open, and I don't particularly want to subject Castellano's workers to an open-air bloodbath —not that they're likely to be morally pure either.

I aim the barrel of the gun at the door and roll my neck. Knots crackle along my muscles, and I hold onto that sense of satisfaction, then I gun the entire door off its hinges.

I step inside the warehouse and come face-to-face with three pistols aimed at my head. Savero and the two Mexicans have stood up at my arrival.

I laugh. "Here you all are. Now . . ." I slide the

glock into my waistband and stride toward them. "What did I miss?"

Savero's eyes are wide. Understandably so—he thought I was dead.

Thankfully, he can't shoot me in front of Miguel and his sidekick. If I know anything about this particular cartel, it's that they don't like infighting or betrayal. They're old-school. A code is a code. If they saw Savero shoot his own brother, their faith in his loyalty and honor—as laughable as that is already—would be called into serious question. This deal would not go ahead.

Miguel flashes an annoyed scowl at my brother.

Another thing I know about this cartel: they don't like surprises.

"*Fratello* . . ." Savero says through gritted teeth, sliding his pistol into his waistband.

I suppress a shudder.

"Seems like you got yourself a good yard here," I say. "Especially for the kind of shipments I just heard you discussing."

The two Mexicans exchange a nervous glance but lower their firearms.

I hold my hands up and sit on one of the metal chairs positioned in the center of the space. The three men tentatively sit but lean forward as though they're ready to spring up at a moment's notice.

"I was just walking our friends out," Savero grits out. "Come. Let's see them off, and I'll bring you up to speed."

I beam him a smile and stand again. No one is

saying what they're really thinking. This is the world I've lived in for ten years running casinos. I've seen great poker faces and terrible poker faces, and I can read them all. And I'm bathing in the awkwardness.

"Great."

I wait for Miguel and his associate to pass. They're still white-knuckling their firearms.

"Hide the guns, will you?" I ask. "This port is a family business."

They both throw me another scowl but do as I ask.

Savero pauses when he reaches my side. He's pissed —either because I've interrupted his meeting or because I haven't died.

"After you, brother," I say, cocking my head toward the exit.

Savero doesn't conceal his gun, but I didn't expect him to. All I needed was a slight upper hand, and I've got it.

We reach the exit, and the Mexicans walk on through, leaving me and Sav still inside. I wrap a hand around the back of my brother's neck, shoving him face-first into the wall. His arm flies up, and I shoot a bullet straight through it before pressing the barrel to his temple. His gun clatters to the stone floor, and I flick it up with my foot, catching it in my free hand. I haven't had as much practice at handling a gun as Savero has, but I've been preparing for this the whole drive here.

Miguel's face appears around the doorframe. Nothing like a gunshot to make a mob man curious.

I cock the trigger of Sav's gun and put a bullet

through Miguel's forehead. When the second cartel guy pokes his head around the frame, he gets one in the side of his face. Both slide to the ground.

A thin smile creeps across Savero's face. "Drink the water, did she?"

"What water?" I test.

"Well, something's clearly happened to your precious woman, and *you're* still alive, so . . ." He shrugs. "Is she dead?" His tongue clicks against his teeth on that last syllable, and I shove his head so hard into the wall blood starts to trickle down his cheek.

"If you think I'm telling you *anything* about that "woman," you can think again," I hiss in his ear.

I press one gun to his forehead and turn him around so he can see nothing but me. Then I press the other to his throat.

The smile on his face is designed to make me crack, but he's getting nothing but steel out of me from here on in.

"Why?" I say. It's not a question—it's a fucking command.

"Why . . . what?" A sneer curls his lip.

Man, he's going to play with me till the end.

I roll my eyes skyward. "Where do I begin?" Then I level him with the kind of glare I'd give a murderer, not a brother. "Why did you try to drown me?"

His right eyebrow inches upward. "I didn't like you."

I grind my teeth. "Why did you try to poison me?"

His eyes narrow into slits. "I still don't like you."

I can't deny the way his words form a fist around my heart. I had no idea his hatred wound this deep.

"What did I ever do to you, brother?"

His sneer sharpens. "You were *born*."

My natural reaction is to step back in shock, but there's a part of me that knows I need to fire at least one of these two guns. Not for me—I can deal with his hatred—but for Trilby.

I step up to his face. "I've done *nothing* to you. I even moved to the west coast because I didn't want to get in your way."

"Until something caught your eye—right, *fratello*?"

My teeth grind so hard I feel like I might soon be spitting them out. "Not that it matters to you, but I met her first, *fratello*."

"Two nights earlier, right?" he says lazily. "I heard."

I laugh in his face. "Bullshit. It was a little earlier than that," I say, cryptically.

"What the fuck does it matter? She was engaged to *me*."

"Because you wanted this port. Not because you wanted her."

He enunciates slowly, so I don't miss a beat. "She was collateral. That's all women are fucking useful for."

My fingers itch to pull the triggers. Both of them.

"And what about Father's hope that I would succeed him?" I taunt. "That had to rub you up the wrong way . . ."

He glares at me as if he didn't think I had the balls to confront him on that. Then he laughs, dark and low.

"Why do you think we find ourselves at this impasse? What do you think started this chain of events?"

"I don't know, Savero. All I know is what Augie told me."

Savero relaxes his chin onto the barrel of the gun. "The fucker always was a little too close to Father for his own good. But let me burst this bubble for him. I didn't find out about Father's succession plan from that rat. I found out from Father himself."

What?

With his uninjured arm, Savero taps at a part of his jacket that covers an inside pocket. "Father wrote a letter. To you."

My jaw drops, which I'm sure is his intention.

"It goes into great detail about how he wants the family to be carved up and managed, with you at the helm. Me?" He laughs again, but there's more defeat in his tone than darkness. "I wasn't even considered fit to be a capo."

My heart drums. Father didn't even want Savero as a capo? That would have had to hurt. In seconds my fingers relax. I'm unsure I have the conviction to pull the triggers anymore.

Then his lips purse into a point, and I hardly recognize him. "But I've fucking shown him. I have some lucrative deals lined up that would have doubled our investments, and a virgin bride I could have thrown around a room for a night."

I let out a morbid chuckle, drawing his gaze to mine. I'm straining to tell him she's no longer a virgin, but that was never all she was, and to gloat about that would be to undermine everything she is.

"You don't deserve her," I say. "And she certainly never deserved you."

His bullet-like eyes swivel to mine, and I know I can't prolong this. I have more important places to be and more important people to be with.

"We could have been epic, you and me," I say, and I mean it. "But you couldn't see through your hate."

His shoulders slump. "Do it, Cris."

I freeze. He hasn't called me Cris since I was a kid, and it was so long ago it feels alien. I don't realize until now how much I've yearned for the brotherly connection we may have once had.

"Don't . . ." I murmur.

His lip curls up at one end, but there's sadness in it. "Would it help if I told you I would have raped her on our wedding night?"

My breath escapes me, and in the blink of an eye, I can see he's taunting me to get it over with. I don't know which way is up anymore. All I know is that a man who has lied to me—hated me—all my life just suggested he'd hurt Trilby in the worst possible way.

He senses my conviction collapsing and moves suddenly to knock one of the guns from my grip. We both make a dive for it and I feel his knee drive up into my ribcage knocking the wind right out of me. I roll onto my back and in a split second he's standing over me, a boot poised just inches above my face. His gun rests casually by his side like he isn't going to need it, but I've always been quicker than him.

"Wait–" I plead.

He twists his foot so he can see my eyes.

"I would have loved you, brother," I whisper.

Just as he catches a breath I cock the gun and shoot him through the jaw.

He drops heavily to the ground and I leap to my feet to take a last look at his dying features. His lips are contorted into a sneer until the last of his breath leaves him. Only then do they soften. Only then does he look like a human being, like the brother he could have been had he not let his hatred eat him up inside.

I stare at him for a full minute, then I snap into autopilot. I shove the glocks into my waistband and pull the two Mexican bodies inside the warehouse, out of sight of the port workers. I retrieve the door from the floor and prop it up, sealing it from the road. At the very least, I'd prefer for none of Castellano's employees to see two dead and dismembered bodies in their place of work. They've earned their dinner—they should be able to eat it.

I flip open my phone and place a call. It's the type of call I haven't had to make in more than ten years, but as it turns out, it's like riding a bike. You never forget.

"I need a cleaner."

A voice speaks at the other end.

"Two," I reply. "Castellano Shipping Co. Warehouse seven. And there's one more . . ." I take a breath. "A Di Santo."

The voice on the other end of the line stills for a moment. "We're on our way."

I hang up the call and bend at the knees. Then I open Sav's jacket and reach inside the pocket. I half-expect it to be a complete fabrication, but there is an actual letter, folded and well-thumbed. I pocket it without reading it and flick the buttons on Savero's jacket, then I rip his shirt apart.

There it is. The Di Santo crest.

I remember us both aged fourteen sitting for hours in the back-alley tattoo parlor, under the watchful eye of our father, while the symbol of saintliness, a dove amid a tongue of flame, was inked onto our chests. Grief floods through me—not for the brother I just lost but the brother I never had.

The brother I did have never deserved that crest. Not in life . . . or death.

And with that final defiant thought, I flip out my pocketknife.

$\mathcal{T}$rilby

Awareness comes back to me in dull waves.

I feel heavy, as though I've been asleep for days. My eyelids are fused together, so I focus on the sounds around me.

There's beeping close by and in the distance. People speaking in hushed voices. Faint footsteps. Someone breathing not far from my body.

A wave of sadness grips my chest. It's so tight and so acute I choke on it.

"Trilby . . ."

Someone's fingers brush my cheek. *Papa?*

"Nurse—"

"God, is she okay?" *Sera.*

"Let's sit her up." This comes from a voice I don't recognize.

I sense two people, one either side of where I'm lying, cradling me as I'm lifted a little more upright. *Where am I?*

"Trilby, can you hear us?" Sera asks.

The coughing just killed my throat, so I nod.

"Oh God, love. You had us so worried." I smell Allegra's perfume close to my nose.

"Don't crowd her, Alli," Papa snaps.

"I'm not crowding her," Allegra hisses. "I want to make sure she can hear us is all. I've been just as worried as you—"

"Quit arguing," Sera says. Someone's fingers slip between my own, and they feel like my sister's.

I open my mouth to speak, but nothing comes out.

"Shh." It's Sera. "She's trying to say something."

"He—" I start, then I swallow. My mouth is dry and scratchy. I try again. "He left."

"Who did, sweetie? Savero?"

My head hurts when I shake it, and I close my eyes. I can't say his name, because then they'll know.

"Savero will be here soon," she says.

I lie back against the pillows and turn my head to one side. Sunrays beam through the window, lighting up the darkness in my heart. I close my eyes against them.

"Cristiano has gone to find him."

What?

My lids pop open, and I turn my head.

"Cristiano found you on the floor of the kitchen this morning and brought you here. He said, um . . ." She looks at Papa and Allegra.

Cristiano came back?

Allegra leans forward. "He thinks you were poisoned, Trilby."

My eyes widen. *Poisoned?* My gaze flits across all of them. The words "I don't understand" come out croaky but clear.

"That's all we know." Sera bites down on her lip. "I'm sure Cristiano will tell us more when he gets here."

Cristiano. The beat of my heart is fast and loud. *He's coming here?*

Hope swells inside my chest at the thought of seeing him again, but the threat of Savero walking in here is like a pin poised ready to pop it.

A shadow falls across the room, and although I feel as though I've been punched repeatedly in the chest, the skin all over my body sizzles. I look up to see Cristiano standing in the doorway. I can't hear much above the loud thump of my pulse, but my gaze is drawn to a box in his hands.

Papa stands impatiently. "Well? Did you speak to Savero?"

Cristiano's gaze finds me, and shadows fall from his face.

"It's been hours since you left for the port. What happened?" I can hear impatience bubbling beneath Papa's words, but it doesn't seem to affect Cristiano at all.

He walks a little closer, still looking only at me.

"Was it . . . *him?*" Papa asks, his words gritty and his teeth clenched.

Without saying a thing, Cristiano drags his gaze from me to Papa, takes the lid off the box, and tips it toward my father. I've never seen Papa go as pale as I do now. He swallows and looks up at Cristiano, then he silently makes the mark of the cross.

"What is it?" My voice is half-croak, half-whisper. "What's going on?"

Cristiano looks back at me. Part of me wilts a little at seeing him so soon. It means I'll have to say goodbye to him again, and I thought I'd already lived through that torture.

I stare at him. I need answers. "My family says you brought me here. You think I've been poisoned?"

He steps forward again but remains at arm's length. "That's right."

His voice seeps through my consciousness and lights me up inside. It's a reaction I don't want but can't control.

"But you left . . ."

"I came back."

His sharp response narrows my eyes. I'm not in the mood or any fit state to play games. I want—*I need*—the truth.

"Where's Savero? Where is my *fiancé*?"

I hope the last word wounds him, because I can't have this man in my life if he isn't going to stay. It's simply too hard. The pain it inflicts on my heart is worse than the pain of poison. And I can say that now from experience, it seems.

I take the exact same power his presence wields over

me, double it, and channel it through a glare. "Will someone *please* tell me what is going on?"

And when I say "someone," I mean the man my gaze is burning holes in.

Cristiano lifts the box and tips it toward me.

It takes a few seconds for me to comprehend what I'm seeing, and even then, I can't make sense of it. "Isn't that—?"

Sera leans over to look and then promptly sits back down, retching into her hand.

It's the Di Santo crest. A dove in flight amid a tongue of fire.

Tattooed onto a slice of flesh.

I recoil slightly while my eyes catch on mundane things. Blood streaking across the bottom of the box. A piece of cloth doing a poor job of soaking it up. It's like my awareness wishes to acknowledge anything but the thing right in front of me.

"That's Savero's tattoo." My whispered words come out all dry.

Cristiano bites out his words. "Savero didn't deserve to wear it."

"But . . ." I can't get past the fact it's in a box. "It was on his chest."

I glance at the expanse of purpling ink, its flesh-colored edges curling.

"There's only one way you could—" I look up sharply.

Cristiano looks different. He's wearing the same suit he left the house in earlier, but he seems taller, sturdier.

His features are sharper. He's watching me not with the apologetic expression of someone who might have had a minor argument with my future husband, but as someone who shot a man twenty times over and meant every single bullet.

"You killed him." My gaze slides down his jacket and his slacks to his shoes, and there my stunned eyes stare at the floor.

I can't believe it.

Suddenly, he's somehow inches from my shortened breaths, blocking out everyone else in the room. Hot breath grazes my cheek. "He almost killed *you*. He didn't deserve to bear the family crest. So I cut it off his body, the same way we denounce any undeserving member of the family."

The fact settles in my chest like the ash from a flame.

"I don't understand," I mutter. "This doesn't make any sense."

A whisper of air brushes my arm, and he settles on his knees beside my bed. "It wasn't his intention to poison you, Trilby," he says. "The poison was meant for me."

"Why?" I whisper. Poisoning anyone is nonsensical, but to poison your own brother . . .?

"He found out Father wanted *me* to succeed him as don, not Savero."

My mind whirls. Now it makes sense. This is why Savero was so intent on establishing that he was the don, not his brother.

"But your father let you go . . ."

"He did. He asked to come back many times, and I always said no. He never said *why* he wanted me back here so badly, but now I know it was because he wanted me to succeed him."

"And you didn't want to?"

"I didn't want to work with Savero."

"And now? Do you want to lead the family?"

He reaches for my hand. "I want to be honest with you, Trilby. I don't know. I haven't decided yet."

My mind feels fuzzy. I haven't long been awake, and this is information overload. "So let me get this straight. Savero, the same brother who saved you from drowning when you were eight, has just tried to kill you because your father, who is no longer here, wanted you to succeed him?"

Cristiano bites his bottom lip. He looks almost proud of me for thinking this through. "That's almost correct. I've come to learn he never saved me from drowning, Trilby. He was the one holding me under."

A gasp makes my chest ache even harder. "So, if he wanted you dead back then, why did he wait so long to try again?"

He shrugs. "I moved away. I was no longer a threat to him."

"And now?"

"I was getting in the way of his alliance with your father."

Alarm and realization halts my breath. "And he suspected there was something between me and you…"

"Yes." Cristiano grazes his thumb over the top of my hand, sending tendrils of fire along my arm. "Enough that he began to see me as a threat to your wedding."

"Why did he care? Surely, if the wedding didn't happen, he'd have taken the port from under us anyway."

Cristiano sighs and stares at the movement of his fingertips curling around and across my palm. "It was the principle. He was already pissed at finding out Father's plans. For me to be the one you wanted, not him, was another nail in the coffin."

"How did he find out your father's plans?"

Cristiano reaches into his inside jacket pocket with his free hand and pulls out a dog-eared piece of folded paper. He sandwiches it between his forefinger and his middle finger and waves it in front of me.

"He found this in Father's office." A dark emotion crosses his features like rolling thunder.

"What is it?" I ask quietly.

"It's a letter Father wrote begging me one final time to reconsider coming home. In it, he lays out his plan to announce me as his successor. It's dated three days before he died. It was never put in the mail."

Shock renders me breathless. "You think Savero killed your father?" I whisper, bracing my shoulders.

"I know he did. He told me."

"What?" I mouth in disbelief.

"Right before I put a bullet in his skull." Cristiano's grip around my hand tightens. "There's more."

I swallow, because I don't have any words right now for anything.

"Savero was planning to traffic people into the country via your father's port."

"He was *what*?" My hatred for the man grows overwhelmingly.

Cristiano's tone is grave. "I overheard him talking to associates of the Mexican cartel."

My eye sockets are starting to ache from staring in disbelief.

"I shot them all."

My chest braces, and he sees it.

"That deal will never happen."

I may loathe violence, I may hate everything Papa's involvement with the Di Santos has stood for over the years, but that doesn't mean I haven't learned a thing or two.

"At what cost?"

"I don't know yet. But it won't be long before the cartel discovers their associates are dead. Then we'll find out."

His words settle on me like acid rain. I know what this means. It means war. And Cristiano will believe a war is his doing. He won't want to return to Vegas now and leave the rest of the family to pick up the pieces.

He sighs. "I swear, this couldn't have happened any other way. The second I heard their conversation and figured out what they were planning, I had to stop it from going any further. I had to kill my brother."

Then he leans in, his long lashes fanning my hot

skin. "But let me be clear, Trilby. That wasn't *why* I killed my brother." He moves closer, so I'm certain no one else in the room can hear, then he cups my chin and lifts my gaze to his. "I killed him *for you*."

I do my best to stare into his orbit, but the vision moves in and out of focus, my peripheral blurring into something I no longer recognize.

I close my eyes and feel his forehead resting against mine.

"I know you hate this," he whispers. "I know you hate the violence, the death—all of it. But I know you, Trilby. I *see* you. Think back to the person you were before your mama died."

I try to shake my head, but he reaches up and holds me still.

"Remember how you'd run into the sea in all weather? You'd dive off the rocks. You'd camp in the forest without telling anyone where you were. You had no problem visiting the shooting range and being a better shot than guys twice your age."

His words spin around images that fly at me— slowly at first, and then thick and fast. Images that depict me throwing myself headfirst into freezing-cold waves, sleeping alone under the stars, firing bullets with absolute precision into targets designed for men and women much older and more experienced than I was.

"You were wild once. Untethered. Unashamedly courageous."

I nod. I remember.

Then something jolts me out of the memories.

How *the fuck* does Cristiano know who I once was?

I jerk away from him, and his expression shifts. His eyes flit from side to side as if anticipating my reaction.

"How do you know?"

"Know what?"

"How do you know I used to do those things?"

"I grew up around here."

"But I don't remember you." I feel almost ashamed to admit that, because even as kids, the Di Santos were practically royalty on Long Island. But I was only ten when he left.

"Maybe not." He rubs his chin, drawing my attention to a layer of stubble. "But I remember you."

My brain scrambles around for a memory, a fragment. "Were we . . . friends?"

"Not exactly."

"Cristiano." I drop my head wearily. "Now is not the time for vague answers. Can I please just have a straight one?"

"We met once. You were about eight years old. You'd found a dead bird, and you were trying to nurse it back to life." He wipes the smile from his face with a thumb. "I sat with you while you operated on it with sticks and grass, then you sang it a lullaby."

I blink. "Did we talk?"

"Kinda. I was your consultant, really. You asked me for my professional medical opinion on a couple of matters. I gave it. But you went ahead and did your own thing anyway. I was just amazed at how you were able to lose yourself in that tale. I envied your ability to transcend our lives and embody this character and this purpose you'd created in your head." He bites the inside of his cheek.

"So then what happened?"

He glances over his shoulder. Papa, Allegra, and Sera are speaking with a doctor. Then he drops his gaze to the floor.

"Your mama saw us talking, and she pulled you away."

"Why?" I say, breathless.

"She didn't want you talking to a Di Santo I expect."

I narrow my eyes and try to remember.

"You weren't happy about it. You were beside yourself at having to leave the bird behind. I promised to look after it, and I did."

"You did?" I whisper.

He shrugs. "Yeah, as well as anyone can look after a feathered corpse. I found a box in my grandfather's boat shed, and I gave it a proper burial service."

I can't help my smile. "Really?"

"I'd just helped you perform extremely intense keyhole surgery under highly pressurized conditions—I was pretty invested by that point."

His expression is so earnest it squeezes my heart, then my smile fades.

"I'm so sorry about Mama . . ."

"Don't be." He wraps his hands around mine. "She was trying to protect you. And she did—for a long, long time. I'm grateful to her."

"But you . . ." I rub my eyes. "You hadn't done

anything wrong." I gaze at him, my eyelids heavy. I've just taken in a mountain of information in a small space of time. A lot of death and a lot of violence.

"You need to rest," he says before I can suggest it myself. "We can talk more later."

He doesn't wait for a response. Instead he stands, turns to my family, and announces they're all to leave me alone for a few hours.

He places my hand back onto the bedsheets and trails his fingers along the top. "Rest, Trilby. I'll be back in a few hours."

I don't appreciate being told what to do, but right now, I'll gladly surrender to his instructions. I let my eyelids flutter closed and listen to the slow, methodical beeps of the heart monitor as I drift into a dreamless sleep.

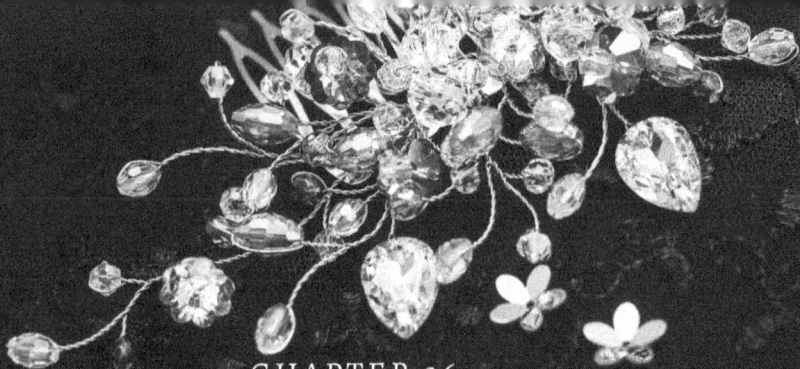

CHAPTER 36

*T*rilby

I lay on the hospital bed with my eyes closed, listening to the bleeps of the monitors. It all feels a bit extreme really. I've been here for ten days now and I'm pretty certain the poison is out of my system.

The Dolls Eye poison that is.

There's a whole different kind of poison running through my veins now.

Savero has gone. Dead. I'm no longer engaged. Papa has his port back. Everything has gone back to how it was before, except nothing feels the same.

Like a brain that has been put through serious trauma, I'm changed.

Sera, Tess and Bambi have visited daily with news of how the scandal of Savero's deceit and subsequent murder has spread all the way from New York to

Chicago. Poison is the coward's weapon in the Cosa Nostra. And though it hasn't yet been proven, everyone suspects Savero killed his own father, the revered don, Gianni. For that reason, he's been put six feet underground without so much as a sidelong glance from a priest.

Allegra has popped in to bring me an array of delicious cannoli that I'm not allowed to eat. Papa is the only one who's had to stay away because the port had to be untangled from all the deals Savero had set up.

Apart from the aforementioned metamorphosis, I feel pretty good; the doctors are pleased with my progress. I should have been discharged by now.

But *someone* won't let me leave.

And that someone is leaning up against the doorframe watching me 'sleep.'

I refuse to open my eyes because I don't think I can look into his.

Two days ago, while I was 'sleeping,' he confessed he's finally agreed to fulfil his father's wish and assume the role of don. Someone called Augie is his new underboss and Nicolò's loyalty has been rewarded with a new job out in Vegas, running a sizeable casino business.

Cristiano is now the don of the Di Santo crime family.

"I know you're awake." His voice slips beneath the sheets and slides across my skin making me feverish. "You've been awake for six days."

FML.

"When are you going to acknowledge me?"

I lift a finger.

There. Acknowledgement made.

I can hear his smile, damn it. Right before his footsteps close in on my bed.

I do my best to affect an air of boredom. "Shouldn't you be at 'work'?"

He stands over me. "Work can wait."

The bleeps quicken and I silently curse the heart monitor. It is now obvious to Cristiano that his presence has a physical effect on my heart rate.

"Open your eyes, woman."

I don't mean to, but my annoyance at his command and the use of that word overrides my best intentions. Those full-bodied irises are the first thing I see and I sink into them.

When I finally drag myself out of those depths, he's shaking his head, his arms folded across his bloody enormous chest.

"How do you do it, huh?"

I inhale sharply, unable to tear my eyes away from him. "How do I do what?"

"Get more fucking beautiful every day without lifting a finger? And that one…" he points at the finger I just lifted, " doesn't count."

My insides swirl like a whirlpool.

I swallow and the air sticks in my throat. "Why are you here, Cristiano?"

He blinks and the smile falls from his face. "I want to make sure you're ok before we get you discharged."

"I'm fine. I want to go home."

He opens his mouth to protest but I beat him to it.

"I'm no longer engaged to a Di Santo," I say slowly. "I'm not at risk of imminent death anymore. I haven't been home in ages and that's where I want to be."

He nods as if he's trying to convince himself he's in agreement. "Fine. When you're settled you can come to the house and pick out anything you want to keep from the closet I got you."

"Can't you return it?"

He shrugs. "Too much hassle."

"More hassle than having me come round and dilly dally about which clothes I want to keep?" *Has he met me?*

"Having you visit will never be a hassle."

His soft tone jabs me in the chest.

"Cristiano…"

Suddenly, he's crouching by the side of the bed, his face level with mine. It takes my breath away. This is why I kept my eyes closed these last few days; I knew he would weaken my defenses with a mere *look*.

"Do you want to know what I want?"

A puff of air escapes my lips and I snap them shut. *Yes.*

"No."

"I'm going to tell you anyway, because you need to hear it."

I go to turn my face away but he grips it in place.

"I want *you*."

He stares at me while those words sink in. They send tendrils of heat across every nerve ending.

"I've wanted you since the night at Joe's. Fuck, I've wanted you since we were kids; I just had no idea we would meet again."

I purse my lips together because nothing good would come of me opening my mouth right now.

"I know you hate this life, Trilby. There's nothing I can do about that. It's taken me a long time to realize it, but this is where I need to be. I owe it to my father to continue this family in the way he would have wanted."

There's such sincerity in his eyes, I can't look away.

"And, I hate to admit this to you but..." His gaze roams my face as though he's trying to find a way in. "Coming back here, putting my ammo to use in your honor whether you asked for it or not, it's made me feel *alive*. Killing my brother for what he did to you? That's the greatest satisfaction I've gotten from doing anything, *ever*. I would do it all again, for you."

His grip eases.

"Why?"

"Because... I think I was made for you."

"Made?"

His brows knit. "In every way possible."

The damn heart rate monitor is having a conniption.

"It doesn't all have to be about the life, Trilby." He takes hold of my hands. "It can also be about us. I want to give you everything. Children, art, your family, your freedom..." He glances away, briefly, "to a point."

I hike my brows and his face softens into a devastating smile.

"I want to give you so many fucking orgasms you can't walk."

I blush up to my hairline.

"I want to kiss you until you can no longer feel your lips."

My gaze drops to his without thinking.

"I want you to be the lady of *my* house. I will never be able to spend enough money on you, but God help me, I'll try."

My mind spins back to the confessions he made outside the restaurant. They made my legs so weak I could barely walk. Now, my resolve is weakening so much I don't think I can refuse him.

He leans into me so that his breath coasts over my lips and my eyelids flutter shut.

"Remember what I said, little one."

My thighs tremble at the pet name he's adopted for me.

"There's violence…"

My lids pop open just enough to see the fire in his eyes, then he flicks out his tongue to tease the top of my lip before pulling away. "…and there's *violence*."

My lips part in a gasp and he closes his mouth over them, thundering into me with a kiss so hot and unbridled I can't breathe.

The force of him pushes me into the bed and I mindlessly thread my fingers through his hair, holding on to him tightly.

A growl rumbles through his chest and into my mouth and his tongue licks around it, making me heady with lust. He's on his feet, his hands stroking over my face, my throat, my shoulders. I wriggle upwards trying to free myself from the bedsheet because I'm so hot I need air. The heart monitor is going berserk so I yank the wires from my body and the beeping stops.

Cristiano lifts his lips to murmur against my skin. "I was enjoying that."

I curl my fingers into his hair. "Don't gloat." Then I pull him back onto my mouth.

Within seconds I'm lost again.

His hands slip below the sheets and tug up the nightgown I've been forced to wear.

"This is sexy," he says softly.

I adopt my most sultry voice. "Wait till you see the bed pan."

He rewards my sharp tongue with a nip and shoves the sheet down over my thighs.

Then he gives me what I need. All of his weight.

He stills while I revel in the length of his cock pressing into my thighs and stomach. I tip my head backwards and let out a long breathy moan.

"Oh fuck, Trilby," he whispers hoarsely. "Stop doing this to me."

I lower my head and frown. "Doing what?"

"Making me want to fuck you in public places when anyone could walk in and see us. We're in a hospital in case you hadn't noticed."

I lift my head and bite his bottom lip earning myself another growl. "I don't care."

"Then I have to, for your sake." His torso stiffens but I can feel his conviction slipping away with each kiss I press to his jaw.

"Stop it," he moans.

I smile against his neck. "No."

"Oh good lord." He gasps when I slide my hand down to his pants and cup as much of his cock as I can through the fabric. It leaps into my hold and he buries his face into the pillow muffling a frustrated groan.

"Just fuck me for heaven's sake," I murmur into his ear. "I've been waiting for ten damn days."

He lifts his head and spears me with a hooded brow and a look of pure filth.

"Spread your legs."

Yes.

I wriggle my legs out from under him then a crack pierces the air and I slide head first into the head board. Cristiano's weight rolls off me, while I fold up like a concertina at the top of the bed... half of which is now collapsed on the floor.

"Jesus!" Cristiano is standing over me in seconds and scooping me up in his arms. "Are you ok?"

I look around myself in shock. "What happened?"

He lowers my feet to the floor. "We broke the bed."

I pan back to him, my brows arched.

He holds up his hands. "It wasn't just me, Castellano. There were two of us on it. And it wasn't one of the standard issue ones. That fucker was *flimsy.*"

I narrow my eyes and smooth the cotton down over my legs. "It's held up just fine for four days."

When I look up again, he's staring at me.

"What?"

"Marry me." His tone is sharp and unyielding.

I frown. "Don't tell me what to do."

A corner of his lips ticks up until he wipes it away with his knuckle. "Ok then, *please* will you marry me?"

My chest flutters. "I'll think about it."

He grabs the back of my head and swallows my petulance in a messy tongue kiss. When he releases me, he shakes his head. "You are pure insolence, woman."

I smile and shuffle after him in my bare feet and apparently sexy hospital gown.

CHAPTER 37

*T*rilby

The gates open slowly, bringing the Di Santo residence into full view. My heart skips about like the butterflies that have taken up permanent residence in my stomach.

Sera puts a foot on the brake and turns to face me. "Do you want me to wait for you?"

"No, it's okay." I smile. "I'm sure Cristiano or one of his men will take me home after I've collected the clothes."

After much pestering on his part, I've finally come to collect the closet Cristiano bought for me. Though the pestering wasn't so much about collecting the clothes— it was more about having me move in with them. With *him*. But, as per the marriage proposal, I've been changing the subject. Not because I don't want to do those things—because, actually, I want nothing more than to move in with Cristiano, to marry him, and to build a life with him—but because it feels a little too much like we're dancing on Savero's grave.

Despite the fact he was an evil son of a bitch, it's too soon.

"Anyway, you must be exhausted after letting me drag you around all the galleries today."

"Nonsense. It was my idea, wasn't it?"

"Yeah, well, who can me blame for accepting your invitation when I'm about to lose you to the Hamptons for the next school year?"

"I'm not going yet. I have another month."

"Then there are many more gallery visits in our future." I smile. "How did you manage to secure a placement so quickly?"

Sera eyes me suspiciously.

"It's not a trick question," I clarify.

"No . . ." She shakes her head. "It's just . . . I thought you knew."

"Knew what?"

"Cristiano arranged it. One of his former casino managers runs one of the big country clubs. He put a word in for me."

"He did?" My eyebrows inch up toward my hairline. "He kept that quiet."

Sera takes my hand and gives it a small squeeze. "There's a lot he's been keeping quiet. He's helping Tess get into the dance school she wants, he's upgrading the security at the port, he's had Allegra's car fixed. But it's not for us—it's all for you."

I fall back against the headrest. "Why hasn't he told me any of this?"

"He doesn't want to overwhelm you," she replies in her lovely soft voice. "That happily ever after we all want? He's already there, Tril. He's just patiently waiting for you to catch up to him. He doesn't want to scare you away."

"He just killed his own brother. If I were going to run away scared, I think I'd be long gone by now."

She smiles sweetly. "Then what are you waiting for?"

I breathe out slowly. "I don't know."

After she's driven away, I turn to look at the grand house that, not so long ago, was going to be mine. I take in the white weatherboards, the wraparound porch, the beautiful gardens. It's even more beautiful now only Cristiano is in it.

I walk up to the main door and press the bell. I expect to see a staff member, so I'm taken aback when Cristiano himself opens the door.

My breath escapes at the sight of him in a white button-up with rolled-up sleeves and a pair of slacks, sending the butterflies in my stomach fluttering in more of a frenzy.

"Hi," I whisper.

A smile tugs at his lips. "Hi to you."

We stand on the porch and stare at each other. Then he leans forward and presses a long, warm kiss to my mouth. When he pulls away, I'm lightheaded.

His gaze burrows under my skin, into my bones, heating every inch of me. "I missed you."

"You only saw me yesterday," I say, arching a brow.

"So? I still fucking missed you."

I look past him into the house. "It's quiet. Where is everyone?"

He shrugs. "A few people left after . . . well, you know." He turns around, and I follow.

"After you killed and carved up your brother? Yeah, I can imagine that isn't to everyone's taste."

He laughs, and it makes my skin tingle.

"There's no point in me hiring more staff right now anyway."

"Oh?"

He pauses to look over his shoulder. "Well, I'd expect the new lady of the house to do that."

My heart beats loudly in my ears. "Uh-huh."

I follow him through to the lobby, where the staircase rises. "I had it put in the east wing," he says. "Come find me when you're done. I'll make dinner." His fingers find mine and curl around them. My breath escapes me at the simple, unexpected gesture.

"I will."

He leaves a feathery trail along my fingertips then leaves me to climb the stairs. I try not to picture the last time I was at the top of them, but the terror of that night is still fresh in my mind. The memory of Savero standing over me with his hand around my throat, threatening my life, is so clear I can feel it. It doesn't matter that he's dead now—it brought home to me just how vulnerable I really am. I grew up with a lot of bravado. I lost it after Mama died, but it was always inside of me, itching to emerge.

The only times I've felt safe since she passed have been in Cristiano's arms.

I sigh heavily and turn the door handle. Then I have to blink, because I'm not sure what I'm seeing.

The door swings inward, and I shake my head, trying to figure out what's in front of me. I haven't been back to the apartment since this morning, so why does it look like I'm back there right now?

I walk over to the antique console that sits in the hallway and rest my purse on it. Then I look around at the plant pots, the paintings I've thrifted from flea markets and vintage fairs, and the shoes normally laid out on the floor of my closet. I frown at the rows and rows of clothes that look alarmingly familiar, the easel and the paints, the pieces of art I've created over the past few years . . .

I don't understand.

But then again, I do.

This isn't just the closet Cristiano bought me when I was staying in his apartment. This is *all my stuff.*

A soft knock sounds at the door.

"Um, yeah?" I murmur.

I hear the door open and close behind me, and even though I haven't turned around, his presence fills the room.

"What is this?" I whisper.

"I thought you might want to feel at home."

"This isn't my home."

"It can be, Trilby. Just say the word."

"I . . . I'm confused. How is all my stuff here?"

"The last time I asked you to move in, I didn't get the answer I wanted, so I'm not asking again. You know what they say—it's better to ask for forgiveness than permission."

I turn around and stare at him wide-eyed. "You . . . you want me to move in with you?"

Cristiano draws his hands from his pockets and stalks toward me. He invades my space, breathing heavily, and lifts my chin up until my eyes reach his. "How many different ways do I have to say it, Trilby? I want you to be my wife. That generally means I'd like you to live under the same roof as me."

I blink at him numbly.

"And I know how fucking weird you are about your closet, so I figured, let's just get everything here, and then you won't have to worry about it."

"But . . . how?" My head is spinning. He would have needed a small army to move all this stuff in just a few hours.

"It doesn't matter." His voice softens. "What matters is it's here. And you're here. That's all I care about. Everything else, we can deal with together, all right?"

I nod, words eluding me for the first time ever.

He bows his head toward me, and I smell toothpaste, fresh sweat, and musky dust. That's what transporting antique furniture and vintage clothes does to you. "Now, after the calamity that was the collapsing hospital bed, can I *please* fuck you?"

I rise up onto my tiptoes and brush my lips over his. "I thought you'd never ask."

We launch for each other, grabbing at one another's skin, hair, and clothing. I want to feel him everywhere.

"Are you mine?" he murmurs into my mouth.

I nod.

He grabs my hair in his fist. "Are you *mine*?"

I gasp. "I couldn't be anyone else's."

"Yes, you could." His tone is gritty. "You could belong to anyone you wanted. Don't think I haven't seen the way other men drool over you. The way they can't take their eyes off you."

I coast my fingers through his hair and grip it like he's gripping mine. "Those other men?" I stare into his eyes and mean every word. "They fell for my smile. But you?"

His eyes search mine.

"You fell for my tears."

He stares at me for a long moment. Then he releases my hair and drops onto my lips with a grievous moan.

My eyes drift shut as Cristiano lowers me to a rug that only this morning was laid on my bedroom floor. He straddles me on his hands and knees and stares at me with dark eyes. I lick my lips, and he emits a low growl before shifting his feet downward. He hooks a leg and props it up, then he licks a hot, wet line from my ankle to the crease of my knee. It's slow and torturous, when all I want is him inside me—now. I didn't dare believe it would happen again, so now that it is happening, I can't wait any longer.

His lips skitter over my upper leg, his hot breath curling my toes. Then he's inching his way toward the apex of my thighs.

"Cristiano . . . please . . ." I need to feel him inside of me. It's a need I don't have the words for.

He lifts his head, a frown line creasing his brow. "You're trying to stop me from eating you out?"

I nod, but before I can explain myself, his brows knit together, and a low growl erupts from somewhere in his chest.

"What the actual fuck Trilby? I'm starving for you, and I didn't fight my way to the top of the food chain to be a vegetarian."

Breath rushes out of my lungs. Well, *fuck*.

He pushes my knees outward, and I curl my fists. His molten breath drifts across my panties, and his tongue darts out to tease at the lace.

"Please don't rip another pair," I whisper hoarsely. "French lace doesn't grow on trees."

He pauses and smiles against my pussy. "It does in my garden." Then he gnashes his teeth over the strip of lace and tears it clean off my body. Cool air whips across my damp skin, making me shudder, before his whole mouth covers me, hot and wet and *ravenous*.

My fingers find his hair and tug at it mindlessly while he makes an actual meal out of my clit. A long lick is followed by a taut suck, then he circles his tongue around the hardening nub, making me squirm. He presses his hands into my thighs, exposing more of me to him—more that he can devour. Unanchored whimpers and moans escape my mouth, and I toss my head from side to side.

"That's it, little one. See what happens when you stop fighting me?" he taunts in between sucks.

Ugh, just don't stop.

"Please, Cristiano . . ."

"Yes, baby?" He laps at my clit as though he's licking an ice cream, seemingly oblivious to the mess I'm becoming.

"Please make me come."

"With pleasure." He wraps his lips around me and rims my entrance with soft thumbs while he sucks hard.

The room turns white as my spine arches, and I push my hips up to him. He hums triumphantly as I come apart beneath him.

I pull my heavy head up to see him drag the back of his hand across his mouth. Like a predator about to devour its prey, he crawls up to me, and his cock finds its way to my entrance.

I suck in a breath. Despite having an orgasm my first time, it still hurt.

He pushes his way in by a couple of inches. My body wants to hyperventilate.

"Look at me." His commanding voice anchors my thoughts, and I lift my gaze to his. "I want to see your face when I fill you with my cock."

His words send a ripple of lust through my bones, and I pull my knees in toward myself. He takes one in his hand and presses it into my shoulder. Pain radiates out from my hip, distracting me from the feel of his cock sliding in to my very edge.

Now I can feel him in my stomach.

His gaze doesn't waver, but his jaw has hardened like steel. "You take every. Single. Inch of me, Trilby." His voice is filled with wonder. "You wrap around me so tight. So warm. So fucking perfect."

He lowers his lips and kisses me slowly. I silently thank God that Cristiano's doing all the work, because I'm immobile.

He pulls my bottom lip between his teeth and draws back, letting it pop out gently. "Do you need me to take it slow?"

I swallow and nod. "Can you?"

"I can do whatever you need me to do."

He lowers his elbows to the floor and presses kisses to the corner of my mouth as he begins to move. At first it feels like a freight train is trying to pass through my body, but as my walls soften and allow him space, it gets easier. It gets . . . *nice*.

Little gasps are pushed out of my lungs with each gentle thrust. I look up to see his jaw clenched tight.

"Kiss me," I whisper.

He lets out a fractured groan and complies, catching my lips in a restless dance.

"God, you feel incredible," he murmurs. "Just *fucking* incredible."

He ignites that place within me that turns me inside out, and from here on, I'm an unraveling mess.

I'm right on that edge, ready to tip over, when he stills, removing the friction I need to chase to put an end to this pressure. I claw my gaze to his, and he's looking at me with devious intent.

"Marry me."

I blink. Did I just hear him right?

"Marry me, damn it."

I suck in a breath. "What? That's blackmail."

He pants as though it's taking every ounce of his strength to hold back. His voice is tight. "It's only blackmail if there's something in it for me. I'm dying of blue balls over here."

"I'm not being coerced into marriage."

His hands are balled into fists, buried in the rug, and his upper arms are starting to shake.

"No one's coercing you, Trilby. I want you . . ."

I arch my brows.

"I *love* you. I want you to be my wife, for fuck's sake."

My entire body smiles even though he's in agony right now. *Wife.* Not sister. Wife.

"Yes," I whisper.

"What?" His teeth are clenched, and the veins at the side of his face are thick and throbbing.

"I said yes. I will marry you."

He collapses onto me and begins moving again, but this time it's slow and just overwhelming enough.

"God, *woman*," he drawls.

I've never been so pleased to hear that word fall from his lips.

He litters my face with a million kisses and whispers soft curses and no-sweet-about-it nothings. "You've had it now. Oh fuck, this is good. I'm going to screw you like this every night. Jesus, this is unreal. You're a fucking heathen. I can't get enough of you, little one."

And my favorite one of all: "Be careful what you wish for, Castellano. I'm going to worship you for the rest of my life."

I sigh into his skin as I get closer to that edge. "What *are* you going to call me when I'm no longer a Castellano?"

"That's easy." He looks up with dark, dangerous eyes. "My queen."

CHAPTER 38

Cristiano

I sit on the edge of the bed and just stare at her. I've already blocked three calls and silenced my phone, because I can't bring myself to move. I just want to stare, drink her in, bask in her warmth, inhale her scent. I want to be the first to see her open her eyes in the morning. Every morning. Starting with this one.

Her lips part, and I hope a little snore works its way out, because I want to absorb every single sound she makes.

"Are you going to stare at me all morning?"

I smile to myself. "If you'll let me."

She opens her eyes. They seem a brighter blue in the light of the master bedroom. "I'd rather not. It's weird."

I wipe the smile away with my thumb. "I have to go."

"Oh." She sits up and rakes her gaze hungrily over my freshly laundered suit. "Where?"

I trace a finger along her cheekbone. "To Benny's. I have papers to sign and businesses to run."

Her shoulders stiffen. "Oh, right." She takes a long breath. "What kind of businesses?"

I grind my teeth softly. "You want to have this talk now?"

We're getting married—she's going to find out the details of our operation before long. She's also not a typical Mafia wife-to-be, and I'm not a typical don. I want her to know everything about me, and that includes the work of our family. I don't expect her to get involved, but I don't want to keep secrets from her either.

"Well, there's the laundromat and the manufacturing business—they're the biggest. We have some small waste-disposal businesses, click farms, and a growing data-mining enterprise."

She nods slowly. "And the unions?"

"Yeah, those too."

"Drugs?"

"Cocaine," I affirm.

"Firearms?"

"Fewer now, but yes."

I can see a moral war waging behind her eyes. I can't bear to watch her slip away when faced with the reality of who I am now, but neither can I lie.

"Will you make it worth it?"

At first I don't understand her, but when she looks at me with hope in her eyes, I know what this is. She knows I can't change what a don does, but she's asking if a marriage to me will make up for the compromise—the *sacrifice*—she's making in going along with something she's feared for so long.

"I'll make it worth your while ten times over."

I mean every word.

"We can start by converting the ground floor."

She blinks. "To what?"

"A studio," I reply. "The light through the French doors is the best in the entire property. It's spacious. We don't have a need for a breakfast room, dining room, bar, utility, and kitchen. We can open up the whole side of the house. It can be yours to use however you wish."

"Are you serious?" Her eyes dart about as she formulates a plan in her head. "What about my career?"

I fold my arms and frown in concentration. "What career?"

"Well, now I've finished up the year, I can either go on to further study, or I could look for work in local art galleries, or I could quit altogether."

"What do you want to do?"

"I'd like to work in a gallery."

"So do it." I stand up and button my jacket.

"Really?"

"Yeah, of course."

She narrows her eyes. "This is too good to be true."

I grin.

"No, I mean it. There has to be a catch. You're the Di Santo don—my marriage to you will put a price on my head again, right?"

I inhale a sobering breath. "Right."

"Will I be safe working in a regular job?"

"If you pick a gallery in a part of the city I own, you'll be fine."

Her eyelids pop open. "And which parts do you *own*?"

I cock my head to one side and narrow my gaze as I recall. "Pretty much all of them."

"And the Marchesis?"

"We've squeezed them out of Lower Manhattan, Brooklyn, Staten Island. Newark aside, they've moved north. Otherwise, they won't be a problem for us."

She stares after me as I walk to the door.

"By the way," I say over my shoulder, "I've invited your aunt and sisters over for lunch."

"Why?"

"I didn't want you to feel lonely on your first day in your new home."

She looks panicked. "Do you, um, have food in?"

I rest my hand on the door handle and turn to face her. "I have more than food. I have staff. Not many, but the important ones. Lunch will be served on the terrace whenever you request it."

"Right. Okay." She nods. "Thanks. Um, Cristiano . . ."

"Yeah?"

"Are you sure you want to marry me?"

I almost laugh at her question, but she's deadly serious.

"Queen, I killed my flesh and blood for you. I've never been more sure of anything in my life."

$\mathcal{T}$rilby

I'm still walking through the rooms filled with all my stuff when I hear giddy voices making their way to the front doors. I lean out the window and see a few male members of Cristiano's staff offering their assistance, their bulging eyes set on Tess.

"Why is Trilby still here anyway?" Bambi whines.

Sera shrugs and hides a smile. "I've no idea."

She's such a bad liar.

"Lunch had better be decent." Tess. "I'm starving."

Our third sister is always starving. Eighteen years in, and I'm still at a loss as to where she puts it.

"Don't be vulgar," Allegra chastises. "We've been invited here by the don. We must always behave respectfully."

Tess goes to protest, but Allegra halts her with *that*

glare. "And that means not eating him out of house and home."

Tess frowns.

"And one of these days, your metabolism is not going to burn through the amount you put away, dear," Allegra warns. She runs a finger up and down her own form in a rare show of self-effacement. "Case in point."

It shuts Tess up at least.

"Up here!" I call out, and four heads swivel toward me.

They forget their petty quarrels and hurry into the house.

I run out of the room and down the stairs, colliding with Sera at the bottom. She throws her arms around me and buries her face in the crook of my neck.

"I've missed you," she whispers.

"*Caspita!* You only saw each other yesterday." Allegra walks by as if she owns the place already.

Sera holds my face inches from her own and shakes her head. "I know it's only been one night, and I know you're just down the street, but . . ." She drops her gaze to the floor and then looks up through auburn lashes. "I feel as though you're moving on, slipping away."

My brows knit. "I'd already moved into this place when Savero, well . . ." I'm not sure how to refer to my relationship with my discredited, dead ex-fiancé, but it doesn't matter, because Sera places a finger over my lips.

"It feels different this time," she says in a soft voice. "This time, you want to be here."

I bite the side of my cheek. "Do I?"

"It's obvious, Trilby. You're smitten with each other."

My chest fills with a combination of dread and warmth. "How do you know?"

She laughs quietly. "Ever since he invited us to join you at the bridal gown fitting, I've watched the way you are around each other. You're like mirrors, bouncing light off each other."

"What?" My whisper is breathless. "If it was obvious to you, then . . ."

The lightness in her face fades. "It was obvious to me because I care so much about you. No one else seemed to notice, but they weren't looking closely enough."

"Savero knew," I admit. "Or at least he suspected."

Sera trails her fingers down my cheek, and sympathy floods her eyes. "That explains a lot."

I force myself to smile as Bambi skips from room to room, assessing which TV to watch first. Then a thought occurs to me.

"Sera . . . how did Cristiano move all my stuff in just a few hours?"

My sister can't hide her smile. "Allegra."

Cristiano has been speaking with my aunt?

"With the help of a few of his soldiers and some U-Haul trucks."

I turn around to see my aunt poised with an arched brow.

"You're not supposed to just ship my stuff out on a whim." I frown.

"Oh, Trilby," she says with a dark chuckle. "This was no whim."

"When did he talk to you?"

"A few days ago," she replies.

I'm about to say how that sounds like a whim to me, but she raises her brows.

"But I knew it was on the cards the second he showed up with half his brother's chest in a box."

I pin my lips together and dart my eyes to Sera, who turns green at the memory. I slip my arm through hers and guide her to the terrace. "Come on. I don't have you for much longer—I want to hear all about your plans for the Hamptons."

"Can I come back tomorrow with my bathing suit?" Bambi asks. The water ripples out from where her feet are dipping in the pool.

I help myself to more of the pink lemonade one of the servants placed on a table. "I can't see why not."

"I don't suppose you can click your fingers and magic up an early dinner, can you?" Tess's sunglasses glint at me from her pool lounger.

Allegra tuts from her own lounger but doesn't appear to have the energy to challenge her niece.

"We should perhaps wait for Cristiano to get back.

This doesn't feel like my home yet." As I say the words, I wonder if it will ever feel like my home. It's huge and stately, and I never dreamed I'd be a "lady" of any house, let alone one of the grandest on Long Island.

Just as she's about to huff out a sigh of supposed starvation, voices echo through the house, and my chest warms at the familiar timber. When Cristiano appears on the terrace, I have to fight every urge to run to him. Instead we saunter toward each other, biting back smiles, knowing the eyes of every member of my family are watching feverishly.

I reach him and inhale deeply as he bends to press a chaste kiss to my cheek. Then his lips brush the shell of my ear.

"Fuck, I want you alone." He pulls away, taking my breath with him.

"Hi," I rasp. "Good day at the office?"

His gaze coasts over me and warms with hunger. "Would rather have been at home." He threads his fingers through mine and steps to the side.

Another figure looms large in the doorway—an older man, with thick brows, salt-and-pepper hair, and an expression too kind to be marred by Mafia blood.

"Trilby, this is Augie, my underboss."

Underboss? He looks too old to be second-in-command to the don of a highly active crime organization.

I swallow and hold out my free hand. "It's a pleasure."

Augie steps toward me, and as if to prove my

judgment is impaired, he rolls up his sleeves. His arms are *enormous* and laced with ink. His grip is like steel, and his expression is solid, as though a world of opinions is racing around behind it, but no one would ever know.

"Trilby," he says with a smile. "I'm pleased to finally meet you."

Finally? How long has he known I exist?

More steps echo through the house, and Benito Bernadi appears behind Augie. His eyes unashamedly roam the terrace until they land on something and harden like flint. I cast a look over my shoulder to see what his gaze has settled on.

Tess is stretched out on her lounger, one knee bent, her arms resting overhead like a Hollywood starlet.

"Augie and Benny are joining us for the evening," Cristiano says, drawing my gaze back to his.

"Actually," Augie says, "I'm just going to stay for a quick bite, then I need to pay Beppe a visit."

Cristiano shoots him a questioning look.

"There's been a bit of trouble with the Marchesis, but nothing for you to worry about . . . yet," Augie says.

Sera bounds over and throws her arms around Cristiano. "Congratulations!" she squeals. "Welcome to the family."

I flick my lids shyly up at my fiancé, only to see him gazing down at me with an assured smile.

"Thanks, Sera. Welcome to mine."

"Oh, um . . ." My sister stutters her thanks. Clearly,

she didn't consider she'd be joining the Di Santo family herself through my marriage.

"Let's sit," Cristiano says brightly.

Tess leaps up at the suggestion of imminent food and doesn't even tug down the hem of her dress. I catch Benito's discreet glance at her bare thighs and the movement of his Adam's apple as she slides onto a chair.

We tuck into grilled seafood, fresh salad, and stuffed eggplant and talk mainly about the house and the casino business Cristiano has handed to Nicolò. It's too soon for any talk of Savero or the port or our impending wedding.

Cristiano's thigh rests against mine, and his hand occasionally reaches down to graze the bare skin beneath my dress. I don't need to glance up at him to feel the force of his presence. My heart flutters permanently these days, whether he's around me or not.

On my other side, Augie turns to me every few minutes to share an anecdote from Cristiano's past, making me giggle and almost spit out my food. The more I get to know him, the more I'm thankful he's still in Cristiano's life.

"You loved Gianni, didn't you?" I ask Augie as the sky begins to darken.

He smiles. "Like a brother," he says, then he catches himself. "Like a brother *should*."

I place my fork on the plate. "I wish I could have met him."

"I wish you could have too. He'd have adored you."

My chest warms at the thought.

"He certainly wouldn't have forced you down the aisle with Savero." He takes a long slug of wine.

I follow suit and sip at my lemonade.

"Poison," he mutters. "The weapon of the weak."

I place my glass down carefully. "I thought poison was known as the woman's weapon."

He brings a napkin to his lips and then looks sideways at me. "Frankly," he says, "I find that an insult to women."

I run a tongue over my teeth and grin. I like Cristiano's underboss.

He places the napkin on the table. "It's been a pleasure, Miss Castellano. And before I go, may I just say thank you?"

I peer up at him as he stands. "For what?"

"For bringing our boy home." His eyes flick in Cristiano's direction. "If it weren't for you, he wouldn't have stayed. Dead brother or no dead brother."

"That's not true," I whisper, hoping Cristiano can't hear me.

Augie leans toward me. "He is the rightful boss of this family, but he hasn't taken that role out of some sense of duty to his father. He's taken it to protect you."

I blink. "Protect me from what?"

"The only way he can guarantee no one else will come along and try to take the port from under your father is to assume the deadliest title this side of Chicago. The *only* way."

My mouth falls open.

"But don't misunderstand me, my love," he says with a wink. "He was born to do it."

He waits for the smile to form on my lips, then he walks around me to say a few words to Cristiano before darkening the doorway again as he leaves.

The rest of the night is filled with the sound of my sisters getting tipsy and Allegra rolling her eyes. Cristiano and Benito are locked in a conversation about things I probably don't want to know about, but every now and then, I notice Benito's gaze coasting to Tess. She's utterly oblivious, which is probably for the best. Benito is possibly one of her least favorite people in the town, though I don't quite know why.

It's almost midnight when Allegra gets unsteadily to her feet. "Our car is outside, girls," she says. "Serafina, help me carry Bambi."

My youngest sister is asleep on a sun lounger, having grown bored of the adult chat.

"I'll carry her."

We all turn to see Benito stride forward, not waiting for agreement or objection. He bends down and scoops Bambi into his arms as though she's as light as a puff of air.

"We would have managed just fine," Tess says in a tight voice.

He stops and drags his eyes over Tess. "You of all people shouldn't be settling for 'fine.'"

Tess's brows knit together as we follow Benito through the house.

Cristiano threads his fingers through mine again and

pulls me back to let everyone walk ahead. I'm drawn into the shadows under the veil of his gaze.

His lips brush mine, igniting every nerve ending. "I cannot stop thinking about you, Mrs. Di Santo."

I smile against his mouth. "I'm not your Mrs. yet."

"Maybe not on paper." He punctuates this by gripping my ass in one hand and squeezing it until I yelp. "But you are in every other way. Let's see your family out, then I'll show you *exactly* what I mean."

I shiver under his promise.

"Oh yeah," Cristiano whispers. "Why does your sister keep asking me what time I was born?"

I suddenly remember Sera's obsession with creating birth charts and relationship forecasts and pin my lips together to stop a smile as I shrug. "I have absolutely no idea."

We catch up with the rest of them. Tess is dragging her feet behind Benito, who has single-mindedly ploughed ahead with our little sister in his arms.

Cristiano puts a hand on Allegra's shoulder. "Thanks so much for coming, and for all your help yesterday. You must visit us again soon."

Allegra blushes like a beet and mutters something incomprehensible.

We wait for Benito to emerge empty-handed through the gates and watch as he settles a disgruntled Tess and a grateful Allegra into the waiting car, then he nods curtly and climbs into his Ferrari.

When the sound of tires has disappeared, I take a deep breath and turn to Cristiano. "What's going on with the Marchesis?" Augie mentioned a problem with them and I don't want to be kept in the dark.

His gaze softens. "I don't want you to worry about them."

"But they killed my mother, Cristiano. And I heard Augie say earlier there's been some trouble . . ."

Cristiano sighs as his gaze roams my face.

"I can take it," I assure him. "I know what I'm marrying into, and I don't want you to keep secrets to protect me, especially when it comes to the Marchesis."

He clears his throat. "It turns out they too were in partnership with the cartel associates I shot at the port. They're not happy about the fact I eliminated two people who would've made them a lot of money."

My voice drops to a whisper. "Were they trafficking humans too?"

"I don't know the details." He grits his teeth. "But it wouldn't surprise me."

I take another deep breath before asking the one question I'm really afraid to know the answer to. "What's going to happen, Cristiano? Are we going to war?"

He nods slowly. I knew it, but seeing his response only makes me feel heavier.

Then a smile spreads across his face before he bites his bottom lip.

"What are you smiling at?

He chases his teeth with a swipe of his tongue. "You said 'we.'"

"What?"

"You said, 'Are *we* going to war?'"

I stand up on tiptoes and brush my lips across his. Augie's words are still fresh in my mind. Cristiano stayed to keep my family safe.

"We're in this together, Di Santo. Your war is mine too."

"Oh, Castellano." His eyelids drift shut, and he gently licks my top lip. "I will burn down the whole of New York for you."

The End.

WHERE WILD HEARTS DANCE

*B*enito

3 months earlier

If my eyes were bullets, the back of Savero's head would be leaking blood like a fucking sieve.

Each step I take along the church aisle is punctuated by the sound of my teeth gnashing together. I shouldn't be here. None of us should be here. This funeral was never meant to happen. Not yet. Not so damn fucking soon.

Gianni Di Santo was young for a don. Exceptionally

young for a don who had the whole of New York at his feet. The man wasn't even sixty, and he was the fittest fifty-something fucker I knew. I'm half his age, and he could run rings around me—literally. He ran ten miles every morning and lifted weights every day. Had to, he said. Not every war could be won with a gun, he said. Sometimes, good old-fashioned fistfights weren't only essential but good for the soul, he said.

The steel in my waistband presses firmly against my back, reminding me of the threats that are never far away in this world. I wonder if I'd feel any better had it been a bullet that took Gianni's life in the end, not the heart attack none of us were prepared for.

My heart cracks a little wider the closer my footsteps take me to the final goodbye.

Gianni treated me like a son way more than my own father did. Not that my own father deserved the title. Gianni recognized something in me when I was in my late teens. Potential, perhaps, or maybe it was the insatiable hunger I felt to destroy anything that crossed my path, with little to no empathy. I guess it was better to have someone like that on side as opposed to against.

My eyes bore into Savero as if it's his fault his father died. I know this is how grief works—I've watched enough men die in my line of work. Hell, most of them died by my own hands. Very few I actually cared about, but for those I did, the process was the same: get angry, kick a few things, blame the person closest. When I learned of Gianni's passing, I screamed at the sky. I punched a few walls. And now I'm blaming Savero.

One minute, Gianni's here, commanding his capos from the quiet of his office, moving money and assets around the city like pawns on a chessboard.

The next, he's gone.

One minute, Savero's a nobody—a capo by name, an incendiary fucker by nature.

The next, he's King of New York.

Sure, he was Gianni's firstborn, but we all know he isn't don material. He's too unpredictable, too unhinged, to be a mafia kingpin. Locked and loaded soldier? Maybe. Don of the biggest crime family this side of Chicago? Fuck no.

Yet here we are, following the loosest of cannons into a church where we're to bury the greatest Italian leader who ever lived. Coincidence? I'm not convinced.

The anger tastes bitter as I swallow it, then my eyes catch on something to my left. My chest hardens in recognition.

Only capos and their families were given access to this church service—not even soldiers were granted that privilege—so why the hell is Tony Castellano, a mere *associate*, and his entire fucking family taking up a whole row?

I watch for any change in Savero's manner that might suggest a huge mistake. Maybe I can prevent someone from getting their neck snapped in two for the oversight. Instead I breathe a sigh of relief when he walks past Castellano, his sister, and his four daughters without so much as a pause.

Beppe lowers his voice when I arrive at his side. "What are *they* doing here?" the capo asks.

I stroke a hand down the tie I reserve for funerals and only the most formal of legal negotiations. "I was going to ask you the same thing."

I glance to my right, and my annoyance abates at the sight of Cristiano, Gianni's second—and substantially more pleasant—son. He has his head bent, scrolling through his phone, while he ignores the Mafia charade unfolding around him.

"Must be something to do with the port," Beppe mutters under his breath.

My eyes narrow.

Gianni and Tony Castellano had a good arrangement. Tony let Gianni ship a few illegal consignments through his port, and Gianni paid him handsomely for it. Savero's always been vocal about wanting more—a majority share, in fact—though none of us really know why. This must be why Castellano is here. It's the only explanation. And since Savero's inherited me as his new consigliere, it pisses me off he hasn't kept me in the fucking loop.

"Yeah, you're probably right," I concede. *Though it doesn't explain why the entire family got an invite.*

The church begins to quieten, and I turn to see the priest walking our way, his head bowed. I'm about to do the same when I feel a hostile pair of eyes burning into the side of my face. It's not an unusual sensation—most people despise me—but it's one I wasn't expecting at Gianni's funeral of all places.

I search for the culprit and have to do a double-take.

That is not what I was expecting.

Not what I was expecting *at all*.

One of the younger Castellano girls is *glaring* at me as if she wants to rip me apart with a blunt blade. I indulge the urge to stare back, which seems to incense her even more. Her lips are full but pursed, and her arms are folded firmly across her chest, long, black-nailed fingers drumming against smooth alabaster skin. I slowly stroke my gaze over her, enjoying her obvious fury. She has one leg crossed over the other, and she wears a floor-length black satin dress that falls open midway up her thigh.

My gaze crawls back up her body to her eyes. I can't confirm the color, because they're narrowed to slits, but I catch a flash of green when she blinks. Her hair is jet-black, long, and pinned to one side. It's the sort of hair I'd normally wrap around my fist.

She's catastrophically beautiful, which is irritating, because the least I can do today is give my full focus to remembering Gianni, a man who practically raised me as his own, and not a seething beauty who's sticking metaphorical pins into me for some unknown reason.

A sharp elbow in my ribs signals the service is about to start. The corner of my mouth ticks up, and the girl's eyes narrow even further. Then, with an inhuman amount of willpower, I turn back to the priest.

My attention is feigned though. I can't shake the image of those catlike eyes burning shards into my skin, making even my tailored suit feel scratchy and uncomfortable.

What is her problem?

I piss off a lot of people in my line of work. Very few of them have the guts to show it.

But I have a feeling this one might just give me a run for my money—and fuck me, am I ready for the race.

ACKNOWLEDGMENTS

This is my first foray into mafia romance and I really couldn't have done it without one hell of an amazing team.

First, I must thank all the hugely talented authors already rocking this crazy genre and writing stories that have simultaneously inspired and freaked me the dickens out (how can I rise to such an incredible standard?)

Second, the utter professionals who've guided me, supported me and taken this book to entirely new levels. Farrah, your covers are works of art and I hope you will forever humour/ignore/blow out of the water my lame briefs. Heidi, you guided me throughout and I am indebted to you for the invaluable advice. Bryony, your comments and edits kept me going to the end and I'm so grateful for your detailed and experienced eye. My awesome beta readers, Demi, Allie, Lynne, Kerri, Debbie and Shannon. Your input was beyond helpful and ensured I've stayed true to those critical reader expectations. My ARC team, especially those who journeyed with me from a previous pen, I love and appreciate you all so much I could cry right now. And I'm peri-menopausal so I'm not even kidding.

And finally, to my husband whose words (and tats) never fail to inspire me. Thank you for continuing to support me in all the ways as I pursue my dream. And for doing the school pick-up. I love you most Ardingly. (deliberate typo)

ABOUT VICTORIA HOLLIDAY

Victoria Holliday is a contemporary romance author who writes dangerously delicious romance. When she isn't daydreaming about her husband or dirty dons and hot heroines, she can be found running around after either a) a small child b) a dog with slippers in his mouth c) one of three flighty chickens, or d) all of the above.

tiktok.com/@victoriahollidaywrites

instagram.com/victoriahollidaywrites

www.ingramcontent.com/pod-product-compliance
Ingram Content Group UK Ltd.
Pitfield, Milton Keynes, MK11 3LW, UK
UKHW041041140425
457384UK00002B/76

9 781739 865726